The Man Who Bought the World

Hope you enjoy reading the book

Fiona

The Man Who Bought the World

Fiona Lamont

This book is a work of fiction. Names and characters are the product of the author's imagination or are used fictitiously. Any resemblance to real people, living or dead, is purely coincidental.

Copyright © 2021 Fiona Lamont

All rights reserved

ISBN-13 9798759680970

Published by Lamont Worricker Ltd.
www.lamontworricker.co.uk

Dedication

This book is dedicated to all the wild swimmers
In the Outdoor Swimming Society, whose posts on our
Facebook page never fail to inspire me, and to wild
swimmers everywhere.

Cover design by Fiona Lamont
Cover image by Oliver Sjostrom from Pexels

Prologue 1

Chapter One...3

Chapter Two 13

Chapter Three...21

Chapter Four...28

Chapter Five 34

Chapter Six 41

Chapter Seven 48

Chapter Eight..54

Chapter Nine 59

Chapter Ten 69

Chapter Eleven 72

Chapter Twelve 75

Chapter Thirteen...83

Chapter Fourteen 95

Chapter Fifteen 100

Chapter Sixteen 112

Chapter Seventeen..121

Chapter Eighteen	130
Chapter Nineteen	134
Chapter Twenty	144
Chapter Twenty-One	151
Chapter Twenty-Two	153
Chapter Twenty-Three	160
Chapter Twenty-Four	169
Chapter Twenty-Five	173
Chapter Twenty-Six	177
Chapter Twenty-Seven	183
Chapter Twenty-Eight	187
Chapter Twenty-Nine	197
Chapter Thirty	204
Chapter Thirty-One	212
Chapter Thirty-Two	224
Chapter Thirty-Three	227
Chapter Thirty-Four	232
Chapter Thirty-Five	235

Chapter Thirty-Six..242

Chapter Thirty-Seven 246

Chapter Thirty-Eight 257

Chapter Thirty-Nine 260

Chapter Forty..266

Chapter Forty-One..270

Chapter Forty-Two 274

Chapter Forty-Three 280

Chapter Forty-Four...284

Chapter Forty-Five 289

Chapter Forty-Six 293

Chapter Forty-Seven 305

Chapter Forty-Eight..308

Prologue

July 2012

Gazing through the circular window, the girl watched the flicker of headlights between the trees lining the lane, heralding the arrival of her father. Her feeling of foreboding increased as the big, black SUV turned into the drive and came slowly up to the house, wheels crunching on the gravel. The car door opened, and her father got out, carrying a small overnight bag. He walked to the door with his usual brisk impatient steps and rapped firmly on it.

She heard the door open and her mother's voice, 'well you're here at last, Ross. How was your flight?'

'The same as all transatlantic flights, tedious. I hope you're not overreacting, Mary. She is thirteen now. Teenagers do all sorts of weird shit.'

They went inside and she couldn't hear her mother's reply. The girl shivered. Her father sounded so unconcerned, if she didn't know him better, she would think her problems over now he had arrived.

He was always like that, unconcerned, laid back. He never got angry though occasionally he would raise his voice. Not because he was annoyed, but because he wanted to speak louder than you. He needed to make sure you understood what he said went. She wouldn't have to face him tonight; her mother told her he would talk to her at breakfast tomorrow. A miasma of apprehension filled her bedroom, breakfast would be the time of the reckoning.

She already knew the likely outcome of tomorrow's talk; her father would take her away in that ominous black car to a place where adults would ask her questions and not listen to her answers. They thought her mad because she worried the rivers would become too polluted to swim in. 'What a thing to be anxious about,' the doctor had said in her patronising voice.

The girl changed into her swimsuit and swivelled the circular window open. Taking care not to make any noise, she scrambled down the thick wisteria stems to the flower bed. She would go to the river and swim up to Harpers Brook and back, a four-mile route. The full moon cast a brilliant light, such a beautiful evening to go swimming.

She walked along the lane, anticipating the sensation of moving through water, the feeling of weightlessness. She would swim tonight because tomorrow she might be in prison. Anywhere could be a prison she thought, anywhere you were forced to go and not allowed to leave was a prison. People could be caged as well as animals.

The moonlight glinting on the water told her she had reached the riverbank. She slipped into the water thinking of her favourite books, The Wind in the Willows and The Water Babies. Maybe tonight she would become a water baby and float away and never come back.

Chapter One

February 2019

In winter snow defines Russia and here the snow was black. Fat black snowflakes swirled down from the weighty brown sky to land on Seville Campbell's upturned face. A thick blanket of charcoal coloured snow covered the woodland floor. Adamantine jet crystals glinted and solidified on the tree branches and stained her scarlet ski jacket with black streaks.

It was a long drive from Novosibirsk airport and snow had followed them throughout their journey, but as they entered the Kuzbass region, the nature of it changed. They had driven from a winter wonderland into this sinister, apocalyptic landscape, which held a strange, eerie beauty.

'Welcome to Siberia,' said her companion. 'Welcome to the Kuzbass, home of our coal mining industry.'

She stared at the black substance covering every surface, a layer had already formed on the roof of the Land Rover. Seville had come to Russia to document water pollution, but she had never imagined pollution that caused snow to become black. She glanced at her driver. 'What causes this? It must do so much damage to the environment.'

Taras Alexeev barked out a brief chuckle. 'Never mind damage to the environment, think of the damage done to the people. High cancer and tuberculosis rates, lower than average life span. The authorities do not like us journalists to write about this. A shield has broken so the coal dust is always in the atmosphere and when it snows, it paints the snow black. Come, we will go into Kiselyovsk, and you will see how beautiful this makes the town.'

'Does the government do nothing about it?' she asked. 'Aren't there any laws to prevent this sort of pollution?'

'To smoke a cigarette in a public place is illegal,' said Taras. 'They will fine you for that. Pollute the air and fill everyone's lungs with coal dust and there is no punishment. If I make too loud a noise about pollution, they may punish me. Dissension is always punished.'

Seville followed her companion back to the battered Land Rover. They had spoken little during the five-hour drive from Novosibirsk to Kiselyovsk. She felt disorientated by the long flight and the scale of the

Siberian landscape, and Taras's quiet authority intimidated her. They drove through the woods into the town.

'Oh my,' she said, the inadequacy of her words made her feel like a thirteen-year-old again. She thought this would make a great setting for a dystopian disaster movie. A situation like "The Road," with the survivors travelling across the snowy tundra into a sinister, deserted town coated in this snow. Only it wouldn't be black, after the apocalypse the industry generating this pollution would not exist. Looking around the mixture of charcoal grey sludge and glittering coal-black crystals that blanketed their surroundings brought on a familiar sense of anxiety.

***

They drew up outside the hotel, a modern building with a desolate air beneath the surface gloss, though inside it was warm. They checked in and Seville took a shower. She would like to swim, she found swimming the best way to dissipate these feelings, but the hotel had no pool. The water flowed over her, and she imagined slipping into a river and letting herself go with the current. The shower was no substitute.

Yet somehow the bland anonymity of the place helped. She packed away her samples and downloaded her photos to her laptop. She tried to sponge the black streaks off her ski jacket and changed into fresh clothes. Glancing at the mirror she experienced her usual surprise when an adult stared back at her. A young adult to be sure, a serious young woman, who didn't smile as much as she should.

They met for dinner in the restaurant. She thought she might be in a play, sitting at the table with this solemn man. An actor playing the role of environmental science student and her words sounded self-conscious and stilted in her ears.

Their desultory small talk stuttered to a halt, then Taras gave her an unexpectedly engaging smile, and asked about her degree, and what she hoped to achieve from this visit. 'I was asked to show a student some of our most polluted places, but how do you intend to use this experience?'

Seville wondered how to express herself without sounding pretentious. 'The purity of water,' she replied, embarrassed by the expression, though this was the title she would like to give her dissertation. Her tutor had advised on one more academic.

Taras raised an eyebrow, 'what does that mean?' His deep and tragic sounding voice added to her feeling of performing in a play.

'This may sound silly to you, but my biggest passion in life is to swim. I swim in cold water to feel alive, in rivers, in the sea and lakes. Only one thing is worse than to find swimming in these places is unsafe because of pollution, and that is not to have water that is safe to drink. About a third of the world's population does not have access to clean drinking water. My dissertation is about the causes of this and how we can change it.'

'Then Russia is bad, half of our people do not have clean drinking water. As always, we excel against the average, we win in our race to the bottom.'

'Unpolluted drinking water should be a basic human right. Because swimming is important to me, it's made me think about how water matters to everyone. In Britain, we take it for granted, though we allow the pollution of many of our rivers and beaches. I want to assess water quality around the world, publish the results and inform people. What does black snow do to the water here? If people know, they'll put pressure on governments and companies to clean up.'

'If the people can organise themselves to protest. My country has plenty of freshwater, but much of it is contaminated. Where are the protesters about that? Kiselyovsk and Dzerzhinsk are typical of many Russian industrial towns, though Dzerzhinsk is an extreme example.'

'My original plan was to travel to India and write about the pollution of the Ganges, but my tutor suggested I should come to Russia. He talked about Dzerzhinsk, and a city called Norilsk. He said Norilsk is the most polluted city in Russia, possibly in the world. I'm going to visit there during my gap year before starting my masters.'

Taras had a curious expression on his face as he

answered, 'Norilsk is a closed city.'

'Yes, I read that but what does it mean?'

'If a city is closed the government avoids scrutiny on what is manufactured or happens in that city. This is a typical Russian situation. It is rumoured there may be sixty closed cities in Russia, some do not even appear on maps. Can you imagine that happening in Britain, cities not shown on your maps?'

'That couldn't happen in Britain, we are such a small country. It would be impossible to hide a village, let alone a city.'

'No roads or railways go into Norilsk. The way in is to fly and to board the flight, you would need the correct papers. These papers are not often issued to foreigners, these papers are not issued to many Russians.'

'There must be roads, how did the city ever get built?'

'Blood and tears. A slave camp built by slave labour. Occasionally a scientist gains permission to visit the area. A British friend of mine was such a scientist, and she met with a fatal accident. You cannot go there,' said Taras.

'What causes the pollution?'

'Primarily nickel mining and smelting, and also from a company called Northern Chemicals. The area is exceptionally polluted, making it an easy place to manufacture the more polluting chemicals. The authorities do not enforce regulations and the pollution grows. Come, it is time to retire, we have much to do tomorrow, and you must need a good night's sleep after your journey. We will drive back to Novosibirsk, then we will fly to Moscow. Forget Norilsk, Dzerzhinsk is a portal to hell.'

***

Busy day or not tomorrow, she was not ready for bed. She zipped up her ski jacket, pulled her hat well down over her ears and set out to take photos of the town by night. She felt slightly guilty at ignoring Taras's advice, a familiar sensation for her.   Seville often ignored the advice of others.

She walked along the road towards a colourful temple with an impossibly long name. Lights reflected off the golden onion-shaped domes of the building. The contrast between the colour and the dark snow made a striking image.

Kneeling to get the right angle for a shot, she stared ruefully at the damp, stained knees to her jeans. She took another photo at a less challenging angle and glanced around the square. A large black car parked by the roadside and two men got out and walked towards the temple. Silhouetted against the floodlights the men looked incongruously matched. One was tall, slim, and smoked a cigar, the other short and plump, stepping cautiously across the snow. Like Seville, he took photos of the building but used his phone.

It started to snow again, big, black snowflakes swirling from the sky, and she took shelter in a doorway to the temple. She heard the two men talk in the square, and they surprised her by speaking in English.

The tall man said in an amused, upper-class English voice, 'you're not going to take a selfie, are you, Donnie?'

The smaller man spoke with an American accent. 'Well, most of the places I get to visit haven't got any views worth taking a picture of. This is something, look at that coloured decoration against the black snow. It won't be the same in daylight.'

'The snow's starting to come down a bit, better put your phone away.'

'Do you want to go back to the car?'

'No, I've lit my cigar now, let's go to that doorway so I can finish it. I've plenty of time before my plane leaves.'

Seville hoped they were not coming to shelter where she stood, but they went to a deeper alcove next to the one she sheltered in. She smelt the cigar smoke and backed in further, she did not want to get involved in any conversation with them.

The men did not speak for a couple of minutes, then she overheard the voice of the American. 'Are you happy about us moving the business to Norilsk? You can't trust these Russians.'

'Relax Donnie,' said his companion. 'We have Ivan Popov; he is well-connected and has much to gain from this. As CEO, he can grease the right palms, he knows who to speak to. Northern Chemicals is already manufacturing in Norilsk. We can move their Dzerzhinsk operations to Norilsk, and it will not appear untoward.'

The name caught her attention. Norilsk, they were talking about the city she wanted to visit, the city Taras said was closed.

'We must move the operation, there is too much focus on Dzerzhinsk now, but I'm still worried about Norilsk. It will be difficult for me George.'

'That's why we employ Popov.'

The American sounded querulous. 'Are we sure it is safe to move all Northern Chemicals operations to Norilsk? The problem is in the mix, George, our new pesticide, and chemical weapons. The recipes are the same, questions may be asked.'

'We've been over this,' said the English voice. 'Norilsk is different. We know the world is suspicious of Russia's involvement with Syria and Syria's use of chemical weapons. The world wants reassurance Russia speaks the truth when it says its stocks of Sarin, and suchlike are destroyed.'

The American sounded panicked by this, he shushed the Englishman and told him not to name the materials.

The Englishman's voice became more clipped, he sounded like a teacher speaking to a stubbornly stupid pupil. 'We need to move out of Dzerzhinsk, and Norilsk is the ideal new location. The focus is on the pollution from the mining and metallurgy plants.'

'Alright for you, George, but I'm the man on the ground in Russia, the buck always stops with me. You can claim you know nothing; hell, you always claim you know nothing. You're a proper wise monkey.'

Seville listened intently and her heart began to race. This visit to Russia was becoming increasingly surreal. These Western businessmen appeared to be discussing the manufacture of chemical weapons. The thought she had strayed into a film set crossed her mind, and she smiled at the notion.

After a moment's silence, the Englishman spoke. 'The so-called weapons are a by-product, we're manufacturing pesticides. Do what we said to clean up the Dzerzhinsk operation. Dump any stocks of the by-products and make sure no evidence remains to show recent manufacture. No problem in dumping I guess; there are whole lakes of the stuff in that city. Remember Donnie, Sarin was originally a pesticide.'

The American replied in a sullen voice. 'You make things sound so easy, George, you're here for the meeting and off you go. No staying in crappy towns covered in black snow.'

'Stop worrying, this is serious money. We're producing our new pesticide and the "newcomer." The Russian government looks favourably on anyone manufacturing the "newcomer." Think of the bright side, no more visits to the factories at Dzerzhinsk. Norilsk may be a shit hole but at least the life expectancy is more than mid-forties. What is it in Dzerzhinsk, forty-two for men?'

'Don't joke about this George. Since that poisoning in Salisbury, Western governments don't look kindly on companies manufacturing Novichok, it'll be on the banned list before long.'

'Why do you think we make it over here, Donnie.'

A man left the alcove next to Seville and walked towards the black Range Rover parked on the road. He reached the car, and the headlights came on, so she shrank back in the doorway. A kaleidoscope of fragments of the conversation spun around her mind. She tried to corral them into an ordered sequence. The car drove off, she forgot about the American and stepped from the shelter of the alcove.

Seville walked across the open space, and a voice behind her called, 'hey, where did you come from, just hang on one tiny minute.'

She turned around and the short, plump man appeared from the deeper recess next to the door. The surprise made her pause for a moment, then she ran. The reaction was instinctive, and a frisson of fear coursed through her as the man chased her.

She was faster than him. He slipped on the ice and cursed, she glanced back and saw a small pool of light from his mobile phone. He sat on the ground and fumbled with it. Seville guessed he would call his companion. That would mean reinforcements with a car she would not be able to outrun. Seville ran on wondering which way to go.

Why are you running away, she berated herself? She hadn't done anything wrong. Why not pretend to be Russian, shrug her shoulders, act like she didn't understand. She was a student, not a spy, she had no reason to run, but she couldn't stop now she had started. Car headlights appeared in the distance and drove towards the temple, she needed to get away from the roads. The Range Rover loomed up, gleaming darkly against the lights illuminating the building.

She fought down panic, was she right to run? What reason had the man to call after her, why were they chasing her? Was it because she was stupid enough to run away? What harm could a couple of Western businessmen do to her? She did not know but thought it better not to wait to find out.

Seville decided not to go directly back to the hotel and ran in the opposite direction to put them off her tracks. She did not worry she would lose her way. Her sense of direction was instinctively accurate, her own internal satellite system. She ran down an alleyway before doubling back towards the hotel.

She went to the rear of the building to try to gain entrance, her heart pounding industrially, making her shake. The American was likely to stay at the same place; Taras had told her this was the best the town had to offer. She found a door ajar with a pile of cigarette butts next to it. This must be the staff smoking spot. Checking no one watched her, she slipped through the open door. If questioned, reception would not know she had returned late.

Seville went up the back stairs to her room and sat on her bed taking deep breaths to calm herself. She did not think the man had a chance to take a proper look at her. He would think her a young Russian local sheltering from the snow, and unable to understand his conversation. He might recognise the red ski jacket though. She would wear her blue jacket tomorrow even though it was not as warm. She did not want to risk identification.

Seville showered again to warm herself up and pondered on what she had overheard. Those men sounded like ordinary western businessmen, and she had acted like they were the KGB, not that the KGB existed anymore. She had watched too many spy films. Yet their conversation alarmed her. They mentioned Sarin and Novichok, both were chemical weapons. Should she tell Taras, was this dangerous knowledge for a Russian environmental journalist, would anyone in Russia care?

She dried her hair and hummed to herself. She was much faster than that fat American, and he'd looked ridiculous sitting in the snow. Seville thought she should not have run, but why did he call out to her? She decided to make a note of the company they had spoken of, then if anything came up in the future about this, she would share what she had overheard.

***

At breakfast the next morning, Seville mulled over the conversation from last night. What a strange coincidence they had mentioned Norilsk, the city she wanted to visit. If she could organise a trip there, perhaps she could check up on Northern Chemicals.

Seville sighed, she could scarcely turn up at a factory and ask for samples of what they were manufacturing. She watched the other guests, checking if any of them looked like the American. Maybe he was staying elsewhere. As they checked out, a small plump man crossed the reception area. A staff member greeted him with 'good morning, Mr Brown,' and the man replied with an American accent.

When she walked to the door Mr Brown appeared to notice her for the first time and stared at her. This time she met his eye and walked confidently past him, giving him a brief nod to acknowledge his presence. I should have behaved like this last night, she thought. The American continued to stare, then he appeared to relax. Was it her confident stance or her blue jacket?

Chapter Two

February 2019

Ross Campbell did not consider himself a family man, yet somehow, he had seven children, and in most people's eyes, that number of kids constituted a family. Too many children were an inevitable product of having three wives. But no more, today he would take back control, this afternoon he would have the snip and that would end his breeding days. Any future wives would have to make do with pet dogs.

He settled back in his chair in the Harley Street waiting room and glanced around for a distraction. Stern notices forbade the use of mobile phones, a particular hate of this consultant judging by his Twitter feed, which he presumably updated from his laptop. Ross never engaged with social media himself, empty vessels, and all that, but he liked to check out the Twitter commentary of anyone he had any involvement with.

He spotted a newspaper, folded back to reveal a crossword. Idly he picked it up and studied the page. He took a pen from his briefcase and without reading any clue, filled in nine across. The word POWER neatly filled the five spaces. He paused for a moment, then again without checking he completed two down, CONTROL, seven letters this time. Control and power, which came first?

The receptionist came over to Ross and whispered, 'Mr Frost will see you now sir.'

He left the newspaper and considered what the correct answers to nine across and two down were. To be honest, control and power were always the right answers.

***

When Ross returned to his office, he wished he had thought to wear baggier trousers. The consultant had been breezy about telling him there would be no pain at all, though he must expect some discomfort. He wondered what constituted pain to the medical profession. Red hot poker up the arse maybe. He should have demanded an exact definition of "discomfort" from his surgeon before the operation.

As he walked through the reception area of his company, he was conscious his gait had a slight "just got off my horse" roll to it. He imagined a sign floated above his head, a finger pointing down in Monty Python style, saying, "this man is emasculated." For all his laid-back demeanour, Ross liked everyone to take him as seriously as he took himself and the comic walk did not help.

He decided he would tell his driver to avoid the road with the speed bumps. He preferred to be the man at the steering wheel, but it took away from his authority. As CEO of Atlas, the world's largest private company, he had to have a driver. You could not be God and drive yourself, at least not to and from the office.

***

Ross never arrived home in time for the kids' bedtime and thought the boarding school was among the more civilised features of English family life. Of course, both his children with wife number three were still too young for school, boarding or otherwise.

Home was outside Cambridge. Though not a man generally concerned with environmental matters, he had checked out projected sea level rises. Cambridge appeared safe unless things went catastrophically wrong. He had not chosen a house near a river. Ross disliked extreme landscapes and found Cambridgeshire reassuringly flat.

Ross said goodnight to his driver and entered the house to find a whirlwind of activity generated by his wife, Madrigal. Like much about Madrigal, her name gave a misleading impression. It was a romantic name, unlike those of his first two wives, Mary, and Susan. Ross admired exotic names and felt proud of the imagination shown in the names bestowed on his first five children.

He was delighted to meet a Madrigal, especially a beautiful Pre-Raphaelite style redhead, with hair hanging below her waist. Her old hippy father was some sort of Lord complete with a manor, and he thought he had bought into the dream. A different vision greeted him today, Madrigal stood with her hands on her hips, and positively scowled at him.

'You're late,' she said. 'You'd better get changed quickly. You can't go to the Capell's in those jeans.'

He sighed. When he returned to England, he had prided himself on bringing a Californian vibe to his stuffy City of London office. It lulled people into a false sense of security, thinking the jeans showed a casual laid back attitude to business, a lack of concern about status. How wrong they were. 'Mads, you don't expect me to wear a suit?'

Madrigal's voice rose. 'You cannot turn up to dinner wearing jeans. God knows what they make of you in the office turning up dressed like that, but when you are out with me you have standards to maintain. Get your suit on.'

Ross went to change. If only I didn't like fucking her so much, he thought. He always found her sexy, particularly when she behaved like Nurse Ratched. He imagined Madrigal in a nurse's outfit, then shook himself, now was not the time to engage in those fantasies. Still, he had outmanoeuvred her today, no more kids for her, well, not from him.

***

The Capells were useful people to know, or at least Edward Capell was. The male guests did indeed wear suits. Ross guessed they were either civil servants or bankers, two breeds of men who made up the last bastions of those who wore suits to dinner.

As always, the food and wine were excellent, and many of the guests showed interest in Madrigal's charity foundation. Her grumpiness vanished as she spoke about the work, "Safe Water for All," did. To listen to her one would have thought that she had dug the wells and installed the purification units.

They passed the port around the table, the Baccarat crystal decanter glinting in the candlelight. Their hostess, Lady Fakenham, aka Angela Capell, turned to Ross with what he thought of as a mugger's smile. 'Ross, I wonder if I can count on your support for an initiative I'm pursuing with the government.'

'Angela, if the initiative is right, you will have my 100% support. Convince me.'

Madrigal frowned at him, and he grimaced back at her. Jesus, he couldn't roll over on his back and say yes to every proposition put to him. He had no problem with donations, hell, he'd happily give money to any cause, provided it would gain public approbation. Supporting initiatives was a different matter. Some may become political, and he never overtly involved himself in anything political.

Angela helped herself to a chocolate truffle from a silver dish of antique appearance before replying. A large diamond sparkled on her finger reminding him her family had connections to diamond mines in Africa.

'We are promoting an initiative for greater transparency in business. I'm sure you would not want your pension funds invested in a company that caused environmental damage or used child labour. We will score against an index of environmental and social responsibility measures. Pension fund managers will publish annually how the companies they invest in perform against these KPI's.'

Well, what a shitty idea, thought Ross. One where he needed to be inside the tent and in full knowledge of the strategy. 'That sounds like an interesting initiative, Angela. Atlas will want to be fully on board. I'll allocate one of my directors to support you with it. Give me your card and I'll put them in touch with you.'

He noted with satisfaction that she appeared surprised by his response. He was no idiot, when something to your disadvantage came up with obvious popular appeal, one had to embrace it publicly and deal with it privately. Ross prided himself on lack of transparency; only a fool let the world see their true self.

***

The next morning Ross summoned his sustainability director, Jason Harris. He thought Jason a worthless piece of shit, but a necessary worthless piece of shit. He felt the same about most of the board of Atlas, apart from the Trading Director, a ball-breaking bitch. She controlled her team with a rod of iron and was worth every penny he paid her. His first wife, Mary, was also worthy of her place. He smiled, appreciative of the irony that the worthwhile directors were women. Women were always best at selling crap to people. After all, they were the ones that liked buying it.

Jason entered Ross's office and hovered by the door, waiting for an invitation to take a seat. Ross clicked his fingers and pointed to a chair. Jason hastened to sit, clutching his iPad like a swimming aid. He projected an aura of disbelief that he had landed such a prestigious and well-paid role only four years out of university. Disbelief shared by the rest of the board and all Jason's friends and relatives.

Ross considered Jason ideal for the job. The last thing he wanted was a sustainability director who knew what he was talking about. He required someone young, naive, and enthusiastic, to spout the right words without taking any effective action. Someone who could write the socially aware policies without following them through. When Jason eventually became old and wise, he would be toast.

He handed Lady Fakenham's card to Jason and saw with satisfaction how he raised his eyebrow at the title, obviously impressed. It amused him how exposure to minor aristocracy affected some people. In his experience, many a rampant left-winger became reduced to gibbering obsequiousness when introduced to royalty.

'Angela Capell, that is Lady Fakenham, is setting up this new foundation for transparency in business. I told her we would be delighted to support her organisation. Contact her and see how she thinks we can help. Your budget is £100k to spend on collaborating with her. I want a report on how they propose to work with industry by the end of next week.'

'I'll call her, it sounds like an exciting initiative,' said Jason.

Ross turned to his laptop and made a tick against a column on a worksheet, then waved a dismissive hand at Jason. He considered his "Bollocks Bingo" spreadsheet. "Exciting Initiative" steamed ahead this week, closely followed by "Demonstrating Diversity."

He opened his desk drawer and took out a mobile. He selected the number for George Fenton and smiled, this conversation would be unlikely to score many Bollocks Bingo hits. A business discussion with George was always straight to the point.

***

He met George for lunch at No. One Piccadilly, not a venue Ross would choose. According to rumour George's wife was a shit cook, so he always fed himself up at lunchtime. Oak panelling and dinner wheeled around on carving trolleys didn't do much for him, but as CEO of Gaia Chemicals, George was a valued employee, and if No. One Piccadilly did it for George, that was where they would lunch.

As the public face of Gaia Chemicals George kept a low profile. They met today to discuss a new development, a substitute for DDT, the pesticide banned in much of the world. Ross believed in meeting face to face to talk about such issues. The email was not your friend, the written word, even in electronic form, could always come back and bite you on the bum.

'How was Russia?' asked Ross.

'Cold,' said George, 'cold, dark and uncomfortable. Remember

I wasn't visiting Moscow or St Petersburg. Hotels in those industrial towns, it's impossible to get any decent wine.'

George waved away the wine list with a sad expression, and they ordered the obligatory bottle of sparkling mineral water instead. Ross knew George fancied himself as a wine expert, but no one drank at lunch these days unless of course, one was at a business meeting in France. They exchanged pleasantries and George updated him on general progress at Gaia.

Ross looked on glumly at a trolley that held an array of roast meats. He preferred a sandwich at lunchtime. George enthusiastically selected roast beef, roast potatoes, roast vegetables, two Yorkshire puddings and a bucket's worth of gravy. Ross asked for one slice of the beef, peas, and a few parsnips. The waiter served him with a sniff of disapproval.

George liked to concentrate on his food when eating, so they ate in silence for a while. Ross chased his last peas around the plate, and he saw George had already finished, despite having at least twice as much food. He marvelled how George remained slim, assuming it must be the exercise from all that hunting, shooting, and fishing he did at the weekends.

The waiter cleared their plates and tried to interest them in a dessert, before going off to fetch coffee and the bill. George glanced regretfully after the vanishing dessert menu, then leant back in his seat with the air of a man who in an ideal world would now have lit a cigar.

The waiter brought the coffee and handed the bill to George, clearly assuming that the man in the Saville Row suit would be the one paying. Ross sighed and pulled it towards himself. An idle thought crossed his mind, should he buy No. One Piccadilly and bring the whole place bang up to date?

The coffee arrived and they moved on to the primary business of the day. 'DDT, wonder chemical to eradicate malaria, or villain that kills wildlife?' asked George, posing a question Ross had never considered.

'Banned in the Western world where malaria's eradicated, used in Africa and India where they still suffer from it,' said Ross.

'Got it in one. Many environmental groups are calling for a worldwide ban, and we have a substitute that would facilitate this. We'll clean up in that market.'

'Sounds good to me, what's the issue?'

'The formulation destroys pests without getting in the food chain, eradicates mosquitoes helping to prevent malaria, though it is unstable in production. Once the compound is complete there are no issues, but the manufacturing process produces a by-product that causes health problems. Safe disposal of this substance would make manufacturing prohibitively expensive.'

'Is unsafe disposal a possibility?'

'That depends on where we make it. The new company we bought, Northern Chemicals, could be the ticket. They manufacture in sites so polluted no one will notice a bit more. To be honest, the by-product offers an opportunity, but a strictly illegal one. It's the sort of product that countries ruled by nasty dictators use against human pests.'

'Never discount a commercial opportunity. Let's face it, George, the world needs pesticides.'

'Indeed,' said George. 'There are too many pests in the world.'

They laughed and toasted the witticism with their coffee cups. Ross thought he thoroughly approved of pest extermination.

Chapter Three

February 2019

They did not need to cross the River Styx; they drove into hell along the M7 from Moscow. Seville soon understood what Taras meant when he said Dzerzhinsk was a portal to hell. Black snow in Kiselyovsk seemed benign in comparison. She could not imagine anyone ever swam in the wild here.

Taras had arranged to meet with a local activist, Uri Turgenev. He told her they had never met each other, although they had corresponded for several years. Uri hugged Taras, 'My friend, we meet at last, and you bring a beautiful woman to see me.'

He embraced Seville, and the greeting took her aback. She found it difficult to reconcile someone calling her a beautiful woman with the image of herself she kept in her head. Stop thinking of yourself as a child, she scolded herself. You are a woman now.

'Are you well?' asked Taras. 'Shall we take a drive out to the White Sea? I fear we will not want to swim in that sea.'

'Swimming in our White Sea is not the way to a long life,' said Uri. 'I understand you want to show your friend our beautiful lake, but we must be careful, it is a forbidden place, although no one guards it.'

They got in the car and Taras drove out of the city, the countryside had a grubby, dusty appearance. The landscape rapidly became industrial, armies of pylons stretched across the horizon and the ubiquitous tall chimneys, striped white and red, billowed out smoke. For all his activism, Uri appeared to be nervous at undertaking this journey. Seville could not stop herself looking back to see if anyone followed them, she thought the pursuit in Kieslyovsk had unnerved her.

They turned down a small road and drove through wasteland punctuated by bushes and sickly-looking trees. A strong smell of sulphur began to pervade the car and made her cough. They reached the White Sea, a 100-acre lake of pale grey chemical sludge. The acrid stench overwhelmed them; they dared not stay long enough for Seville to obtain a sample of the liquid, the process felt too dangerous. She collected soil instead and took photographs of the bleak surroundings.

'It contains 17 million times the legal limit of phenol,' said Uri. 'All these chemicals seep through into the water table and pollute our water. We must not linger here.'

Seville stared at the lake and shuddered. She found it incredible no one in the West wrote about this. Her tutor was right, everyone knew of pollution in India and China, few ever considered the pollution in Russia. Apart from Chernobyl of course, though that was in Ukraine, not Russia. Perhaps scientists in Russia had to toe the government line, and that was why her tutor had recommended her to get in touch with a journalist for her trip.

They returned to Uri's village, a few miles outside the city. Taras drove much faster on the return journey, Seville noticed his eyes returning to the mirror every few minutes. She winced when the car bounced over a deep pothole. They reached the weed-strewn gravel lane to Uri's house and relaxed. Taras parked the car outside and Uri led them into his tiny kitchen. 'Would you like a drink of water?'

'Oh yes please,' said Seville, unthinking, her mouth dry from the chemical atmosphere of the White Sea.

Uri turned on a tap and poured water into a glass. The liquid dribbled out in a dirty grey colour. She backed away from the glass in horror. Uri laughed as he poured the water away. He gave her a bottle of water from his fridge.

'Yes, like you, I would not drink this water. But my neighbours drink it. Ten years ago, no one would drink it, now the authorities have allegedly cleaned up the city, though it only appears clean to those who have known much worse. We are a poisoned people.'

Seville exchanged a glance with Taras, neither knew what to say. They left the claustrophobic house to drink their water in Uri's small garden. She regarded the well-tended vegetable plot with unease. She didn't fancy eating anything grown in this soil. A neighbour of Uri's came by, and they exchanged a few words, ending with the neighbour laughing.

'What did he say?' Seville asked Taras.

'He asked where we had been, and I told him the White Sea. He said no one goes there. If you would walk your dog by that lake, you must want your dog's life to end. Cheaper than the vet. Come, Uri has arranged for us to talk to some people.'

***

They sat in the hotel restaurant in Dzerzhinsk and drank vodka. Somehow water did not appeal in this place. Seville had no appetite for food either. She thought she may swallow poison with every mouthful. This place had the lowest average life expectancy in the world.

The horror of what they had seen and heard today made Taras appear less remote to her. He no longer seemed like a stern guide, more of a colleague. 'Why do people stay here?' she asked him.

'Who can guess, maybe they have nowhere else to go. There is always work here and people need to work. For many people, it is not so easy to decide to move on.'

She glanced around the restaurant, blonde wood, pale grey walls, and a profusion of pot plants as if to compensate for the lack of greenery in the city itself. It had a gloss of sophistication, though she found the blue and grey colour scheme cold and unwelcoming. Seville thought there could be no welcome here.

The stories from the people they interviewed were too awful. The production of chemical weapons ended, but the legacy of the manufacturing of them had destroyed this place. When the government disposed of the chemical weapons, they buried them in the ground and dumped them in the lakes. The consequences were severe, the water pollution unimaginable.

Seville glanced over her shoulder. She had developed a need to check that no one watched them. All the people they interviewed were keen to talk about their experiences, yet nervous, fearing retribution for any criticism. She felt gripped by their collective paranoia.

Taras poured himself another vodka. 'So, you have seen Dzerzhinsk, and everyone tells you how improved it is. Ten years ago, this was a closed city, like Norilsk, and now the city is open, and its people consider it cleaned up.'

Seville shuddered thinking of those conversations. People told them that during the manufacture of chemical weapons in Dzerzhinsk, babies were born with their hearts on the outside, no heads, no limbs. It made her feel sick and anxious to even think about it.

Taras poured more vodka into her glass. 'Dzerzhinsk is dammed by its past. All those deadly chemicals dumped in the lake. It is also dammed by its future, a thousand varieties of chemicals are produced here, and the pollution continues.'

Seville thought about the conversation she overheard by the temple and debated whether she should share it with Taras. She was afraid to appear naïve. He might give that brief, barking laugh of his and say, 'of course, do you think there are no western companies involved in manufacturing harmful chemicals? You think it is only Russian companies?'

She took a sideways glance at him, not wanting to stare. She thought he was at most ten years older than her, but he came over like a person from a different generation. He had an aura of one wearied by the world, remote and absent from everyday life. Taras made her think of a holocaust survivor who had lost everything and everyone.

He gave her his sad smile, then stretched over and lightly tapped her hand. 'At least you care. You are working in this field; you can make people aware. After you qualify as an environmental scientist you should train to be a journalist.' Absently he gazed around the restaurant, then he appeared to focus and smiled. 'Seville is an unusual name.'

She overcame her surprise at this move into normal small talk, though to be fair many people were curious about her name. 'My parents being pretentious, particularly my father. He likes to think he is cool. He thought it so unconventional to name us all after where we were conceived. I suppose it could be worse, they might have chosen wine grapes or fruit. You know, Merlot and Chardonnay, Apple and Kumquat.'

Taras gave his bark of a laugh. 'Name you all? I guess you have siblings then?'

'I'm their only child, I was five when they divorced. But I have an army of half-siblings. Classic successful businessman behaviour, all your possessions need renewal and updating. Resulting from the updates I have six half brothers and sisters. Four by wife number two and two by wife number three. Wife number two went along with the place names. Wife number three is English minor aristocracy and thought calling children after places working class. My youngest siblings are Imogen and Charlie.'

'Very correct,' said Taras. 'What cities were the other ones called after?'

'Wife number two was a Californian surf child. The unfortunate offspring are Sacramento, Havana, Kingston and Kapalua. Very nearly Kumquat.'

'My God, are they in therapy?'

'Their friends are Brooklyns and Moonbeams, so they fit right in.'

'What names will you give your children?'

'I don't intend to have any,' she replied. 'I would not want to bring children into this world.'

'And your stepmother, with all the children, is she a Californian hippy?'

'Californian mindful. Lots of crystal healing and jade eggs. She makes the kids drink their urine at breakfast. Nothing toxic is allowed in the house, everything from natural products. Somehow I can't laugh at her today sitting in this shithole of a city.'

'Yes, you have a point. Still, it is the luxury of having first world problems to deal with,' said Taras.

Seville tried to imagine stepmother number one in this place. It was impossible to conjure up the image. She remembered her Californian stepmother examining the contents of her wash bag when she visited as a young teenager. Scrutinising the products to make sure none of them had any parabens. Parabens would be the least of her worries here.

She stretched back in her chair and thought it was time to go up to her room, the day had tired her. The exploration of this place had aroused too many emotions. She sat up abruptly. The American called Mr Brown walked into the restaurant. He looked around the room and appeared to double-take when he saw her. Taras glanced over at him, then tapped her on the arm.

'That man is a Westerner profiting from this pollution. He is a director of a big chemical company called Gaia Chemicals. I think they bought our Northern Chemicals because there are fewer regulations here. They can manufacture products they cannot manufacture in America. He is called Mr Brown, a quiet, innocuous name do you not think?'

'Do you know his first name?'

'Donald, I believe.'

'Donnie,' muttered Seville.

He looked at the man again. 'Do you know him? He is staring at you.'

'Dirty old man syndrome, time to go up to my room now. I've drunk enough vodka for one night.' Taras stood, shook hands in his formal way, and wished her a good night's sleep. She left the restaurant and thought she could feel Mr Brown's eyes following her. She dared not turn around to check.

Chapter Four

March 2019

Ross Campbell hated charity events and three months in the year were the worst for them. The pre-Christmas push in November, the competition to get events in before diaries filled up with Christmas activities. In June people held charity balls in marquees before everyone went on holiday. An expression of the hopeless optimism of the British, to expect dry, sunny weather then. The tax year ended in March, making that the time to make those tax saving donations.

So here he was at a grand dinner at the Royal Academy, for UNICEF UK. About which he knew nothing other than it was a children's charity. Madrigal was on top of the detail and her water charity collaborated with them. Ross understood rich men must give generously and donated about a billion pounds a year to various charities, which made him the number one donor in the UK.

Money itself meant nothing to him, it was what one bought with it that mattered. Not things, though things were useful to impress others, the best use of money was to buy power. Investing in the purchase of power was a virtuous circle generating more money and through that more power.

Certain events made Ross think about his ordinary suburban background compared to how he lived now. He never expressed those thoughts; he had buried his past and buried it deep. He had no intention of boasting about his humble origins and how far he had climbed. No, a clever man shared as little information about himself as possible, his history was an abandoned coat, mislaid in a foreign cloakroom.

Sadly, maintaining wives demanded a substantial amount of cash, particularly the maintenance of Madrigal. Her charity, their properties and most of all her family's old manor house all cost him a fortune. He would swear he had spent many millions on that old heap, it was nothing but a breeding farm for woodworm. It would be cheaper to pull it down and rebuild from scratch, though he had met with shocked outrage when he suggested this solution.

Ross swiped a last glass of champagne from a passing waiter as he made his way to the table. People milled around looking at the seating plan. There were twelve guests to a table and Madrigal had organised the seating plan for their table. He discretely removed a card from his pocket with the names of the people on either side of him and professional and personal details about them.

The wife of a famous author sat on his right. The author's wife was in her seventies, with environmental issues as her special interest. He groaned, not another evening with people telling him not to fly anywhere.

The Secretary of State for the Environment would sit on his left. He was out of luck tonight. He should lean back and let them talk across him. Still, to be fair, this Secretary of State was a left-field choice for the role. Linked to the fossil fuel industry and rumoured to be a climate change denier, she was not hot on saving the environment, particularly if it cost the government any money. The current government seemed to judge success by how little cash each department spent; he could tell them that was a false economy.

Once they sat at the table and introduced themselves, Ross

thought he detected a gleam in the eye of the author's wife as she eyed the politician. As a Hampsteadian lady of a certain class and age, he felt she would wipe the floor with the none too honourable member. Introductions over, he smiled benevolently on them both and leaned back in his chair.

***

Once the meal was over, there was a short interval to abandon one's table and network before the charity auction began. The wine flowed copiously. Ross guessed many guests would wake up tomorrow and wonder why they had bid for that monstrous object they were now the proud owners of. He reckoned a goodly number of the objects put up for auction originated at the event last year and had been donated back once the buyer's remorse set in.

Ross excused himself to his neighbours and went to find his first wife, Mary. She still owned ten per cent of Atlas. He fought her for that, but the judge awarded her this share. Truth to tell, he got on well with Mary these days. She was a clever businesswoman and a useful asset to the company. Mary hosted a table tonight on behalf of Atlas and Ross would speak to her even if it did piss off Madrigal.

Mary still looked good, she was of Anglo-Indian descent, with long straight black hair and unlined olive skin. He made a double take as he approached the table. A young woman, even younger than Madrigal, also sat there with long straight black hair and smooth, unblemished olive skin. He recognised his daughter, Seville, another bloody environmental nutcase. She should be studying for her finals rather than hanging out at charity dinners. Typical of students, they could never resist a free drink.

He summoned a benevolent smile for wife number one and his eldest daughter and glanced shiftily over his shoulder to ensure Madrigal was not looking. 'Mary, Seville, great to see you both, how are you enjoying the event?'

Mary frowned at him, 'I am here to promote our company, not to enjoy myself.'

Ross winced when she said that. He felt physical pain in his heart when she said "our" company, it was his company, and he did not like to share. One day he would need to sort this out but now was not the time. 'Seville, I hope you are at least enjoying yourself. I trust it's worth taking the time off from university.'

'She is home to work on her dissertation for a few days. Anyway, Seville needs to make contacts, a couple or so months more, and she will be working,' said Mary. 'She can't spend her entire life worrying about the environment, once she has her degree, she must get a proper job.'

Seville fidgeted with the cutlery and avoided her father's eye. What was it about his eldest daughter he wondered, why did she always appear defiant in that goody two shoes sort of way? The problem with that kid was she just took life too seriously.

Ross regarded her cynically, 'you want me to arrange something for you with Atlas? I'm not sure what roles need a degree in environmental science.' He paused, 'I suppose you could be the buyer for environmental products for us. We're bound to stock them, we sell everything.'

Seville narrowed her eyes, 'I have no intention of working at Atlas.'

He shrugged. 'No problem for me, honey, you work wherever you like.' Definitely for the best, he thought. He should keep Seville far away from any of his business interests.

Ross glanced at Mary who tightened her lips and glared at their daughter. He guessed this was an ongoing discussion he did not intend to get involved in. As far as he was concerned, he had done his bit when Seville suffered from all those panic attacks when she was a young teenager. Time to move on. Kids, better never to have any. Well, he would not have any more.

Ross took out his mobile phone and checked the notes with Madrigal's instructions. 'Tables where you must acknowledge people.' He noted Mary's table was not on the list. 'Table 3, people of note; Head of UNICEF UK, the two Right Honourable Members who are candidates to be the new party leader for the Conservatives.

Table 5, people of note: Head of Friends of the Earth UK and the Turner Twins.' He sighed; it would be a long night.

He headed over to table three, Right Honourable Members were more important than celebrities. Ross dealt with politicians by having them under obligation to himself. For total control, it was necessary to have senior politicians in your pocket. Any prime minister and his or her cabinet were but puppets, puppets manipulated by the puppet master. That was a role he aspired to, the shady figure behind the scenes who pulled all the strings, a person anonymous and unaccountable.

He meandered up to the politicians' table exchanging waves and nods with several people. He had no idea who the fuck they were, but if someone waved at you, you had to wave back. Ross despised these ministers, though they were useful, their simple motivations made it easy to manipulate them. Sycophantic smiles greeted him as he approached their table. He noticed the chap from UNICEF brightened when he saw him, realising Ross was more likely to donate money to his cause than any politician.

Ross constructed a broad smile that radiated insincerity. 'Glad to see you support children's charities in person, ministers, even if your government cannot support them in public.' He slapped the skinnier politician on the back with considerable force causing him to splutter on his champagne. He winked at the Head of UNICEF who allowed a small smile to cross his face. The current government was not known for its generosity towards children, particularly refugee children.

'I hope this is a successful fundraiser tonight, John.' With an effort, he remembered the head of UNICEF's name. 'We have a nice big cheque to present to you. I always find that better than bidding at the auction.' he said with truth. He waved away the thanks and with an 'enjoy your champagne,' he left their table.

Revitalised by this sowing of dissension, he could face the celebrities on table Five. Head of Friends of the Earth and those celebrity tossers, the Turner Twins, environmental nutcases all. Well, he would not donate any cash for those causes.

An urge for nicotine overcame him, and he decided to indulge it before engaging in more small talk. Along the length of the room, long double windows opened out to small balconies overlooking the street below. Ideal smoking spots.

Ross opened a set of windows and stepped out on the balcony; he found his lighter, then lit his cigar. He didn't hear the door opening again, but it must have done because now he had a companion. Ross couldn't place him, though he seemed familiar. An 'Everyman' character, of medium height, medium build, nondescript colouring with pale blue eyes, instantly forgettable in appearance.

The man smiled at him, and he smiled back. Both men puffed on their cigars. 'Politicians are hollow men; would you not agree?' asked the man.

Ross wondered if the man was a journalist or politician, come here to trap him into an indiscretion. 'Public servants, doing their duty,' he replied.

'Trapped between existence and nothingness, like all who crave attention. Fuelled by adulation, burnt by condemnation, then tipped into the abyss by indifference. When celebrity fades, they are nothing, they no longer exist.'

His companion's words impressed Ross. 'Hollow Men,' he liked that as a description of politicians. The same might also be said for celebrities, though many politicians these days considered themselves celebrities, public service replaced by self-service. He thought only fools sought fame.

The man inhaled deeply on his cigar. 'To win, you need to be in control, you must own them,' he said.

Ross stared down at the street, where had he met this man before? He turned to face the man, but he had gone. He had left as silently as he had arrived.

Chapter Five

April 2019

Seville sat on the branch of an ancient oak tree and watched the glassy water slip by underneath. The sun shone in a blue sky, dotted with painterly clouds. Small pieces of flora floated on the river's surface, they glistened against the water and made irregular patterns as they spun in the current.

She slid from the warmth of the branch to the exhilaration of being in the cold water. In April the river was chilly enough to make her skin burn, and she gasped at the sensation. Nothing in the world beats this, she thought, her body powerful and weightless, able to move more freely in this medium than on land. The water energised her, gave her clarity of mind and vision. Her doubts about herself, her feelings of anxiety all vanished.

Seville swam with strong breaststrokes, marvelling at the dragonflies hovering over the surface, the sun glinting on their iridescent wings. Two stately swans glided by her, seeming to move without any effort. She kept an eye out for kayakers and narrowboats, but Seville didn't mind sharing the river.

Her favourite book was, "The Wind in the Willows." She fancied herself as otter, quick and sleek, appearing from the water to say hello to Ratty and Mole. Her thoughts caused a pang of loss for an imagined idealised childhood she had never known. Thoughts of her grandfather brought a sharper pain; he'd taught her to swim in this very river. The tales he told her were not of otters and water rats, but of swimming in tributaries of the Ganges with shy river dolphins, whilst watching out for crocodiles.

Today the water was clear of obstacles, so Seville flipped over to her back and studied the sky. The current slowly took her downstream, and she imagined letting herself float with the river down to the sea. She became wholly relaxed, her anxiety dissipated once in the water, her natural element. Here there was no parent to criticise or display indifference.

Her slim frame held a Pandora's box of emotions, which she needed to keep tightly locked because if opened, she would screech out of control, her anxiety, and her neediness would engulf her. She had let go in her early teens and the consequences temporarily shattered her. Now she had learnt how to dissemble and hide her emotions.

Seville turned over once more and swam back against the current using a strong front crawl. Water, she thought, the most important substance in the world. Life could not exist without water to drink, and for her, there was no life without water to swim in.

***

Seville cycled home in her swimsuit, amused at the consternation this caused some drivers. Many people would not think of April as an ideal time to take a dip in an English river, even on a warm, sunny day. She swam regardless of the season, though if it was cold enough, she paid tribute to winter and wore a wetsuit.

She cycled through the wide gates framing the entrance to her mother's house. The garden enclosed within the stone walls already displayed early flowering shrubs and spring bulbs. Seville got off her bike and walked up the drive, the better to take everything in. She thought she must move away from this beautiful, idyllic spot. It had never been a proper refuge, but there was a comfort in home, even when home was not the happiest place.

As she entered the house the housekeeper called to her, 'Seville, is that you?'

'Yes Amrita,' she replied, as she climbed the stairs to find a towel to dry her hair with.

Amrita came to the base of the staircase and called up, 'Your mother rang for you.'

Seville wrapped the towel around her head and came down, wearing a gown over her swimsuit. 'Let me guess, she said that girl never answers her mobile.'

Amrita put a hand to her mouth to hide her smile and ignored this. She was an expert in avoiding taking sides in any conflict between mother and daughter.

'Your mother would like you to meet her at the office and go for dinner tonight. She said to bring an overnight bag and you can stay in the London flat with her.'

Seville felt a flash of anger, her mother still treated her like a small child. Why did she think she could just summon her? She considered making a point and ignoring the summons, but she had put off this discussion for several months and now, it must be faced.

She deliberately did not pack an overnight bag, deciding to catch a train home instead. She dressed in jeans and a white shirt, as she had no intention of dressing up for dinner. If her mother had booked somewhere too fancy for this outfit she would need to cancel. Seville gave a wry smile, the truth was, if you were rich enough, you could dress as you like no matter how fancy the venue.

***

Seville walked into the reception area of Atlas's British headquarters. She had not been here for many years and the lone evening receptionist did not recognise her. A security guard stopped her before she even reached the reception desk. He asked if he could help her, in a tone of voice that suggested he thought that was unlikely.

'I'm waiting for Mary Campbell, could you tell her I'm here please.'

She couldn't understand why her mother had not reverted to her maiden name after the divorce. Mary told her people found it difficult to pronounce "Acharya," so she found staying as Campbell easier, but Seville suspected her mother wanted people to know she was part of the ruling Campbell clan and no mere employee.

The security guard led her to the gleaming brushed steel desk and the receptionist asked whom she should say was waiting.

'Seville.'

The receptionist raised an eyebrow and looked her up and down with an air of incredulity. 'Surname please.'

'Just tell her Seville.' No way was she going to identify herself as a Campbell around here.

The receptionist pursed her lips and picked up the phone. Seville found a seat and prepared for a long wait. It wasn't too bad, Mary appeared from the glass bubble lift after half an hour and made a big performance of hugging her daughter, and exclaiming 'Darling' loudly.

Seville felt guilty at her stab of pleasure at the disconcerted looks on the faces of the security guard and the receptionist. She was glad to see no sign of her father, although he certainly wouldn't hug her and call her darling. 'Hi honey' and a brief wave would be the most she could expect.

Outside the building, Mary dropped the devoted mother display and reverted to type. 'Really Seville, you could have made more of an effort in how you dressed.'

'Are we going somewhere where it will matter?'

'Luckily not, we're going to the Hansom at St Pancras. Where is your overnight bag?'

'I thought I'd go home tonight. I've got a lot of work to do for my finals.'

Mary frowned. 'It would be nice if just for once, you did what you were asked to do. You are so unappreciative of what people try to do for you. Here's our taxi, come on, we don't want to be late.'

***

Seville was too braced for combat with her mother to enjoy the meal. Her life seemed like a series of battles, all signposted and expected, with both sides gearing themselves up for the fray. Her childhood was a fight she had lost and fighting it had caused her much pain. University was the first battle she won, her mother couldn't fill in the UCAS application for her, couldn't force her to take a degree in business studies or law.

She gained her place at Durham University to study environmental geoscience in the face of her parents' opposition. On her last visit to her therapist, when she refused to attend any more appointments once she was eighteen, the therapist pointed out at length how unwise her choice of degree was.

'Environmental matters make you anxious. I have always advised you, Seville, to avoid situations that cause you anxiety. I believe this choice of degree subject is misguided.' It might have been her mother speaking.

'What do you intend to do once you have finished your degree?' said Mary. 'With your issues, I think it is important you have clear goals, and you get to work without any delay. You need a routine to keep order in your life. Despite that ridiculous degree you're taking, I can help you find a role in a suitable business.'

Seville had been avoiding this conversation, it was easier to deal with low level nagging from her mother rather than giving her a specific grievance to work on. Now was the right time though, she would return to Durham at the weekend and wouldn't be back until after her finals. 'I'm taking a gap year.'

Mary rolled her eyes and shook her head. 'Is that wise? Surely it would be better to find a job straight away. What would you do with a gap year, you can't just hang around the house for all that time?'

'I have no intention of hanging around the house. I'm going to take a year out for travel and research on water pollution. Then I'm going to do a master's in environmental sustainability at Glasgow.'

'Glasgow, that's in Scotland.' Mary spoke as if Scotland was a dangerous foreign land.

'I know it's in Scotland,' said Seville, her voice rising. She fought against her anger.

'You need to be in London, if you must continue studying at least take an MBA, that will be of use to you.'

'Mum, watch my lips, I'm not going to take a job in business, nor am I going to become some sort of corporate lawyer. An MBA is of no interest or use to me. I'm not a child, I make the decisions about my life now.'

'This is all your father's fault.'

Seville frowned at her mother, 'how?' Her father had scarcely encouraged her to take this route.

'Giving you all that money when you were twenty-one. I told him it was a mistake, that it would take away the motivation for you to earn a living and make something of yourself.'

What conflicting views on money everyone has, thought Seville. Ross Campbell, a man who would donate a million to a charity without a second thought, always said his children must succeed on their own. Ross's idea of succeeding on your own was to give each child a million pounds on their twenty-first birthday and then tell them not to expect any further handouts. When he announced this strategy to the wider family there were a variety of receptions.

Mary disapproved of the gift as she thought it took away the need to make a success of yourself. Suzie, wife number two, also protested, 'how could Ross be so mean?' Why a million pounds or 1.2 million dollars was barely enough to buy each child a decent house to live in.

Madrigal, wife number three, had a few years before any of her children reached twenty-one. She appeared to have decided she did not need to take this battle on now. Ross told them he did not understand what the problem was, when he died all the children would be extraordinarily rich indeed.

Seville thought of this gift as her dirty little secret, and it made her feel like a fraud, an actor in the role of concerned environmentalist. But she held on to the money, it represented freedom and independence from her parents and their world. She consoled herself with the thought she could donate it to environmental causes once she was earning a living for herself.

'Sometimes, Seville, I think you plan your life to spite me. You must know I want you to join Atlas eventually. Yes, you should build up credentials by starting your career in another firm. But I have not invested so much of myself in the company for all the benefits to go elsewhere. Imagine Suzie's children taking over Atlas, or more likely Madrigal's. I intend my shares to go to you, and you need to actively participate in how the company is run.' Mary gave her daughter a reproachful look.

The familiar guilt returned. She resented how her mother manipulated her. 'We've been over this before, Mum. It's not what I want to do with my life.'

'It is your duty, Seville. I am wealthy; you will inherit it all one day and such wealth brings obligations. You cannot accept the income without taking responsibility for the company that generates it.'

'Mum I don't want money. If you died tomorrow, I would sell my shares and donate the money to environmental charities. I can't live my life to your plan.'

Mary's face took on a cold, shuttered expression. Seville had seen this many times before, this was her mother's reaction to people opposing her. She imagined her father was familiar with this face.

'You do know Seville, that with your history, responsible adults might need to take action to protect you from yourself. Your father and I must ensure you don't do anything that might damage your mental health again.'

Seville stared at her mother, she understood this thinly veiled threat. Taking a deep breath she said, 'what would you like for dessert, I fancy sorbet.' She must not allow herself to display any anger, her only protection was to keep all her emotions under strict control.

Chapter Six

May 2019

Ross hated flying; his life was too important to him to entrust to the skills of some random stranger, who had probably been up partying all night. It made no difference if it was the company private jet or a commercial flight, the pilots would be equally untrustworthy. Unfortunately, if one wanted to travel anywhere outside of Western Europe, flying was an unavoidable evil.

He shifted in his seat, supposedly the height of luxury, a first-class 'suite' in a plane. God, he felt sorry for those poor sods in economy. OK, the seat turned into a sort of bed, but a bed too short for comfort, and he was unpleasantly aware of the proximity of his neighbour. This was what came from deciding not to take his private jet.

The company plane was becoming an issue, Lady Fakenham's nasty little initiative had become far too influential. It became the fashion to name and shame companies on their environmental credentials and running a private plane was about as sinful as a company got, just short of refusing to offer vegan options in the staff canteen.

Jason brought the problem to the attention of the board. He

stood in front of his audience all bright-eyed and bushy-tailed saying how Atlas could lead the way and dispose of their jet, what a fantastic public relations statement. Most of the directors glared at him as if he were Joan of Arc telling them to recant their claim on France.

Jason's proposal did not go down well, the finance director was apoplectic at the thought he should travel with B list celebrities and foreign businessmen in first class.

'I work on the plane' he insisted, 'we can't take the risk someone may look over my shoulder and read confidential information.'

The rest of the board eagerly seized upon this reason for not travelling with the hoi polloi, except the trading director. 'I always travel with my team,' she said,' and we don't want them getting used to travelling by private jet.'

They had a vote, the trading director and Jason voted to ditch the private plane, Mary and the remaining directors voted to keep it. That swung the issue for Ross, and he told them the jet would have to go, sod democracy. He enjoyed these small exercises of power; it kept his board on its toes and showed them whose opinion mattered.

The meeting broke up acrimoniously, several of the directors popped in and out of each other's offices to whisper their fruitless rebellion. The finance director sat with his door firmly shut, studying the seating plan in the British Airways first-class section. Ross had whistled happily to himself. If he hated flying, he saw no reason why any of the others should enjoy their trips.

He had returned to his office and tapped the keyboard on his laptop and opened the bingo spreadsheet. He'd ticked "developing sustainable solutions" and smiled. Jason could keep the spreadsheet going single-handedly. He also ticked "disruptor." Jason's final verbal flourish was 'this is a disruptor that I think we may find has legs.' Fabulous.

Ross thought of that board meeting as he gazed out of the window, today's trip was one better kept anonymous. Tomorrow he would travel to Delhi to meet with an Indian trade minister, but today was other business, business unrelated to Atlas. He stared down at the closely gathered buildings of Mumbai and saw opportunity. All those people who did not understand their potential economic power. The teeming masses of the poor of India, waiting to become consumers. Always a pleasure to do business in a place where money had the most powerful voice.

He preferred to travel alone and found the time never wasted. When you travelled you were captive to time, nothing would shorten the journey, many things conspired to lengthen it. If alone, that captivity was time to think things through. Life required planning to sculpt it into the image one desired, to be in total control. It was impossible to concentrate with someone droning on in your ear.

He stretched and sighed. An hour or so to kill at Mumbai airport. Enough time to drink a coffee and pick up a newspaper. Then on to Bhopal, somewhere he had never thought he would visit, especially not the area of the Gareeb Nagar district around the old Union Carbide factory.

Ross was at school when the Bhopal accident occurred. He had a vague memory of the news of it. The incident was still the world's worst industrial accident and that was saying something when you thought of Chernobyl. The Chernobyl explosion rated higher on his consciousness, but Bhopal happened a mere two years before. When George Fenton rang him and said he wanted to talk about Bhopal, he thought he connected the name with a disaster. If George had rung him about Chernobyl, he would have been on the exact page straight away.

He mused on the comparative news value of disasters, any nuclear accident made front-page news, you did not need to live next door to the disaster site for it to affect you. But a chemical accident in India was of strictly localised impact. He wondered what capital George thought they could make from it.

***

Ross arrived at Raja Bhoj Airport and walked through arrivals.

George was waiting for him; he knew better than to have a driver standing around with a Ross Campbell placard. You never knew who might be around. They shook hands and made their way outside to a black limo.

Donnie Brown waited for them in the car. Donnie was useful, but he generated a perpetual aura of anxiety. Ross dreaded to think what his blood pressure must be like. He greeted him with a 'Hi Donnie.'

'Do you want to book into your hotel or go straight to the factory?' asked George.

'Let's go to the factory first.'

'We'll take the scenic route by the lake,' George instructed the driver. 'You might as well see the best parts of the city. Bhopal is one of India's greenest cities.'

They followed the lake road, then drove through a mixture of streets and green spaces until they came to a deserted site, filled with the husks of rusting, disintegrating buildings. As in all man's constructions that he has abandoned, nature had made a vigorous attempt to reclaim the place. A solitary security guard stood at the derelict entrance. Ross did not imagine any of the locals would try to gain access to the site.

When the limo parked in front of the factory, Donnie caused consternation by donning a face mask.

'What the fuck are you doing with that, Donnie?' inquired George.

'It's to protect against any pollution, I have a couple for you and Ross,' replied Donnie.

'Donnie, the accident happened thirty-five years ago. We're going to be here for ten minutes. You don't need a bloody mask.' George's voice began to rise.

'A photojournalist was hospitalised after photographing the inside of the factory only a few years ago,' said Donnie. 'I'm just taking precautions.'

'We're not going in the buildings. I want to show Ross the place before negotiations start.'

Ross slapped Donnie on the back. 'Hey, Donnie, you look a right twat in that mask but if it makes you feel better, keep it on. George, if Donnie wants to make a twat of himself, then it is his human right to do so. Come on, let's check this out.'

They got out of the car and the security guard saluted them. George waved a languid hand at him, and they passed down the rutted earth drive.

'He knows who you are?' Ross pointed at the man in the shabby uniform.

'No,' replied George. 'But he would wave through any Westerner who turns up in a big black limo. After all, what would a Westerner want to steal from here.'

They walked past decaying buildings and tanks. Donnie walked behind and muttered to himself; he had kept his mask on.

'What has this got for us, George?' said Ross. 'Everything here needs demolishing.'

George paused and glanced around. 'What do you know of the Bhopal disaster?'

'Not much. When you spoke about Bhopal it rang a bell, but I thought the accident happened in the seventies or something. I was surprised it was only two years before Chernobyl.'

'December 1984 when the disaster happened. A leak of highly toxic gas affected half a million people. They reckon about 8,000 people died of the effects within a fortnight along with 2,000 animals. Lots of blame slinging followed, the facility was half-owned by Union Carbide and half-owned by the Indian public and the Government. They claimed poor maintenance caused the leak, but also raised the possibility of deliberate sabotage by a disgruntled employee. The true cause was never established.

'United Indian Chemicals owns the site now, and they are mainly owned by the Indian Government. As you know our strategy is to buy up as many of these small operators as possible, and this site is about the full extent of United Indian Chemicals. You can tell they haven't cleaned up the site. It is an ongoing embarrassment to the government, and I think they would sell the whole works to Gaia Chemicals for a song. 'We could make a noise about bringing justice to the people. We would flatten this, construct a new factory. Build a hospital and give free treatment to the locals. Do enough for the local community and no one will question what we are manufacturing here. The new pesticide looks promising. Once we have finished the tests, we could produce it here as well as in Norilsk. Let's face it, India will be among the major markets.'

'I think you've got something there, George,' said Ross. 'We need units where we can manufacture more economically. With the bonus of doing this Government a favour, and I like Governments in my debt.'

'Donnie and I have a meeting with the minister today. Are you happy for us to progress this, I should have the detail for us to go through by tonight?'

'You go ahead, George, as always, my name must not come into it.'

Donnie stopped walking. 'I don't think we should go any further. My eyes are starting to sting.'

Ross and George regarded Donnie, Ross with amusement, George with exasperation.

'You know Donnie, I might send you to another place that came up for sale cheaply because of a disaster,' said Ross. 'You ever heard of Gruinard Island?'

Donnie shook his head, but George nodded. 'That was the place the government bought up during the war for British experiments with chemical warfare. They infected the island with anthrax and killed a load of sheep?'

'Got it in one George. Took them years to decontaminate it, then in the nineties, they sold it back to the original owners for £500.'

'Doesn't sound like much of a bargain to me,' sniffed Donnie. 'I'd never believe it was properly decontaminated.'

'The owners felt a bit like you, Donnie,' said Ross. 'I bought the island from them in the early 2000s, not for £500 but still cheap. I built a luxury sanatorium type place there, for my pharmaceutical business to use for medicine and vaccine trials. Once a volunteer is on that island they can't get off until we've finished monitoring them. So, you see Donnie, there is a purpose in buying up old plague and disaster houses.'

Donnie shuddered. 'Rather them than me. Come on, we've been here long enough.'

'For God's sake, Donnie, stop panicking. You spend your life on these sorts of facilities,' said George.

'That's what worries me,' muttered Donnie.

Ross laughed. 'I don't think we want to go any further until it's cleaned up here. India is a good place to have the government under obligation to you. We must take a world view; we need to ensure no territories are out of bounds to us. You can go ahead George.'

George nodded and they walked back to the car. Ross contemplated Donnie sanitising his hands. Donnie could keep companies in line at a local level. He knew how to keep in with the right people, he ensured there was no trouble with the staff. But useful as he was, Ross was becoming concerned about him. Donnie seemed to be getting increasingly flaky. For now, he was still useful, but he could become expendable. He made a mental note, get George to watch out and be prepared to deal with Donnie if necessary.

Chapter Seven

June 2019

A thrill of pleasurable anticipation ran through Seville, she was soon to meet Taras at the Natural History Museum. When she caught sight of her reflection in a window, she marvelled at the stranger that looked back. Silver sandals and long earrings embellished her normal jeans and t-shirt. She was slightly embarrassed to have taken such care with her appearance.

She got off the train at St Pancras and descended the escalator to the lower concourse. The crowds were like a river she thought, a slow river pulling you along in its general direction if you did not resist the current. The dominant current pulled towards the underground, where it swirled and eddied off to the various tube lines on offer. Seville flowed in the direction of the Piccadilly line, intent on making her way to South Kensington.

She entered the museum into the great Hintze Hall. It was like entering a cathedral with the vaulted ceiling soaring above and the decorated glass windows. The huge skeletons displayed gave a warning of the fate of all living creatures. She stood underneath the skeleton of a flying dinosaur and stared up, mesmerised by the thought of the world populated by this creature, so different from that of today. 200 million years ago the planet would be hot and dry, much of the land covered in deserts without polar ice caps. Are we returning to those times she wondered? She found an obscure comfort in the thought the earth would survive, even if mankind did not.

'Seville,' a voice exclaimed behind her. She turned around to see Taras, and he grasped her hand and shook it vigorously. 'It is so good to be back in London,' he said. 'I love the spirit of the place, and especially I love this museum. It is my favourite here, possibly the best in the world.'

'That's a bold statement,' said Seville. 'How many natural history museums have you visited?'

He shrugged, 'I have never been to America, but I have visited many museums in Europe and Beijing, and this is the best of what I have seen. Come, shall we look and talk?'

They wandered around, admired the marvels, and caught up on each other's news. Taras seemed a different person in London, thought Seville. Less sad, more relaxed, here he felt more like a friend than a guide. She could not believe she had ever found him intimidating. By early afternoon they were hungry and went for lunch, Taras insisted on eating at the T Rex Grill.

'How can you resist a restaurant with such a name?' he said.

Although designed to appeal to children, he ate his burger with relish. Once he'd finished, he asked Seville what her plans were now she had completed her degree.

'I'm taking a year off before I start my masters,' she replied. 'I thought I would spend the time researching.'

'What will you research?' asked Taras.

'I'm going to investigate the effects of pollution from farming and manufacturing, and the impact on drinking water supplies. I'm going back to Russia, then to Peru and finally to India. I'm going to the most polluted city and river in each place.'

He raised an eyebrow, 'so where in Russia will you go?'

'Norilsk, then to the Techa River and Lake Karachay. Do you think those are the right choices?'

Taras took a deep breath and pushed back his shoulders. 'Seville, do you know how dangerous this would be. Yes, the authorities have filled in Lake Karachay, but the level of radioactivity is still dangerously high, as it is along the Techa River. Radioactivity is not the issue in Norilsk, yet you cannot visit there. It is a closed city and forbidden to most Westerners. Come to Russia and let me show you somewhere beautiful. Do you not want to see what is good in my country?'

'Of course, I would love to.' She flushed with embarrassment; she did not want Taras to think she saw his country as a complete environmental disaster. 'It would be great to visit the beautiful parts of your country, and I understand visiting places of high radioactivity is not sensible, but I do intend to go to Norilsk. I'll find a way.'

He shook his head. 'There is no way for you to visit Norilsk, believe me when I say this. You went to Dzerzhinsk, let that suffice for your Russian investigations.'

Life had taught Seville not to enter into dispute with people who are trying to prevent you from doing what you want to do, but to step around them and go your way regardless.

'Where would you show me?' she asked.

'Where would a Siberian take a friend who loves to swim? They would take them to a lake in Siberia which is also the most beautiful lake in Russia, possibly the most beautiful in the world. I would take you to Lake Baikal.'

'Lake Baikal? Is it supposed to be the largest lake in the world?'

'Not supposed, it is the largest and deepest. You would love it, Seville, come in August when the water is warmest.'

***

They spent the rest of the afternoon looking around the museum, then Taras said he would go back with Seville to St Pancras station. They found the underground so crowded they decided they would walk. 'I need the exercise,' he said.

It was a bright, early summer day, not too warm, and they worked up an appetite by the time they reached St Pancras.

'Would you like dinner?' Seville asked him. 'My treat but it will be somewhere a bit more sophisticated than where we ate for lunch.'

'I can eat with sophistication,' said Taras. He looked up doubtfully at the St Pancras Renaissance Hotel. 'As grand as this?' he gestured.

Seville laughed, 'no not as grand as this. Come along, it's around the corner here.'

They went down an alleyway that opened out into a yard with tables in front of a restaurant.

'This place serves Spanish food, tapas and wine or even sherry if you are adventurous. Is it OK?'

Taras gestured to Seville to take a seat. 'I feel adventurous, I will drink a sherry, although I have never before drunk such a drink.'

***

They had an easy and relaxed evening. Taras told her about the subjects currently of interest to journalists in Siberia, Seville talked about her dissertation and her hopes for her results from her degree. The sherry went down better than expected, although Taras changed to brandy which he said he preferred to vodka. The evening started to cool, so they decided to go inside for one last drink.

It seemed dark inside after being out in the sunlight. They sat at a table and continued their conversation. Taras leaned forward and took Seville's hand.

'Don't turn around now; a man on the table behind you is staring at us. I wonder who he could be, he seems familiar, but I cannot place him. If you get a chance let me know if you recognise him.'

'It might be my father,' said Seville.

'Surely your father or anyone who knows you would say hello?'

She made a face, 'my father might not, he might be thinking how can I avoid my daughter seeing me? Is there a woman there?'

'No, only two men.'

'I'll go to the loo,' said Seville, 'then I'll check on the way back.'

She got up and left the table, wondering who the man was. She thought it likely it was someone who worked for her father who thought, correctly, he had recognised her. Coming back from the loos she squinted at the man, who was too far away to be made out in the dim light. She tried not to be obvious and prepared to nod hello if formally acknowledged. She glanced again as she approached her table.

For the first time in her life, she understood the sensation described as "your heart in your mouth." A strange sensation, like your heart giving an extra hard pump and moving upwards. She knew the man at the next table, he was the man who chased her in Kiselyovsk, and she would bet the name of the other man was George.

The expression on Taras's face told her that he too recognised the man. Taras rose from the table and took her hand. 'Come, let us pay our bill.'

The man semi-rose too, but his companion pulled him back. Seville was too distracted to notice that Taras paid the bill. They left and walked hurriedly to the station.

'I recognised him,' said Seville. 'He was the man at Kiselyovsk and Dzerzhinsk'

'Mr Brown of Gaia Chemicals. Why was he staring at us, he was looking at both of us, not just you?'

Seville took a deep breath. She wondered if she should tell him about the overheard conversation. Not yet, she thought, after all, Taras was a journalist. Now she had finished her degree she needed to consider what she had overheard and what action to take. This confirmed her resolution to visit Norilsk.

'He recognised us from Russia and was surprised to see us again. It is quite a coincidence.'

'I did not like his expression. Maybe because I am Russian. I come from a country with a history of keeping people under observation. I become concerned when a stranger takes an interest in me.'

They parted at St Pancras with a warm embrace and the promise to email. Taras would return to Russia the following evening.

'Lake Baikal sounds fun,' said Seville. 'Let's get dates in August.'

She sat on the train and gazed at her reflection in the window. Lights became further and further apart as they left London and the suburbs. The relaxed, happy mood of the day vanished, replaced by a sense of foreboding.

When the train finally pulled into the station, Seville decided to sleep in her car. She had drunk too much to drive. As she tried to make herself comfortable in the back seat her thoughts took her back to Kieslyovsk. She thought of the colourful temple and the black snow, and those men talking about the manufacture of Sarin and Novichok. Men who made money from poisoning the world. Seville wondered if she had anything to fear from them.

Chapter Eight

June 2019

Ross had no idea why Maria, the au pair, was so scared of him. His strategy always was, the lower in the pecking order a person is, the less demanding one is of them. Hell, if he was paying someone a six-figure salary they needed to jump when he told them to, but a minimum wage slave deserved consideration. He heard a knock at his study door, it opened slowly, and Maria's timid head came into view. 'Mr Campbell, sir, you have a visitor.'

Maria never appeared intimidated by Madrigal, who could be sharp with the minions, yet she seemed terrified of him. Perhaps it had something to do with coming from some Southern European Catholic country. The patriarchal society and all that. Well, no matter what the women's libbers, or whatever they called themselves now said, it was a long time since Britain had been a patriarchal society.

He would not mind Maria's timidity if he was one of those lecherous types, but long-ago Ross decided he would never make a move on a member of his staff, be it at work or home. Only complete idiots or men over seventy went in for that stuff these days. No one from the "Me Too" movement could call him out.

His board was perfectly balanced, four women and four men. His ex-wife Mary, as business development director, and the trading, marketing, and HR directors were all women. Mary slotted nicely into the double role of being of mixed race. It was a shame none of them were lesbians.

Four male directors, himself, finance, operations, and logistics. Logistics directors had to be male, that was a hard stereotype to break. Luckily, the operations director was gay, though sadly not black as well. The next time he had a vacancy on the board he would make sure they found a gay black, male, or female, it didn't bother him. Of the non-board directors, who were legion, he'd swear every bugger they made a job offer to demanded the title of director; at least Jason, the sustainability director, was black.

He smiled patiently at Maria, 'do show my guest in.'

George Fenton had asked to meet him. Ross never met him at the office, he liked to keep his business relationship with him away from scrutiny. Ross stood and shook hands with George and motioned him to a chair. Gaia Chemicals was not a company with concerns about politically correct boards. The only woman in a Gaia Chemicals board meeting would be taking the minutes or delivering the refreshments.

'You said you needed to speak to me urgently.'

George steepled his fingers and gazed out of the window. 'Yes, something has come up that may be an issue.'

'Do you want to enlighten me?'

'Can we deal with the good news first?'

'OK, do tell.'

'We've got the Novichok contract.'

'Now that is great news, Ivan's contacts with the Russian president must be strong.'

'Oh yes. We will, of course, keep this quiet, Novichok is not on the list of banned chemical weapons yet, but there would be powerful condemnation if Gaia Chemicals involvement in the manufacture was known.'

'So, what's troubling you?'

'A series of coincidences. You remember in February this year; Donnie and I went to Russia to finalise the purchase of Northern Chemicals. We met up with Ivan in Kiselyovsk,' said George.

'Yeah, I remember.'

'Before we went to the airport we stopped at a temple. Place with a snappy name, the Temple in the Honour of an Icon of the Mother of God of Skoroposlushnits. Donnie wanted to take a picture.'

'Jesus, George, you were there on business, not as fucking tourists.'

'You know how he gets. It started to snow heavily, and we sheltered in a doorway while I finished my cigar.'

Ross snorted. 'So, the truth is you wanted a smoke before you got to the airport.'

George ignored this. 'We discussed the need to move the facility from Dzerzhinsk to Norilsk. Then I went back to the car. When Donnie left, he saw a young woman, we had not seen her before, and she must have sheltered near us. He shouted to her to stop, and she ran away.'

'What do you expect? If I was a young woman in a dark place at night and Donnie called out to me, I'd run away. Probably some Russian girl thinking an old American man was chasing her.'

'Exactly what I thought. He rang me in a panic, and I came back to help him find her, but she had vamoosed.'

'Yeah, a second man joining the chase, that's going to reassure her. You were lucky she didn't go to the police.'

'Pretty much my take. The next day, Donnie noticed a young British girl staying in his hotel.'

'The same girl?'

'He couldn't tell. The girl at night wore a red jacket and the girl at the hotel was wearing a blue jacket. He thought both had long dark hair, but he hadn't seen her clearly and couldn't say she was the same person.'

'Please don't tell me he has been worrying about this since February. He's got to get a grip.'

'No, I think even Donnie wouldn't be concerned if it was just that. Anyway, he went back to Dzerzhinsk to rubber-stamp all the relocation arrangements. He spotted the girl again at his hotel, with a Russian. He checked, and the Russian is a journalist for the Siberian Times.'

'OK, now you're beginning to worry me. But this was four months ago, I take it there hasn't been anything to trouble us in the Siberian Times?'

'No, at least not yet. However, the last coincidence caused me to become concerned.'

'Do tell.'

'Donnie and I met for dinner in London last week. The girl and the journalist were at the same restaurant.'

'Now that doesn't sound too clever. This journalist, does he write in any particular field?' said Ross.

'Yes, he writes about the environment.'

They sat in silence. Ross considered berating George about discussing company business in public, but there was no purpose now. His finance director could have a point about having privacy on the private jet. Hell, they discussed business out in the open at Bhopal, the security guard could be a stooge for a newspaper. He understood how it happened.

'Who is the girl? Some British environmental journalist?'

'We have no idea who she is. Donnie took a photo, but we were not able to identify her. Do you want to look, he emailed me a copy?' George tapped at his mobile.

'Let's see.' Ross held out a hand for the mobile. He stared at the picture. 'That's my daughter,' he said.

'Your daughter? Are you sure?'

'Of course, I'm sure, I know what my own fucking daughter looks like.'

George put his hands up. 'Of course, you do. What's your daughter doing with a Russian journalist?'

'There's the million-dollar question,' Ross said. 'Wait a minute, I remember Mary telling me about Seville going to Russia, part of her degree.'

'Is her degree in Russian?'

'No. Some environmental thing, something to do with water. Jesus, I'm surrounded by women who are obsessed with water. Leave it with me, I'll find a way to update us on what she's been up to. Hell, it shouldn't be difficult to clip her wings and the journalist's wings. Brits can't travel to Russia and Russians can't travel to Britain without visas. That might be a route to pursue. Don't you worry, I'll sort this out.'

'What shall I tell Donnie?'

'Tell him half the truth. Tell him it's my daughter. She got herself a Russian boyfriend and now we've blocked her from Russia. Tell him the situation is under control.'

George sighed, 'Donnie will worry regardless, but, as I have told him, no one unauthorised can gain access to Norilsk. The facility is secure.' He paused then continued, 'if I may ask, is your daughter sound?'

'Sound, what woman is sound? She's like that mad Swedish schoolgirl, all she does is go on about the environment, though I'm sure she didn't catch a train to Russia. These young people love to go on about environmental issues, yet they all want to fly around the world, they all want mobiles and internet access. All these young people George, they don't appreciate the world we've made for them.'

'Environmentalism is a fashion among the young.'

'Yeah, and they mainly grow out of it.' Ross thought of his daughter, worrying about farming discharge polluting their river when she was only a young teenager. Sitting outside a farm with a placard and the farmer calling the police. He'd dealt with her then, but he was under no illusions, Seville had not grown out of it. He must be prepared to deal with her again.

Chapter Nine

June 2019

Ross felt the will to live slipping from him as he followed Madrigal through the marquee, and she pointed out the flaws in the arrangements to the unfortunate event manager. Each year in late June, Madrigal hosted a ball for her charity, "Safe Water for All." In her eyes it was the event of the season, even a royal wedding would be secondary to this.

He mused on the irony of these events. You did not need to be an accountant to work out the charities would make more money if everyone who attended just donated whatever they would spend directly to the charity. Tonight's bash would cost him a fortune. Madrigal's policy was to donate all the cash from the tickets to her charity. This meant the money for the night's entertainment; marquee, food, drink, music, and assorted performers, had to come from somewhere else. That being Ross, and he would be delighted to donate the money directly to avoid all this, but show was all in charitable donations.

Then there was the auction. Madrigal had commissioned a painting to be the star prize. Call him old-fashioned, but he did not see the point of buying something to auction. Why not donate a painting they already had around the house, or better still, a piece of old crap from her parents' house?

Admittedly paintings of rosy-cheeked children asleep in the cornfield, or one of the many hunting scenes infesting Lord Sedley's manor house were not the height of fashion in the art world. Still, enough people at the ball tonight had strictly first-generation acquaintance with high society and would be delighted to own a painting previously owned by the aristocracy.

The painting flaunted itself on a dais next to the top table, entitled 'The Dilemma of Social Media.' Ross thought that told you everything you needed to know about both picture and artist. He squinted at the picture, it looked to him like a collection of body parts.

Ahead of him, Madrigal pointed, sighed, and clicked her fingers. Various events management staff jumped quickly to make the alterations she demanded. As he plotted his escape, his eldest son, Sacramento, entered the marquee carrying a box that appeared to be full of little golden bags.

Sacramento approached his father with a sullen expression. His mother, wife number two, had decided he needed more father time and should spend summer with Ross in England. The summer holidays started early for him after expulsion from his latest school for some activity associated with illegal drugs. Ross sincerely hoped Suzie didn't intend to force him to find a school for his son in Britain. If that was the plan, he would need to research schools in Scotland, the Outer Hebrides sounded attractive.

Sacramento made a gesture with his head towards Madrigal. His hands were too full to allow for hand gestures. 'It's like she thinks like I'm a servant or something. Man, she's a bossy bitch.'

'A women's voice reminds me to serve and not to speak. Steely Dan,' said Ross to him.

'Like what? Is that some old person stuff? You're doing my head in with all your old person shit,' whined Sacramento.

'You're not the only person having their head done in,' said Ross, as he eyed his son sourly. He would organise a whole load of faraway business trips; it was going to be a long summer.

'Hello Dad,' came a voice behind him.

Ross turned to see his daughter. The charity ball was the ideal excuse to invite Seville over and engineer a chat with her. He wanted to understand what she was up to. 'Hi, honey. Hey, look who's here. Sacramento is over on a visit; bet you can't believe how much he's grown since you last saw him?'

Sacramento rolled his eyes and made a sound like air escaping from a balloon. He walked up beside Madrigal and placed the box heavily on the table next to her. She glanced severely at him.

'Do be careful with that. Well, why are you standing around, there are two more boxes to bring. Come on, chop, chop, you're sixteen, not sixty.'

With a deep sigh, Sacramento walked slowly from the marquee.

'I hope she hasn't put me on the same table as him,' said Seville.

'You'll have a wonderful time honey,' replied Ross. He was sure Madrigal would put Seville and Sacramento on the same table, with several other low-ranking guests. If he remembered rightly a couple of well diggers were attending tonight, Madrigal thought it important for authentic charity workers to be present. They would all be on the unimportant guests' table, well diggers and unwanted stepchildren. Add a woodcutter or two and it would be like something out of a fairy tale.

***

Ross may have lied to Seville when he said she would have a wonderful time, but to be fair, he wasn't having such a fun time either. He hosted a table populated by various heads of retail companies who wanted to provide themselves with a few environmental credentials. They saw supporting a water aid charity as a simple but effective way of doing this.

Madrigal believed High Street retailers were socially unacceptable, so she had placed all these shitheads on his table. Oh yes, and Jason. He'd have done better on the kids' table, he appeared out of his depth among these adults. On one side of Jason sat Anita Bradley, a woman who had set up a successful chain of sex shops. She eyed Jason hungrily, and Jason seemed nervous. He edged towards his other neighbour; a prim woman married to the chief shit head on the table.

The chief shit head was the sort of person Ross hated most in the world, a professional self-made man. He ran a discount supermarket where it was impossible to find an item not wrapped in single-use plastic. The USP of his supermarket chain was multibuys, and as they thought the customer too stupid to understand how many items might be in each multibuy, or even worse, might try to buy a single item, they bundled up all the deals together in plastic. The self-made man liked to win every race to the bottom.

To prove their environmental credentials, this chain now donated five pence to "Safe Water for All" from every purchase of a four-pack of water. Wrapped in plastic and bottled in plastic. An irony lost on their supreme leader.

Jason instigated a controversial conversation by talking about Lady Fakenham's initiative for transparency in business. Ross thought Jason mentioned it so he could keep saying the name 'Lady Fakenham,' hoping to impress his audience by showing how familiar he was with the aristocracy.

'Transparency in business,' spluttered the self-made man. 'Now that is a terrible idea. I don't want my rivals to know all my business, why would I be transparent about what my business does?'

'The idea is to be transparent about business ethics and sourcing or production. It is not about giving away trade secrets. It's about things like an ethical supply chain, equality of opportunity, showing that BAME people, the LGBT community and women are represented on the board and among senior management,' said Jason.

'When did people stop being people and become a collection of initials?' asked the self-made man rhetorically. 'Well though you can't say this anymore these days, I don't have any of that political correctness rubbish on my board. No, my directors are the best people for the job, and if they all happen to be white, heterosexual and male, well that's because they were the best people for the job.'

Yeah, thought Ross. The people with the brownest tongues, the people who'll agree with everything you say and laugh at your shitty jokes. They're always the best people for the job. You need sycophancy to make you feel powerful. With real power, you don't need any sycophancy, merely obedience. He considered the retailers, these people with their little kingdoms, they had no idea of real power. Just as well, there was only room for one at the top of the tree.

The professional self-made man slapped the bum of a passing waitress, said 'eh up lass,' to emphasise his humble northern roots, and laughed at such scintillating humour. His wife looked on dourly. Ross wished they would hurry up and serve the dessert, then he could legitimately say he must go and greet guests on other tables.

***

Breakfast was late the following morning. Ross came into the morning room to find everyone over three years old there. Sacramento tucked into an enormous plate of cooked breakfast, heavy on the bacon.

'I thought you were a vegetarian?' said Ross.

'I thought you were a vegan?' Seville joined the attack. 'You shouldn't even be eating the eggs. Have you drunk your wee-wee yet? Maybe a bit polluted after the champagne you downed last night.'

'I'm on tour,' said Sacramento, 'so no telling tales. I threw up everything before I went to bed. Man was I sick. Drank about two gallons of water after that, so my pee will be fine today, nice and clear.'

'Don't tell me you drink your urine,' said Madrigal in horror.

'How and why would you do that.'

'I use a glass. I don't drink it out of the bowl or go straight to source. Hey, you would need to be really flexible to do that. Quite an idea though, you could give yourself a blow job.'

'That boy,' said Madrigal to Ross, 'is sixteen going on thirty. I have never heard so much filth from one so young.' She turned on Sacramento, 'don't you dare use any glass in this house to wee in. That is such an unhygienic habit.'

'Why would I be drinking my wee here? I'm not the looney, that's my mom. Listen I'm on holiday, I'm going to use this time to put as many chemicals as possible into my body.'

Seville raised her eyebrow. She was under the impression it was down to putting lots of chemicals into his body that landed Sacramento over here in the first place.

Ross debated how to get Seville on her own so he might find out what she was up to. Madrigal was bursting with self-satisfaction, even conversation with her stepson could not dampen it. She'd already taken several calls from people congratulating her on such a successful event.

Her biggest triumph of the evening was raising a quarter of a million for the hideous picture. Viscount Starck was the successful bidder, and Ross made a mental note to tell Madrigal not to hand over the painting until Starck handed over the money. Ross's experience of the aristocracy was although they may have assets, they rarely ever, apart from a few noble exceptions, had any cash.

'Do you think the weird guy who bought the picture was tripping?' asked Sacramento, unwisely in Ross' opinion.

'That is no way to speak of Viscount Starck,' snapped Madrigal. 'What on earth would make you think that?'

'Yeah, well it was your party and all that, but he smelt a bit like the people who hang out around dumpsters in the U.S. You know, like homeless people, he was, like, dirty. I wondered if he had a bad trip and forgot to shower.'

'There used to be a programme on people like that,' said Seville.

'It was called Too Posh to Wash.'

'That is like so English. At home, we all wash, well apart from the people who hang out on dumpsters of course.'

Madrigal regarded the stepchildren with disapproval. 'What are you both intending to do today? I don't want you getting in the way of the events company while they're trying to clear up.'

'I thought I'd go for a swim, it's such a beautiful day.' Seville gazed out of the window to the sunlit gardens.

'Tell the gardener and he can turn the heating on in the pool,' said Madrigal.

'I don't want to swim in the pool, and if I did, I wouldn't want the heating turned on. No, I thought I would drive to the River Cam. You can swim between Trumpington and the Fitzwilliam Museum.'

'Why would you swim in a river when you've got a perfectly good pool here?' asked Madrigal, her voice rising.

'Are you nuts?' asked Sacramento. 'I could understand if you were going down to the sea to surf, but why swim in a river, isn't it dangerous?'

'No more dangerous than snorting a load of cocaine up your nose then downing two bottles of champagne.'

'I'll come with you,' interrupted Ross.

That silenced everyone. They all stared at him in amazement.

'I can find my way Dad,' said Seville. 'I don't need you to drive me.'

'You can drive,' said Ross. 'I meant I'll join you at swimming.'

Madrigal threw her hands up in the air. 'This is like having breakfast at the zoo. I'm going to find some people who can talk sense. I'll get more sense from Charlie and Imogen than I will ever get from any of you.' She left the morning room.

'Hey, you can't leave me behind,' said Sacramento. 'The bitch queen has got it in for me. Don't they do that strange English thing in Cambridge, punting? You two can swim and I'll take a punt out.'

Ross shuddered at the idea of Sacramento endangering all other river users in a punt. Oh well, best to take it on the chin. Madrigal might kill Sacramento if he left him behind and at least he could talk to Seville while they swam. He could deal with any devastation caused by his son after the conversation with his daughter.

***

The river was chilly. Ross found it strange and slightly undignified to scramble down a riverbank and get into the water. It was unnatural. To be fair he was none too keen on swimming in the sea, but he could cope with feeling sand between his toes. It felt wrong to feel mud squelch between them. He wondered what other creatures might be in there in the water with him.

Still, the most dangerous creature on the river, his son, was thrashing about in a punt further upstream. Ross could envisage a few compensation claims coming his way by the time Sacramento finished his session. Seville trod water as she waited for him to join her. Here goes, he thought, as he committed himself to the water.

They swam up the river against a gentle current. 'So, what are your plans? asked Ross.

'Mum told you I'm taking a gap year, and then starting a masters?'

'Yeah, sure. Your mother told me.'

'Hmm,' said Seville. 'Mum's not too happy about it.'

'It's your life, not your mother's.'

Seville turned her head to him and gave him a blinding smile. He thought that was a first.

'Thanks for being supportive Dad.'

'So, what are you going to do with the year off before you go back to your education?'

'More research. I'm checking out areas where industrial pollution is affecting drinking water supplies and documenting the exact nature of these problems.'

'Hey, how about taking time out to be young and have some fun? At your age, you don't want to be worrying about pollution. Plenty of time for that when you are older.'

'Dad, if we don't take action today, in ten years there will be real consequences from climate change and pollution. If all young people decide not to worry about it now, there will be no impetus for change.'

'Yeah, well at least give yourself a year's break from it, and enjoy yourself. You can't buy your youth back you know.'

Seville turned to look at him again. 'Dad, our youth has been sold. One generation must take a stand, must not put everything off for another generation to sort out. Anyway, I am going to have fun.'

'Tell me what your idea of fun is, I can't wait to find out.'

'I'm going to go swimming in Lake Baikal.'

'You have a strange idea of pleasure Seville. Isn't Lake Baikal in Russia, why would you want to go to Russia?'

'It's the biggest lake in the world.'

'Honey, Russia isn't a fabulous place to go to. Well after this excess of 'fun,' where to next?'

Seville did not reply for a moment. 'I'm not sure, I'm going to check out places known to have problems with clean drinking water because of industrial pollution. I'm planning to travel to places in Russia, Peru, and India. I will work out an itinerary, I'll also need help at a local level, for access and translation. I'll need to spend a month or so working out a plan.'

'You haven't identified any specific places yet?'

'There is a place in Russia, called Norilsk, but I understand access is difficult. Hey Dad, you know lots of people, would you be able to help me with that?'

Oh yes, thought Ross, I'll be able to help with that.

Seville continued to regard him earnestly. 'I think it important Dad, for everyone to understand what a crucial resource water is and how we are damaging it. People must realise the environmental implications of how they lead their lives and what they buy.'

'Anyone would think you were Suzie's daughter.'

'Suzie isn't interested in environmental matters; she only cares about herself and her immediate family. You know, her body is a temple, she's worried about her health and looks, not what happens in the wider world.'

'Harsh but true. Listen, Seville, you do whatever you want, but remember people are concerned about the environment only to a certain level. People like things to be cheap and convenient. Live and let live is what I believe, you do what you want, I won't interfere in any way,' he lied.

'Thanks, Dad. I wish you would talk to Mum. I think you are wrong though, if people understand all the issues and damage their lifestyles cause, they will want to change.'

'Time will tell,' said Ross with cod wisdom. 'In the meantime, remember, you're only young once. Why don't you go and do some fun travel, get a backpack and see the world as other young people do.'

Seville's lips tightened. 'The world is changing Dad. Young people aren't so easily bought off.'

Ross watched his daughter as she swam off ahead of him. Seville was a problem, and she wasn't improving with age.

Chapter Ten

July 2019

It was the summer of drawing the short straw, thought Seville. The atmosphere in her mother's house had become too tense, so she had moved to the Atlas company apartment in London. She hoped not to be there too long, but she needed somewhere to stay while she planned her research trips and contacted people in each country who could help her. Sharing the apartment with Sacramento was not part of her plans.

Ross told her Madrigal had banned Sacramento from the house, for being a bad influence on their children. Seville assumed Charlie and Imogen were picking up some colourful language. Ross had decided London was the best place for him, under the supervision of his half-sister.

Ignoring her objections, father and son arrived the following Saturday. Ross parked his Bentley Bentayga on the double yellow line outside the apartment block and summoned both Seville and the concierge to help with unloading the car.

'That car is so much an old man's car,' said Sacramento. 'It's got like quilted leather seats in beige. Beige, who'd want a car with beige seats, and quilted leather, please? But the bitch queen likes it.

Man, she may have the tits and ass, but she's like a fifty-year-old in that ginger head of hers.'

'Don't speak about your stepmother like that,' said Ross mildly. The comments on the car seemed to distress him more than those about Madrigal. 'Sacramento, you behave yourself, I'm giving you £500 a week and not a penny more. Seville, don't lend him any money.'

'Like I would,' said Seville scornfully.

'Well, you've only yourself to blame if I have to sell my ass on the streets,' said Sacramento. He gave his father a cheery wave goodbye.

***

Once their father left Sacramento followed Seville into her room. She tutted at him. 'This is my room.'

'Yeah, yeah,' he replied. 'I want to see what's in here. I'm nosey, it's normal to be interested in other people. Hey, what's on your wall?'

'I thought even you would recognise a map of the world. Do they not teach you geography at school or is it all mindfulness rubbish?'

'We do geography, but I've never seen the world all flat on the wall before. We use an atlas but that fuck off wall map makes everything seem out of proportion.'

'In what way?' asked Seville.

'Man, Russia looks way too big. The weird wall map thing makes Russia look about three times the size of the US.'

'It is twice the size. Why are you surprised?'

'I always thought the US was the biggest country in the world. No wonder Americans always go on about Russia. Scary dude, a country double our size.'

'Showing yourself as a true man, one for whom size matters.'

'Hey, size does matter, twice as many Russians as Americans is not great.'

'Your grasp of world statistics is shaky. The population of the

US is twice that of Russia.'

'Whoa, you're doing my head in. Double in size with half the people. How does that make sense?'

'You need to travel,' said Seville. 'Much of the land is uninhabited and uninhabitable. Russia is an amazing place.'

A calculating expression came over Sacramento's face. 'Did you say you were going to Russia this summer?'

'Yes, and so what?'

'Take me with you.'

'Why on earth would I want to do that?'

'Hey, I'm your brother. It would be so cool to go home and say I'd been to Russia. Mom would go mad. She thinks they all suffer from radiation sickness even if they don't realise it. Chernobyl you know. She reckons loads of kids born after the disaster are either missing bits or have extra bits and the Russians are keeping it quiet. She's into nuclear disasters, always reading about them and their effects on people.' He dropped to his knees and clasped his hands, 'take me there with you.'

'Why would you want to go. It would bore you. I'm going there to swim.'

'Hey, there's bound to be jet skis on a lake. Or we can bring one with us. After punting in Cambridge, I decided water sports are more than just surfing. Man, that was fun. You should have seen all those old people getting out of my way. And all those la di dah motherfuckers. Wearing straw hats and all that shit. Let me come along Seville.'

She felt guilty. People didn't normally beg to be in her company. She was sorry for Sacramento, neither parent appeared to want his company, he was here in London, without any friends. She sensed much of his attitude was bravado.

'I'll think about it,' she said. 'Dad would have to agree, you'd need a visa and at your age, a parent must give permission.'

Sacramento grinned, 'where there's a will there's a way.'

Chapter Eleven

July 2019

Although Ross owned the most influential social media company in the world, he despised social media and thought of it as a pointless waste of time. Unless, of course, one wanted to check up on somebody, he always checked out the postings of anyone he was proposing to do business with. Often that gave him the edge in negotiations, know thy enemy and all that.

Atlas owned The Book of Friends, the most popular platform in the world. It had twelve times as many daily users as Twitter, and many of those on Twitter also used Book of Friends, making Ross the most influential in that milieu.

Politicians were aware of this; they understood his importance in this world. Now he needed a favour from a politician. He rang the Home Secretary on his private number, knowing he would pick up straight away. James Holt hoped to replace the current incumbent in the top job and was savvy enough to understand Ross may influence that outcome.

'Ross, how the devil are you?' the Home Secretary's voice boomed over the phone.

'Never better. Can you spare me five minutes? I want some advice.'

James sounded surprised, Ross normally advised him, not the other way around. 'Naturally, happy to help if I can.'

'I have a problem with my eldest daughter.'

James made sympathetic noises; he was a man reputed to have many problems with his offspring.

'Among the many issues with being a billionaire,' it never hurt to remind politicians how rich he was, 'is that unscrupulous people target your children. There's a lot of gold diggers around.'

'Of course, Ross.'

'My daughter Seville has become involved with a Russian who as far as I can tell is after her money. I'd like to keep them apart.'

'Naturally. No problem with that, let me know his name and I'll ensure he can't obtain a visa for the UK.'

'Thank you, James, but I am also concerned that she is planning to travel to Russia.'

'No issue there either, a word in the right place, and a visa won't be issued to her. Give me full names and dates of birth and consider it sorted.'

'Thanks, I'll send the details to you. We ought to meet for dinner soon, let's put a date in the diary.'

'Sounds marvellous. My PA will contact yours.'

A few more platitudes and Ross rang off. He looked out of the window and smiled. Simple, no need for any drama. Once Seville found out she could no longer visit Russia, she would turn her attention elsewhere. Oh, to resolve all problems so easily.

***

Having sorted out his eldest daughter, he needed to deal with his eldest son. He was right; Suzie had schemed to move Sacramento's education to Britain. She emailed Ross to say no school in the entire

USA would accept Sacramento, even if they did offer to pay a pupil premium.

Ross did not believe this and set his secretary to contact schools across America to find if any would take Sacramento. After she reported back that over fifty schools so far had rejected him, Ross told her not to bother anymore. He felt grudging admiration, what had his son done to be so firmly blacklisted? He must have inherited the anarchy gene.

If Sacramento had to finish his schooling in Britain, it would need to be somewhere a long way from Cambridgeshire. Ross's secretary, a woman of supreme efficiency, managed to locate a school in Scotland suitable on every count, apart from the fact they insisted on meeting a parent in person before allocating a place.

The location of the school whilst being ideal to keep Sacramento well out of Ross's hair, was inconvenient for a parental visit. It was in a converted castle in Dunvegan on the Isle of Skye. With only a single runway airfield for small private planes, it was difficult to fly directly to Skye. Ross hated flying in small planes, they took away his sense of his invincibility.

The trip preyed on his mind, he dreamt he stood on the battlements of a castle in the middle of an island, looking out across a loch towards mountains. The view reminded him of standing on Gruinard Island and looking across the bay to the sea.

He had a misty awareness of having fought a battle and won, and imprisoned in the dungeons below were all those who had opposed him. High above his prisoners, he was king of the castle. The horizon tilted in a vertiginous manner, and he grasped the battlements to steady his balance. Now he could gaze over the entire world, and it was his. He awoke knowing he was the emperor.

Chapter Twelve

July 2019

Sacramento did not give up once he had an idea in his head. He sensed weakness in Seville and regularly returned to the attack. She asked Taras what he thought, and he appeared more amused than concerned by the notion Sacramento might come on the trip.

'You don't know what he is like,' she protested.

'We will tire him out with activities. I like the idea of an American teenager coming to Russia. I have never met an American teenager; this will be an interesting experience for me.'

That was one way to put it, thought Seville. She told Sacramento he could come, but he needed a parent's permission for the visa. He said he would ask Ross as no way his mom would give permission.

Ross appeared surprised when approached by his son and gave his permission after a show of reluctance. He enacted the role of a parent who would not prevent his children from travelling to wherever they wished to go. They duly applied for visas, and Seville was shocked when one came through for Sacramento but hers was refused. She rang Taras to ask for his advice.

'I don't understand why they won't issue me a visa. I had no problem the last time.'

'I wonder if it has anything to do with your last visit. You came on a student visa that time?'

'Yes, but this was a tourist visa application. I thought they would refuse a student visa as I'm not currently studying at an institution. I was told that is the correct thing to do.'

Taras was silent for a moment before he spoke. 'Yes, that was the right thing to do. Tell me, Seville, you haven't applied to gain access to Norilsk at any time?'

'No, I wanted to discuss it with you first. I don't think I've done anything that would upset any official. Do you think I should see if my father can do anything to sort this out? I don't want to ask him for help.'

Taras became silent again. She heard him tap against his mobile.

'I think it will be tied to your research in some way. I do not see how anyone noticed it but there is a whole apparatus of investigation in my country. Do not laugh at me, I may sound paranoid, but I wonder if it is anything to do with those men in the restaurant?'

'You don't sound paranoid to me. Something was going on. If they identified me, would foreign businessmen be able to get someone banned from entering Russia?'

'If they are important to the establishment, yes. But how would they identify you?'

It was her turn to be silent for a moment. 'My father is high profile, I did attend one of his charity events, there might be a photo of me.'

Taras gave a brief laugh. 'How the other half lives, I forget your background. But why would those men be interested in you in the first place? Is there something you are not telling me?'

She sighed, 'yes, there is. Look, sorry to go all 007 on you, but I don't think we should discuss it on the phone.'

'What is 007, oh yes, your James Bond. Let me think about this, I need to speak to a friend of mine in England. I might ask him to contact you, his name is Colin Wilton. If he contacts you, it is OK to speak to him freely. I will be in touch again soon.'

'Speak soon, I hope we can sort this out, not just for the holiday, but also for my research.'

'Hey, that sounded interesting.' A voice came from behind Seville.

She swung around. 'Sacramento, that conversation was private.'

'I'm your brother, what secrets can you have from me?' He put up his hands in a gesture of surrender as he saw the expression on her face. 'Hey, my holiday is going to be ruined too.'

'This is a problem. It affects all my plans if I can't go to Russia. I don't know what to do. Should I speak to Dad?'

Sacramento shrugged his shoulders. 'My philosophy is to share as little information as possible with parents. But he's not anti-Russian otherwise he'd never have signed the form to allow me to apply for a visa. Thing is, he's a businessman, why would the Russian government pay any attention to what he says? He's not like important, only in his own business.'

'I'm not too sure about that,' Seville replied. 'Even if he can't do anything himself, he knows people. He's here on Thursday evening, I'm going to ask him then. There's still time to reapply if he can sort it.'

***

Sacramento had left Seville to negotiate with their father. He came out of his room once Ross had left to see if she'd had any luck.

'How did it go with the old man?' he asked.

She put the coffee pot down with unnecessary force. 'He said he can't help. He was quite dismissive. He said, of course, he couldn't help, and I would need to research somewhere else. When I pointed out I was initially going for a holiday, he said I should take you to a

Greek island. He laughed and said go to Lesbos and help with the refugees if I must make my holiday worthwhile. He didn't take it seriously.'

'Yeah, well, dude, his parenting skills are pretty sketchy.'

Seville thought this surprisingly percipient of Sacramento. Her mobile rang and a number she did not recognise showed on the screen. She answered the phone and listened intently. Sacramento strained to hear anything.

'Yes, Taras said you may call.' She listened then replied. 'Come over this evening, we're in Queens Square, near Russell Square Station.' Silence, 'yes that would be fine.'

'Who was that?' asked Sacramento.

'A journalist called Colin Wilton. Taras gave him my number.'

'Is he coming here tonight? What time?'

'Eight, but you'll be out. I thought you were going to that rap thing at Brixton tonight?'

'Hey, I can go to rap things any night. I don't want to miss out. Don't tell me to mind my own business. You're my sister, what's your business is my business.'

Seville shrugged. She adopted the Ross strategy with Sacramento, take the line of least resistance.

***

Colin Wilton arrived promptly at 8 p.m. that evening. Seville was not sure what to expect, but she thought he would be younger. He was in his early to mid-fifties, of medium height and build with a thick shock of silvered hair and sharp blue eyes. He had the florid complexion of one who enjoys a drink, and Taras had warned her to make sure she had superior quality single malt scotch for him to drink.

Colin looked surprised when Sacramento joined them and put his feet in grubby trainers up on the white leather sofa. He gazed in approval at the glass of Talisker Seville poured him and tutted in disgust when Sacramento requested the same, asking for it to be topped up with coke.

'That is sacrilegious Sonny. If you're going to drink it with coke, stick to Johnny Walker. Anyway, aren't you too young for scotch?'

'Dude, you should try being young in California. You can't buy alcohol until you're twenty-one and my mom is completely against alcohol. She thinks it's like poison. I'm making the most of it while I'm here.'

'To be fair,' interjected Seville, 'it's illegal for you to buy alcohol here at sixteen.'

'Man, who'd be a teenager. The world is against you.'

Colin appeared amused. 'Still a waste of good scotch. Anyway, young man, finish your drink and run along, I need to speak to your sister in private.'

Sacramento made a rude noise, Colin stared evenly at him. The standoff continued until Sacramento knocked back his drink and said, 'OK, I'm out of here, Seville will tell me everything anyway.'

Sacramento planted his glass with some force on the table, grabbed his jacket and left the room. Seville watched him go in surprise.

'Wow, how did you manage to do that? I can never get him to do anything I want.'

'Force of personality. So, I understand you have problems in getting to Russia.'

'Yes, my visa application was refused. I don't understand why, I got a student one no problem, but they've turned me down for a tourist visa.'

'Taras mentioned some sort of incident you never fully explained to him. Would you care to explain to me?'

Seville looked away from him and wondered what to do. This man was a journalist, though also a friend of Taras's. She'd decided she would discuss the incident in Kiselyovsk with Taras, but Taras was not here now. Colin unnerved her; he had the aura of a man who pursued his aims ruthlessly. He reminded her of her father, and she was never sure if she could trust her father.

He saw her hesitation. 'Seville, if I am going to assist you, we need mutual trust. I will be stepping outside the law to help you, and if I do that, I must trust you.'

She met his steady gaze. If Taras trusted him she should too. She told Colin what had happened, the overheard conversation, how the men pursued her, coming across Mr Brown in Dzerzhinsk, then seeing both men in London and how they reacted to seeing her and Taras.

'Do you think they identified me and got the government to refuse me a visa?' she said.

Colin thought before speaking. 'Possible but a bit unlikely. Had you applied to go to any restricted places, places that might ring an alarm bell?'

'No, not yet. I was going to apply when I got back from Lake Baikal. I intend to try to travel to Norilsk.'

A strange expression passed across Colin's face. 'I would advise against going to Norilsk, but it will be impossible for you. Even if you obtain a visa for Russia, you would not be able to visit Norilsk.'

'That's what Taras said, I don't understand. I don't understand any of this.'

Colin held out his glass for a refill. 'Let's put all the serious stuff to one side. In the meantime, you wanted to go to Lake Baikal for a holiday.'

'Yes, Taras's descriptions make it sound incredible. Imagine swimming in the deepest freshwater lake on earth. I do want to go there.'

Colin took a sip of his Talisker. 'I'm going to come at this from a different angle. Most people in the world are not free to travel wherever they like. I'm in the same position as you Seville, I can't obtain permission to visit Russia. I'll tell you why some time, it is to do with Norilsk. I do not need to go to Russia right now, but if I did, and I had enough money, I would be able to arrange it. You live in this expensive apartment; do you have any money or access to money?'

This surprised her, it seemed a strange question to ask. She hated to discuss money; her wealth made her feel uncomfortable. She nodded her head.

'If you have money, and I'm talking about more than a few hundred, it is possible to set up a false identity for yourself. You need a passport in a different name, you need a second identity. I can get you a passport, driving licence, bank account and credit card in another name. Then you can apply again.'

'Wouldn't that be illegal?'

'Yes of course.'

'This all sounds quite criminal.'

'There were times in my life when following the rules was not the right course of action for me to take,' Colin said. 'There have been times when by not following the rules I have positively committed a criminal act. If one makes a conscious decision not to follow the law, one must accept any consequences. You must understand the potential risks.'

This troubled Seville. 'I don't know, I'm not sure I should commit a criminal act just to go on holiday.'

Colin nodded, 'that is a sound judgement.'

'But it might be worth it for my research. I guess I might want to commit all sorts of criminal acts throughout my life. I might want to go to places those in authority don't want me to go to. I may choose to trespass; I may choose to protest when protesting is illegal. If governments are trying to hide things, exposing them may always be illegal. What the hell, let's go for it.'

***

In the end, they got fake papers for Sacramento too, they increased his age to eighteen, so he did not require parental permission. Colin suggested this would be wise as if he travelled on his own passport, he might draw attention to Seville. They examined the documents detailing their new identities critically, Sacramento objected to taking the name of Ben Smith.

'That's such a meh name, sort of anonymous,' he said.

Colin shrugged, 'anonymity when travelling on false documents is something to be desired, young man.'

'Yeah, your rules seem a bit sketchy to me. There's one rule for me and a different one for Seville. Her documents say she's Ophelia Macbeth, I mean dude, Ophelia Macbeth?'

'Listen sonny, you can't choose your names, we have to use dead people's identities.'

Seville smiled, she liked Ophelia Macbeth, at least she wouldn't forget it. She looked at her documents again, then gave Colin an uneasy look, he appeared to be so comfortable working outside the law. She always thought of false passports as the territory of terrorists and criminals, and she would not expect a journalist to be so familiar with the process of creating a false identity. Of course, she may be naive, this might be an essential part of investigative journalism. But in her mind, she filed a question mark against him.

The visas were issued without any problems this time, and they booked their flights for mid-August. They told their parents they were going to Ibiza. Seville found herself in the unusual position of having both parents approve of her actions. Ross said, 'excellent choice, I'm pleased you're lightening up.' Mary said this was an island with business opportunities and gave her the names of some people to look up. Even Madrigal complimented her on taking Sacramento with her.

Seville wondered how difficult it would be for her to get to Norilsk. This trip could be used to assess how easily she could travel through Russia. It seemed unlikely once you were in a country, there could be places that would be impossible to travel to. She looked at the map on her wall and considered how vast an area Siberia was, with few cities. She experienced a frisson of apprehension as she realised travelling to Norilsk was a journey she would need to undertake on her own.

Chapter Thirteen

August 2019

Ross found it hard to believe now, but when he was young, he had suffered from foolish naivety on some subjects. When Seville was born, Ross thought how much easier life would be once she grew up, when she was independent, a proper person. Now he knew his mistake, small children were a doddle compared to teenagers and young adults.

While your offspring were small you could employ staff to take care of them, once they became a bit older, you packed them off to boarding school. Then they grew up more and burst out of these confines, they started to believe they were in charge, not you. It depressed him to think he had five more children growing up, all about to exponentially demand attention. At what age were they no longer a pain in the arse he wondered?

Well, the two currently old enough to be a nuisance were out of his hair for three weeks, gone to sunny Ibiza. Once they returned, he would pack Sacramento off to his prison school and with any luck, Seville would have started a holiday romance. That would take her mind off sticking her nose into things that were none of her business. It was about time she got a boyfriend, or indeed a girlfriend, he didn't care which.

Madrigal stomped about the house organising everyone. They were going to a 'House Party' at her father's, which involved dinner and shooting the following afternoon. In Ross's mind, a house party meant some unfortunate parents had gone away for the weekend and their offspring had invited all their friends around to trash the place and wind up the neighbours.

Normally Ross would find an excuse not to attend such an event, but people of interest to him were attending. Seville's father was a member of the House of Lords. Bearing in mind the 1999 act taking away the automatic right of hereditary peers to sit in the House of Lords, he was amazed the old man had managed to cling on to his right to rule.

He could not imagine Lord Sedley added anything of value to the process of government, but the old boy loved sticking his finger into lots of pies. Allowing Madrigal's father to become involved in one's pie-making, inevitably led to confusion and culinary disaster.

Lord Sedley sported long, flowing grey locks, and often favoured clothing that made him resemble Gandalf. He supported a strange mixture of both left-wing and right-wing ideas and causes. He thought Brexit was a good move as it would enable Britain to manage its own affairs. In contradiction, he also thought the United Kingdom should open its borders and allow all Syrian refugees in, as indeed should all Europe.

On a holiday to Egypt, visiting Cairo and the Pyramids, he met a relative of the al-Assad family. This 'very charming man,' explained to him the problems in Syria could be resolved, if all the people who disagreed with the Bashar al Assad regime were allowed to peacefully leave the country and settle elsewhere.

It sounded like a marvellous and civilised solution to Lord Sedley, and he adopted this as one of his causes. It ranked slightly higher than his previous two favourites, 'Stop all Fracking' and 'Relaunch the Cornish Tin Mining Industry.' But lower than his all-time favourite, 'Government Grants for all British Historic Buildings Over 400 Years Old.' One had to get the priorities right, thought Ross.

In pursuit of bringing his influence on this mass resettling of refugees, Lord Sedley had invited The Home Secretary, some Russian Oligarch responsible for sourcing all the equipment for the Russian armed forces, Ross, and the European Commissioner for Migration and Home Affairs. Oh, and of course, their wives.

The oligarch was reputed to be the richest man in Russia, a desirable choice as far as Ross was concerned. A Russian contact like this could be of significant use to him, so he was prepared to endure a night at the Abbey. Luckily, it was summer. He would never stay at Ashworth Abbey in winter again. Jesus, he still remembered the dreadful Christmas when he got up in the morning and found ice on the inside of the windows.

***

They drove up the long, curved drive of Ashworth Abbey. Ross thought it must be a mile from the entrance to the door. He hoped the postman came in a van. The grounds had an end of summer air with all the green parched out of the grass, and the lake shimmered in the distance. Just as well Seville was not with them, he thought. She'd be in the water like a shot, and it was probably full of blue-green algae.

They arrived at the front of the Abbey, and Ross gave a smile of satisfaction, his Bentley Bentayga was by far the most impressive car. OK, it would be lost on the commissioner, the French weren't so into cars as status symbols, but it would establish the pecking order with the Russian and the Home Secretary.

Lord and Lady Sedley came to greet them with much hugging and kissing and exclaiming about how big Charlie and Imogen had become. 'Come and have a drink in the library before you get dressed for dinner,' said Lord Sedley. 'The others will join us once they've finished their tour. My secretary is showing them around.'

Ross frowned; no one had said anything about dressing for dinner. He caught Madrigal's eye, and she scowled at him. 'I am dressed' he mouthed at her.

She shook her head, 'No you're not,' she mouthed back.

Ross regarded her father's current attire. He guessed the patchwork denim coat could well be thought a bit outré by the guests at dinner tonight and assumed his host had decided that if he had to change, then everyone had to change.

The nanny took the children to the nursery, and the adults made their way to the library. Ross was glad to see a fire burned in the cavernous inglenook fireplace. It may be August, but the Abbey was still chilly inside. Lord Sedley produced a decanter and asked, 'sherry anyone?'

***

An hour later Ross brushed his teeth to get rid of the taste of the sherry. 'Does he get that stuff from Lidl or something?' he said to Madrigal. 'It tastes like shit.'

Even Madrigal knew the sherry was bad. 'It'll be from some supermarket; he thinks he's getting a bargain when he manages to buy a bottle for £5.'

He shuddered. 'Just as well I brought the wine for tonight. You will make sure he uses ours and doesn't serve us his old bargain basement shit. Christ knows what the French chap from the EU would make of that.'

'Don't worry, I've told Daddy he must use our wine. God that sherry was rank. He pours it into a decanter so no one can tell it's from a supermarket. I told him to place the actual bottles on the table, so you'll be able to check.'

Yeah, thought Ross. I wouldn't put it past the old skinflint to decant all the decent wine into the decanters and pour his old shit into the bottles. He decided not to share that thought with Madrigal.

Dinner was in the oldest part of the abbey, the chilly vaulted great hall. A highly polished oval dining table stood like an island of wood, crystal, and silver in the middle of the cavernous space, the illumination from the candles and the vast glittering chandelier not extending to the more distant corners. The ladies clutched their wraps about their shoulders. His father-in-law had changed into some sort of long green velvet frock coat, and Ross felt indignant he'd had to change into a dinner suit.

Lord Sedley kicked off the conversation with a lengthy and rambling tale about the ghosts that haunted the abbey. Both the Home Secretary's and the Russian Oligarch's wives seemed interested in this, while everyone else focused on filling up their glasses. James Holt, the home secretary, brightened up when he saw what the wine was. Ross guessed he had visited here before.

Madrigal asked the Russians, Albert, and Anna Tolstoy if they were relatives of the great man. Ross suppressed a snigger, he had googled the Tolstoys, and their origins were somewhat humbler, especially those of the beautiful, blonde, Mrs Tolstaya. Mind you she wasn't a patch on Madrigal he thought. Another area where he scored number one, Madrigal was without a doubt by far the most stunning woman here and the youngest. Best car and best wife.

The Commissioner took a sip from the antique crystal glass then held it up to Lord Sedley. 'My dear William, this is excellent. I salute you, too often the British do not pay enough attention to their wine.'

Anna Tolstaya took a substantial swig from her glass. Ross thought she was more of a Lidl girl. In his opinion, fine wine was wasted on Russians. Any nation where vodka was the national drink would never own much of a palette. Albert Tolstoy made a show of sipping and exclaimed, 'superb.' James Holt filled his glass to the brim, taking no chances on what Lord Sedley might serve next.

Small talk dominated the conversation until they had finished dessert. The quality of food was excellent at Ashworth Abbey as it was all sourced from the estate. Lucky for them thought Ross. He would hate to see what would be on the menu if the old buffer had to pay for it. He sighed as he thought of the uncomfortable night's sleep ahead of him. Madrigal's father hadn't invested any of the enormous sums Ross had handed over to him in buying new mattresses for the guest rooms.

Once the table was cleared, Ross swiftly decanted the port himself. He wasn't going to give his father-in-law the chance to exercise any sleight of hand and substitute Aldi's best for the vintage port he had brought.

Lord Sedley gave a little cough and turned to his wife. 'Now my dear, I think we gentlemen are going to claim our traditional right of asking the ladies to retire while we pass the port.'

Lady Sedley stood. Madrigal tutted and said, 'really Daddy, how sexist of you. Why not say you want to talk about business. Surely you are the ones who should leave, not us?'

'Madrigal,' said her mother.

Madrigal shrugged, 'well I'm sure our conversation will be more intelligent without the men. Ross, please make sure you do not stay up too late. I don't want you disturbing me once I'm asleep.' As the women left the room, Madrigal collected several bottles from the long sideboard.

Ross brought the port over to the table. Lord Sedley smiled at his guests with the delight of a man realising he has a captive audience.

'So, I must confess, I do have an interest close to my heart I would like to talk to you all about, particularly you, James, and you, Sylvain.'

The Home secretary poured the ruby liquid into his wine glass, ignoring the smaller port glass. He had the air of one settled in for a long night. 'Always happy to help William if it is in my power.'

'It's this war in Syria, it needs to be ended.'

'My government is working towards that,' said Albert Tolstoy. 'We are supporting the lawful government to enable them to end this disastrous conflict.'

'But that is part of the problem,' said the European Commissioner. 'Which faction is the lawful government? The people of Syria rejected the al Assad regime.'

'My understanding is it was only some troublemakers.' said Lord Sedley.

'Quite a substantial quantity of troublemakers,' said the Home Secretary. 'It is said a mere 25% support the al Assad regime and a civil war has been going on for nine years now.'

'Yes, but that was explained to me. The rebels successfully gained a considerable amount of territory, so people who supported Bashar al-Assad fled into government territory, and that is where most of the population is. If Europe said they would give a home to all those Syrians who are unhappy with the official government, those people could leave, and the war would end.'

Sylvain Bonnay raised his hands in horror, 'Lord Sedley, I can tell you Europe cannot accept any more refugees. We understand there is a problem, and our preferred strategy is to support those adjoining countries to host the refugees until the conflict is over and then aid them to return home. The situation is not helped by outside interference.' He glared at Albert Tolstoy.

'Yes, that is the strategy for Britain as well,' endorsed the Home Secretary.

'Indeed,' said the Commissioner, turning his glare on the Home Secretary. 'I would have thought now might be the time for Britain to step up and take its share of refugees. Even the United States has taken more than the United Kingdom.'

'Yes,' interrupted Lord Sedley, 'an excellent point my dear Sylvian. But listen to what I have to say. Both Europe and the United Kingdom are suffering from the demographics of their populations. Too many old people, like myself,' he said with a self-deprecating smile. 'We would benefit from an injection of young, vigorous people. Bring these people in and settle them in the countryside rather than our cities. Why there are vast swaths of Europe that are underpopulated, parts of Britain too, look at Scotland, James.'

'William, I must say it does not seem like a practical idea to try to settle Syrian refugees on Scottish mountains and moorland. What will they do to earn a living?'

'They can become crofters,' said Lord Sedley with the blithe disregard of one who has never tried to scrap subsistence from the side of a mountain. 'I have gone into this quite scientifically and I believe Europe could increase its population by 5% and benefit from this.'

'How do you work that out?' said Ross, amused.

'Consider population densities. Goodness, the entire population of Syria is 18 million. If 75% of those support the government, that would mean four and a half million would want to leave. That would only increase the population of Europe by 0.6%. It would increase the overall population density from 33.8 people per square kilometre to 34 people per square kilometre.' Lord Sedley sat back in his chair triumphantly, in his mind he had made his point.

Ross whistled, he had to hand it to the old boy, you couldn't fault him on his figures. Practicality, low. Sound statistical analysis, high. He looked around the table to judge how this proposal had gone down.

The Russian laughed and slapped Lord Sedley on the back. 'You are needed at the United Nations, my friend. You would solve all their problems. Please excuse me one moment, my nicotine craving is calling.'

Ross pushed back his chair. 'I will join you, come I'll show you where we can smoke.'

They left the vaulted hall for the grounds; it was noticeably warmer outside. The gravel crunched under their feet as they made their way to a long bench under a magnificent rose arbour. Albert Tolstoy offered Ross a cigar and he accepted gratefully.

Ross rolled the smoke around his mouth, enjoying the flavour of the tobacco. 'Tell me, Albert,' he said, 'how important is it to your government that the status quo is maintained in Syria?'

Albert Tolstoy eyed him with interest. 'It depends on what you mean by that.'

'Rule by Bashar al-Assad is what I would call the status quo.'

'It is of the utmost importance to my country. We have made a significant investment in Syria. Obviously, the current situation is not ideal for profiting from those investments, but it would be disastrous for us if the opposition, the terrorists, took over. Our colours are nailed firmly to the al-Assad flag. There is no profitable way back.'

Ross leaned back against the bench and blew smoke rings into the roses. He gave a small smile of self-admiration as one ring momentarily formed a perfect circular frame to a rose. The air was laden with the scent of roses and the sweet cigar smoke. He tapped the ash from his cigar and turned to face his companion.

'I have a business acquaintance whom I occasionally introduce to other acquaintances when I think their interests may coincide. He is the CEO of Gaia Chemicals, his company has interests in Russian chemical manufacturers, specifically Northern Chemicals. They might be able to help your government take decisive action in Syria. The country is exhausted, and the West has lost any patience it ever had. Nine years is a long time to be at war. Maybe brutal means are needed, one extreme push to wipe out the opposition would be the best for all concerned.'

Albert Tolstoy regarded Ross sharply. 'There would be much outcry.'

'Not if it was quick and conclusive, the methods used to establish peace would soon be forgotten.'

Tolstoy studied his cigar. 'It would need to be completely decisive. The methods I believe you are talking about have been applied in a small way, but because of treaties and conventions, only a small amount of the, what shall I say, material, is ever manufactured.'

'Why not speak to my associate and see what Gaia Chemicals could do for you. I believe they could vastly ramp up manufacturing without any obvious trail. The chemicals used for manufacturing pesticides are the same as those used in warfare.'

'I know of this company, they are already producing a certain substance for the government, but it is a legal substance, at least for now. What would they expect for progressing this further?'

'As I said, there are many uses for these chemicals. Gaia Chemicals manufacture pesticides, fertilisers, and other chemicals. These will all be needed as Syria is rebuilt.'

'And what is in it for you, Mr Campbell.'

'I am a businessman. Stable markets are good for my business. I am always happy to put a word in here and there and to introduce people, so they can work together to build world stability. I need no more than that.'

'A stable world, an admirable aim. But that involves control. The world can be destabilised by people asking for their so-called freedom. The people do not always understand that 'freedom' does not always deliver the stability and prosperity they look for.'

Ross smiled, 'those are philosophical matters well beyond me. I'm only a businessman. I have a simple view of the world; I think of myself as a simple man.'

'A remarkably successful businessman. Your view cannot be that simple.'

He shrugged. 'I introduce people to each other to manage the more complex businesses of the world. For myself, I simply sell goods to people. With me, what you see is what you get.'

Albert Tolstoy chuckled, 'I think you are being disingenuous Mr Campbell. But give your friend my details. I will be interested to speak to him.' He shook his head and muttered 'a simple man,' then laughed once again.

'Room for a small one?' said a voice. They looked up to find James Holt had joined them, not a man generally described as a small one.

Ross and Tolstoy shuffled along the bench which creaked loudly as James Holt lowered his weight on it. He refused the offer of a cigar, saying the scent of the smoke was enough for him, and took a large swig of port from his full wine glass.

The men stared up at the stars, then Albert Tolstoy started the conversation.

'Lord Sedley chose an interesting subject for our discussions tonight. The affairs of Syria are close to the heart of Russians.'

'So I have heard,' said James Holt, 'but Albert, do tell me why. I have never understood what Russia gains from supporting the Al Assad regime. Naturally, Russian interests need protecting, though sometimes it is better to cut your losses and run.'

'Russia has made substantial investments in Syria, but there is more to it than that. To understand you need to know the Russian psyche, you need knowledge of what is important to Russians. Syria is our oldest and closest ally in the Middle East, if the government changed this may no longer be the case. Most crucial of all is for Russians to believe they are a powerful force on the world stage. The conflict in Syria is perceived as an easy war, not a place where we are sending young Russian men to their deaths. This is a battleground where our superior technology humiliates the enemy. We cannot retreat. What we started we must finish. Do you not agree, Home Secretary?'

James Holt shrugged. 'Nothing to do with me old chap, I'm home secretary, not foreign secretary. Invade whoever you like.'

Albert Tolstoy frowned, 'we have not invaded Syria, we are merely supporting the Syrian government.'

'Of course, of course, but as I say, none of my business. Try not to send too many refugees our way, eh. I know your father-in-law is keen on them Ross, but they don't go down well with most of the electorate. There's nothing to be gained for Britain in this war, so we don't have an interest in it.'

Albert Tolstoy gave James a hard look. 'Britain is fighting to leave Europe; we expected the British government would be friendly towards Russia and see new opportunities once they had cast off the yoke of the European Union.

'In politics, rumour and speculation always abound. It is a wise man who knows the truth,' said Ross.

'It is a foolish man in politics who speaks the truth,' replied James. 'The public don't want facts.'

'There is no such thing as truth,' said Albert.

Ross eyed them both. His view was you had to be careful with facts. For most people, the truth was too frightening, they preferred beliefs. How could a government tell people there may well be no God, that religion was based on belief, not facts? How did you tell them society will always be unequal, that the winner will always take all?

He thought if you rubbished people's beliefs you made them unhappy. The trick was to leave them to believe whatever they wanted, but properly inform yourself. Critical thinking was not an art most of the people of the world excelled at. Make sure your life was not at the mercy of other people's foolish emotion and belief-driven decisions. Ultimately if enough people understood what was true and false, there would be trouble.

Ross regarded his two companions, both men of power and influence. Holt, as a politician was not in total control of his destiny, there were limits to his power. Tolstoy was different, he was a man like himself, rumoured to be the richest man in Russia, he controlled the oil industry as well as sourcing military equipment. But he had a high public profile which made him vulnerable, if those ruling Russia saw his wealth and power as a threat.

For Ross, it was only acceptable to be powerful enough to be in complete control, but he did not need to advertise his authority. He gazed up at the stars and smiled with sly satisfaction, these men were his puppets, and he would set them to do his bidding.

Chapter Fourteen

August 2019

Travelling with Sacramento brought its problems in addition to the normal challenges posed by the aviation industry. Seville proposed they travel to Russia overland. She explained to Sacramento her concerns about the effect of flying on the environment. He protested they had three weeks, and he was not going to spend half his holiday travelling.

They planned to meet Taras in Irkutsk, but it was impossible to fly direct, so they flew to Moscow and took a second flight to Irkutsk. Their stopover seemed interminable, as time always moves slowly when your companion asks, 'how much longer till boarding is called,' every five minutes or so.

The next leg of the journey was more trying. The passengers travelling from Moscow to Irkutsk appeared somewhat less cosmopolitan than those on the flight from London to Moscow. Sacramento looked alarmed when a man with an unfeasibly black and luxuriant moustache sat on the end of their row. He produced an enormous cloth handkerchief and began vigorously blowing his nose.

'Man, how unhygienic,' hissed Sacramento to Seville.

'Will you please be quiet; he might understand English.'

Sacramento subsided into silence until the cabin crew served their meals. He gazed at his tray in dismay, 'Man, what is this?'

Seville regarded her meal. To be fair the offering was unusually beige. Meat, or what she presumed was meat featured heavily. Two gherkins and a frill of lettuce represented the vegetable world, accompanied by a dollop of soft white potato. A pale bread roll and a packet of beige biscuits completed the offer.

Sacramento prodded a slice of the meat, of various shades in the beige pallet, they trended from off white, to palest brown. He picked up a gherkin and waved it around. 'Hey Seville, this looks like something the Russian dude on the end might sneeze out.'

She shuddered. 'Either eat that or leave it, but please don't play with your food. I think I might try a biscuit.'

Sacramento examined the biscuits. 'Briz, have you ever heard of biscuits called Briz before? Is that tomato ketchup, guess I could dip them in it?'

Seville made a face and passed her tub of ketchup to him.

***

They arrived in Irkutsk without any major incidents. Seville experienced a thrill of anxiety as they approached passport control, she thought this would be the first time their false passports would be properly scrutinised. She shifted from foot to foot as they waited in the slow-moving queue.

'Dude, you are giving out 'look at me, I'm an international criminal,' signs. Stop looking so guilty.'

'I can't help it. I've never done anything illegal before.'

Sacramento stared at her. 'What never? You must have done something illegal.'

She flushed, 'don't stare at me like that, it's perfectly normal to go through life without breaking the law.'

'If you say so. Man, it doesn't seem natural. Aren't scientists supposed to question things? Surely when you question things you end up breaking laws because the laws are stupid?'

Yet again, Sacramento surprised Seville by showing unlooked-for wisdom.

'Well quite. That's why we're here now.' She thought of all the times she had disobeyed her parents, but that was not the same as doing something illegal. There were consequences though, they'd curtailed her freedom. Thinking about this made her more fidgety.

He nudged her. 'Time to show your illegal document.'

Their bickering had prevented her from noticing they were now at the front of the queue and the official clicked his fingers and tutted at her. He examined her passport with great care, stamped it with vigour and waved her on. Both passed through without incident. As a bonus, their luggage also arrived, always a surprise on a journey involving changing flights.

'What now? Where do we meet your friend?' Sacramento fired questions at Seville.

'Taras is meeting us here. Then we are going to drive straight to the cabin.'

'Hey, that sounds cool. Will that be like a log cabin?'

***

Seville soon found Taras, and they loaded their luggage into the hired car. He had bought provisions including copious quantities of vodka. His lips twitched every time he regarded Sacramento, and Seville thought he had lived up to Taras's expectations.

They drove south for about an hour to Listvyanka, a tourist village on the shores of Lake Baikal and stopped for lunch.

'Now we leave civilisation,' said Taras as they finished their substantial meal. 'The roads, they will be bumpy in places. We drive northeast towards Khargino and our cabin. But do not worry, we have food and vodka, and we will have the water and the mountains.'

***

The roads were bumpy, potholed tracks would be a more exact description. Seville was hot, dusty, and tired, and longed for the embrace of the lake. The countryside was starkly beautiful with forested slopes rising steeply from the water.

'People swim in the lake all year round,' said Taras. 'In winter they make a hole in the ice and get in the water, some swim under the ice.'

'What the fuck?' said Sacramento. 'Are they freaking loonies?'

'Many Russians are loonies,' replied Taras. 'It is in our nature to love extremes.'

'I wouldn't mind doing that,' said Seville.

Sacramento eyed her with disbelief. 'I can't believe we share genes. Hey Taras, are we nearly there yet?'

They arrived at the cabin an hour later. Two cabins nestled against a wooded hill with a strip of shingle leading down to a sandy beach. The larger of the two was a strange mixture of the decorative and the primitive. A form of marquetry covered the exterior, creating the outline of a many-branched tree with no leaves. The windows were elaborate, painted in a pale blue with white wood filigree trim. Here the gingerbread cottage resemblance ended, the roof was of grey corrugated iron and the external walls had random solar panels attached haphazardly. It was, however, much more impressive than its neighbour. This construction had green lichen coating the sagging wood walls and an insecurely fitted corrugated iron front door.

'Which is ours?' asked Sacramento in a cautious tone.

'Our cabin is first-class,' said Taras. 'Come and I will show you all the luxurious facilities inside.'

Brother and sister exchanged glances and shrugged. 'Just remember he's your friend,' said Sacramento.

Both paused for a moment to check which building Taras would make for, neither felt sure it would be the gingerbread cottage. They smiled with relief when Taras opened the pale blue door rather than the rusting corrugated iron one and followed him into the building.

Their gingerbread cottage had plain wood floors, wood-panelled walls, and a preponderance of floral decorations. Sofas, cushions, curtains, crockery, and vases all featured floral motifs. Sacramento examined the décor with an air of disapproval.

'Man, this is like some old lady place.' He opened another door and a smile spread across his face. 'We've got a sauna. How do you turn it on, Taras? I'm going to take a sauna and then I'm going to bed.'

'I'm going to swim while it heats up, then I'll have one too. I'll wait a bit before trying to sleep,' said Seville.

'Let us bring in our luggage, then I'll fire up the sauna,' said Taras. 'I will join you while we wait for the sauna to heat up.'

Seville unpacked, changed into her swimsuit, and ran down to the lake, an immense body of water, sparkling away to a distant horizon. She crossed a small band of shingle and walked across coarse sand into the water. The translucent water was inviting, cool and fresh on her skin, banishing her tiredness from the journey. She swam out to about a mile from the shore and floated on her back. Seville became wholly relaxed and hoped the others would take their time before they joined her.

Although both Sacramento and Taras were competent swimmers, they were not confident enough to swim out as far as Seville. She was in her own space, with a sapphire sky above, royal blue water around her, and views of the mountains surrounding the lake. She wanted to stay here forever; all anxiety exorcised. Seville flipped herself over on her front and dived down, it was so deep she could not see the bottom. She broke through the surface again and gazed up at the sky.

Seville felt like a ship in a bottle floating on the lake, contained within this beautiful bubble of sky, water and mountains. 'How strange,' she thought, 'in this country, there is the horror of Dzerhinsk and the beauty of Lake Baikal.' That was the way of the world, both beauty and horror, and she intended to expose the horrors to public scrutiny, even if that did lead to punishment for her.

Chapter Fifteen

August 2019

Ross thought of it as his annual punishment, going on holiday with his family in August. Left to his own devices he would not bother with holidays, he struggled to understand the attraction in them. But Madrigal was clear, it was socially unacceptable not to holiday at least once a year with one's family. The fact he went skiing with her in February did not count.

So here he was in Northern Italy, ensconced on a private island on Lake Orta. A resort open to the public would not do. He thought Madrigal had delusions of grandeur, maybe she imagined paparazzi would try to photograph her in her bikini as if she were a vacationing royal.

Not that they were on their own. The regular nanny was set free for a month and holiday cover nannies hired. The villa came with a quantity of staff, how many, he did not know. Madrigal invited what seemed like every casual acquaintance, to come and spend a few days on their island. She thought it a waste not to fill every room in the ten-bedroom villa, the staff occupying premises on the grounds.

She pinned up a calendar in the room assigned as his study, so each morning he could check it with low-level apprehension to note whom she was inflicting on him. Ross wondered if she intended to publish her version of Hello magazine, with an array of the rich and well-known, interspersed with some of her relatives. He reckoned she planned to make them all donate to her charity before they left. He had to hand it to Madrigal, she was top gun when it came to getting money out of people.

Ross checked the calendar; the first guests were due tomorrow, and he thought he had better get himself up to speed on who was going to be infesting his palazzo. The Capells and their two brats, Horace, and Octavia headed the list. Who on earth would ever think Horace a suitable name for a child? He thought at least he would remember his name. Ross was not too hot when it came to remembering the names of people's children. He could not see the point; he would never talk to them, so why did he need to know their names.

The next name was more ominous, Dido Richardson, she was down for the month. He groaned; Dido was Madrigal's best friend. She never had a partner; most men were far too sensible to become involved with her. She took life seriously and had a monopoly on deep and meaningful conversation. Meat and alcohol never passed her lips, and she embraced veganism with the enthusiasm of a true puritan. Ross never fathomed out why anyone would want her as a best friend.

He frowned at another name on the list, Jason Harris, Jason fucking Harris. What the fuck was Madrigal doing inviting his employees on holiday with them. Had she lost her mind? 'Madrigal,' he called.

Getting no response, he went to search around the villa, or palazzo as Madrigal insisted on calling it. It was impressive, but the rooms with the restored frescoes on the walls would need to be out of bounds to the children. He could see the results of sticky little hands over those damned paintings.

He found Madrigal in the entrance hall taking delivery of what appeared to be a warehouse's worth of boxed goods and giving instructions to an army of staff. Impressively she spoke to them all in rapid Italian, a more effective method than that adopted by her father of speaking louder.

'Madrigal, why is Jason on the list of guests?'

She paused in her commands, 'Ross do you ever listen to anything I say to you? I went through the guest list with you and clearly explained whom I have invited. I invited Jason for Dido; he is a handsome man, and I must find someone for her. He is a couple of years younger and of course wouldn't be suitable as a permanent partner, but she has to start again somewhere with men.'

Ross found himself in the unusual condition of being speechless. He was unaware Dido had ever started with men, so 'start again' confused him. He felt sorry for Jason, no one deserved to be paired off with Dido, hell, he wouldn't wish that on his worst enemy. Ross collected himself, 'Madrigal, business needs to be kept separate from family.'

She waved a dismissive hand at him, 'what nonsense, we often have business connections to dinner, why everyone does, we were always having business acquaintances to stay at the Abbey when I was a child.'

'Business yes, but employees no. You never invite your employees around unless it's a company event.'

'Rubbish, anyway I don't know where I'd find another man like Jason, he's handsome, interesting, and different.' Her voice rose on the last three words.

'You mean he's black,' said Ross raising an eyebrow.

Madrigal had the grace to flush slightly. 'Well yes, I thought he might interest Dido, none of our crowd has ever been any good with her.'

'How long is he here for?'

'I invited him for a fortnight, which should be enough time for him to make an impression.'

'God help us,' muttered Ross. 'Anyone else I should be warned about?'

'If you paid attention you'd know. Mummy and Daddy will come for a week after you've left, along with the Minister for Overseas Development and her husband. Daddy wants to speak to them about his Syrian idea. The Capells and their family are here for a few days from tomorrow, Charlotte and David are coming with their sweet baby, as David is filming in Milan, and he's got a weekend free. Hugo and Fraser with that little African boy they've adopted, and Rachel and Simon are bringing their three along too.'

Ross shuddered, 'I will need to work. Make sure no kids are allowed anywhere near my study.'

'The children are staying in a house on the grounds with their nannies. I have invited some people for you too.'

'Whom might that be?'

'Well, I told you, the Home Secretary and his family, they're your friends, and that charming Russian couple Daddy introduced us to, Mr and Mrs Tolstoy. I'm hoping he might support my charity; Daddy says he owns all the oil in Russia.'

'Oil and armaments apparently. Yes, he's a major player. What makes you think you're inviting them for me?'

'They're business people, you only enjoy talking to business people or politicians. Anyway, I didn't exactly invite them, they sort of invited themselves, I found myself in a position where it would have been most impolite not to extend an invitation.'

This piqued Ross's interest. What did Albert Tolstoy want from him?

***

Ross cited the claims of business and spent the day hiding in his office. He could cope with the evenings once the nannies put the children to bed, though dealing with Dido was challenging. They gathered for dinner on Monday evening, at a table on the terrace, overlooking the lake. Ross and Edward Capell ambled down together, clutching cocktails. Edward appeared overstimulated by the presence of the nannies, and Ross had to extract him from the poolside in the nanny house.

The Capells' nanny at home in England was a matronly, middle-aged woman. Angela had too keen an eye for the frailty of man to employ any pretty young thing. Madrigal was so confident of her shimmering beauty that such a concern would never occur to her. She had employed two attractive young Italian girls to look after all the children, both excellent swimmers and fully conversant with all first aid procedures, she informed her guests. Edward had popped down to check how they were coping.

With reluctance, he allowed Ross to lead him from the nanny house to the main terrace outside the palazzo. Finally, accepting the inevitable, he turned his attention to updating Ross with the latest political gossip. Edward was head of the civil service so in a strong position to be up to date with political gossip.

'Word is out there will be an election before the end of the year. Everything is going to hell in a hand cart. Brexit is crippling politics.'

Ross nodded, 'crippling business too,' he said insincerely. He felt his business interests were fairly Brexit proof, how wise he was not to be in financial services, agriculture, or manufacturing his products in the UK.

'Too right old chap, too right,' replied Edward. 'My political masters have completely lost the plot. All the parties apart from the SNP have not a clue what they're doing, they're all over the place. None of them has a strong, credible leader, our current prime minister is a complete disaster. Spends more time correcting his civil servants' grammar than controlling his party.' Edward lowered his voice, 'not popular with the electorate either, he patronises them too much.'

'Who should be the leader then? I take it only the Conservatives have a chance of winning an election?'

'My God, yes. No one over twenty-five will vote for Red Peter, the Liberal Democrats cannibalise the vote for the right-wing of

Labour and the left-wing of Conservatives. The problem is without a popular leader for the Conservatives, we're back to a hung parliament and continued chaos. Doris was unpopular, but Tristan is no better. I'm beginning to wonder if James Holt should be the man.'

Ross gave a small smile of self-satisfaction. James Holt was his choice of leader. He had supported Tristan because at that time James Holt had no chance of being chosen, he was not considered serious enough. Now the party had a 'serious' leader, and no one liked him. 'Do you think the party would vote for him?' he asked.

'Six months ago, no. They perceived James as having no gravitas, more interested in making witty comments than developing policy. That is why they made him Home Secretary, it was a bit too gloomy and sombre in that department, what with the Windrush scandal and all that. The party needed someone to lighten things up there. Now the whole country is at each other's throats, we need someone who doesn't take it all so seriously.'

'Would it be credible for the Conservatives to have another leadership election so soon?'

'Well, it wouldn't be ideal. Still, if public opinion is strong enough,' he tailed off.

'You must keep an eye on my social media site,' said Ross. 'Book of Friends gives a clear idea of how the public thinks. Check if there are anti-Tristan and pro-James sentiments expressed strongly there.'

Edward smiled back, 'I will indeed,' he said.

The arrival of the women interrupted the conversation, Madrigal stunning in a short, floaty flower print silk dress and Angela in a cream linen shift dress that emphasised her tan. Dido appeared dressed for a funeral, her long, grey dress in complete contrast to their sunny, colourful surroundings. Ross wondered what she would wear to the pool. Her face was bare of any makeup, and her blonde eyebrows and eyelashes, along with pale mousey hair, gave her the aspect of a ghost.

'Where's Jason?' asked Ross.

'He arrived half an hour ago, so he's freshening up before joining us.'

'Better have a stiff drink waiting for him then,' said Ross, gesturing at a member of the staff.

Madrigal frowned at him.

***

They sat down to dinner and Madrigal seated Jason next to Dido like a sacrificial lamb. The boy wasn't as stupid as he appeared thought Ross. As Jason approached the table a wary expression came over his face when he saw two men and three women. The penny dropped, he'd been invited to even up the sexes, Dido was his.

Jason shook hands with the men, air-kissed Madrigal and Angela, and almost imperceptibly paused before Dido. Before he had a chance to decide on a handshake or air kiss for the woman you don't know, Dido embraced him and said she was so glad to meet him, and she had heard so much about him from Madrigal.

Ross would have sworn Jason paled, he politely disentangled himself, sat and moved his chair away from Dido. He seemed nervous and kept calling Ross Mr Campbell.

The conversation was difficult, Madrigal and Angela watched Jason and Dido intently, like mother hens with their new chicks. As the sky darkened and lights came on around the lake, Dido kept putting a hand out, like a lollipop lady halting the traffic and asking them if they could feel a presence in the air. Edward became restive and said he would go and check up on the children, Ross decided he had an important call to make from his study. It would be too painful to watch how Madrigal and Angela might manoeuvre to leave Jason alone with Dido.

***

The Capells left, replaced by Hugo, Fraser and their spawn of the devil adopted child, who needed 666 tattooed on his forehead to alert people of the danger. Ross imagined the birth parents were glad to see the back of him. One nanny resigned, and he had to promise an unfeasibly large bonus payment if she agreed to stay and deal with the devil child. He made Sacramento look tame, thought Ross.

Loud shouts from the side of the lake distracted him from his midday conference call. The devil child, appropriately named Damien, had found a silk wrap of Madrigal's, and thrown it in the lake. He then threw stones at a couple of swans that came up to investigate. That was a big mistake, the enraged birds left the water and showed themselves to be as tall as the child. Damien fled, the swans gave chase and when Hugo nobly interposed himself between them and his adopted son, the swans satisfied themselves with attacking Hugo instead.

The group retired to the villa, Madrigal helping the injured Hugo. They barred the doors, and the swans stalked around hissing viciously for a while, before retiring to the lake. Fraser insisted they would replace the damaged wrap, an action that would set them back hundreds of euros, and a nanny applied first aid to Hugo.

Ross realised the extent of the problem when he saw Damien disciplined.

'Damien, come to me,' said Fraser.

'Won't' said Damien.

'Damien, you must apologise to Madrigal for ruining her lovely wrap, and you need to go and kiss daddy better on all those cuts and bruises he got defending you from the swan.'

'Won't' said Damien.

'Damien, you are being a naughty boy and naughty boys are punished. Now come and sit on the naughty step and think about what you have done.'

'Won't' said Damien.

Fraser wagged a finger at Damien. 'What happens to naughty boys?'

'They get ice cream,' said Damien, a broad smile breaking across his previously sullen face.

Fraser gave a guilty smile to Madrigal and Ross. 'Oh dear, he's not wrong really. The last time he got cross with one of his small friends, we made him sit on the naughty step, and he was so devastated he cried and cried until he made himself sick. Poor little thing, we had to buy him ice cream to cheer him up.'

They exchanged glances, neither of them came from that school of parenting.

***

Hugo, Fraser, and Damien left their party to commit acts of terrorism at the villas of other unfortunate friends in the South of France. The Tolstoy's arrived, thankfully not accompanied by any 'little ones,' and the Home Secretary and some members of his family also turned up.

Ross always thought of James Holt, the home secretary, as a fellow traveller in life. He too had complicated family arrangements, though generally, he did not marry the mothers of his children. The current partner held out for marriage, then promptly delivered twins. James looked in need of a holiday, he was a man with a short attention span, and twin toddlers demanded more attentiveness than he could give. He appeared to be so relieved to dump the twins on the nannies, he didn't register how attractive they were.

The interminable fortnight rolled on, yet again they sat at the dinner table on the terrace, once more Dido droned on about how they were all cutting their lives short by eating meat and destroying the environment. Ross thanked God he had not committed to the full month and used the excuse of having a business call to leave the table and retreat to his study.

He filled a glass with an expensive single malt, exited through the veranda doors and walked down to a pontoon at the edge of the lake. A table and four chairs stood on it, and he sat bobbing up and down with the movement of the water. Two swans swam by in a stately manner. Ross eyed them warily, he hoped they weren't the ones the devil child had attacked.

He glanced up at the sky, it seemed a mass of stars. He'd recently read an article about light pollution in Northern Italy making it impossible to see the Milky Way anymore, but the night sky was good enough for him. Hell, he had no idea what the Milky Way looked like.

The pontoon rocked vigorously, and he turned and saw Jason walking across the boards towards him. Ross sighed, he hoped Jason wasn't about to use him as an agony uncle, it would be a waste of his time.

'Hi Mr, er Ross, can you spare me a few minutes of your time?'

'Of course,' said Ross with false bonhomie. 'What can I do for you?'

Jason adopted his most earnest expression, he gazed directly at Ross with brown soulful eyes. Ross thought he'd better not gaze at Dido like that or there would be no escape. Jason would be getting up early each morning for the yoga session, followed by a tasty breakfast of a glass of green gunk.

'Greta Thunberg,' he said, in an earnest tone of voice.

'Yes,' replied Ross, 'Swedish teenager, autistic, short, pigtails, obsessed with the environment, crosses the Atlantic by boat. Do I get full points?'

'It was after having further conversations with Angela, Lady Fakenham. I thought how fantastic it would be for Atlas to link up with Greta Thunberg.'

'Link up with her in what way? She's not one of those YouTube influencers you know, you can't bung her a couple of hundred grand to say how wonderful Atlas is.'

Jason became agitated, 'of course, I know she is not a celebrity for sale. Dido thought if Atlas could collaborate with her in some way, help her promote her message, sponsor her like Kingfisher sponsored Ellen MacArthur. It would establish our green credentials.'

Ross regarded Jason; he did not get it. He didn't understand Greta Thunberg's influence came from not linking up with commerce, that she was uninterested in fame or money-making opportunities. That she was a genuine nutcase, only concerned about the environment. She did not need sponsorship like a sportsperson. Still, it might distract him from spending too much time on Lady

Fakenham's 'Transparency in Business' initiative.

'Well, I can't see you having any success but feel free to have a go.'

A smile spread across Jason's face, he grabbed Ross's hand and shook it energetically. 'I knew I was right; Dido didn't believe me when I said you would be interested in promoting Atlas's green credentials.'

This pricked Ross's interest. 'So how are you getting on with Dido? I assumed you were coming to me for advice on how to shake her off.'

'Oh no, Dido has a beautiful soul. She feels deeply about things. I have never met anyone like her before.'

Indeed, thought Ross, neither had he. Well, Madrigal had that one right; some people you could fool all the time. He always put Dido down as a narcissistic, self-obsessed neurotic, but hey, what did he know. He watched Jason hurry off back to his inamorata and shuddered at the thought of having sex with Dido.

Ross leaned back in his chair to contemplate the sky and felt the rhythm of heavy steps on the pontoon once more. It was going to be one of those evenings. Albert Tolstoy and James Holt joined him, with the aura of men making a strategic escape.

Albert sat down, clutching a substantial glass of brandy. He raised the glass to toast Ross, 'my compliments on your excellent brandy my friend.'

'And on your excellent wine,' said James, waving a bottle at him. He sat down heavily, making the pontoon rock, so he had to clutch the bottle of wine.

'My pleasure.'

The men stared up at the stars, all feigning an interest in the beauty of the night. Ross considered his companions, he knew what use Holt could be to him, and James Holt knew how important Ross was to his ambitions. But what did Tolstoy want? He had a strong suspicion it was James Holt that interested Tolstoy.

'How is your government progressing with Brexit?' Tolstoy

asked James.

Ross raised an eyebrow, no beating about the bush he thought.

James Holt appeared taken aback by the question, presumably, the answer was 'not at all.'

'My country may be able to help you,' said Tolstoy. 'Britain will need allies once it leaves the EU and America is an untrustworthy partner. Russia and Britain have been good friends in the past, my namesake wrote the great novel, War and Peace, celebrating a time when we joined together to defeat the imperialism of Europe.'

'Steady on old chap,' said James. 'Hopefully, we're not at that stage yet. Still, we are both major powers, maybe we do need to link up against the hideous regiment of French and Germans.'

Albert Tolstoy passed James his card, 'informal channels of communication are often the best, I think. Every September I hold an exclusive party in Geneva, I think you would enjoy it, I will have an invitation sent to you.'

James pocketed the card carefully. 'Yes, indeed, what is life for if not to enjoy. Mind you, Ross, enjoyment appears to be a foreign country to that friend of your wife's.'

'Well enjoying her food seems to be alien to Dido. That was some lecture we sat through condemning everything on the table.'

'My God,' replied James, 'what does that woman actually eat? I've never heard anyone so passionately condemn a dessert of panna cotta and honey. Where's the meat in that?'

'She's a vegan James. She can't consume any animal products, the honey was stolen from the bees and the panna cotta is made from milk and gelatine, both of which come from animals,' said Ross.

'Quite puts one off the food, listening to her rant on. Not the cheeriest dinner companion.'

Albert Tolstoy knocked back the last of his brandy. 'There are too many people like that in the world today. People worrying about the environment rather than fighting to preserve our way of life. These people encourage governments to create barriers for industry, luckily my government resisted going down that route. We will not let the environmentalists sabotage us.'

'Just so, just so,' said James. 'The liberal elite are divorced from the reality of making a living.'

Ross smiled to himself, it was a bit rich he thought, James Holt, talking about other people being divorced from the reality of making a living. A hollow man indeed.

Chapter Sixteen

August 2019

In the largest country in the world, is a massive, ancient lake, surrounded by mountains and forests. In the depths of winter, the lake freezes over, but in summer it becomes a wild swimmer's paradise, its water among the purest in the world. To Seville, it had a fairy tale quality, a quality she felt much of Russia shared.

Their days passed with a simple rhythm, get up, swim, come back and eat breakfast outside the cabin. Each day an excursion. A hike into the mountains, or a drive along the coast of the lake to find a different place to swim. Swimming in rock pools in a river, a visit to a nearby village to try local specialities and once hiring ponies to trek into the countryside. Sacramento accepted this healthy living with surprisingly little complaint.

Taras had brought along paddleboards, and Sacramento loved this new sport. He had an excellent sense of balance and entertained himself by capsizing the others. They were all out on the paddleboards one afternoon when a couple of glossy black SUVs arrived and parked in front of their cabin, with complete disregard for anyone occupying it.

Seville paddled over to Taras, 'who are they?' she asked.

Taras sighed, 'Muscovites,' he said in the same tone one would say 'cockroaches.' He glared sourly at the SUVs. 'The young and the rich from Moscow. They will camp outside our cabin with no concern for us, then they will party until they are too drunk to stand.'

Sacramento joined them. 'Sounds like my sort of people,' he said. 'I'm going to go and introduce myself to those dudes.'

Seville laughed, 'surely they will not stay long? The gravel isn't the best surface to camp on.'

'They will be here one night. They will build a fire even though it is warm, they will play shit music too loud. They will drink vodka, jump in the lake, and scream because they will think the water cold. We must make sure Sacramento does not let them use our sauna. Tomorrow they will go somewhere else.'

'Just a brief invasion,' said Seville.

'As Shakespeare would say, a plague on their houses. To Siberians Muscovites are the devil, they are the serpent in our garden of Eden. Let us hope they do not tempt Sacramento to move on with them.'

***

The unwelcome guests consisted of five girls in their late teens or early twenties, and three young men. The girls teetered down to the water's edge in wedge sandals carrying armfuls of bottles of Beluga vodka. They filled a plastic tub with water and then placed the bottles in it. The boys wrestled with expensive-looking high-tech tents they were pitching a few yards from the log cabin. Loud music echoed off the cliffs at the side of the bay, while Sacramento helped the girls to cool the vodka bottles.

Even though they were a similar age to herself, the Muscovites made Seville feel old. They were uninterested in Seville and Taras, but the girls showed interest in Sacramento.

'Hey,' called Sacramento. 'I told them they can use our

bathrooms.'

'So,' said Taras. 'You will be the one to clean the bathrooms tomorrow.'

'Hey man,' replied Sacramento, 'relax, they won't leave the bathrooms in a funky state.'

'Then cleaning tomorrow will not be too bad,' said Taras.

'We're going to dig a pit on the beach and barbecue.'

So, you'll be filling that in tomorrow as well,' replied Seville. 'Taras, shall we drive to Khargino to eat tonight?'

'Exactly what I was thinking,' replied Taras. 'Maybe we should look for a hotel as well.'

***

They did not pursue the hotel option and bitterly regretted it when they arrived back. The Muscovites were committed party people and the music echoed off the cliffs and resounded over the water.

Due to the difficulty of remaining upright whilst dancing when intoxicated on a gravel beach, half of the group had commandeered the wooden deck, while the rest had moved down to the sandy part of the beach. This had the disadvantage of being further from the music but the advantage of being nearer the vodka bottles kept cool in the water.

Seville decided to go for a late-night swim to move out of range of the noise. She swam out until all she could see of the party were small pinpoints of light, but still heard the music, albeit in a muted way that almost made it seem musical. She sighed and began to swim back to literally 'face the music.'

After lying in her bed for an hour or so and miserably failing to conjure up sleep, she decided to make herself a hot drink and try reading sitting on a chair. As she walked through the living area, she saw Taras sitting under a reading lamp.

He smiled, 'you cannot sleep?'

'God no. I feel quite middle-aged, I guess I'm not much of a party person.'

He laughed, 'one day I would like to see you party Seville. I imagine you dancing in a woodland glade, like a dryad, though truly you are a rusalka.'

'What is a rusalka?'

'It is the Russian name for a river spirit, and you are a spirit of the water.'

Seville blushed; this was the most romantic thing anyone had ever said to her, better than previous attempts ranging from 'you've got the best legs in Durham,' to 'you've got nice hair.' Comparison to a water spirit was a proper compliment.

'Would you like some tea?' she replied, in a typically English manner. As the kettle boiled, she wondered what Taras thought of her. She found herself becoming increasingly attracted to him on this holiday, he was clever and witty, patient, gentle and well-informed on the environment. But he did not suggest that he saw her as anything other than a friend, and she was scared to make any advance that may end in rejection and risk their friendship. 'Rusalka' she muttered to herself, the best compliment ever.

The night stretched out forever. At about five in the morning, the music stopped. The sound of general partying had ended some time before and all Seville could hear was vigorous retching from the decking area. She made a mental note to ensure Sacramento cleaned up any remains.

They sat reading together until Taras got up, stretched, and said he was going to try to sleep in his bed again. He kissed Seville goodnight chastely on her forehead, and she wondered what his reaction would be if she followed him to his bedroom. She dismissed the idea, she knew safety lay in self-control, it was dangerous to reveal her true emotions.

She must have fallen asleep because she woke in the chair with a pain in her face from resting against her book, leaving her with an imprint across her cheek. Feeling groggy and disorientated she decided a swim would clear her head.

She opened the door to Sacramento's room before leaving the cabin, his bed was empty. With trepidation, she went outside, apprehensive of what she may discover. A scene of minor devastation met her eyes. A body laid in a foetal position near the edge of the decking, covered in a towel. Seville guessed he or she had been the one retching.

Vodka bottles were scattered everywhere, some smashed in the bottom of the fire pit, which possibly accounted for the small explosion she heard in the early hours of the morning. An SUV stood with a door open, and a figure curled up in the back seat. The rest were presumably in the tents. She tiptoed past them and made her way to the water.

Seville swam away from the shore with rapid front crawl strokes, then changed to breaststroke to admire the scene surrounding her. This was better than having a morning shower. She made out the cabin and a couple of black dots that must be the four-wheel drives. Flipping over on her back she regarded the sky, a view sublime enough to grace the Sistine Chapel ceiling.

She could think of no sensation to compare with swimming in this landscape. Seville revelled in the glory of it, with no one to stop her. She thought of laws and regulations that prevented people from doing as they wished, even though what they wished to do would cause no harm. She had experienced the ultimate restriction, when those with authority take away your freedom, just because you think differently to them.

Seville swam along the coast, putting off the moment when she would return and face a crowd of hungover people. Would Sacramento expect her and Taras to cook breakfast for all, would they be vile and inhospitable if they refused to entertain their uninvited guests. Distracted by these thoughts, she swam further than she intended to, and it was two hours later when she got back.

She swam towards the shore and saw no sign of the black SUVs. It seemed optimistic to hope the party of Muscovites had upped camp and left, but sure enough, there were no tents on the beach nor any shiny black vehicles.

She picked up her robe from the gravel and walked back to the cabin. Vodka bottles still lay scattered about and the fire pit dug in the sand remained like a black plague buboe. Split plastic glasses and assorted snack food packaging covered the decking, and she noted with interest the remains of a packet of Brix biscuits.

Before going inside, she peered around the back to check there were no SUVs hidden there. She thought she needed to prepare herself if she was going to have to face the Muscovites, but they had gone.

Cautiously she opened the door, voices came from the living room. She went in, still half expecting a rowdy group to jump out at her. Sacramento sat on the sofa next to Taras, looking surprisingly perky after his night of excess.

He turned to her with a radiant expression on his face. 'Oh man, Seville, I'm in love.'

Behind him, Taras rolled his eyes. Seville was unsure of how to respond.

'With one of the Muscovites?' she asked.

'Dude, did you see her? She is so beautiful, the one with the long blonde hair and the blue eyes. Her name is Vera.'

'Vera? How did you communicate? You don't know any Russian.'

'Man, she speaks American of course. With this sexy accent. I'm so in love.'

'What name did you give her?' said Taras. 'Did you tell her you are called Ben Smith?'

'Dude, I couldn't lie to her, I love her. You can't start a relationship telling someone your name is Ben and months later say you're really called Sacramento. They'd never get it right in their head again. Anyway, she thinks Sacramento is a cool name.'

Seville and Taras exchanged glances. 'So how are you intending to pursue this relationship?' asked Taras. 'They went off swiftly this morning.'

'Today is the last day of their holiday. They had to return the hire cars to Irkutsk and catch a plane to Moscow. Vera must get back to work, she works for a studio, called something cool like My Duck's Vision. Me and Vera are going to meet in Moscow, you said we have two days there before we fly home.'

'Young love,' said Taras with a laugh. 'I think you will be seeing the sights of Moscow on your own, Seville.'

***

Seville had been for a last swim and sat on the decking, towelling her hair dry in preparation for moving on. Taras came and sat beside her. 'Have you enjoyed your holiday Seville? Will you miss our beautiful lake?'

Seville thought she would miss him as well as the lake but wasn't going to say so. 'You can't imagine how much I will miss this place.'

'You should come back in winter; the landscape is spectacularly beautiful then. People swim under the ice and skate on top of the lake, this is where I learnt to skate.'

'I want to come back. Sacramento might make me come back.' She hoped he would and Taras would want to come with them.

Taras smiled, 'if the young love lasts. Vera works for a video company that produces viral videos for YouTube. "My Ducks Vision" promotes the Russian as conqueror and mocks some American institutions. Who knows what Sacramento's American friends would make of them? She is of what my parents would call the new Russia. These young people have parents who suddenly became rich whilst most of Russia was becoming poor. They work to amuse themselves rather than to earn money or have a serious career. None of them want to be doctors, or journalists or teachers. They want fun, not responsibility or hard work, they do not know what it is to go without.'

Seville gazed into the distance, 'I guess that is where Sacramento and I come from too, neither of us has ever gone without.'

Taras shrugged. 'None of us can help what we are born to, but we can help what we become. Look at yourself Seville, you have rejected that life, you will help Sacramento to reject it too.'

She made a face, 'maybe I have shown him how he can have a Russian version of it. Oh well, Moscow here we come.'

***

They spent a night in Irkutsk before flying to Moscow. Seville and Taras sat up late in the hotel, discussing her plans to visit Norilsk. Taras was against it, he said it was impossible to obtain official permission and to do it unofficially would be too dangerous.

'Are you sure this idea has not just become a great adventure for you?' he asked her. 'What productive research do you think you could carry out there. Will you knock on the factory door and ask them to tell you what they are manufacturing? How would you get any evidence of what they manufacture?'

'Soil and water samples, I could collect these and bring them back to the UK. I would also like to see the industry with my own eyes, I'd like to take some photos.'

'But to what purpose Seville? My government will know what goes on in Norilsk, will your research change anything?'

'It might do, the British government might be interested in my research. But also, if anyone is manufacturing chemical weapons or nerve gas there, that needs to be exposed. It adds to the information on the dangers and helps to drive public opinion to reject the products produced in this way.'

Taras smiled, 'if we had convincing evidence of damage my newspaper would print this. An environmental movement is beginning to build in Russia, but progress is slow. It is of interest to Siberians as we are the ones who suffer from pollution. I will talk to people, and I will check if anything can be done. But I warn you, I do not think we can make this happen.'

***

Seville felt sorry to say goodbye to Taras, she would have enjoyed visiting Moscow with him. Now she would see Moscow on her own and leave Sacramento to his own devices. He vanished once they booked into their hotel, with a cheery wave and instructions he would feed himself and not wait up for him.

Seville spent two happy days wandering around the sights of Moscow. She enquired at the hotel about swimming, and they directed her to a spot on the banks of the Moskva River. Not up to Lake Baikal standards but still better than the hotel swimming pool or an artificial beach.

On their last morning, Vera joined them for breakfast. She appeared softer than Seville had expected, she had built up a picture of a brash, entitled rich girl in her mind. The reality appeared reassuring. Vera told Seville she was just eighteen and having a gap year before going to university. She said she was interested in the environment and admired Greta Thunberg.

'I would like to have joined in the Friday school protests,' said Vera, 'but in Moscow, it is illegal to protest if you are under eighteen years old, and once you are eighteen you can only protest alone. Every protest with more than one person must have government approval. We are behind in Russia.'

Sacramento beamed at Vera, 'isn't she fantastic?' he asked Seville.

Seville smiled at them both, she thought it would be a long journey home.

Chapter Seventeen

September 2019

Seville and Sacramento arrived in London, tired and bad-tempered, to find a message from Ross telling them he needed to speak to them the next day. Her brother seemed unconcerned, but she could not prevent the familiar tinge of apprehension such messages from her father always caused. Had he discovered they had gone to Russia? Were they about to suffer consequences from that trip?

Over breakfast, Seville continued to read the Lonely Planet guide to Ibiza to be able to give a convincing account of their supposed holiday. She would deny that they had gone anywhere else. She was not at all confident about Sacramento's ability to withstand any inquisition on Ibiza, but no one would be surprised by his lack of grasp of any detail on the island.

At 9 a.m. Ross arrived, and Seville persuaded Sacramento to join them for coffee, he emerged, bleary-eyed, reluctant, and grumpy from his room.

'I need to speak to you Sacramento,' said Ross.

Seville felt a surge of relief that she was not the focus of her father's intentions.

'Yeah, well I'm like still asleep,' replied Sacramento. 'Don't ask any difficult questions.'

'I take it you both enjoyed your holiday?'

'Yeah, it was sweet.' Sacramento yawned.

'Yes, we had a fantastic time,' added Seville, wishing she had chosen a destination she had visited before. She hoped Ross would not be interested in the detail.

'So, Sacramento, your mother has been in communication with me. She cannot find any school anywhere in the USA prepared to offer you a place.'

Sacramento perked up. 'Wow, how awesome. Absolutely nowhere, not even some dumb ass hick place in Alaska? Hey, what am I saying, I don't want to go to school in Alaska, although…?' A thought appeared to hit him, and his voice trailed off.

Seville saw straight through him. She knew he was thinking, with his improved grip upon the geography of the world, that Alaska was near Russia.

Ross regarded his son sourly, 'your mother does not see it as such an achievement. She decided you need to go to a boarding school in the UK.'

'Oh no,' said Sacramento, 'I'm not going to some la di dah posh boarding school in England.'

'You are so right. I can't imagine any la di dah posh school would want you. No, you are going to the sort of school designed to sort out people like you. You are going to the Thistle Academy, charmingly located on the Isle of Skye, far away from the temptations of any bright lights. They claim their regime will make a man of you.'

'Dad, I am a man, let me show you my winkie.' Sacramento stood and dropped his pyjama bottoms. 'I don't need any help to become a man, here is the evidence, a genuine penis.' He gestured in the direction of his genitals.

'Pull your trousers up,' said Ross with studied patience. 'You know perfectly well what I mean, you need some discipline. You failed every exam you have ever taken, and I do not believe it is down to stupidity, or at least not congenital stupidity. Tomorrow you go to Scotland, if you achieve a good report, you can fly home to California for Christmas. After two years at this school, you should be able to go to the university of your choice.'

'Man, this is so unfair, I've been so well-behaved over here, I even went on holiday with my big sister without complaint.' Sacramento stopped talking and frowned with concentration. After a moment he said, 'I can go anywhere in the world to university?'

'Yes, that's what I said.'

'You going to give me your word?'

'I'm your father, I don't need to give you my word.'

'Listen, Dad, we can do this the easy way or the hard way. I can go to Scotland without any fuss, or you can drag me there kicking and screaming and watch me escape. Don't think I don't trust you, but I want you to guarantee in front of a witness that if I go to this school and pass whatever exams they put me in for, I can go to university in the country of my choice.'

'You have my word, but you'll need to deal with your mother if she objects to where you choose.'

'She won't be the one paying for it,' said Sacramento.

Seville was impressed, she had the advantage of being able to read Sacramento like the proverbial open book. Vera would take a gap year then go to university; Later Sacramento would join her at whatever establishment she attended. She guessed after listening to a couple of Sacramento's telephone conversations with his mother, exile for as many years as possible was presumably his mother's preferred choice.

She could tell her father was anxious to finalise the arrangements for his son's banishment. He told his son he'd arranged for a driver to pick him up early the following morning and take him to Skye. It was all organised.

'Dad,' said Seville, 'why don't I drive Sacramento up to Scotland? It'll be easier for him than going off with someone he doesn't know, I promise I'll get him safely to school.'

'You've had him all summer, I'd have thought you'd be grateful to see the back of him.'

Her brother put an arm around Seville. 'Hey man, I want my sister to take me to school. I don't want some swanky driver to take me.'

Ross shook his head. 'You never fail to baffle me, Seville. OK, I'll tell the driver to drop the bags around, but I'll be checking up he arrives there. Don't complain to me if he drives you insane on the journey.'

'I managed on a much longer journey,' she said without thinking.

Ross frowned. 'You do know where Skye is, don't you? It must be a twelve-hour journey; the school isn't expecting Sacramento before midnight, and you'll have to stay the night before driving back. They had a room for the driver, so I'll tell them it will be you instead. You'll find the drive longer than getting on a plane to Ibiza.'

Sacramento nudged Seville. 'Yes, well it seemed quite long at the time,' she said.

'Believe me, this will seem a lot longer,' said Ross.

***

They set off on time, but Sacramento got in the car and promptly fell asleep. He slept till they stopped in Durham for lunch, at a favourite venue from Seville's student days. His first question was, 'are we nearly there yet?'

After they passed Glasgow Seville stopped again for a break. Sacramento glanced around the stunning view of mountains and loch, it appeared to depress him.

'Hey dude, there isn't much up here, it's like being back in Russia again. Do people live here?'

'I wouldn't mind living here. I think one day I will come here to live.'

'Yeah,' said Sacramento looking out over the loch. 'There's nothing but fuck off big lakes around here.'

'Scotland is so beautiful, lots of water and few people, what's not to love?' asked Seville.

'You are such an old lady,' said her half-brother.

***

They completed their journey in good time and at 11 p.m. they arrived at the Thistle Academy near Dunvegan. It had once been a stately home and its crenellated battlements made Seville think of Hogwarts. Sacramento stared at it in horror, it was quite uncalifornian.

'Think of Vera, university in Russia,' said Seville to encourage him.

'Man, I'll never last two years here. Seville, Vera will be in touch with you. She wants to do some sort of environmental degree and I told her you were the best person to speak to. You'll help her, won't you?'

'Of course, I'll help, you never know, she might be able to help me.'

'I'm going to study Russian,' said Sacramento. I have to take these things called 'A' levels and Russian is among the choices.'

'That's a clever idea Sacramento,' said Seville, surprised. 'Helpful if you end up going to a university in Russia. Are you good at languages?'

'Never tried. Come on, we'd better go and meet the jailers, man I'll bet they're a bunch of weird, creepy dudes.'

***

The following morning Seville left after breakfast without being able to see Sacramento again. She felt sorry for her stepbrother, he wasn't that bad, only a bit out of control. A complete contrast to her, she spent her whole life controlling herself. She examined the map and decided to first drive to Portree and take a couple of days to journey back.

Portree proved to be a small fishing village, given over to

tourism of the active type, a mecca for walkers and climbers. She found a café overlooking the harbour and settled herself at a table outside, in the warm September sun.

The view was stunning, brightly coloured boats bobbed about, and in the distance, a shimmering mist hung over the mountains. Seville studied her map, planning where she would stop for a swim. She picked up a newspaper from an adjoining table intending to catch up on the news, she had not bothered checking what was going on in the world while on holiday. The headline shocked her. It told of the poisoning of a Russian dissident living in Britain, supposedly by Federal Security Service agents using the nerve gas Novichok.

She read the detail with a growing sense of concern. The journalist expressed indignation that Russians could do this on British soil, but how much worse would this outrage be if it was a British owned company producing the nerve gas. Seville wondered if she should contact the journalist reporting on the story and tell him of the conversation she had overheard.

Seville thrummed her fingers on the table, considering what action to take. Would any journalist believe her without evidence to back her claim, anyone could make up such a tale? She decided she must find a way to visit Norilsk and the factory the men had mentioned.

A voice with a strong London accent interrupted her reverie. 'Hi Ophelia, do you mind if I join you?'

Seville started, not getting the reference. Then she thought, Ophelia Macbeth, of course. She smiled at the intruder, 'Hi Colin, what are you doing here?'

'I might ask you the same question,' said Colin Wilton. 'You are the last person I would expect to meet here. You're back from Russia, how did the trip go? I hope all the paperwork passed scrutiny.'

'It worked well, though I was nervous about going through passport control with a fake passport. I think coming back into the UK was even worse than getting into Russia.'

'Yeah, I get that,' said Colin. 'UK border control tends to suspect all arrivals of being potential illegal immigrants. Still, you were returning to the country from Russia, not Africa, and though you are not quite the right colour, at least you are not black.'

Seville raised her eyebrow, 'been investigating the Home Office recently, have you?'

'Strangely enough, I have, though not for crimes against humanity like denying the Windrush generation passports. It is an officer of the Home Office I am investigating, to be exact, the Home Secretary, the Honourable Mr James Holt.'

'James Holt, I think he is an acquaintance of my father's. He always says he likes to have a few tame politicians in his pocket.'

'Indeed, does he now? Do you know Seville, you might be a valuable friend to me? I am a humble East London boy who has done well to become a journalist, but you are in a different league. You sit at the top table so to speak.'

Seville flushed; she hated any reference to her privileged background. It was one of the reasons she liked Taras, he treated her like an ordinary person. He was aware she came from a wealthy family, but he never behaved as if she were rich. 'I try to keep away from all that as much as I can.'

Colin smiled a nasty smile. 'Yeah, but I'm being honest with you because I like you. We could help each other, you could be my secret agent and find out the low down on some of these shady deals, and I can find information for you on environmental issues. We can scratch each other's backs.'

The conversation took her aback. 'I might share information with you if I thought it was for the right reasons,' she replied. 'I realise that when your interests aren't the same as the government's interests, it might put you on the other side of the law. I guess it's because the laws are made by the government, and they put their interests first.'

'Yeah, I could tell you about a load of things that are legal but wrong. So, Mr James Holt. Your father's social media machine started promoting him since the vote of no confidence in that streak of pompous piss, Tristan Douglas Home. Mr Holt appears to be the favourite for the new Conservative leader.'

'My father always says he's neutral in politics, he never donates money to any political party.'

'The action of a wise man, nothing like having no affiliations so no one can call you out on them. Anyway, we digress, what brought you up here?'

'My brother has been sent to gaol up here, not a proper prison, a boot camp type school for troublesome teens, located in some sort of medieval castle at Dunvegan.'

'Yes, the young vandal who pollutes decent single malt scotch with coke. I thought he was American?'

'He is, but he appears to be banned from every private school in the US. I think my father sent him here because Skye is a long way away from Cambridgeshire and even if he breaks out, it should be possible to recapture him before he makes it home.'

'Did he take his fake passport with him?'

'Ah, yes, he did along with a secret mobile. But he hasn't got access to any money if he wanted to escape somewhere.'

'Though he might make a call to his sister.'

'I'm braced for it, though it would be most likely to come in the New Year which is when I intend to return to Russia again.'

'Winter swimming in Lake Baikal?'

'No,' said Seville. 'A trip to Norilsk.'

'I think I told you before, Norilsk is not a place to visit.'

'Have you read today's headlines; nerve gas used upon a Russian dissident?'

'Of course, but what do you think you can do about it?'

'If I can find concrete proof that a factory owned by a British company is producing Novichok, I'm sure I can convince a newspaper to publish that. I'll pass the evidence on to you and you can write about it. I'd send all the details to Extinction Rebellion, and they would make a noise about it. All I need to do is get there and gather the evidence.

'No Russian official is going to permit an environmentalist to visit Norilsk,' said Colin. 'They will ask you why you want to go and if you say to investigate whether nerve gas is being produced by a factory owned by a British company, they're not going to say, oh yes do come along, how can we help.'

Seville felt tears of frustration pricking at her eyes. Colin made her feel young, foolish, and naïve, but she would not sit on her knowledge and do nothing.

'What do you know about Norilsk?' asked Colin. 'Did Taras tell you about it?'

'No, just that a friend was killed there, and it is a closed city.'

'It is the most northern city with more than 100,000 inhabitants and Taras's great grandfather helped to build it. He was a political prisoner in the Gulags, forced labour built the city and it is there to support the mining industry,' said Colin.

'Taras's great grandfather was in the gulags?'

'Oh yes. He was an educated man at a time when being educated was problematic, always the danger you might think for yourself. There are rich mineral deposits in Norilsk, but the mining devastated the area, and yes contamination from nickel mining caused that river to run red. The prisoners built a railway, but the railway is not operational, you cannot get to Norilsk by train or by road. To get there you must fly or go by boat from the Arctic Ocean, and you need a special permit from the FSS, the Federal Security Service.'

'So, you are telling me, difficult but not impossible.'

'I'm telling you, unwise to attempt it. Taras's friend was a girlfriend of mine, that's how I met him. She was investigating pollution and met with a so-called accident. It was murder, they organised a car crash and left her to freeze to death in the car. You never read about that in any paper. Neither Taras nor I will help you with this, he would be risking his career and his life by getting involved. There are many other places in the world where drinking water is polluted, investigate those.'

Colin's steady gaze made Seville feel guilty. She had imagined visiting Norilsk with Taras but had not thought about the issues that could cause for him. She had the money and contacts to buy her way out of trouble, not everyone had her safety net. The same rules did not apply to everyone, most people had to earn a living and try and stay out of trouble. If she was to go to Norilsk, it must be on her own, and maybe she would find her money and contacts counted for nothing in

Chapter Eighteen

September 2019

Ross sat in his study, behind his desk in his Herman Miller chair and thought all was right with the world. He appreciated having the house to himself. Delightful scents came from a cafetiere of Blue Mountain coffee and a restful silence reigned.

This was better than any holiday. Two weeks without any family present and working from home while business ground to its normal August halt. No annoying members of staff to deal with, no sitting in meetings listening to people trying to impress him by talking a load of shit. He would return to the fray reinvigorated.

He poured himself a coffee before opening the news on his laptop. The press worked itself up into a state of indignation, over the supposed poisoning by Novichok of a Russian dissident who lived in Britain. It read like an old-fashioned cold war tale, with a touch of James Bond thrown in for extra excitement. He felt a sense of pride he was at the heart of the story, his nerve gas, made by his company.

Ross thought the press were in their comfort zone with a good old anti-Russian piece. But although it was easy to persuade the public and the media to perceive Russia as an enemy, the view of the Government was different. They knew Russians rich enough to buy their friendship, and for some in government, money always has the loudest voice. They would express outrage but take no effective action.

He heard a noise and turned around to see the door open and a tall man enter his study, clapping his hands in applause for Ross. He shook his head and the vision vanished. He glanced around the room, half expecting more of those figures who haunted him.

His mobile rang and he saw the name Ganak Reddy on the screen. From one shadowy phantom to another, he thought. Ganak was the CEO of Ross's company, Assist Pharmaceuticals, a man he could never trust. Ganak was just too transparent in his raw ambition. He accepted the call.

'Ross, it's Ganak. Have you read my proposal?'

He had read the proposal, and it was quite extraordinary. Ganak wanted a substantial budget to develop a vaccine against an imaginary disease he had named disease X. It was a quite incredible request, but Ross knew that Ganak was for all his faults, a clever man.

'Yeah, I read it. But you haven't convinced me, why would I invest in a vaccine against an imaginary disease?'

'My God, Ross, research and development is a constant ongoing process. We're not talking about an imaginary disease here; we are talking about something that is likely to happen within the next five years. All the modelling suggests a global pandemic, most likely a respiratory disease, will occur, and we need to be ahead of the game with a vaccine that can be tweaked to deal with the specific disease.'

Ross had already decided he would invest the money, but he didn't want Ganak to know this yet, he would keep him waiting, he would make Ganak work for the funds. 'I need more information; I want to see all the technical detail. I must see all the probability figures. I want to understand how this is being prioritised and what research this will downgrade.'

'Fine, fine, we will send you more detail, but I assure you this is most important.'

Ganak's voice sounded irritated, Ross knew he hated being challenged in any way. A thought occurred to him, would Ganak create a virus that only he could find the cure for? It wasn't a pleasant thought and Ross wouldn't put that past him. Ganak was stupendously clever in some ways but transparent in his raw ambition. He began his career at Assist Pharmaceuticals as a research assistant and rose over a mere eighteen years to become CEO. His stellar rise came from his ability to steal other people's work and add his own extra ingenious twist to it, and a positively Machiavellian attitude to company politics. Ross thought that if he dug up the grounds of Assist's research facility at Reading, he would discover many bodies with a knife in the back.

'I need to have more information, I'm disappointed in you Ganak, I would have thought by now you would understand I don't make decisions without fully understanding all the issues.'

'These are technical issues, you are a businessman Ross, not a scientist. I thought you would prefer just to know the concept and not get bogged down in detail.'

A broad smile spread across Ross's face; he had really got up Ganak's nose now.

Ross did not enjoy being patronised by his employees. George understood that, but Ganak was too self-obsessed to pick up on the reactions of others. Ganak hung up with a huffy, 'goodbye' and Ross continued his own investigation into pandemics.

He drank his coffee and studied on his laptop the results of his searches on upcoming pandemics. It made uncomfortable reading. Ganak did not need to manufacture a virus. There were many candidates for the next pandemic. Ebola, Zika, SARS and the snappily named Crimean-Congo Haemorrhagic Fever to list a few.

He guessed Ganak had seen some modelling suggesting which would be most likely.

He could see the opportunity for making money, but it would be acclaim and plaudits that Ganak would chase. Ross glanced out of the window and thought of the horsemen of the apocalypse, the pale horse that represented plague. He needed to keep Ganak close to him he decided, he must be ready to clip his wings. He would not allow this pale rider to unseat him.

It would be intolerable for anyone to challenge Ross's supremacy; such an event had never happened. Ross sipped his coffee and thought, to stay ahead you must be prepared for all eventualities. If a pandemic arose and someone came forward with a vaccine, that person would be a hero. But one can be a hero one day and a villain the next.

If a story spread on social media that the man who created the solution and the man who created the problem were the same, he would move from hero to villain overnight.

Jamaican Blue Mountain coffee was his favourite, thought Ross. He took another sip, drinking coffee always helped to focus his mind. It was important to know when people outlived their use. To be able to cut the ties between those who had become a liability and yourself, to cut them without fuss and at the right time. Ultimately one had to travel alone.

Chapter Nineteen

September 2019

No map showed a route to Norilsk. A single road connected Dudinka, Norilsk and Talnakh, and went no further. Three closed cities with access to the rest of the world strictly limited. The only way in was to fly, or travel by sea from the Arctic Ocean along the River Yenisei to Dudinka.

Seville sat on the floor of the London apartment, surrounded by a multitude of maps of Russia, none of which helped in showing a route to Norilsk. Taras and Colin were right, to get there one would need to fly or walk. The alternative was to wait till summer and go by boat up the Yenisei River. But that was an organised tourist trip and did not seem a practical way to investigate a polluting factory.

Krasnoyarsk appeared to be the nearest city to Norilsk Seville could travel to, without getting official permission. No roads connected the cities, but she thought perhaps she could hire a snowmobile and make her way overland using satellite navigation. The distance was daunting, almost a thousand miles, and she spent much time researching Canadian internet sites about long distance travel on a snowmobile. Depending on the terrain the journey might take as little as three days, or as long as a week.

She gazed at the maps surrounding her, none were at a level of detail to make such a trip practical. Oh, for an ordnance survey map she thought. It seemed suicidal to set out on a snowmobile armed only with a compass and large-scale map of Russia, to try to navigate one thousand miles. She clicked hopelessly on Google maps, all it showed was a featureless terrain of mountains and forest.

Seville flicked back to website pages offering snowmobiling lessons in Norway, she would not give up that easily. Surely, she could learn about winter survival and how to plot her way across unmapped territory. Her phone rang and an unfamiliar number flashed up. She recognised it as a Russian number and answered eagerly.

'Hello, Seville speaking.'

'This is Vera. Sacramento gave me your number. You remember me?'

'Yes, how are you?'

'Good, thanks. I need a favour, your brother said you would help me.'

'Of course, what can I do for you?'

'I wish to come to London and stay with you. Only for four or five days.'

Seville was surprised, from what she knew of Vera's circumstances she did not need to beg for free accommodation. But perhaps her parents did not want her to come to London and would not pay for a hotel. 'Of course, when were you thinking of coming?'

'It must be soon, in two weeks, will this be convenient for you?'

'Yes, I have no plans for the next fortnight.' She hesitated, 'is there any particular reason for your visit Vera?'

Vera laughed, 'when I come, I will explain.'

***

Vera treated Seville's suggestion of taking the Piccadilly line from Heathrow with scorn. When she arrived at the apartment it was obvious why the underground did not appeal, she wore six-inch-high stilettos not designed for any form of travel requiring walking any distance. Seville marvelled she had managed to navigate airport corridors in them.

To be fair, it was not just the footwear that was troublesome. Vera also brought an enormous Louis Vuitton suitcase, the size of an old-fashioned 1920s travel trunk that would admirably suit a journey on the Titanic.

'How long are you planning to stay?' asked Seville.

'I have five days,' said Vera.

She wheeled the trunk through the door to the centre of the reception room and opened it. Less than a quarter of the trunk was full, and the contents consisted of the tools needed for a stringent beauty regime. There were many electrical appliances Seville presumed related to hair maintenance, and others of mysterious purpose. There were few clothes.

Vera caught Seville staring at her trunk. 'Today I must shop, I have much space to fill with clothes and shoes. You will come shopping with me? I always go shopping with a girlfriend. We will go to Selfridges and Harvey Nichols, and we will buy outfits to wear tonight when we go to the club.'

'Club, what club?' said Seville in horror.

'You live in London; do you not know what clubs to go to?'

'Vera, sorry to disappoint you, but I don't go to clubs.'

She frowned. 'So, what do you do on a Saturday night?'

What did she do, Seville wondered? Her life was empty of youthful activities. She researched issues relating to water pollution, she read, she swam, she met a few friends at the pub or a restaurant, or she went to the cinema. She did not imagine any of this would be acceptable entertainment to Vera.

'We could go out for dinner,' she offered.

Vera flopped to the ground and took off her shoes. She

massaged her feet, then gave Seville a blinding smile, all perfect white teeth, and ruby lips. 'OK, we have four quiet nights where you tell me everything about environmental studies, you teach me everything you know and five days we shop. This will be good.'

Somehow, thought Seville, Vera had manoeuvred her into spending five days on an activity she loathed. 'Would you not prefer to shop on your own?' she asked, already recognising this as a lost cause.

'No, it will be more fun shopping with you. Now I will change, and we will go to Selfridges.' Vera smiled, evidently feeling she had made immense concessions.

***

Seville mused on Dante's circles of Hell and decided shopping was well suited to them. The shopping circle would be the deepest one, reserved for extremely bad people. The eighth circle where the fraudulent resided, punished for the alchemy of taking the ordinary and pretending to change it into gold, by the addition of a designer label.

She sat on a spindly chair in the Gucci shop in Selfridges, while Vera tried on a sweatshirt of extraordinary ugliness and fantastic price. The Gucci logo was woven into the fabric in gold metallic thread, so there was no chance the person in the street would fail to recognise the wearer had invested in some egregious bling.

Seville realised Vera took shopping seriously when she changed from the six-inch stilettos to trainers. Admittedly flashy looking Louis Vuitton trainers, with a substantial wedge sole making them impractical for any form of sporting activity, but never less, much more comfortable looking than the stilettos. After three hours of sifting through designer brands at Selfridges, Seville begged for a coffee.

'Oh, let's find the champagne bar, I don't want coffee,' said Vera.

'We'll compromise, we'll find one that does coffee and champagne. Come on, choose a pair of sunglasses, and we can go for a drink. I'm so thirsty.'

Vera hovered over the twelve pairs of Dior sunglasses in front of her, picked up two pairs and paid for them. It puzzled Seville she needed sunglasses, it was October, and it was unlikely Vera would find sunglasses useful during a Moscow winter. It seemed even more unlikely that anyone so devoted to conspicuous consumption, could be interested in a career in environmental conservation.

***

They ate dinner that night at a family-run Italian restaurant near Russell Square. Vera was uninterested in what she ate but took a close interest in what she drank. A minor crisis arose when she discovered the restaurant did not stock Champagne, but Seville persuaded her Franciacorta had a similar taste to Champagne and was nothing like prosecco. Vera told the waiter, unambiguously, that she hated prosecco.

Half a bottle of Franciacorta later peace was restored. Vera told Seville Sacramento planned to return early from California after Christmas and go to Moscow. This plan involved Seville helping Sacramento by applying for a visa in the name of his false passport and then meeting him with the necessary documentation at Heathrow. Both showed a touching faith in Seville doing this without any objection.

'Yes, I'll sort that out for him,' said Seville, 'but is he allowed to make his own way to and from the prison school?'

'He said at the end of each term the school considers they become the parent's responsibility. They take them in minibuses to Glasgow airport and station and let them loose. At the start of term, they pick them all up again from wherever they dropped them off. This school is different from what I know?'

'Different from most schools,' said Seville. 'When do you go to university?'

'I have not decided yet. To follow environmental studies in Russia is difficult. Irkutsk University teaches a degree in ecology engineering, but it is focused on green energy rather than anything broader. I think I will study abroad, Sacramento told me you studied at Durham University in England.'

'I can give you information about that and I enjoyed my studies. But tell me, Vera, why do you want to study the environment? What do you ultimately want to do?'

'I wish to be a protester,' said Vera. 'Our generation, we are fucked and few of the old people care.'

Seville blinked in surprise; she was not expecting that. Sacramento said Vera was interested in the environment, but Seville had seen no evidence of this.

'I have read books,' said Vera, '2050 is mentioned as a year when irreversible changes to the world will affect how we live, when parts of the world will be too warm to live in or will be underwater. To these old men who are in power, it is nothing but a date. The worst of the old men, the president of America, he will be dead, I will be forty-seven. There will be no more shopping in Selfridges for me. There will be no shopping in Selfridges for anyone then.'

'Yes, but that is the worst case, we can do something about stopping global warming before then.'

'We won't without protests,' said Vera bleakly. 'My plan is, first I must understand the subject, I must have knowledge. So, I will complete a degree in environmental studies. Then I need to protest, but I cannot be Greta Thunberg. I cannot protest in the streets of Moscow, no one could join me, and on my own, I will be ignored. My parents will stop my allowance. So, I need to be clever, I must be subversive.

'I am working at My Duck's Vision to understand how to make videos. I will set up my own YouTube company and I will make subversive videos. They will show all the bad things pollution does to the world, and we will film the old men saying nothing is happening. My videos will be factual and satirical, and I will stay anonymous.

'I come to London with the credit card my father gives me, and I buy many clothes, many sunglasses, many shoes. I behave like a stupid rich girl; I am careless of the environment. My father, who makes his money from oil, he will finance my subversion, he will not think it possible anything apart from shopping interests me. What do you think?'

Vera's scope of imagination impressed Seville and made her feel inadequate. 'Sounds a fantastic idea,' she replied. 'But think about doing a degree in media studies and bring in environmental expertise. That would be more logical.'

Vera looked thoughtful. 'Maybe you are right, I must consider this.'

***

After four days of shopping, Seville had made acquaintance with parts of London previously unknown to her. New Bond Street, Sloane Street and Knightsbridge had not featured highly in places she visited when in London. A Dolce and Gabbana swimsuit, in a vivid green tropical print, tempted her. A fitting outfit for the water spirit Taras had compared her to, the Rusalka, but the £500 price tag appeared inappropriate for a creature of nature.

On her last night, Vera asked Seville what she would be doing next. She sighed and felt anxiety creeping over her.

'I'm not sure. I had planned to visit sites where industry has polluted the local water supply, to document the effects, take samples of the pollution and interview people locally.'

Seville paused for a moment then decided she would share her ambition to visit Norilsk with Vera. 'But now I want most of all to visit Norilsk. I want to go because I believe a British owned company is manufacturing chemical weapons there, and I need to expose them in the British press. But my friend Taras, the man who was with us at Lake Baikal, tells me it is impossible.'

'Why would it be impossible?' asked Vera.

'It is a closed city. Do you know about Norilsk?'

Vera shrugged. 'It is one of those places in Siberia no one wants to go to. Siberia was the land of the gulags, there are places people only go to because they have no choice. Northern Siberia is a terrible place, the ground never thaws out even in summer. In winter it is deadly cold, summer is not much better, but these days every place makes a statement on their touristic attractions. I will get us to Norilsk.'

'Us?'

Vera smiled at Seville. 'I have an idea. You might be right, and it is media I should study. I should learn to become a great filmmaker, good for more than just YouTube. This could be our experiment, we go to Norilsk, you search out the pollution and I film it. You can be my environmental expert and I will be the filmmaker expert. After Christmas, we will go to Norilsk, and we will make our protest film.'

'How will we do that; everyone has told me this is impossible?'

'Nothing is impossible. I accept the challenge. It is men who have told you this, men, what do they know?'

Seville raised her glass in a toast to Vera, 'if you can get me into Norilsk, I will be your environmental expert.'

***

Vera left on Wednesday, with her trunk considerably heavier than on arrival. She pushed it out to the taxi, teetering on high heels and encrusted in makeup, a well disguised environmental activist. She kissed Seville goodbye and with an airy wave she left, leaving the apartment unnaturally quiet.

After waving Vera goodbye, Seville returned to the living room and found a parcel addressed to her. She unwrapped it to find an expensive-looking box embossed with the Dolce and Gabbana logo. She opened the box, peeled back the coloured tissue paper, to reveal the swimsuit she had admired. Seville held it up and considered it; a symbol of all she despised, it represented pointless and frivolous expense. But the swimsuit was beautiful.

'I'll just try it on,' she thought. She wriggled into the swimsuit and looked at her reflection in the mirror. It moulded perfectly to her slim, muscular body, the design in shades of green complemented by her dark olive skin and long, straight black hair. It made her feel like a Rusalka. She took it off and examined the costume for any obvious logos, but she saw none apart from a label inside. 'Perhaps I can keep it,' she thought guiltily, after all, no one would know what brand it was.

***

Seville was not convinced Vera intended to come to Norilsk with her, but in less than a fortnight, she had worked out a plan. A plan that sounded both thoroughly researched and comparatively simple. 'Don't stereotype people,' thought Seville, yet again surprised by Vera's inventiveness.

They could only reach the city by air or water. To visit one required authority from the Federal Security Service, and this permission was hard to come by, especially for foreigners. There would need to be an exceptionally good reason for the authorities to approve.

Vera had a cunning plan, appropriately centred on swimming. Norilsk had a swimming club, known as the Norilsk Walrus swimming club. The members swam all year round, even in temperatures of -50°, and without wetsuits. The sort of activity that would only appeal to hardcore swimmers. Krasnoyarsk also had another famous winter swimming club, the Psychrophile Winter swimming club.

Vera constructed a cover story around making a film about an English swimmer coming to Russia and seeing if she was able to cope with Russian winter swimming. She approached local officials who all liked the idea, and they helped her to get authorisation from the FSS. The security service would ensure they had an official escort, but Vera saw no problem in either losing them when convenient or bribing them to look the other way when she filmed the pollution from industry.

Seville's visions of secretly making her way through hundreds of kilometres of forest on a snowmobile, camping at night in polar conditions and trying to avoid frostbite, happily vanished. Vera's solution appeared to have more chance of success and of keeping her extremities intact, though less exciting, and dramatic. They settled on dates in late January 2020, which gave them time to arrange all the detail and acquire the necessary permits.

Excitement bubbled up inside her at the thought of the trip, though she wished Taras was part of her party. She missed him, and they had no planned date to meet again. She resolved to shed her inhibitions and get in touch with him after her Norilsk trip, the worst that could happen would be a polite refusal. In the meantime, she prepared for a journey with no maps.

Chapter Twenty

October 2019

It created a sense of invincibility when all your endeavours came together as you wished, thought Ross. Of course, that is what should happen if you planned well. Still, you couldn't discount the chance of some random factor slipping out of the woodwork and causing disruption. The best-laid plans and all that.

In the world of Ross Campbell, plans succeeded in a manner likely to generate illusions of God like prescience. Or as Jason would say, he stood on the right step on the strategic staircase. One day he would reach out to Jason. Reach out and grab his head and bring it into sharp contact with the table they sat around.

He had almost tipped Ross over the edge during a meeting to discuss the marketing proposal, "Ethical Fashion, it's in our Jeans." Jason had piped up. 'Can I pull together all the major stakeholders on this, for a thought shower on how we communicate to the customer how this product fits all our sustainability criteria.'

Stakeholders was bad enough in the wanky expression lexicon, but "thought shower," what pratt came up with that one? For a moment Ross gazed wistfully at the sprinkler system installed above their heads. How marvellous if he could programme them to come on every time anyone said, 'thought shower.' That would give them something to have a thought shower about.

Ross thought it was fashionable in both business and politics to use opaque language, weasel words to twist the truth. How valid was that old saying, "empty vessels make the most noise?" Aptly proven in the political arena.

The Conservative party was making a lot of noise, as they rejected their last choice of leader and sought another. Constant commentary in Book of Friends that Tristan Douglas Home was an archaic, elitist snob, who wanted to ban abortion, reinstate fox hunting, and privatise the National Health Service, had worked its effect.

James Holt, short, fat, and jovial looking, appeared to fit the bill, primarily by being the opposite of Tristan. As far as Ross was concerned, James was ideally suited for the role of prime minister. The vote for the new leader and therefore de facto prime minister was tomorrow. Ross invited James and his wife to dinner on Saturday evening. All concerned expected it to be a celebratory dinner.

***

On Saturday night Ross lounged on his bed. He watched Madrigal with admiration as she dressed for dinner. God, she was so sexy and beautiful, and her stern autocratic ways were such a turn on. It always sent a frisson of desire down his spine when he heard her lay down the law in her 'Nazi Ice Queen' way. Who wanted a doormat for a partner, how unexciting would that be?

He found it satisfying to look at his wife and know she wouldn't have given him a second glance if she had met him when he was eighteen. It showed how far he had travelled in life. Though, to be fair when he was that age, Madrigal hadn't been born. But if they were the same age, at eighteen Ross would be no more than a speck of mud on Madrigal's shoe.

This applied to all his guests tonight, apart from the Tolstoys. He was sure that no one else's father was a postman or had a mother who worked in WH Smith. Luckily, his parents had obligingly died when he was seventeen. The compensation from the accident set Ross up to begin his journey to rule the world. The details of his childhood, of his handicap, would remain his secret alone.

He'd enticed James Holt to dinner tonight, with the promise of introducing him to big hitters from industry, who might be interested in donating to the Conservative party. James always followed the money. Lay a trail of banknotes from the door of number 10 to the gates of Hell, and James would gaily trip along, picking them up with no care for where the path might take him. Everything had gone to plan, no longer humble home secretary, now James was prime minister.

One might have thought a new prime minister would have better things to do a mere two nights after achieving that position. James, however, never missed a free dinner and the opportunity of influencing rich people. While the country waited to see who James selected for his new cabinet, he had more interest in meeting people who could sponsor the party and himself.

Tonight, Ross had invited a select group to dinner. George Fenton and Donald Brown attended as lobbyists for the chemical industry, Ganak Reddy for pharmaceuticals and Albert Tolstoy as the obligatory Russian Oligarch. The guests would be cosmopolitan. Himself, James, and George represented England, Ganak for India, Tolstoy for Russia, Donnie for America, and not an EU European in sight.

***

Once everyone arrived, they made their way to the table. It pleased Ross to see the sly, lustful glances most of the men gave Madrigal. Not Ganak nor his partner of course. James's looks were none too discreet, and his wife glared at him. Octavia Holt, though young and pretty in a girl next door sort of way, always made him think of a hamster. She was rumoured to have political ambitions herself, and Ross thought she would need to ditch James before she could ever succeed with those.

George, astoundingly for a man of such wealth and no physical disadvantages, still had wife number one. She was an attractive fifty-something blonde, very much of the hunting, shooting, and fishing set. She and Madrigal clicked straight away.

Donnie was on wife number six. She was a woman with no class and the improbable name of Scarlett. No wonder he always appeared stressed and nervy, thought Ross, he'd hate to think of Donnie's monthly alimony bill. Scarlett was an over made-up blonde. She wore so much mascara that she kept blinking to stop her eyelashes from sticking together and had invested in at least one boob job too many. Her bosoms protruded like two massive, unyielding boulders, portable deadly weapons.

Encrusted with a king's ransom's worth of jewellery, Anna Tolstaya reminded him of a Ponte Vecchio shop, massed glittering gems behind a blank glass facade. Ross hoped they were facsimiles and the real jewels safely stowed in the bank.

The most striking couple were Ganak and his partner. Ganak was tall, dark, and slim, a man considered desirable by both men and women. His Russian boyfriend lacked any obvious physical attractions. His round bald head, unembellished by any facial hair, thick glasses and short hunched demeanour made Ross think of a cartoon mad scientist.

The boyfriend, Alex, was rumoured to be a strategic and mathematical genius. Ross assumed it was his mind not his body that attracted Ganak. He thought Alex's modelling work had informed Ganak's assumptions of an imminent pandemic.

As always on these occasions, the conversation began with polite small talk. Ross proposed a toast to James and poured everyone a glass of vintage Krug, except Ganak and Alex. They toasted James with fizzy water.

Discussion moved on to Madrigal's water charity, and George and his wife expressed interest in this. Madrigal radiated good humour from their attentions and Ross made a mental note to include them on guest lists going forward.

Indeed, everyone began to express so much interest in charitable works that James Holt started to look grumpy. This should be his night, and he was not happy at sharing the limelight with Madrigal. His wife, Octavia, also appeared disgruntled, she too involved herself with charitable works, but no one seemed interested in her charity. Ross could have told her this was the wrong audience for a cat charity. Cat charities worked best with old ladies. Or indeed Bridgette Bardot, who, come to think of it, was an old lady now. What was it with cats and old ladies?

Eventually, Ross interrupted the sycophants and moved the conversation on to other matters. Albert Tolstoy spoke at length about field sports in Russia. The thrill of the chase. The excitement of slaughtering the Asiatic black bear, the Russian grey wolf, and the snow sheep, rather than shooting pheasants and grouse. To be fair, if snow sheep were anything like British sheep, shooting them wouldn't be much of a challenge.

Octavia Holt looked horrified as Albert talked about trophy hunting and offered to show photos of some of his kills. At this point, reading the room correctly, George interrupted with talk about the importance of agriculture today. How to feed a growing world, and the necessity of the crop protection industry.

Ross had to hand it to George, if you talked about pesticides at the dinner table people eyed you with disapproval. Mention crop protection, and they all nodded sagely and agreed on the importance of growing enough food to feed the world. George had a way with words, he could explain away any crime.

'We at Gaia Chemicals would love to be manufacturing more in the UK, but there are so many regulations imposed upon you by the EU that we find it difficult to manufacture here.' said Donnie. 'If your party can get Brexit done Prime Minister, you will be doing

British manufacturing a favour.'

'How much do you manufacture in the UK?'

'Well, we are not currently manufacturing in the UK,' said George smoothly. 'But we intend to commence manufacturing here once the UK leaves the EU.'

'The world needs effective chemicals,' said Donnie.

'And effective medicines,' said Ganak, unable to sit quietly any longer. 'My company invests billions of dollars every year into research.'

Ross tore his bread roll into small pieces and fixed Ganak with a critical stare. He felt a pang when he heard Ganak say 'his company.' It was, in fact, Ross's company, Ganak was merely CEO, and he had better not get any ambitious ideas above that.

Ganak's partner, Alex stared at James intently. 'Tell me Prime Minister, what preparations have Britain made for any eventual pandemic?'

James seemed puzzled; perhaps he thought this question below his pay grade. 'Well, the Department of Health is always looking at that sort of thing. What are the chances of there being any pandemic in the West? Obviously, any medical crisis will always be of interest to people like yourselves in the pharmaceutical industry.'

James grasped the champagne bottle and poured the last of the Krug into his glass before anyone else could lay claim to it. He chuckled, 'a pandemic would be a great business opportunity for your industry. We all need to keep an eye on you to ensure you don't manufacture one to grow your business. Ha, that would be enterprising.' He laughed heartily at his wit.

Ross eyed Ganak with concern. Jesus, out of the mouths of babes and all that. He wouldn't put it past Ganak to engineer a pandemic just so he could show how clever a cure he could invent. Truth could so often be stranger than fiction.

'But Prime Minister,' said Alex, 'do you use modelling to predict future events and to prepare for them. In your party's campaign to leave Europe, you must have used modelling to predict how people would respond to your message?'

'I'm sure some back-room bods were looking at that sort of thing.' James spoke from a position of blissful ignorance. 'People beavering away on their abacuses. Marvellous thing statistics, not my forte of course.'

'In today's world data is power,' replied Alex. 'Do get your people to speak to me if you need any help with this.'

'Of course, of course. Got to choose my cabinet tomorrow, so I'll make sure one of them is good at maths. Better be the chancellor, eh. Can't have a chancellor who can't add up, though we don't want one who's too sharp with the figures. Don't want the treasury to be a growth prevention department. Sometimes we have to spend to promote our country.'

Ross kept his face straight. He could see a lavish redecoration of Number 10 in the pipeline.

Chapter Twenty-One

November 2019

Ross read a report from Jason. Greta Thunberg was not interested in working with Atlas. Well, what a surprise, though only a surprise for Jason. He smiled and shook his head; people could be so blind when it came to understanding other people's motivation. His mobile rang, the call was from George.

'Hi, George.'

'Ross, have you seen the papers today?'

'Not yet, why anything to cause concern?'

'Maybe, Novichok has been added to the list of banned chemical weapons.'

'Does that mean any issues for us?'

'Russia refused to comment, but Ivan Popov spoke to the Russian president off the record. Novichok is an organophosphate, the ingredients used in manufacture are the same as those used in our new pesticide. The Northern Chemicals facility in Norilsk was the one factory authorised by the government to produce Novichok and this authority continues, despite any ban from The Hague.'

'Unofficial production I presume?'

'Yes, Russia is a signatory to the chemical weapons treaty. However, an element of blackmail is involved.'

'Is this us blackmailing Russia or Russia blackmailing us?'

'Russia strongarming us, Popov was told to speak to our good friend Albert Tolstoy. Both contacted me, they don't know anything about your involvement.'

'And what did our Russian friends say?'

'The president of Russia made it clear he could, if he felt so inclined, inform the world that when the British were in uproar at a Russian dissident being poisoned with nerve gas on British soil, the gas in question was produced by a British owned company. He insinuated that may cause a scandal, not merely in the UK but among our European allies.'

Ross counted to ten, anger flooded through his body, he did not enjoy being threatened. 'What favour is he asking for?'

George was silent for a moment. 'The Russian authorities wish to end the war in Syria. They want to make a final push on Raqqa, it's held by the Kurds, and is seen as a key centre. They're looking to use chemical weapons, and they want us to supply them.'

'Won't that give them leverage over us?'

'No,' said George. 'If they expose us, we are in a position to expose them. The world may consider poisoning your dissidents with Novichok a little Russian peccadillo, but they will take supplying Sarin to the al-Assad regime for mass use against its people seriously. They need to be able to deny that one.'

'I'm not happy about this, George.'

'Indeed, the Russian government is not a comfortable bedfellow.'

'I don't want governments blackmailing us. We need more leverage on them.'

'Well, I await your instructions.'

'We have no choice, do what they say, and George, I want some dirt on our friend Albert Tolstoy.'

Chapter Twenty-Two

December 2019

It was December, the time for peace and goodwill for all mankind. Goodwill was sadly lacking this year, half the country hated the other half, divided along lines of pro or anti-Europe. Seville found it ironic. The EU was formed to prevent the countries in Europe from going to war with each other, and now her country had engaged in a civil war over Europe.

Britain had experienced the unusual disturbance of a December election, and the inevitable happened, the Conservatives remained in power, but now with a decisive majority. If not for her upcoming trip to Russia, depression would paralyse Seville. The new government appeared to have no strategy for the environment and to give no thought to the young. They were the forgotten people.

But her arrangements progressed well, Vera told her to expect her visa and authority to travel to Norilsk to come through any day now. Seville tried not to get too excited in case something went wrong. It was never comfortable to be dependent on the whims of bureaucrats. She guessed there were many people in Britain could confirm that.

Christmas offered no relief from gloom; Seville and her mother were going to Paris for the festive season. They found no seasonal appeal in the two of them celebrating Christmas on their own in the big house in Wadenhoe. Surrounded by other people in a luxury hotel in Paris would at least create the illusion of a festive spirit. Seville wished her mother would find another partner, then she would not feel so guilty at not living up to her mother's expectations. But work seemed to be the most important thing in Mary's life.

Her father extended a casual invitation to her to come over during the holidays and told her he would understand if she was too busy. She decided to take him up on the offer, partly to annoy Madrigal, but also to make sure he wasn't plotting anything. Seville saw how he had dealt with the inconvenience of Sacramento. She worried both parents may gang up on her if she did not pay lip service to the role of obedient daughter.

***

On Christmas Eve Seville flicked through news stories on her phone. The headlines were shocking, there had been a major attack on the city of Raqqa in Syria. Human Rights Watch suspected the use of chemical weapons, there were pictures of children crying, people lying in the streets while others tried to help them. Doctors from Médecins Sans Frontiéres spoke of an appalling atrocity, said the hospitals could not cope with the number of people affected. They pleaded for help and money. The government backed Syrian army was moving in on the city.

Seville read these reports with horror and thought she would not let anything stop her trip to Norilsk now.

***

The stage was set for Christmas, twinkling lights and Santa Claus in one part of the world, pain and death in another. Seville hoped the atrocity in Syria would register more response than merely asking for prayers for the afflicted during the Christmas mass.

They arrived in Paris on the Eurostar. Mary dressed for travel as if on the Orient Express, bejewelled, and elegant in designer clothes, Seville dressed for travel comfort. When they met at St Pancras station, Mary regarded Seville with displeasure. 'Really Seville, if you must always wear jeans, you should at least have a decent jacket to wear with them. We must try and visit Dior while we're in Paris.'

Seville thought she'd already succumbed to temptation by the devil when she accepted the Dolce and Gabbana swimsuit. She had no intention of allowing a Dior jacket to tempt her, though she guessed it would impress Vera if she turned up in Russia wearing one. Mary became surprisingly emotional over this rejection, claiming most daughters would be overjoyed if their mothers offered to buy them a Dior jacket.

Seville thought most daughters would worry that their mother had robbed a bank if offered such a trophy. But she accepted the gist of the argument. They arrived at the hotel, Mary's eyes bright with unshed tears and Seville enveloped in a cloak of guilt. Not the best start to a Christmas holiday. First world problems, Seville reminded herself, they both needed to get a grip.

Inspired by her guilt, Seville expressed suitable delight in the magnificence of the decorations and the luxury of the facilities. When Mary said she had specially chosen a hotel with a swimming pool, Seville hugged her, internally scolding herself for being a bad daughter. She did not dare tell her mother she had found a spot for wild swimming in a Parisienne canal. The Paris Swimming Society swam in a tributary of the Canal de Saint-Martin all year round and often at night. She'd contacted them and planned to meet the group for a swim.

***

Seville felt like an actor, performing in a play about Christmas. It was the opposite of a nativity play. There a refugee woman gives birth to a child in a stable, here they celebrated Christmas in a luxury hotel, drinking Champagne at the breakfast table. They each guiltily eyed the present received from the other. Constructing smiles and compliments on the choice and secretly wondering how to dispose of the unwanted gift.

Seville could not imagine herself ever wearing a diamond encrusted Chopard watch. The beautiful limited-edition book of 1001 Arabian Nights illustrated by Salvador Dali, which daughter gave to her mother, also seemed to be a mistake. When Mary said how much she loved Salvador Dali's work, she meant when hanging on the wall visible to all, not hidden in a book.

They went for a walk after breakfast, walking down festive streets lined with shops selling luxury goods. Seville nodded her head and made anodyne replies to her mother's commentary, conscious of an unbridgeable gap between their reactions to this place. She gazed at the homeless people huddled in luxury shop doorways. She thought of their empty stomachs, while she and her mother would return to a sumptuous banquet that they would be unable to finish.

When they reached the Dior store, Mary stopped to exclaim over jackets displayed in the window. 'We really must come here, it's impossible to shop Dior online. Look at that jacket Seville, it would be ideal for you.'

Seville looked at the jacket, a snip at 3,000 €, then the young woman sitting in the doorway caught her eye. She looked like a refugee from North Africa or the Middle East, her hair covered with a scarf. Momentarily they stared at each other, separated by a vast abyss of privilege and luck. Seville had to look away, there go I, she thought, except for an accident of birth. She thought her Christmas dinner might choke her.

***

Late that night Seville hurried through the dark, cold streets, to find redemption in a canal. Unable to resist the pull of a midnight swim, she made her apologies, pleaded tiredness, and went to join the Parisiennes from the swimming club. She knew she had drunk too much to swim, but her saviour from excess was to immerse herself in the chilly waters of the canal.

If this was a morality play, Seville told herself, she would drown, and her mother would come to realise how unimportant all the trappings of wealth are. But it is real life, not a play. The black icy waters surrounded by industrial buildings revived her, and she swam safely before returning to her luxurious cage. She took a long route back to pass the Dior store, half fearful she would see the migrant woman frozen to death.

She stopped to withdraw 200 € from a cash point. Moving carefully, so as not to wake or alarm the woman lying in her sleeping bag, she pushed the notes next to the woman's back. With a final glance around to make sure no other desperate person had seen her action, she returned to the hotel. Seville felt like medieval aristocracy buying an indulgence, but unlike them, she did not think herself absolved.

***

Sacramento had a four-hour gap between arriving at Heathrow as Sacramento Campbell and leaving for Moscow as Ben Smith. Seville found herself eager to listen to Sacramento's adventures as she waited for him at arrivals. He finally came through, wheeling a Vera sized suitcase and looking grumpy.

'Man, I've had such a bad journey,' he complained. 'You'd think it would be OK in first class, but I might as well have been in economy with the dudes who use laundry bags for hand luggage.'

Seville shook her head, and they manoeuvred their way to the taxi rank. Seville had booked a meeting room in an airport hotel. She would have walked there but Sacramento's case required assisted transport.

They made themselves comfortable in the room and ordered coffee and beer.

'Is Vera meeting you at the airport?' asked Seville.

'Yeah, she certainly is,' said Sacramento with a wide smile. 'I tell you, dude, it's time I got laid again. It's not healthy for a teenager to go that long without sex, it does strange things to your body, I can tell you.'

'Please don't,' she replied. 'You're giving me too much information now. I don't want to know about your sex life.'

'Aren't you concerned about my health?'

'Not your sexual health.'

'Dude, you are such a prude. Do you like that word, I learnt it at school?'

'Yes, very unamerican. Anyway, what was school like?'

'Man, that school is some sketchy place. We sleep in these dormitory rooms like we were in the army or something. I had to ask Mom to send over all my ski clothes, we've no heating so I had to sleep in my ski thermals. It's cold all the time, the showers are cold, the classrooms are cold and that's supposed to be "character building." They make us go for these runs up hills and then swim in the lake. Hey, it would suit you, Seville.'

'Not the dormitories,' said Seville with a shudder. 'I have that only child syndrome of always needing my own space.'

'Yeah, well there's some really cool dudes, one stole his dad's credit cards and went on an around the world trip. They arrested him in Thailand, but he'd already been to Cambodia, Vietnam, and Laos. Another was at one of your la di dah public schools and set up a gaming syndicate, it all went well until the wrong horse won the Grand National. He owed over £100,000 and someone grassed him up. I've learnt a lot there.'

'Indeed.' Seville thought the exile to the boot camp school wasn't having the effect Sacramento's parents wished. 'How's the Russian going?'

'I'll let you know after Moscow. I think I'm doing great, but when I speak to Vera in Russian she just laughs. Hey, she's told me you two are taking a road trip there in January.'

'Yes, so we are. All the papers came through before Christmas. I'm excited about it, but I hope Vera doesn't get into any trouble through it.'

'Like she'd care. I wish I was coming with you. Man, when I get out of the prison school, I'm going to travel. Vera's going to come to California this summer, you should come over too, bring that Taras dude with you. We can have a road trip to remember.'

California was in the right sort of area to visit the Rio Grande, thought Seville. Would Taras want to come, she wondered? She would not tell him about the Norilsk trip, but she wanted to see Taras again, no one else had ever called her a water spirit.

Chapter Twenty-Three

December 2019

Sacramento left in a state of high excitement, leaving Seville pondering on young love. 'It must be absence makes the heart grow fonder,' she thought. She had never felt like that about any of her boyfriends at university. She took another coffee to fortify herself for the journey to her father's house. It was a shame Sacramento could not come with her; he would be her moral support in a house of dubious welcome.

The traffic was still in Christmas holiday mode, making the drive from Heathrow to Cambridge painless. Seville wondered who might be in residence, it was unlikely there would not be several house guests. She thought Madrigal liked to display her perfect house and life, to promote envy and admiration in others.

She drew up outside the house and parked near the long open-fronted barn that sheltered the household cars. Her father's impossible Bentley had plenty of space around it, no one would take the risk of scratching his car from a carelessly opened door. Further along was Madrigal's bright red mini convertible, the people carrier and the nanny's golf. At the end was the ostentatious black limo that took Ross to and from work.

He just needs a couple of motorcycle outriders surrounding that limo, and he'd look like a proper tinpot dictator, thought Seville. When Sacramento first saw the limo he exclaimed, 'what the fuck, you've made yourself president or something?' That had not gone down well, and Sacramento was in prison school now. Seville was thankful to be an adult.

Maria, the au pair, opened the door. The role of au pair in this house seemed to be that of a general servant. The nanny took care of the children, the cleaner cleaned the house, the cook did the cooking, and the gardener did the gardening. Everyone treated Maria as a messenger and fetcher and carrier of items no one else could be bothered to fetch or carry. Opening the door to visitors appeared to be a major part of her role.

'Hi Maria,' said Seville, 'is my dad around?'

'Mr Campbell, he is shouting at people on a conference call,' said Maria.

'OK, I'd better not interrupt him then. Is Madrigal around?'

'I take you to Mrs Campbell, she is planning the New Year's Eve party in her study.'

I guess she won't be pleased to see me either, thought Seville. Oh well, I need to let them know I'm here.

Madrigal waved an arm at Seville indicating she should sit down. She was speaking in a kind, conciliatory way to someone on the phone. Seville guessed it was not anyone responsible for organising the New Year's Eve party.

'But of course, you must come, it wouldn't be the same without you. Just avoid those people.' Madrigal listened for some time while the person at the other end responded at length.

'I do keep telling you not to get involved in those Twitter conversations, those sorts of people will never see your point.' An even lengthier silence.

'We can't have an exclusively vegan buffet; I have spoken to

Ross about it, and he said under no circumstances. But we will provide an outstanding vegan option and when people see how appetising it is, they might avoid the meat.' A short silence.

'Alright, give the cards to people if you want to, but don't let Ross see you do it.'

After another five minutes of soothing sounds, Madrigal hung up. She regarded Seville with disapproval. 'Well now you're here, you can help me with the arrangements for the party tomorrow night. What are you doing with yourself these days?'

Seville was surprised, Madrigal had never shown any interest in her before. 'I'm completing some research before I start my masters. I'll be going to Peru and India to investigate the pollution there, and the impact on drinking water supplies and water usage in general.'

A spark of interest came into Madrigal's eyes. 'Are you studying water pollution? No one has ever told me that.' She gave Seville an accusing glare.

If you don't listen you don't hear, thought Seville. 'Why, are you interested?' she asked.

'Of course, I'm interested. My charity aims to supply accessible drinking water for those who do not have it. Water pollution is obviously going to be a subject important to me. You might be of use.'

'Glad to hear it,' said Seville.

The sarcasm was wasted on Madrigal, she was busy making a note in her journal. Seville read the note, it said 'Seville useful on water pollution.' Great when your stepmother finds a use for you.

'Now let me bring you up to speed with details of the party. My best friend has launched a campaign for people in the public eye to support and promote veganism. She did want us to set an example at this party, but your father has been unhelpful. He refuses to have a vegan only buffet which is upsetting for poor Dido.'

'Well, I guess if Dad has got businesspeople coming, he needs to offer them what they like. Dad likes meat, you're not expecting him to go vegan, are you?'

'No, of course not, I like meat myself, but promoting a public image of veganism is Dido's aim. She believes after the meat fest of Christmas; it would be good to show an alternative. So, to balance out we will have two buffets, one meat-based and one vegan. Therefore, we need to make the vegan table look more attractive than the carnivore table.'

Seville thought of the meal on the Aeroflot flight. An array of sliced meats in different shades of beige would do the trick, but she guessed the strategy was not to make the meat buffet so unappealing everyone turned to the vegan choice. 'Why is your friend so keen on promoting veganism?'

'You're the environmentalist, I would have thought this would be of interest to you. Her campaign is "Embrace Veganism to Save the World," with a subtitle of "Eating Meat Destroys the Environment." You must agree with that?'

Seville sighed. 'It's complicated. You could say eat food produced from your own country, and no intensively farmed food. There are lots of environmental issues around vegan foods as well as animal products.'

'Well, I don't know about any of that, but our task is to make the vegan buffet fabulous. Come on, I'll take you through the list of vegan food on offer, and we can work out how to display it.'

***

Seville had to hand it to Madrigal, she knew how to throw an excellent party. Was it a skill the British aristocracy learnt at their nanny's knee? It helped in having such a spectacular venue. The Campbell's house had three wings, built around a courtyard. One wing was devoted to a long room, with French windows on either side, opening out to the central courtyard on one side, and the grounds on the other. This was the party room.

Madrigal had not objected to Ross selecting a modern house and having visited Madrigal's parents' house for the christening of

Imogen, Seville wasn't surprised. Growing up in an old abbey with no central heating or modern conveniences could well make your preferences lean towards modern architecture. She understood the abbey had been extensively renovated at her father's expense since her visit, but she imagined the memory lingered on.

A gigantic Christmas tree rivalling the one in Trafalgar Square graced the centre of the courtyard, illuminated with so many lights it was possible to find your way around the interior of the house without bothering to turn on the lights in any room overlooking the courtyard. Madrigal wore a silver sequin gown and resembled a mobile glitter ball, catching the reflection of the tree lights.

Sequins must be the thing this season thought Seville, looking at the glittering gowns on many of the guests. She felt underdressed in a simple midnight blue silk slip dress. The only glittery thing about her was her Chopard watch. She thought she should wear it to show loyalty to her mother, and diamond-encrusted watches were scarcely out of place here.

Seville stood by the vegan buffet, isolated in this older, sophisticated crowd. She had nothing in common with these people. She smiled warmly at Maria, who was adding some last touches to the meat buffet table. Maria smiled shyly back and hastily left the table. Seville wondered what it was like to be an au pair here. Surrounded by all this wealth and privilege, to see a girl the same age as you, but to have no connection. The gap caused by wealth too immense to bridge.

She glanced around the room; richly polished wood floor, silvered glass baubles and ivy festooned over the walls and ceiling, crystal glasses glittering in the partygoer's hands. The live band playing to an inattentive audience who were too busy greeting acquaintances with loud brays and air kisses to listen to the music. The room perilously illuminated by candlelight and the light from the great Christmas tree in the courtyard.

The guests were a cast of middle-aged men with younger women. Mainly white with a few people of Asian descent. Then

Seville saw a young black man, for a moment she stared in surprise and blushed as he caught her eye. She hoped she hadn't looked like she thought he should not be here. She smiled to correct any negative impressions, and he smiled back at her. He spoke to a woman standing next to him, then made his way over to her.

He stretched out a hand. 'Hello, my name's Jason and I work for your father. I'm correct aren't I, you are Ross's daughter? We met at Madrigal's charity ball this summer.'

Seville smiled back, 'yes I am.' She remembered Jason talking about an initiative for transparency in business, and she wondered if she should know what he did at Atlas. Had he told her; would he think her rude if she asked?

'I'm the sustainability director, with responsibility for company ethics,' Jason enlightened her. 'Madrigal's friend Dido is my partner, and we are keen to promote veganism. I must say the vegan buffet looks splendid.'

Seville smiled, 'veganism for the environment?' she asked.

Jason handed her a card with "Embrace veganism to save the world, eating meat destroys the environment," printed on it. 'It is an important message,' he said. 'But I think the young understand this.'

Jason amused Seville. He was not much older than her and spoke so earnestly. His sincerity was obvious, and she thought he did not intend to be patronising. She wondered if she too sounded that earnest to others.

'The environment is immensely important,' she said. 'But this needs to be understood by more than just the young, and veganism by itself is not enough to save the world.'

Her father joined them. 'Hi honey,' he said, kissing Seville lightly on the cheek. 'I haven't had a chance to talk to you properly yet, did you have a good Christmas?' He glanced at the watch she wore, 'nice watch, present from a boyfriend?'

'Dad, I'm unlikely to ever have a boyfriend who could afford to buy me a present like this. It was my Christmas present from Mum.'

'You need to smarten up on your boyfriend qualifications,

honey. You might not want the boyfriend to buy you the expensive watch, but you want them to be able to afford to do so.'

'Money isn't everything,' said Jason.

'A means to an end,' said Ross. 'So, what does the New Year hold for you'

'I've got a trip planned at the end of January, and I'll be visiting Peru and India,' said Seville. 'Then I'm going to do some research on pollution of the Rio Grande in the summer holidays. Sacramento may come with me.'

'Where's your January trip to and what do you plan to do on it?'

Seville hesitated, instinctively she thought she should not mention Russia. Maybe her father had upset someone in authority in Russia, it might be a visa was denied to her because she was Ross Campbell's daughter. She improvised, 'I'm going to follow the course of the River Danube. There are major problems with pollution from pesticide chemical waste there, but also increasing river traffic from tourist cruises is another problem.'

'Really?' said Jason. 'I always thought river cruises sounded like a fun idea.'

'More like a terrible one,' said Seville, 'unless you sail.'

'My God,' said Ross. 'Soon we won't be able to do anything pleasurable.'

'Dad, if we don't change, the pleasure will be taken away from us regardless. You wouldn't find a river cruise fun, so it would make no difference to you.'

'I wouldn't find any cruise fun, the idea of being locked up on a ship with a whole bunch of people I wouldn't choose to spend time with sounds terrible. But some people would find it fun, and they won't take kindly to being told they can't do it anymore. I'll be interested to hear what you turn up; we'll have to get together when you're back and you can update me on your research.'

Seville blinked at her father in surprise. Ross had never shown an interest in her work before. 'Yeah, sure Dad.'

Jason gazed after Ross with admiration. 'Your father is

marvellous, he is so interested in everything, a truly remarkable man. A renaissance man.'

The renaissance man who came to Seville's mind was of the Cesare Borgia variety. 'Yes,' she said, watching her father cross the room and greet a man she recognised, the Englishman from Kiselyovsk.

Her thoughts started to spin like cogs, that man worked for a chemical firm and now her father showed interest in her research on pollution. Chemicals polluted. That man had discussed chemical weapons and now the world suspected the use of chemical weapons in Syria. After telling her father she intended to visit Russia, her visa application was rejected. Suspicion clouded her mind, what was going on?

She realised Jason was still talking to her. 'Sorry, I didn't catch what you said?'

'I asked if you read about the terrible attack in Syria. I shouldn't ask you. This party is supposed to celebrate the New Year, but it was such a dreadful attack. I can't get it out of my mind.

Tears welled up in Jason's eyes and Seville grasped his hand. He pressed her hand back and shook his head. 'I'm sorry, do excuse me. The thought of those poor people at Christmas.'

'You don't need to apologise; you would need a heart of ice not to be affected by such an attack. I'm the one at fault.' Her voice trailed off.

Jason dabbed at his eyes and looked at Seville in surprise. 'How are you at fault?'

Seville considered Jason, even if he did work for her father, he seemed to be a decent, compassionate person. She stared at the business card he had given her; he was a man who cared about both the environment and people. Was he someone she could trust?

'Jason, am I right? You are involved in an initiative concerning company ethics?'

'Yes indeed, I am collaborating with Lady Fakenham.'

'Do you ever investigate companies; do you check if a company that appears to meet all the rules isn't also involved with a company that breaks the rules?'

Jason was thoughtful. 'I'm not sure if that is within the remit of Lady Fakenham's organisation.'

'Can you be sure Atlas is not involved with less reputable companies or with environmentally unfriendly companies?'

'I'm sure your father would not allow such a thing to happen.'

'Could I ask you to do me a favour?'

'Of course.'

'Do you see that man my father is talking to; his first name is George? I believe he works for a company called Gaia Chemicals. I think he may be trying to develop links with Atlas, and I have reason to believe his company is involved in some extremely environmentally unfriendly practices. Would you be able to check it out?'

Jason appeared excited, Seville guessed his role normally involved writing policies, not checking if they were effective or adhered to. 'That's a clever idea. Your father would be too busy to realise if another company was potentially trying to exploit their relationship with Atlas. I'll see what I can find out.'

'I would appreciate it and please don't speak to my father about this. Let me give you my mobile number and email address.'

They exchanged contact details and Jason shook hands with Seville. 'It'll be our secret,' he said. 'We'll protect Atlas against any associations that might smirch the company name.'

'Yes, let's keep it a secret for now,' said Seville. She glanced across the room to where Ross stood talking to the chemical man. She thought she knew extraordinarily little about her father.

Chapter Twenty-Four

December 2020

Ross gazed fondly across the room at Madrigal. She wore an utterly ridiculous dress, but hey, if it made her happy, he wasn't going to be the one to tell her. If she wanted to dress like a glitter ball that was her business. Regardless of the vagaries of fashion, Madrigal always looked beautiful no matter how absurd the outfit.

He glanced around at his guests, who did he need to speak to tonight? George for one. Ross had taken a call from Donnie, and he was not happy with him. Something must be done.

The new Home Secretary was here, an appalling woman who, according to rumour, had toyed with the idea of setting up her own right-wing party, but on reflection decided the Conservatives were right-wing enough for her. Ross assumed James Holt appointed Amy Morton to his cabinet in the hope she would deal with all those issues he had not dealt with during his year-long tenure before becoming prime minister. She was keen on law and order and deportation.

Her civil servants called her the Butcher of Basildon. Ross watched her lips tighten as she took in the room and saw a few people of colour. He guessed in the old days she would have found South Africa to be her natural home.

He followed her gaze which rested upon, of course, Jason. He appeared popular among Madrigal's crowd as their token black, and Ross wondered what Jason thought about that. He noticed Jason talking to Seville and had joined them intending to find out what she was up to. Unfortunately, he could not confine her somewhere in the manner he used to clip Sacramento's wings.

His conversation with Seville did not give him a major cause for concern. He was glad she appeared to have forgotten about travelling in Russia. Ross considered the Danube, he was sure they did not manufacture anything along that route, but the pesticides used were probably his. He would show interest in Seville's research and ask to read any report she made. At least they would be ahead of the game if the environmental lobby kicked up a fuss about pesticides.

George had that expression of pained politeness the English upper classes were so good at putting on when cornered by a member of the hoi polloi. Anyone as quick at reading expressions as Ross could see George making a mental note never to let himself be in the same room as this dreadful woman ever again.

Ross saw his point. He only invited Mrs Morton because Madrigal's father wanted to talk to her about his Syrian refugees. Now, that was a conversation worth eavesdropping on.

Ross needed to speak to George, so he decided to rescue him. George's wife had long since left her husband to his fate; Anne Fenton would not waste time speaking to Amy Morton. She believed in mixing with her own type and Mrs Morton was certainly not that.

Ross extracted his father-in-law from a discussion about tin mining in Cornwall. He appeared to be promoting the idea of using Syrian refugees to restart the industry, two subjects always close to his heart. 'William, do come and meet the new home secretary, you can bring her up to speed on your refugee initiative.'

'Indeed, indeed, though I am sure James explained all the benefits when he handed over his work to her,' said Lord Sedley.

Ross was sure James had done no such thing. The cabinet was chosen at random with no thought of anyone's suitability for the job. Amy Morton's qualifications were a gleeful thought on James's part that she would rile all the civil servants in the Home Office.

A look of relief came over George's face as Ross approached with William in tow. 'My dear Home Secretary do let me introduce my father-in-law, Lord Sedley. He is keen to talk to you about some initiatives he pursued with your predecessor.'

Lord Sedley grasped the home secretary's hand and shook it vigorously while Ross steered George away.

'Thank God for that,' said George. 'What a ghastly racist the woman is, ghastly everything in fact. I'll be waiting to see how many chief constables across the land hand in their resignations.'

'Yes, I think James will have to move her, Edward Capell told me all her civil servants are outraged. I think he is leaving her there long enough so any cockups he made are attributed to her, and then they'll show her the door. I don't want to speak about her, it's Donnie I'm worried about.'

'What's he panicking about now?'

'Our Russian friends, the delightful Tolstoys.' Ross gestured at Albert Tolstoy who stood with his wife on the opposite side of the room talking to Madrigal.

'Yes, I intended to head over there once I managed to extract myself from that awful woman.'

'I guess you've read about the Christmas atrocity.'

'Of course, fifty-seven people killed, all civilians and many needing hospitalisations but unable to get it because the hospital was destroyed. The Guardian called it the biggest atrocity in this war of atrocities.'

'Now Donnie is in a panic Tolstoy will pass any blame to Northern Chemicals if there is an investigation. He went on about

Christmas, he seems to think the attack is worse because it happened on Christmas Eve. He's getting wobbly George.'

George frowned. 'Yes, I think he's coming to the end of the road, I keep waiting for him to give his notice in.'

'In Donnie's role, you do not choose the end of the road, the end of the road chooses you. We need to exit him, George.'

'OK, we can manage this. We'll send Donnie on a trip to Norilsk. Tell him he needs to ensure no chemical weapon development is still going on there.'

'Fine, and George, we are talking about a one-way ticket?'

'Leave it with me. Now let's go and chat up Tolstoy.'

'I'll join you in a minute,' said Ross. He gazed back across the room to where Jason and Seville still talked. Jason's head was inclined towards Seville as if she were talking quietly. They had the unmistakable look of fellow conspirators. Jason glanced quickly towards him and turned away.

Ross felt the unfamiliar anger rise inside him; it was rare for him to feel anger these days. When he was young it had been outside his control, now he had total control and better still, little happened to arouse the anger. His view misted, but Jason was distinct, Ross saw him standing under a tree, with a blazing tyre around his neck. The practice of necklacing he thought. The mist faded and now the blaze came from the myriad reflection of lights on Seville's diamond-encrusted watch.

Chapter Twenty-Five

January 2020

Donnie Brown's life had not been easy, but that was due to bad decisions rather than bad luck. He was born into a wealthy family. That was good fortune, though you might say being born poor and being a success regardless, showed even greater luck. Donnie understood people like himself took much for granted. Those who had to fight for everything tended to be more clued-up about life.

His father was forty-five when Donnie was born, and when he retired at seventy, Donnie became CEO of the family company. He was but twenty-five so perhaps it was not surprising he made a few dumb decisions at this time. He married the wrong woman, and a year later thought he found the right one. An expensive mistake, his first wife's father was a top divorce lawyer and took Donnie to the cleaners.

Wife number two was another error of judgement. Donnie had never met anyone capable of spending so much cash. The woman could spend the GDP of a small country on filling up her wardrobe.

When a company called Gaia Chemicals came along and offered a substantial sum of money to buy the Brown's family firm, Donnie leapt at the offer.

Gaia Chemicals only kept him as CEO of his family company for a year or so. Then they told him they would incorporate Brown's Chemicals into Gaia Chemicals and his current role would not exist anymore. But not to worry, they would give him a job as operations director which commanded a bigger salary than that of CEO at Browns.

The significant difference was Donnie had to travel, to get on planes and fly around the world. The devil made work for the idle hands of his second wife, and she told Donnie she wanted to leave him. Not as remotely expensive as the divorce from wife number one, but it still cost him money.

He found his third wife in Russia. It soon became clear she was only in it for the passport, and they too came to the parting of the ways.

Wife number four was different. Donnie learnt his lesson and decided no more marrying prostitutes he picked up in foreign hotels. He would marry a regular American girl. Janette was a bit older too, but so was he. What he hadn't realised was how scheming a regular American girl could be.

His job required so much travel, it was hard to keep on top of events at home. When he met Janette through the dating website, it escaped him she had three children. To be fair she did not include this little fact on her profile. She revealed the children after the honeymoon, and the marriage ended right there. Donnie was never cut out to be a family man and protected himself against this eventuality, by having a vasectomy after his first divorce.

Some nights he woke abruptly, heart pounding, hot and sweaty, having dreamt how much money his first wife would have taken him for if they had any children. Janette and her family had to go. But to add insult to injury, Donnie found himself responsible for paying maintenance for children who were not his own. He made a mental resolution to drag his first wife's father out of retirement if he ever got divorced again.

Wife number five was foreign, but not the sort of foreign woman you picked up in the bars of the hotels where businessmen hung out. She was classy, he met her in an embassy reception in Delhi and her father was someone senior in the Indian army. When brutally honest with himself, Donnie never worked out what she saw in him. She was a beautiful, delightful person and he never felt truly worthy of her. She was kind and considerate, and he found it all too much.

It ended when she discovered his affair with his secretary, now wife number six. People like George Fenton described Donnie's current wife as a slapper. To be honest he had to admit the jury would weigh in on the slapper description. Wife number five said a dignified goodbye and insisted she did not need any form of divorce settlement. Just thinking about her brought tears to Donnie's eyes.

So here he was, on wife number six and undoubtedly, he would replace her with wife number seven somewhere along the line. Yet another of the worries plaguing his life.

Donnie found himself unable to leave a job he hated because no other company would pay him so well, and he needed the money. Constantly worried that cancerous growths were overtaking his body, a legacy of all the chemicals in all those unsafe factories. He became nervous about being called out for the sins of his industry. Resentful of George and Ross who hid behind fall guys like him.

The chemical attack in Syria proved to be the last straw. Those pictures of kids on Christmas Eve with eyes and nose streaming, lying on the ground in rows, it was too much. When he rang Ross to protest, Ross said, 'they're Muslims Donnie, they don't celebrate Christmas.' As if that made it any better.

Ross told him no one knew if any of these chemical weapons were made from the materials they produced. Donnie said of course they knew, why was Tolstoy so concerned to destroy certain products if that was the case? Ross replied, just normal precautions.

This didn't fool Donnie, he realised what they were doing, this had always been on the cards. He decided he was not up for it anymore. So, he came up with a plan, he would disappear. Like a snake shedding its skin, he would shed this unsatisfactory life and start a new one.

For some time now Donnie had been salting away money in an offshore account. He'd hoped to amass more, but he would survive with half a million dollars. Hell, he was fifty-five, he would find somewhere cheap to live and go underground. He might take a job in a bar. He imagined himself on a Caribbean Island, living in a small house, working at the local bar, and listening to everyone's troubles and dispensing advice.

The idea became increasingly seductive, no way he could face another five years of this, as originally planned. He'd worked it out. George wanted him to go to Norilsk and meet with Ivan Popov. Donnie agreed to that, he would lull George and Ross into thinking it was still business as normal, and then he was off.

He would go out there and come back on the first leg of the return flight which would take him to Moscow. Once in Moscow, he would invent a family crisis that required his presence in the USA. He'd go to New York from Moscow, and there he would change his identity and fly to Florida.

From Florida, he would fly to St Kitts and board a ferry to Nevis, his final destination. He would shop in Miami for everything he needed, then start his new life as a beach bum and barman on the Caribbean Island of Nevis.

In his mind, he sat in the warm sun with his feet dangling in a blue sea. But before he got anywhere near the warmth, he had to go to the exact opposite. It could hit minus 40 °C in Norilsk during January.

Chapter Twenty-Six

January 2020

A long trip requires a long book and Seville was reading War and Peace. It was a novel she had always planned to read but somehow never found the time. She read for her studies and for relaxation she chose crime novels. She enjoyed the combination of a puzzle, high drama, and the mundanity of the detectives' everyday life, their stories, their problems. Presumably, none were true, but lack of realism did not matter if the story entertained.

War and Peace presented the world on a large-scale canvas. She found herself empathising with Pierre in all his setbacks as he tried to do good, shed some tears at his failures. She could see herself in him, the need to do the right thing, wealth as a millstone around one's neck. But a debauched lifestyle had never attracted her.

Seville had undertaken an exceedingly long journey. She promised herself she would fly as little as possible, so with Peru and India planned later in the year, she would go by train to Russia. The journey to Norilsk could not be entirely overland. Once they reached

Krasnoyarsk there was no alternative but to fly to their final destination.

She had enjoyed planning her route. She found the thought of turning up at St Pancras station and hopping on a train to Moscow romantic. Doing this during the winter months added to the glamour, she imagined herself looking through the train window at a landscape crowned with pure white snow. The gloom and depression that enveloped her on her Christmas trip to Paris vanished. She marvelled at how a sense of purpose transformed her mental well-being.

Seville stayed in a hotel in the 19th arrondissement, within walking distance both for the Gare du Nord, the Gare de l'Est and convenient for an illicit dip in the canal. She met some members of the swimming group late that night, and together they swam in the freezing waters.

The next day she caught the Paris Moscow express from the Gare de l'Est. Stary Novy God celebrations, the Russian Old New Year, had finished and the train was quiet. She had the four-berth sleeper to herself. Her excitement made it difficult to concentrate on her book. Her route would take her through France, Germany, Poland, Belarus and into Russia. Anxiously she checked her papers again, travel through Belarus required an additional visa.

She would meet Vera at Moscow Belorussky station, and they would embark on the more challenging leg of their trip. The distance from Moscow to Krasnoyarsk was about the same as from London to Moscow, but the journey immeasurably more complicated. They would take the Rossiya train to Novosibirsk, then another to Krasnoyarsk, a trip that would take nearly three days.

***

To Seville's surprise, Vera proved to be a patient traveller.

'In Russia, there are many slow things, bureaucrats are always slow. We know when we have no choice but to be patient,' she said.

Their 'guide' met them in Krasnoyarsk. Vera had laid her groundwork well, as a small but enthusiastic reception committee from the Psychrophile swimming club also waited for them. The guide was a young woman, not much older than Seville, who appeared to be in awe of Vera. The reputation of Vera's oligarch father travelled before her. Lena, their guide, spoke English well, far advanced on Seville's pidgin Russian.

The swimmers invited them to dinner that evening, and Lena escorted them to their hotel, 'the best in the city,' she assured them. It was comfortable although the decoration appeared old-fashioned. They went to their rooms, and she eyed her king-size bed longingly, it was some time since she had slept in a bed with so much space.

***

Lena ordered coffee in reception. She gazed at Seville with approval.

'Ophelia, I see you read the great Russian authors, I saw you carrying the masterpiece of Tolstoy, War and Peace.'

Seville smiled back. 'Yes, it is a book I always intended to read, but somehow I never found the time to do so. I'm enjoying it.'

'Literature is most important to Russians, we have much outstanding literature. But the English too have great writers, your Charles Dickens and your Shakespeare.'

'Of course, Shakespeare is known around the world.'

Lena said, 'but I can tell Shakespeare matters to you, or your parents. Ophelia Macbeth, these are both names from Shakespeare.'

Seville wondered if she should have insisted on a more inconspicuous name. 'Yes,' she said, 'my parents thought as our name was Macbeth, it would be amusing to give me the first name of a Shakespearean heroine.'

Lena did not appear to be suspicious. 'They were right, it would be a waste not to call you after a woman in Shakespeare. And no one will ever forget you with a name like that.'

'Are you always a guide, Lena?' asked Vera.

'No, I also work as a translator. The money is not so good, so it helps to be a guide as well. I have a degree in English, I would like one day to go to America, but it would cost much money.'

Vera smiled, this was what they wanted, a guide who needed extra money. 'Perhaps you will earn a big tip from us,' she said.

***

No one doubted Vera's cover story. She disguised her environmental credentials behind Dior sunglasses and the Gucci sweatshirt. Seville marvelled that in the grey winter light Vera could see anything through the sunglasses.

The swimming club members were delighted to be filmed and fascinated a girl from Britain would want to swim with them. It was minus twenty outside, so Seville could understand their wonder. It became clear Vera's father was a well-known oligarch in Siberia from his activities in oil, and all treated her with almost exaggerated courtesy. A local government leader also came to dinner, and everyone talked about the importance of showing the West what a marvellous place Russia was.

Lena almost bowed every time she spoke to Vera and seemed impressed she was going to make a film. Seville hoped she would be easy to manipulate once they arrived at Norilsk and wanted to throw her off.

The following day they made their way to the river at midday. As well as a group of well wrapped up spectators, about thirty people gathered in their swimsuits on the bank, with not a single wetsuit in sight. Clearly, wetsuits were for wimps. Vera filmed them and asked if they ever wore wetsuits. Their audience laughed at this, with many people calling out.

'They are saying who has money for wetsuits?' translated Lena. 'They swim because it is free, a poor man can always swim as the water does not charge them. Our water belongs to all our people.'

'Can you ask them if the water is clean to swim in?' said Seville.

Lena spoke to the crowd, then turned to her. 'They say it is pure enough for the fish, so it must be clean enough for them. They ask if the English girl is afraid to jump in?'

Vera laughed. 'Now, come and jump in the water. I want you to run in from this bank and I want you to scream.'

Seville thought there was little chance of her not screaming once she ran into the water unless the cold took her breath away. She pulled off her sheepskin boots and dropped her fleece-lined wrap. She stood in her swimsuit, shocked by the freezing air, and gave her body some minutes to acclimatise to the temperature before entering the water. Her feet sank into the snow-covered bank, and she glanced around. On the opposite side of the river were buildings, and on this side trees. The branches coated in snow showed as a delicate tracery against the ominous brown sky, which spoke of further snowfalls to come.

She raised her arms in a gesture of victory, ran into the river and dived under the steely surface. Every nerve in her body burnt with cold, and she felt extraordinarily alive. She swam out 100 yards then rapidly swam back again. As she left the water enthusiastic applause greeted her.

Members of the club came down the bank and slapped her on her back. The air no longer felt cold, it seemed positively balmy in contrast to the water. There was much talking and gesturing. 'Now they say you must join them in a race,' said Lena.

Vera filmed a toddler who, dressed only in swim trunks, stood knee-deep in the snow, pointing to the river, and calling out. His mother took his hand and waded into the water with him. Seville tried to imagine Madrigal leading Imogen or Charlie by the hand into this river. The image would not come.

She lined up with the other swimmers, who all clapped her and made encouraging noises. Someone counted to three and they ran and dived in. It was as cold the second time. She found it hard to stretch out her arms and to kick smoothly with her legs in the intense cold and noticed some swimmers pulling ahead of her. Seville made more effort, not worried about winning, but determined not to come last, and pushed herself forward. She overtook a person who had overtaken her, performed a perfect turn and began the swim back.

Her technique was excellent, and she passed a few swimmers, scrambling up the bank to come third, to rapturous applause. Vera interviewed the winner, then Seville, and finally some of the defeated. The people were warm, friendly, inclusive and some attempted to engage Seville in conversation in rapid Russian. The event was a success, and they had proved their credentials. Vera pointed out the local press who gathered to take pictures.

***

That night at the hotel, Vera crept into Seville's room half an hour after they had gone to bed. They needed to discuss their next moves in private, but it was obvious Lena had instructions to always remain with them. Even though she appeared tired, it became clear she would not go to bed before they did. Vera and Seville yawned and stretched and thanked Lena for her efforts and made their way to their rooms. They waited to ensure she would be asleep.

'Today we have had success,' said Vera. 'People will hear about us; everyone will believe we are here to film you swimming. You wait, Seville, all the walrus swimming clubs of Russia will be inviting you to come and swim with them.'

'What happens next?'

'Tomorrow we fly to Norilsk, and we meet the members of their swimming club. They have planned a tour of the place for us as I said we are both keen to visit a closed city. Some of the swimmers work at Northern Chemicals, some at the nickel mining company. I need to meet them to judge who I can bribe.'

'How will we get about? Here the Psychrophile swimmers drove us, will anyone in Norilsk be prepared to take us to the sites we wish to see?'

'I have told Lena we want to hire an SUV. Once we arrive, we can plan how we proceed.' Vera smiled mischievously. 'I have reviewed the film I made today, and it is excellent. I will make two films from this trip, the British at play and the British at war. We are going into battle to defend the environment.'

Chapter Twenty-Seven

January 2020

Donnie gazed sourly out of the window of the plane as it shuddered to a stop, the wheels juddering on the icy surface. Nothing redeemed the view, some grim stands of conifers and flat tundra stretched away towards the horizon, all covered in snow. A blank, unenticing vista. But two days and then he was out of here, out of this shit hole and out of this shitty life. Turquoise waters, blue skies and a warm sun awaited him, and hell, what if there was a hurricane or two in the Caribbean, a man could survive a hurricane.

He pulled his heavy down jacket from the overhead locker and jammed his sheepskin-lined hat firmly on his head. Donnie did not have enough hair to consider not wearing a hat for even a minute in this weather. He tucked his scarf into his jacket and zipped it up to his chin, he tugged on his gloves and slipped out into the aisle. The plane was not full, Norilsk Alykel airport was not a major destination.

An announcement came over the Tannoy, and his fellow passengers muttered to themselves, took off their outdoor clothing and sat down again. What the fuck was going on now, wondered Donnie, why couldn't they make announcements in English? He remained standing and rang for cabin crew. A glamorous stewardess approached him with an ingratiating smile on her face.

'Yes?' she said.

'What's happening?' asked Donnie, not bothering to smile back. He did not think he would hear anything worth smiling about.

'Passengers cannot disembark yet; we have a problem.'

'What problem?'

She shrugged. 'My English not good enough to explain, so sorry there is a problem. You will leave the plane soon.'

'Soon, how soon?' Donnie said.

'Soon as the problem is resolved,' she replied in what sounded like pretty fluent English to Donnie.

One of his fellow passengers tapped him on the shoulder. 'Another plane is in trouble and needs to make an emergency stop here, Polar flying in winter you know. They need to sort it out first before they let us out,' he said in an American accent.

'You American?' said Donnie.

'Yup, we're in the minority here friend. Few Americans get authorised to come to Norilsk.'

'Yeah, and I wish I wasn't among them. I'm Donnie Brown, what's your business here pal?'

'Nickel mining, Andy Baclanova. I'm an engineer and I've flown in to advise on the machinery. The Daldykan river is running red once more, and they want it sorted before the world's press is on their back again. The locals take photos and send them to journalists. They have invested a considerable sum of money since the last 'red river' incident in 2016, but some filtration units need replacing. What brings you here?'

'I'm a director at Gaia Chemicals, come to visit our subsidiary, Northern Chemicals. Pleased to meet you, how long do you think we'll be held up?'

'Apparently, the plane with the problem is attempting to land now. They'll want to move us on before the Krasnoyarsk flight arrives, I don't think they can deal with two planes at once, they never deal with more than one plane an hour.'

The presence of another American reassured Donnie and one that understood Russian too. Maybe he was in luck with this trip.

'Where are you staying?'

'In a company apartment.'

'Me too, hey how about meeting for dinner tonight?'

'Sure, great idea, do you know the Norilsk Restaurant? I could meet you there at eight.'

Donnie sank back into his seat with a smile. Dinner with a fellow American sounded more fun than dining with that cold bastard, Ivan Popov. He would love seeing Popov's face when he told him he was having dinner with a friend.

***

They waited over an hour before they disembarked from the plane. Then passport control shut so they had to wait again. Donnie's new friend told him that normally all the border police went for a coffee break after their plane, the 8 a.m. arrival from Moscow, and did not come back on duty again until the 10.15 a.m. from Krasnoyarsk landed. They saw no reason to change their habits and the Moscow arrivals would have to wait until the Krasnoyarsk passengers had disembarked.

They stood in the disgruntled queue, all shifting from foot to foot and some people sat down on the marble floor. A mistake Donnie thought, his mother always said you could get piles from sitting on cold floors. He heard the thudding of many feet, and the Krasnoyarsk passengers began to join the end of the queue.

The border police arrived, and passport control was back in action. As they shuffled forward, Donnie glanced back at the new arrivals. Momentarily his eyes told him that something was amiss, but his brain did not register what. All his faculties caught up with each other, and he stared in dismay at the arrivals. At the back of the queue, standing out like gold nuggets in a muddy river bed, were three girls. One of them was the girl from the temple, the girl who was Ross Campbell's daughter.

Chapter Twenty-Eight

January 2020

Their plane was not full, it appeared not many people wished to come here. A warm satisfaction filled Seville, she had achieved her aim, she was in Norilsk, well in Norilsk Alykel airport at least. She would like to photograph everything but assumed that would be unwise. Instead, she gazed around intently, resolved to remember every fact about this place she had striven so hard to get to.

A long queue stretched ahead of her to passport control. The queue appeared to be composed of middle-aged men, whom she supposed were Russian. She, Vera, and Lena were the only women on their flight from Krasnoyarsk, the rest Russian men apart from two young Chinese men.

They progressed to the front and eventually passed through passport control. Young women stood out as not the normal species of visitor to Norilsk and their documentation was thoroughly scrutinised. They collected their luggage, Vera wheeling the enormous Louis Vuitton trunk. She told Seville it was their disguise for any samples she gathered. No one would dream of searching such a symbol of wealth and power.

Once they cleared customs, they found a small welcoming committee of dedicated Walrus Swimming Club members waiting for them. Vera caused a disturbance by filming them, but one swimmer was a senior official in the local bureaucracy, and he smoothed over any dispute. Outside a heavy snowfall had begun and they posed eagerly again in the deepening snow. At 11 a.m. the sun started to rise, and the horizon became tinged an orangey pink. They attracted a substantial audience from the other passengers.

They left for the city in the minibus the swimmers met them in. It was bitterly cold, and Seville and Vera huddled together for warmth. Lena seemed better able to cope with the extreme cold. Seville's phone recorded the temperature as -25°. The Walruses gleefully informed them it would be colder the following day when they would swim.

Vera filmed the crowd on the minibus, and they made jovial comments about how they did not think the English girl would manage to swim if it dropped below -40°. She stopped filming and nudged Seville. 'Did you notice that man at the airport?' she asked her.

'What man?'

'I think he was an American, his clothes were not Russian or at least not the clothes Russians around here wear. He kept staring at you.'

Seville frowned; she remembered the last time strange men had taken an interest in her. 'What did he look like?'

'Small, fat, white, middle-aged, smartly dressed. American looking.'

Seville thought of the men she had overheard in Kiselyovsk, one of whom she'd seen at her father's party. This was no coincidence, was her father spying on her, had he sent this man to watch her? How could her father be involved with industry in Russia, and how would he know she was here when she travelled as Ophelia Macbeth? It did not make sense, but she had a strong intuition her father had prevented her from getting a visa under her name last summer. She did not know why, but she was convinced this was all connected.

'We must make plans to get to the industrial areas,' she told Vera.

'I will work out a plan,' said Vera, confident of her ability to succeed.

***

The company that night was loud and jolly. They drank vodka flavoured with black pepper and dill weed. The swimmers were of mixed ages and Seville noticed Vera in deep conversation with another girl of similar age to herself. She engaged Lena in conversation to prevent her from listening to Vera's discussion.

'Why is Norilsk a closed city?'

'They are from the times of Stalin, these are places with industries that needed to be secret, the atomic industry, military industries, chemical and metallurgical industries. Even today they are important to the state, so the state controls access. For Norilsk, it is the chemical and metallurgical industries. You are lucky to be permitted to come here.'

'But why is access still limited?'

'Who knows?' said Lena with a shrug. 'The instinct of the authorities is to keep what they value hidden, why allow people into these places if you do not have to? There are about forty closed cities we know of, but there may be more. The populations in closed cities are always controlled.'

Seville tried to imagine living in a city that did not show on any map, a city the world thought did not exist. What sort of paranoia would that cause she wondered? Just the idea of it made her feel anxious, it brought back memories of the clinic when she was a teenager.

'The industries you talk about, are they all polluting industries? Are the people who live here not concerned about pollution? I read about an incident where nickel spillage caused the local river to run red,' said Seville.

Lena glanced around and lowered her voice. 'The Daldykan runs red again today.'

Seville lowered her voice too. 'Would it be possible to see it, we would show it as a place where we would not like to swim.'

Lena looked troubled, 'yes that would be a powerful image, but I cannot take you there. Like many of my countrymen, pollution concerns me, but it is difficult for us to speak out.'

'What if Vera spoke out on your behalf, she would compensate you for any trouble, then you could visit America?'

Lena appeared fearful, 'I would not get work as a guide again.'

'You might not need to work as a guide again. You should speak to Vera. Lena, can you tell me is the water polluted here, apart from red rivers of course.'

'You have planned to swim here but I advise you, do not swallow any water. Yes, there are problems with the water no matter what colour it may be. They say if you gathered samples of snow near Northern Chemicals, you would find illegal levels of pollution.'

'Would I be able to do that?'

'But you are a swimmer, you are not a scientist.'

'Lena, it is possible to be a scientist as well as a swimmer. As a swimmer, I believe all water should be pure and safe. Your country is blessed with ample supplies of freshwater, it should be safe for all.'

Lena laughed, 'Ophelia, much of the drinking water in Russia is unsafe, never drink from a tap. We must purify our water, we have problems with pollution from chemicals, companies do not have clean technology, dangerous chemicals are dumped in our lakes and rivers. Our country is not modern.'

Seville wondered if she should end this conversation now. She had the feeling she could persuade Lena to help, but she was not sure whether to take the risk. She needed to speak to Vera.

***

Vera and Seville met in Seville's room before breakfast. The young swimmer Vera talked to last night had strong environmental concerns. Better still, she worked as a support assistant at Northern Chemicals and was keen for the company to be held to account for polluting processes. They could not gain access to the works plant, but she would show them where waste products ran off into a lake. Vera had arranged to meet her in the morning with a plan to film the red river.

Seville told Vera about her conversation with Lena, they debated if it was worth taking the risk of discussing their plans with her. Vera decided they had to, otherwise, they would find it difficult to get to the sites they wanted to visit. They decided to talk to her over breakfast.

The breakfast room in the hotel was filled with the hum of conversation as people ate what appeared to be hearty breakfasts. Queues formed at the coffee machines. Seville toyed with toast and coffee while Vera started to speak to Lena in whispered, rapid Russian. Lena looked anxious, sitting stiffly upright with crossed arms, then she began to relax, and her body language became more accommodating. Finally, a fleeting smile slipped across her face and though Seville did not know what Lena said, she felt immensely relieved.

Vera turned to Seville with a broad smile, 'Lena has organised the SUV we asked for, we are meeting my new friend from last night, and we are taking a trip to a river.'

***

It was still dark when they left the hotel at 9.30 am, and bone-cracking cold. The receptionist was most insistent on knowing where they were going, but Vera had told him they were on official business and would visit many different locations. Lena assured him she was their official guide and charged with ensuring they did not become lost. No one in Krasnoyarsk had shown any such interest in how they might be occupying their time.

A disturbing, caustic, chemical odour hung over the city, the smell of pollution Seville thought. Lena was a cautious driver, and they drove carefully from the majestic buildings in the city centre to blocks of flats with colourful cladding where they collected the young swimmer from the Walrus Club. Her name was Irina, and she appeared enthusiastic about their project.

'We need to take the road towards the airport,' Lena told them, 'Irina says the nickel mine is on the edge of town, near the Daldykan river, about twenty kilometres away.'

As they left town they became caught up in a convoy of yellow buses, following each other along the snowy roads. 'Have all the buses been held up?' asked Seville.

Lena spoke to Irina and Irina replied in rapid Russian with many hand gestures. Both laughed as she finished her explanation. 'These are the buses taking the workers to the factories and the mines. They travel in convoy so if a bus breaks down, the people can take another bus. If they had to wait in the open for a bus to come and pick them up, they may get frostbite or hypothermia,' said Lena.

Seville blinked. 'Living here is a serious business.'

Lena repeated her comment in Russian to Irina, who laughed and nodded.

They drove through the dark streets and along a grim road, leading out towards tall, smoking chimneys. Bright lights illuminated a distant industrial complex. The snow lining the roads was a dirty grey and the air thick with acrid smells.

Seville felt anxiety building, her chest tightened, and she did not know whether it was from the polluted air or tension. In this dystopian landscape, she half expected to see people brandishing guns, or machines of war. As they got closer to the complex an unnatural light substituted for daylight, revealing the stark, metallic structures nestling behind low hills or slag heaps.

The surface of the road was uneven, and they bounced up and down despite Lena's cautious driving. Seville expected sunrise but it never came. They passed through a thickening smog that penetrated the car and made them cough. Irina muttered to herself and turned the dial on the air conditioning.

'What does she say?' Seville asked Vera.

'She says this is the dirtiest air in the world,' said Vera.

Looking out at the grey miasma enveloping them, Seville could believe it.

They drove past and over the hills into a thicker layer of snow. Rusting pipes snaked down the hill, and a sinister glow lightened the sky. Lena pulled over to the side of the road and stopped the SUV. They put on more outer clothes, cold seeping into the car as the engine cooled down. Irina spoke to Lena.

'Irina says she wants to show you something first before we go to the river. We must climb up the hill, there is a path beside the pipe.'

Vera and Seville exchanged glances; they could not refuse. Cautiously Seville opened the door and shook as the cold hit her. They got out and pulled their hoods tighter around their faces. With a wild laugh, Irina started scrambling up the slope, beckoning to them to follow her. The glow from the other side of the hill illuminated their way, bright enough to cast strong, black shadows. Puffing hard, they reached the top and looked over into the hollow.

It was like looking into the abyss, anxiety made Seville breathless and robbed her of speech. The scene reminded her of the description of Isengard from Lord of the Rings, an industrial horror of harsh lights, stained metal structures and smoking chimneys. Piles of grey and black sludge heaped against the buildings. Vera began to film.

Irina spread her arms wide and laughed maniacally, she spoke in her slow, deep melodious voice sounding like one describing all the sorrows of the world.

'She says look, Norilsk is deadly beautiful, destructive and eternal,' translated Lena. 'Here is wealth for the few and early death for the many.'

They stood in silence looking down, a pale twilight started to seep over the horizon, a faint pink tinged the sky towards the east, but the industrial lights of Norilsk continued to blaze. It was too cold to cry.

Irina began to move again, 'come, come,' she said in English.

They slipped down the hillside, along the course of the pipes down to the river. Vera clutched her camera and paused to film them sliding down. They reached the water, and to Seville's surprise, the river was not frozen over. Lena told her hot discharges from the plants stopped it from freezing. It was a disturbing maroon red. The discharge had stained the land around the river red, the snow and ice were red, and the free running water was red. All the colour of poison.

Vera continued filming, 'Ophelia, pretend you are going to swim and then back away once you notice the colour of the water.'

Seville approached the river taking her coat off and pretending to strip down to a swimsuit, she regarded the water with an unfeigned horror and swiftly put all her outerwear back on. They all laughed, Seville quite hysterically.

She went back to the car and got her case and the containers for samples. She scooped up water, ice, and earth, longing to assess them to discover what pollutants they held. Irina made a passionate statement to the camera, gesturing at the surrounding landscape.

'Is she not taking a risk saying all that?' Seville asked Lena.

'Vera has said her face will be obscured. Irina, she cares about this,' said Lena.

'I can see that.'

As the light increased their surroundings became clearer.

'May we drive out a bit further to see what the countryside looks like away from the industrial development?' said Seville.

Lena spoke to Irina and replied, 'of course, Irina will tell us where to go.'

They packed themselves and their equipment into the SUV and sighed in pleasure as the car began to warm up as they moved on again. They drove for about twenty minutes then pulled off the road into a shallow depression. It was a fine day, with no clouds in the sky, but no sun could be seen. This was civil twilight, generating only enough light to make the surrounding countryside visible. They left the SUV to look around.

At first, Seville thought the landscape man-made. Organically shaped structures broke through the snow, they were trees, bare and dead but with a strange beauty. The expression 'blasted heath' came to mind. They were among the remains of a dead glade of trees, scoured and scorched by acid rain, no wood spirits lingered here, all life was extinct.

***

They returned to the city for the swim with the Walrus Club. The sun set at about three-thirty, and they had arranged to meet at Dolgoe Lake at four. The meeting place was a banya, a sauna at the edge of the lake, powered by steam from the power plant. Seville felt apprehensive, less for the cold and more because of the water pollution. She hoped she could steam any contamination out in the sauna.

Dolgoe Lake sat between the industrial area and the centre of the city. They would dive into an ice hole, swim underwater and come up through another opening in the ice.

It was dark by the time they assembled at the lakeside but brightly lit by floodlights at the power plant and all the buildings surrounding the water. Clouds of what Seville hoped were steam hung in the air, coloured amber from the lights.

The late afternoon was extraordinarily cold, though the steam clouds generated a clammy warmth when one passed through them. Again, no one wore wetsuits and the swimmers walked through the snow and over the ice until they reached the hole and plunged in. Seville had the fanciful thought the lake was composed of acid rain, and she would emerge, solid and wooden, stripped and barren like the trees she had seen earlier.

Vera called to her, and she snapped out of her reverie. Now it was her turn, and the swimmers lined the way, all clapping as she ran down to the lake, her feet stinging from the bitter chill. She jumped into the hole, rose to the surface, her lungs protesting the cold, then performed a perfect surface dive, pulled herself under the ice, and swam through an enchanted, crystalline world. The colour of the water changed above her, and she struck up towards the air and broke through the surface. Applause, cheers, and whistles filled her ears, and she hauled herself out on the ice, unable to face a return journey under that deadly carapace.

The sauna was sublime, the steam could have been radioactive, and Seville would not have cared. All the anxiety generated by the odours of the town, the bleak industrial landscapes, and the shocking red river, dissipated, soothed by her thrilling ice swim and the luxurious warmth of the sauna. All her cares vanished.

This time the meal was a barbecue on the snowy banks of the lake, with much vodka consumed. The following day baby walruses would come for an ice hole plunge during daylight hours and Vera would film them. The swimmers told Seville to return when she had a child, then her child too could become an honorary walrus.

She found it hard to believe Colin Wilton and Taras were so against her attempting to visit Norilsk, had made it sound such an impossible task. Here she was, an honoured guest of the city, and that morning they had filmed and collected evidence of pollution. Tomorrow evening they would visit Northern Chemicals and her mission would be complete. She longed to see their faces when she told them what she had achieved.

Chapter Twenty-Nine

January 2020

Ross left the board meeting with the alacrity of one released from prison. He thought he would go for a walk, down to Tower Bridge and eat a sandwich at a little cafe. Make like a tourist. He needed to clear his head before the afternoon meetings started.

The trouble with board meetings was people operated on the principle of why use ten words when you could use twenty. Some were worse offenders than others, but oh my God they all had a lot to say. He wouldn't mind if they said something worth listening to. Well, that was a lie. Even if they had anything worthwhile to say, he preferred them to go straight to the core of the matter and keep it brief.

One of the agenda points disturbed him, a point tabled by the Marketing Director. She asked Jason to give a presentation to clarify the issue. It arose from Angela Capell's Transparency in Business initiative. She lobbied some government quango for business ethics, to legislate to make retailers take responsibility for ensuring the goods they sold came from ethical producers.

Ross wasn't concerned about any law ensuring a company only sold ethically produced products. If the government passed a law like that, all the shops would soon look empty. It would be like visiting the Gum department store in Russia during the communist era. Most mass-manufactured goods had a dirty little ethical or environmental secret somewhere along the production or supply chain line.

What worried Ross was this obsession with uncovering connections between companies. A government committee raised a question as to whether it was right that Ross's social media company, the Book of Friends, carried so much advertising for products Atlas sold. The 'committee' was concerned people may not realise Atlas owned the Book of Friends and might think other users endorsed these goods.

Today's presentation from Jason highlighted ten companies scoring poorly against a number of ethical and environmental measures, and whose products Atlas sold. This list included Gaia Chemicals and Best for Babies; a company owned by Assist Pharmaceuticals. It produced artificial baby milk and vitamin and mineral supplements for babies.

The essence of Jason's presentation was all trading departments should first check what they stocked from these manufacturers, then decide if appropriate to continue stocking them. His PowerPoint included a nifty bit exposing each company's particular sin. Gaia chemicals polluted the sites they manufactured at, and Best for Babies pushed formula milk and unnecessary vitamins on third world mothers.

The board responded to this like a collection of wise monkeys who have just had their blindfolds, gags and earmuffs removed. Quite incredible. The Marketing Director allowed a few minutes for everyone to absorb this, then gave her presentation, which effectively repeated what Jason had just said.

Ross switched off at that point and started to think about what action he should take. Not stocking certain items did not worry him. What concerned him was people looking too closely at how companies interlinked, and most importantly, why was Gaia Chemicals named as a polluter. He decided the time had come to put a stop to this.

'No,' he said. Their heads swivelled around in unison, in an expression of universal surprise.

'It is not for Atlas to monitor other companies. Naturally, we will not allow any product that is offensive or harmful to be available. But we are a retailer, not the morality police. Jason, I want you to drop this at once and concentrate on ensuring our working practices are ethical and environmentally friendly. You can start by looking at our power consumption. Can we move to renewables, should all our buildings and warehouses be fitted with solar panels? Let us make sure our own house is in order.'

***

Ross met George for dinner that night, George had promised an update on Northern Chemicals. They met at the Grand Hotel St Pancras, in the Gilbert Scott Restaurant. The menu here satisfied both George's need for high-class English stodge, and Ross's desire for a light meal.

He was already at the table when Ross arrived, scrutinising the wine list with a critical eye. Ross toyed with the idea of taking George to visit his father-in-law. He thought of the immense entertainment it would give him to see George's face when Lord Sedley served up Asda's finest wines. He gazed thoughtfully at George.

The gap between himself and George would have been insurmountable when they were children. It was a measure of his success that he had not only narrowed that gap, but he had also overtaken George. All he and George had in common was a ruthless desire to succeed. George might be the epitome of respectability, but he did not protest against the removal of people who were an obstacle or danger to him. How many of the good and the great were comfortable with giving the nod to others to remove those in their way? He guessed many were, as long as it did not involve dirtying their own hands.

He and George never spoke about anything but business. Ross thought they would struggle to hold a conversation on any other subject. He had heard George speak to James Holt about shooting and visiting wine regions in France, both spoke highly of the small French town of Beaune. At his New Year's Eve party, he overheard George and Madrigal discussing a book they had both read. No one ever discussed books with him.

Not that Ross never read books, he had an extensive library on subjects that interested him. This was not a collection of business tomes, the sort of books Jason no doubt read, books full of cod wisdom and crappy little sound bites. Ross had a passion for history and a library of history books.

He never discussed these books with people at parties. Ross's interest was not general history, but the lives of the men who made history. Alexander the Great, Genghis Khan, Napoleon, rather than the One Minute Manager. He was interested in men who conquered others, who built empires.

He often thought if he retired, he would study for a degree in history. But he would never retire. Retirement was for losers, for those who were no longer able to stay in the game or had never been in the game in the first place.

When people asked Ross, what discipline his degree was in, he thought he should reply history, though he always told the truth. He said he had never gone to university. Then they changed the subject. At eighteen, it was impossible for him to attend university. He was incarcerated elsewhere and once he emerged phoenix-like from the bonfire of his life; university had no purpose.

Ross was different from the people he associated with. They did not have his vision of the world, and nor did they see his visions. He glanced over and momentarily he saw Napoleon Bonaparte sitting at the table with George, thinning hair, wispy fringe, and military jacket. Bonaparte glanced up and smiled at him. Ross shook his head and strode over and grasped George's hand in a firm handshake.

'Hi Ross, I was just about to order a bottle of an excellent Alsace Riesling. Would you like to join me, or would you prefer something else?' He passed the wine list over.

'I'm fine with whatever you're having, I trust you, George. Let's order our food and you can update me.'

They both scrutinised the menu, summoned the waiter and ordered. Ross took a sip of the Riesling, it was excellent.

'George, something came up today that concerned me.'

'Indeed, what was that?'

'A presentation identifying Gaia Chemicals as a firm causing pollution where it manufactures. Have you read any commentary about this in the media? Is this the view of the general public?'

'I think not. Our public relations office keeps a close eye on the press to watch for adverse publicity and nothing has been mentioned to me.'

'Odd. An individual who works for me brought it up. I'm going to dig about to find where he got his information from.'

'Please let me know, sometimes employees cause trouble. We come down hard on that sort of thing.'

'OK. So, what about our friends from the North, Albert Tolstoy and Northern Chemicals?'

'James Holt was a sound choice as party leader. Tolstoy is chumming up to James, even invited him to a few parties I understand. You know how James prefers to attend parties rather than parliament.'

'Yes, Mr Holt is the ultimate hollow man. Playing at the role of prime minister to an audience of Russians sniggering behind their hands.'

'Indeed. Anyway, you'll need to take care our prime minister doesn't become too chummy with the Russians. We don't want their supreme leader thinking he controls our supreme leader, it's all the old double agent, double bluff stuff. However, at the current time, Russia owes Gaia Chemicals more than we owe them.'

'Let's try to keep it that way. James is predictable but needs tight control so when those temptations come up, he jumps the right way. We need an implant, someone working for us. Keep an eye out for the right sort of person who can be a guru for James. We want someone to come up with all the ideas, so James doesn't have to spend any effort in coming up with ideas himself. And George, we must get our man in there before Russia has the same idea and plants their man in there,' said Ross.

'I'll keep my eyes and ears open. Talking about eyes and ears, have you spoken to Ganak Reddy lately?'

'He keeps sending me weekly pandemic reports, it goes through my mind he's the one who launched this virus in China. I can see Ganak as a baddie from James Bond. Can't you picture him sitting and stroking a cat saying, 'now I have released the first virus, and my second virus will be more deadly so give me one trillion pounds. Followed by a manic laugh.'

George laughed then shivered. 'Goose walked over my grave. There is something of the dark side about Ganak. However, tempting as it is to imagine Ganak manufacturing a deadly virus only he knows the cure to, undoubtedly there is an issue in China. Even our Foreign Office warned against non-essential travel there.'

'Ganak spoke about that, he mentioned an increased incidence of pneumonia.'

'WHO identified a novel coronavirus in China as a potential issue a couple of weeks ago. Ganak is using half the facility in Bhopal for his research, and he's focusing on this virus,' said George.

'Well, I don't want to sound complacent,' said Ross. 'But if we accept Ganak is not Dr Evil in disguise, trying to wipe out humanity, these sorts of viruses often pop up in that part of the world. They've had all the SARS and MERS stuff.'

'Not being alarmist,' said George, 'but I'm intending to ban any Gaia Chemicals staff travelling to China until we know a bit more about this outbreak. You might want to think of that for Atlas, I'm sure your buying team are constantly out in the Far East.'

'HR is on it, soon as the Foreign Office advice came out, we stopped all our people travelling to the Far East. Talking of people, we need to talk about Donnie.'

'There is nothing to say about him,' said George.

'Fine, so I can consider the problem solved?' said Ross.

'Of course.'

Ross raised his glass to George. 'Let's toast our old friend Donnie, it was a gas while it lasted.'

'To Donnie,' said George.

Chapter Thirty

January 2020

Donnie stared out of the window of the apartment and sighed. Another twenty-four hours to go before he started his journey to freedom. He was anxious, twenty-four hours could be a long time and besides, he'd seen Ross Campbell's daughter at passport control. Had she been sent to spy on him?

This worried him so much, he mentioned it at dinner to Andy Baclanova. He told him he was concerned his boss had some issues with him, and twice in Russia, he was followed by a young woman whom he discovered to be his boss's daughter. He hoped he didn't sound like a paranoid lunatic.

The story intrigued Andy, bosses did weird things sometimes he agreed. Perhaps the boss was trying to find a reason to sack Donnie, though it was odd to send his daughter as a spy, but that might just be a coincidence. Andy suggested he resigned and found another job, though he might get a good payoff if he was sacked.

Donnie found Andy reassuring, his explanation made sense and anyway he was taking him up on his advice, he planned to leave and without waiting for any payoff. He kept an eye out for the Campbell girl and had not seen her anywhere.

He began to wonder if he imagined spotting Ross's daughter, most young women appeared the same to him once you got past the bare attributes of height, hair colour and weight. Hell, there were loads of slim girls with long straight black hair around, he was getting paranoid. Hadn't George said Ross was going to make sure his daughter couldn't travel in Russia again?

He arranged to meet Andy for dinner again that evening. OK, so Ivan Popov would think him rude, but what the fuck, he didn't intend to ever see him after today. He got the hire car out of the garage and drove off to the Industrial area.

The conditions were worse than usual, still pitch dark at 10 am, even colder than yesterday if that was possible. The freaking smell hanging around this place was exceptionally acrid and unpleasant. He donned his face mask. Everyone in the factory stared at him as if he were mad when he wore a mask, but he would not risk his health in this pollution.

Once he reached Northern Chemicals, Popov took him on a delightful little trip to the areas where they disposed of the deadly chemical waste. Health and safety provisions didn't appear to be in any way followed. Back in Popov's office, he asked if this were legal, Popov shrugged, 'who's to know? We are the ones responsible for sending our samples to Moscow for testing. My people are not idiots, they will not send anything that might cause alarm.'

Ivan ordered coffee and Donnie warmed up a bit as he drank his. He settled down for a long and tedious paperwork checking session. Still, paperwork passed the time, and he was safe sitting in the office. Safer than wandering around the facility, he couldn't imagine what it must be like to turn up to work on the production lines each day.

Popov took a call on his mobile phone. Donnie thought the call was confidential as he left the room after glancing at him. He returned looking slightly embarrassed.

'I apologise, I cannot entertain you tonight, I must go to London this afternoon. The factory manager will tell you about the other places you need to check. You must view a new facility we bought.'

Donnie frowned; it was bad enough inspecting the facilities he knew about without more sprung on him. 'Where's that?' he asked.

'You will have to drive,' said Popov.

Donnie scowled, he hated driving in this benighted part of the world, but he didn't trust Russian drivers, they were all mad, speeding along these icy roads. He felt safer driving himself.

'Well, I guessed I wasn't going to walk. Where do I go?'

'Towards Dudinka, about five kilometres past the airport. You cannot miss it; the factory is well signposted from the road.'

'Are they expecting me?'

'Oh yes. I would come with you, but I have a plane to catch.'

Donnie glanced out of the window; it was dark already. 'I'll need to make a call.'

An hour after Popov left, he rang Andy Baclanova. They had arranged to meet for an early dinner that night as they both were booked on the first flight to Moscow in the morning. Even if he left now, he could not drive to the factory and back to the city in time to meet when they had planned. Andy answered his mobile.

'Hi, I'm sorry pal, but I'm going to be late. They told me at the last minute of another facility I have to visit in the opposite direction to Norilsk, along the road on the way to Dudinka.'

'No problem, I'm held up too. Hey, when are you going?'

'In about another thirty minutes, I'm going to leave as soon as possible.'

'Well, you could do me a favour. My taxi has cancelled, and the alternative is either hanging around here for another couple of hours or going back on the bus convoy. Why don't I come with you, and you can drive me back into town?'

Donnie considered, no one said this needed hushing up, what the hell, it would be good to have company. Driving alone along these dark, empty, freaky roads gave him the creeps. 'Yeah, sure, where shall I pick you up?'

'I'm a mile or so west from you. Come to the main gate, you can't miss it.'

He drove to the mining complex and managed to find both the gate and Andy without any trouble. The car warmed up from a second body and the snow stopped. A thick layer covered the ground and Donnie was glad for the studded tyres.

'Where are we going?' said Andy.

'It's called Dudinka Zavod Odin.'

Andy frowned. 'I've been to that operation before, I thought it had closed down.'

'I guess Northern Chemicals have opened the operation back up again. They said the factory is about five kilometres past the turn off to the terminal.'

'I know where we're going, so we won't miss it,' said Andy. 'Bit of a godforsaken place. In winter there is hardly any traffic on the road between Norilsk and Dudinka once you pass the airport and not after dark. I thought there was an explosion or something there.'

'Very likely,' said Donnie. Gaia Chemicals just loved places where there had been an industrial disaster. The site was probably radioactive.

As they drove out of the industrial area Donnie experienced a premonition of danger. Driving from the harsh illumination cast by the factories and mining operations into the dark of the polar night was disconcerting. The road surface was poor, and the roads were empty with no other traffic going west. They passed a few eastbound cars driving to the city, but once past the airport, the road became deserted with no glow of industrial lights ahead.

The darkness appeared impenetrable, the only light being the beam of their SUV's headlights. He drove slowly, visibility was poor, the air was always full of smog or snow. The world outside the confines of their car seemed sinister and filled with foreboding. Like driving towards the world's end. He longed to see lights from another car.

'It should be somewhere around here,' said Andy, squinting into the night.

'It can't be,' said Donnie, 'they always light these places up like Christmas trees and it's pretty dark out there.'

He slowed the car to a walking pace. They drove along peering into the gloom, and Donnie became aware of a lighter patch among the blackness. They stopped as they saw a sign in their headlights, Dudinka Zavod Odin. He turned into the entrance and up to a set of gates. The factory looked like a place that had given up the ghost a long time ago, the rusted metal gates appeared locked, and they could not hear a sound. They gazed at each other in dismay.

'I must have been given the wrong details,' said Donnie with a tremor in his voice.

'There's nothing here.' said Andy, he sounded unnerved too. 'Let's go back to town, you'll have to tell your people you couldn't find it.'

Donnie thought that an excellent idea, as he was not intending to ever see any of his people ever again. Why the fuck had he bothered coming here in the first place he asked himself. He could be back in the apartment by now, having a warm shower and going out to meet Andy for something to eat and a drink. He would like a scotch now.

'Yeah, let's turn around,' he said and began to reverse away from the gate.

A loud noise fractured the silence of the night, spotlights illuminated their car and the gates. Some sort of military armoured vehicle drove at surprising speed through the compound towards the gates and broke through them. A klaxon sounded, and Donnie wondered if he had strayed into a film set or military installation. The vehicle drove straight at them, spotlights blazing. Andy frantically yelled 'drive, drive.' But their car faced the wrong way.

Donnie tried to turn the car and get on the road, his hands, slick with sweat, slid on the steering wheel. The vehicle was much higher than their SUV and the underbelly level with their windscreen, it hit them and shunted them down the drive, out on the road, and they spun around, entirely out of control. Their car lost its grip on the tarmac and slipped down into the deep drainage ditch by the side of the road. The military vehicle passed them without stopping and lumbered off towards Dudinka.

The silence that followed was if anything, more alarming than the screeching noise of the other vehicle. They hung from their seat belts at a steep angle. A rear window was shattered, and a chill air entered the car. Donnie's heart pounded at a terrifying rate, and he anticipated a heart attack. A voice whispered next to him, 'are you alright?'

Donnie couldn't answer, he began to shake and tried to undo the seat belt. He was aware of Andy hanging below him also trying to free himself. A strong arm grasped him and fumbled with his seat belt clasp. Donnie slid to the side of the car as the belt was released, and somehow Andy propped him up.

He found his voice, 'we've got to get out of here and get the car back on the road.'

'Yeah,' said Andy. His voice sounded shaky.

They managed to lower the driver side window and Andy scrambled out. Donnie was too fat to pass through the window. Sitting on the side of the car Andy grasped the door handle and asked him to push the door up. Between them, they opened the door and Andy helped Donnie out. They dropped down and regarded the SUV, no way they would get it out of the ditch without mechanical aid.

They both stared down the road towards Dudinka, fearful they would see the lights of the military vehicle approaching again.

Andy exhaled a long-held breath, 'What the fuck was that all about?'

Donnie shook his head, but he thought he might know. Ross fucking Campbell, it was all about Ross Campbell. The day had come, as he had always known it would, when he outlived his usefulness to Ross. Well, George and Ivan, he thought bitterly, you wait till your days come, and come they will. If you know too much about Mr Campbell, you are toast once he hasn't got any more use for you.

'Do you think they'll come back?' said Andy.

'No,' said Donnie, although he knew they would be back, but not before tomorrow morning. They would come back to check no one had survived, to ensure they were dead and then alert the authorities. "Foreigners, they are not used to driving in these conditions, their car left the road, and they froze to death. So sad."

'Right,' said Donnie, 'I'm not hanging about here.'

'But we can't leave. We need to wait here until help comes along.'

'Where do you think help is going to come from. Have you a signal on your phone?'

Andy shook his head.

'We'll freeze if we wait here till tomorrow morning,' said Donnie.

'We'll freeze to death if we try and walk anywhere.'

'The airport is five kilometres away; we can walk there easily.'

Andy glanced around, the snow started to fall again, in a steady manner suggesting it was setting in for the night. The wind rose, blizzard conditions could rapidly develop. 'We won't make it, let's dig in here, we can make a sort of igloo for shelter.'

'No way, it's only five kilometres, the area will be lit up, we just have to follow the road and make our way towards the lights.'

It was Andy's turn to object, 'it will be shut, no flights depart in the evening. Everyone will have gone home.'

'I'm going, I'm not going to sit here waiting to die. If you don't want to come, I'm going on my own. Are you coming or not?'

Andy gazed at him sadly. 'Leaving the car is like committing suicide pal. Stay here, I'll make an igloo and we can huddle together for warmth.'

Donnie shook his head, even if Andy's igloo worked, he'd bet the first car to come along here would be one checking they were dead, and if they weren't dead, the people in that car would soon ensure they completed their task. His only chance of survival was making it to the airport.

Donnie collected his briefcase with his documents, he saluted Andy and started to trudge eastwards along the road. He could feel Andy's eyes upon him, but it felt so good to act. He would not wait for death.

There may be no flights tonight, but he was sure the airport would still be open. They did not lock up an airport and all go home. The site would be lit up, there would be security lights. All he must do was follow the road and head towards the lights once they came into sight.

He was sorry for Andy, if he survived the night, he would realise his mistake when morning came, and he had visitors. It was his fault Andy would die. If he had not talked to him on the plane, Andy would be eating his dinner and looking forward to getting back to America tomorrow. Donnie continued walking slowly along the potholed tarmac, conserving his energy. How long could it take to walk five kilometres?

Chapter Thirty-One

January 2020

Their second full day was remarkably busy. They filmed baby walrus swimmers and went to an exhibition of needlework. The authorities organised a guided walk around the centre of the city, followed by dinner in the hotel. Once the officials left, Irina joined them. Lena and Seville did not drink any vodka, but the other two were tipsy and voluble. They congregated in Vera's room to review their plans. Irina spoke in a deep voice, occasionally she broke into giggles which unnerved Seville.

'Northern Chemicals has more security than the mines,' said Lena. 'The area surrounding it is forbidden. But Irina says pipes lead to a small lake, a kilometre behind the factory. We must be unseen when we drive to this place. People do not visit because the smell is bad, and people say there is a gas. I am not sure how you say the gas?'

'Fluorine gas,' translated Vera.

'Yes, fluorine gas, it is dangerous. Irina says here they produce ftor, your fluorine and what you call organophosphates for pesticides. These are deadly chemicals, also used to manufacture weapons. Our nerve gas, Novichok is made from organophosphates. The security is little because no one would go there, especially at night. It is known to be dangerous, but because of this to be seen would be suspicious, unlike the nickel mines where people walk upon the hills.'

'So, we need to be careful, quiet, and unobserved.'

'Yes, that is right Ophelia. There is nothing to stop us from going, it is risky but not too risky if we are not seen. Irina says there should be no one to see us.'

Seville considered this information. 'Vera, maybe Lena and Irina should not come with us. If anyone finds us, would it not cause difficulty for them?'

Irina frowned and spoke to Lena, Lena translated, and Irina gestured wildly. Her voice rose, and she spoke with verve and much gesticulation. She finished by clasping her hands to her heart.

Lena and Vera shrugged and exchanged glances at each other. 'She says she was born to no future,' said Lena. 'Always the pollution hangs over her city and each breath she takes poisons her body. The act of living is killing her, and though the act of living kills us all, some are killed sooner than others. Swimming is free, for everything else, there is a cost, and they are not rich people. She says the world can be beautiful, and she is a warrior for beauty.'

Tears welled in Seville's eyes, she brushed them away with the back of her hand. They lived in a protected bubble, both her and Vera. Wealth shielded them; they could never truly understand the bravery of those with no protection.

'What about you, Lena?'

'I am a Siberian too, we are unique. Our land has both great beauty and when despoiled by industry, immense ugliness. Vera offered me money that it would take ten years for me to earn. I have chosen to be brave for this. If anyone saw you two travelling on your own, they would stop you. You cannot travel here without your official guide.'

'If the authorities stop us, we will say Lena and Irina were trying to prevent us. But we will be careful. Come, let us go.' Vera gathered up her outdoors clothes.

They made their way to the SUV. The snow drifted down without respite, and Seville was glad she was not driving. They drove towards the lake which glittered in the city lights and turned up towards the road to the airport, passing few cars as they left the city. Lena drove steadily into the ominous darkness, the only light a neon glow from the distant industrial complexes.

They passed through the hills and saw hazy clouds from the factory chimneys in the distance.

'We will drive past all the factories and the industrial area into the countryside and approach from the west before we reach the mines, we cannot drive into the factory complex,' said Lena.

It felt surreal to leave the industry behind and drive through the countryside. Blackness beckoned, behind them were the bright lights from the industries. As they slipped out of the lit area back into darkness, Lena told them to look out for the road that would lead off on the right, up towards the hills.

Seville gazed through the window into the opaque night. Although apprehensive over what they might find, her heart felt light. She had a feeling of completeness that was alien to her apart from when she swam. It was like being part of a family, she and these three other girls had the same aims, would watch each other's backs. Never had she been a member of a group like this, her friendships from school and university appeared now as acts of convenience. To belong was a strange and pleasing sensation.

The snow came down so heavily, it was difficult to see beyond the immediate illumination of the headlights. Abruptly the snow stopped, and no longer obscured their surroundings. They all spotted the track at the same time and called out together. Lena turned off the tarmac road and bumped up the track. 'I must go carefully. If we get stuck, we will have to dig ourselves out.'

'Have we a spade?' asked Seville.

'Every vehicle carries a spade here.'

Irina called to Lena, and they came to a stop. Vera and Seville took deep breaths and pulled on more outerwear. Irina handed them each a face mask.

'She says the air is bad,' Lena told them.

They got out of the SUV, the area seemed lit by a strange phosphorescence, which made Seville shudder. Vera took out her camera and panned around the landscape, white fresh snow, dead, stunted trees and bushes, and this strange luminous glow. Ahead of them was a high barbed wire fence, garnished with snow and icicles.

'How do we get through this?' said Seville. This was not the sort of fence they could stretch two wires apart and scramble through.

Irina laughed, the sound alarming in that silent landscape, and the others shushed her. She waved stout wire clippers at them.

'Is it safe to cut the wires,' asked Seville. She had a vision of cutting through the wires and an alarm sounding somewhere within the factory.

Irina walked confidently up to the wires, brandishing the clippers like a weapon, and cut the wire. The other three paused for a moment, but no sound could be heard. They carefully crawled through the gap and walked up the low hill, leaving a deep trail of footprints behind. Seville wondered if the snow would cover them by the time the gloomy morning twilight came tomorrow.

At the top of the hill, they came to a small lake, more of a pool than a lake. This was the source of the phosphorescence, and a harsh, green glow illuminated the water. Even through their masks, they smelt a choking, fetid odour coming from a waxy white scum lapping the edge of the pool. It made a dramatic and unearthly scene.

Vera made them all pose by the lake, gagging from the gases, then swung around to take in the dead vegetation. They gathered samples for Seville, and she, with trembling hands, took samples of the water. Vera filmed the end of the pipe, liquid death dribbling from it. Seville gestured to them they should leave, this place seemed too dangerous to linger in.

They slid back down the hill, clutching the hard-won samples. Vera looked back at the trampled snow and shook her head.

'We must hope no one comes here tonight or they will raise an alarm.'

Seville's apprehension increased, if anyone came across them now, it was hard to think what reasonable excuse they could make for their presence.

Back in the car they drank bottled water and washed any exposed part of their faces. Irina spoke in her slow, tragic voice and laughed maniacally again. Seville looked to Vera and Lena for a translation.

Vera spoke this time. 'She says she sees Shakespeare's Ophelia floating in the lake, holding lilies, and glowing in the dark. She says it would be a strange but deadly beauty and that is Russia, a land of strange and deadly beauty.'

'Tell her she should become a writer,' said Seville.

Vera translated and Irina leant forward and took Seville's hand.

'Ophelia,' she said in strongly accented English, 'Words are all I have.'

'Words can change the world,' replied Seville. 'Dictators hate the written word because it cannot be erased. When they put their lies in writing, they come back to bite them, even if they later try to amend them.'

Vera clapped her hands, 'Irina, you must be a writer. I will be your sponsor.'

They started to drive back down the track when Lena stopped.

'What's the problem?' said Seville. Her voice sounded tight and anxious in her ears.

Lena turned off their headlights. She sounded troubled too. 'I can see lights down on the main road.'

They all became silent as if the distant vehicles could overhear them.

'Who could this be?' said Vera.

'It must be traffic between the factories and the mines,' Lena whispered back. 'They will think it odd if we come from this track, they will stop us and question us. They may come up to see where we have been.'

Seville thought of the tangle of cut wire and the trail of footprints they had left behind them. To have come so far, to have succeeded, then for all her samples to be confiscated. She could not bear to think of this, and what would happen to her friends?

Irina spoke and Lena shook her head. Irina spoke again with more force, and Lena shrugged. Vera appeared troubled.

'What is she saying?' asked Seville.

'She says, Ophelia, another route leads across the hills behind the mines and comes out on the road between Norilsk and Dudinka beyond the airport. If we drive along this path, we will be facing away from the traffic below so our headlights should not be visible to them. We must turn our lights off now till we reach the path. She says she will drive as she knows the way well and it could be dangerous in the snow and dark.'

Seville, Vera, and Lena were doubtful. Irina had consumed a considerable amount of vodka. The mountain track sounded a dangerous route to drive along when sober, never mind when drunk. Irina gestured some more and opened her door and came round to the driver's side. Lena threw her hands in the air, then moved over.

'Is it safe?' said Vera.

Lena shrugged. 'We have done nothing safe tonight, why worry now.'

Irina started the car and drove slowly forward. It was not pitch dark, the bright snow reflected whatever light was in the sky and surrounding area. They edged along and took a right turn and moved westwards. Their progress was painfully slow, but it felt safer that way. Eventually, the track began to descend, and they made their way down to the Dudinka road.

As they hit the road the snow started again, large, fat flakes twirling down.

'What will we say if people are still on the road between the factories and the mines,' asked Seville.

'We will say we drove to the terminal to make enquiries about flights tomorrow and because of the weather, we waited before leaving. If we pass them on that road, they will think we are coming from the airport, and they are unlikely to stop us. If they find us driving down a track from the hills, that will make them suspicious.'

Lena and Irina swapped places. Lena continued to drive carefully in the swirling snow, as they rounded a corner, they saw something odd in the road up ahead.

'Is that a car in the ditch?' Seville squinted through the window.

'I think it is,' said Lena. 'We will stop and check no one is in trouble.'

As they neared, an SUV became visible, on its side in the snow-filled drainage ditch by the edge of the road. Lena lowered her window.

'They have driven off the road; I hope they are alright. People freeze to death here.'

They drew up beside the troubled car and got out to investigate. The SUV was wedged into the drainage channel. In the ditch, huddled up to the car, someone had built a small igloo-like construction in the snow.

Lena and Vera called out 'hello' in Russian and Seville shouted in English.

A voice with an American accent answered in English, 'my God, is somebody there?'

A man scrambled out of the makeshift igloo. 'Who are you?' he staggered slightly and stared at the girls in apparent wonder. 'Are you angels?'

Seville gave a short laugh, 'well we're not devils. Can we help?'

The man tried to climb up from the ditch but had trouble getting his hands to work effectively.

Irina muttered to Vera who said to Seville, 'we need to check him for frostbite.'

Seville and Lena went over to help the man up. They hurried him into their car and turned on the engine.

'Are you American?' asked Seville. 'What happened?'

'Andy Baclanova.' He tried and failed to shake hands. 'We got driven off the road.'

'We? Is there another person in the car?'

'No, my companion set off to walk to the airport.'

Lena translated this for Irina, and they looked at each other in horror. Irina crossed herself. Andy stared at her with concern.

'She says, then he is dead,' said Vera.

Andy began to cry, Seville awkwardly put an arm around his shoulders.

'Listen, we will take you back to the city, to a hospital. They will need to check you for frostbite. If someone forced you off the road, you should speak to the authorities.'

'We must find Donnie,' said Andy. 'We need to make sure he is alright.'

Lena and Vera muttered in Russian, and Vera spoke.

'We will go to the airport and see if we can find your companion before we take you to the city. The snow, it is stopping, so we will have a window of opportunity. We must all watch the road.'

Lena started to drive away. Seville felt cold, her heart jumped when the American spoke the name of his companion, Donnie, though surely this was a coincidence. As they drove on, Andy spoke.

'What were you doing on this road, girls? I sure didn't expect anyone to come along before the morning.'

They exchanged glances; Vera replied. 'I am making a film about swimming in the cold of Siberia. We thought we would drive out at night and film the roads, for atmosphere you know, miles and miles of dark empty Siberian roads with nothing but the snow coming down.'

'Yeah, well that would be one sinister atmosphere. I think you're all crazy, but man am I glad you're crazy. You've saved my life, hey who would have thought it, my life saved by crazy angels.'

Vera translated for Irina and Irina began her maniacal laughing again, 'crazy angels. I am crazy angel, a crazy angel writer.'

'Keep watching the road,' said Lena, and they gazed out of the windows. They had a false alarm once, a snow-covered hump looking like a man's body, revealed itself as a pile of debris. A glow appeared on the horizon, lights from the terminal.

They reached the road to the airport. The snow was thick and unmarked.

'No footsteps,' said Seville.

'It has snowed so heavily they could be covered,' said Lena.

Irina opened the door and jumped out of the car. She went to examine the road and called to them. Lena joined her then both returned.

'Footprints are leading down here. Look, they can just be seen under a layer of snow.'

'Hey, he made it,' said Andy. 'Perhaps he was right, he might be sitting in the departure lounge, waiting for the first flight tomorrow.'

Lena and Irina exchanged glances and shook their heads. They drove cautiously down the road till they came to a fence and gates. Slumped by the locked gates, was the snow-covered body of a man. Andy let out a cry.

They left the car and stepped down into the deep snow. Andy called out 'Donnie,' but the man did not move. They went to him, and Seville brushed the ice crystals from his face, lifted a flap of his hat to feel for a pulse, but she found nothing. Vera got out a small mirror and held it in front of his mouth, no mist formed. The man's fingers were entwined in the wire mesh of the gates. Seville tried to loosen one, it was impossible without breaking it.

'He is dead.'

Andy turned his head away. 'Poor man. Shall we try to get him in the car?'

'I think we must leave him where he is,' said Lena. 'We will inform the police, this is no accident, careless driving drove you off the road.'

'It was more than that,' said Andy. 'It was like a setup, his company told him to visit a factory, but the factory was closed and derelict. This military-type vehicle came out from the compound and deliberately forced us off the road. I don't understand any of this.'

'Come, we need to go back to the city. We will take you to the hospital, and they will contact the politsiya. Let us leave before the snow starts again.'

It wasn't just the harsh weather worrying them. They all looked up the road, feeling a frisson of dread in case a military vehicle might be driving towards them.

As they drove away anxiety started to overcome Seville. How would they explain their presence on these roads to the authorities? Who was responsible for the attack? Was it the Russian authorities or was someone else involved? She recognised the man, it was the man from Kiselyovsk, the man in the tapas bar in London, the man whose companion was at her father's New Year's party. The man linked with Northern and Gaia Chemicals.

***

They reached Norilsk without meeting any vehicles, unsurprisingly as it was now 2 am. Lena dropped Irina off first and they impressed upon Andy, he must not mention her, that she would be in trouble going on this night-time trip with them.

They arrived at the hospital and awoke a sleepy doctor in casualty. Lena explained what had happened and the doctor rang for the police, then took Andy off for examination.

The police arrived and at first, treated them as if this was some drunken story. They breathalysed Lena and appeared disappointed when the result showed her in the clear. They shook their heads and asked many questions as to why any of them were out on those roads.

This stopped when Vera intervened, she told them she was going to ring her lawyer, and at the mention of the lawyer's name, the policemen paled. Vera mentioned who her father was, the police consulted among themselves anxiously. They said they must speak to the American and asked Lena to be their translator. The police told Vera and Seville to wait while they questioned the American.

They sat on uncomfortable benches in the casualty reception area.

'What if they ask to check your films?' said Seville to Vera. 'What if they examine the car and find all the samples?'

'They will not dare,' said Vera confidently. 'But we are not going to get much sleep tonight, Ophelia.'

The policemen returned with Lena. Andy would be kept in overnight and could not go anywhere now, but the police would like someone to accompany them to the airport and the scene of the accident. They agreed they would all go. They thought it unfair to leave Lena to deal with this on her own, and they were not sure what treatment she might receive if Vera were absent.

None of them wanted to return out into the freezing night. But they clambered into a police car and dozed in the back as they drove to the airport, accompanied by a police van. Donnie's body remained in position, with his hands frozen to the gates. They left the scene of crime officers in the van to deal with Donnie, and they went on to the place of the incident.

This scene caused consternation for the police, they examined the shattered gates to the derelict factory and the smashed front of the SUV and shook their heads. They spoke to Vera, and she replied sharply. They got back in the car and headed back to the city.

The police spoke at length to Vera, then muttered to each other with much shrugging of shoulders.

'They asked us to come and give a statement tomorrow morning, but I told them we are on the first flight out, and we cannot delay our departure. They will take our statements now, then I think we return to the hotel and pack and wait for the taxi to take us to the airport.'

Seville shrugged, 'fine by me, I don't want to hang around for another day. It's not like we can tell them much, we didn't witness anything.'

At the police station, they told their story, and no one questioned why they would choose to film that road. The authorities knew about the swimming and that alone marked Vera and Seville as crazy girls. If they were prepared to pay good money to come from Moscow and London to make a film about swimming, why wouldn't they go driving out into the countryside at night in a snowstorm? They were rich and crazy.

The police thanked them for their help and allowed them to return to their hotel. It took a while to get everything out of the SUV and even longer to safely pack all Vera's filming equipment and Seville's samples. The taxi arrived, and they made their departure from the city that had obsessed Seville for so long.

Chapter Thirty-Two

February 2020

Jason Harris stared at his laptop screen, not reading the information displayed. Ross Campbell's daughter asked him to check out Gaia Chemicals and the man who ran the company, George Fenton. He was a fully paid-up member of the establishment, educated at Eton and Cambridge, old family pile in Rutland, married to the daughter of a duke.

Jason could unearth no scandal or gossip relating to Fenton, apart from details of him attending various functions showcasing the great and the good. Ascot, Glyndebourne, Wimbledon, the Royal Opera House, garden parties, George graced all these events with his presence. He did not feature on social media, and any other media mention of him suggested boring respectability.

Gaia Chemicals, however, proved to be more interesting. Finding any information on them involved digging deep. The company itself did not appear in any report of environmental issues, but when Jason checked out companies that appeared in such reports, inevitably Gaia Chemicals owned them.

The investigation was a slow and complex process. He read through newspaper websites for old articles on industrial pollution and chemical spillages. There were many occurrences across the world, and he didn't remember reading about these when they happened. A plant in West Virginia contaminated the water supply, red toxic sludge in Hungary killed four people and polluted the Danube. It would take months to compile a book on all the incidents. Gaia Chemicals owned many of these chemical companies.

Jason's findings shocked him. It never occurred to him he would find so many incidents related to pollution from industrial accidents in the chemical industry. He presumed only the major disasters received much publicity, the others were of purely local interest.

He could not believe British owned companies allowed such pollution to happen. Jason always imagined foreign companies caused these incidents, in countries with governments noted for corruption and taking bribes to ignore health and safety lapses. His naivety and his unconscious racism embarrassed him, assuming the British behaved in a superior manner to foreigners. As a black British person, he should know better.

Jason came from a middle-class family and his father was a lawyer, but the police did not realise that. They judged all books by their covers, and they did not recognise that beneath his black skin, he was a respectable middle-class boy. When stopped and searched Jason's accent caused confusion. Some police accused him of taking the piss when they heard him speak. One said, 'so what do you think you are, some African prince's son?'

It concerned him that Ross had a friend like George Fenton. He presumed Ross would be horrified if he knew his friend ran a company that damaged the environment. Jason was unsure of how to alert Ross, but Angela Fakenham's initiative seemed an ideal way. It surprised him when Ross cut any idea of that dead. It sowed the first seeds of doubt as to whether Ross was aware of the damage his friend's companies caused.

He hadn't spoken to Dido about this because it felt a bit too close to home. Dido was Madrigal's best friend and Madrigal was Ross's wife. A seed of caution sprouted deep below Jason's enthusiasm and naivety. Some instinct told him to be careful. The obvious solution was to pass on all he had discovered to Seville. She might be Ross's daughter, but she had asked him to check out Gaia Chemicals. She would understand how to deal with her father and alert him if he unwittingly supped with the devil.

As Jason composed an email to Seville, he wondered what would happen if Ross had intentionally invited the Devil to dinner. He guessed if Ross chose to dine with the devil, he'd buy himself a long spoon.

Chapter Thirty-Three

February 2020

Colin Wilton sat at a small table in his small kitchen and contemplated his bank statement. He'd made a considerable sum of money from his book on those icons of pop, the Turner Twins. Enough that he gave up his job as the political correspondent on a tabloid and set up as a freelancer. But it was amazing how fast his cash went and currently, his outgoings exceeded his incomings.

He decided not to depress himself any further and filed away the statement. He would invest in a bus pass and forsake taxis. Fewer coffees on the go would help as well, he spent over £50 a week on coffee. He remembered a time when that covered his pub bill. Colin sighed, powered up his laptop, and clicked on his emails.

Colin saw he had an email from Taras and thought it might be interesting. He opened it and the attachment and stared in disbelief. It was a copy of an article in a Siberian newspaper called Norilsk Gazeta. Colin could not read the article, but he could translate the picture. It was a night-time scene by a river or lake, and the photo showed a young woman with straight, long black hair, pulling herself up from an ice hole.

'Colin, a local paper sent this story to the Siberian Times. It is of an English swimmer, Ophelia Macbeth, who came to Russia to experience what it is like to swim in extreme cold. She swam with both the Krasnoyarsk Psychrophile and the Norilsk Walruses, and all were impressed by the ability of this British girl.'

He continued reading. 'Seville visited Norilsk, and I hope she managed to leave the city. I am getting this checked out now. I presume she must be safe if the papers are publishing stories about her.'

Colin whistled, he had to hand it to Seville, how the fuck had she got to Norilsk? That girl could develop a distinguished career as an investigative journalist. Maybe he needed to take up swimming. He agreed with Taras, if a Russian paper published details about Seville's swimming feats, it seemed unlikely anything untoward had happened to her.

A couple of hours later he received a call from Taras. 'Colin, have you read the email I sent?'

'Yes, quite a woman your friend Seville.'

'Now she is famous in Siberia, Ophelia Macbeth the English swimmer. A film on YouTube shows her swimming exploits, made by a young woman called Vera Tolstaya, whose father is the wealthiest oligarch in Russia. Now I know this girl, Seville's half-brother, Sacramento claims to be in love with her.'

'Hey, wait a minute, this is all going too fast for me. You are saying Seville travelled to Siberia with some oligarch's daughter who is the girlfriend of Sacramento?'

'That is correct. They plotted together, and they went to Norilsk.'

'Well, that shows considerable enterprise, not an easy thing to do. Do you think Seville did any of her 'investigations' there?'

'I am convinced she did, she does not give up. She would not go just to swim.'

'OK, are there any consequences? Did she get out OK?'

'I do not know about consequences. No immediate problems but I think this will not be consequence-free. I have a contact in Norilsk and there has been an incident that is not reported on.'

'OK, what might that be?'

'Two Americans were attacked, one died, one survived. The one who survived did so because he was rescued by Seville and Vera.'

'That girl needs to start investigative reporting. How did she become involved in all this?'

'I do not know. The story from the survivor is he met the other American on the plane, a Mr Donnie Brown. The man who died worked for Gaia Chemicals, the company that owns Northern Chemicals.'

'Who attacked them?'

'They were visiting a factory. The American who lived, a Mr Baclanova, said his taxi had cancelled, so he hitched a lift with his new acquaintance. Brown told him he had to visit a new facility his company had purchased out on the route to Dudinka. Baclanova was surprised when he heard the name of this place because he thought it was closed down.'

'So Baclanova is an accidental passenger.'

'Yes. They arrived at the factory and found it shut and derelict. A half-track vehicle came storming out from the site, drove straight through the gates and ran their SUV off the road into a ditch. They could not push the car out of the ditch so Baclanova thought they should hunker down and try to build a shelter in the snow. The temperature was -40° so dangerously cold. Brown refused to stay, he said the airport was only five kilometres away, so he would walk through the snow. Baclanova told him it would not be open, but he would not listen.'

'How very foolish.'

'Indeed. Then along comes Seville and Vera with a Russian guide. As if by magic they pop up on a road from nowhere to nowhere. They rescue Baclanova, they drive to the airport and discover the body of the other American. Is that not a strange tale?'

'A strange tale indeed. So, what do Northern Chemicals say?'

'Northern Chemicals tell the authorities they are surprised. No one asked Mr Brown to visit any factory, they cannot think why he would go there. The police decide Donnie Brown is dealing with the Russian Mafia, in drugs, or guns. They believe a deal went wrong and this was a punishment. They do not think Mr Baclanova was involved; they think he was merely unfortunate.'

'Did Gaia Chemicals make any statement?'

'I got a colleague to contact them. They said one of their directors passed away in an accident in Siberia. They claimed it was not on company business, and they hoped the family's privacy would be respected at this difficult time.'

'So, what is rotten in the state of Denmark?'

'Ha, you quote Shakespeare at me, and from the play with Ophelia. You are right my friend; something is rotten. This Mr Brown was among the reasons Seville decided to visit Norilsk. She overheard him talking about chemical weapons being produced in Norilsk and look what happened in Syria on Christmas Eve.'

'An outfit like Gaia Chemicals would be in trouble if they were called out for manufacturing chemical weapons.'

'Extremely big trouble. Brown recognised Seville in London when she and I had dinner together. He was with another man, even more powerful, he was with a Mr Fenton, the CEO of Gaia Chemicals. Seville overheard them both talking about chemical weapons when we were in Kieslyovsk.'

'Have you heard from Seville?'

'No, I thought I would come to London. I told my news desk I am on the trail of a story, and they authorised the trip for me. Then they told me my visa application was rejected. This is strange; I have never had a problem with a visa before.'

Colin thought for a moment. 'Right, I think our best idea is for us to meet with Seville. Can you come to Paris?'

'I will ask, it must be through the Siberian Times, I cannot afford to go travelling around Europe unless I am paid for my expenses, Paris is an expensive city.'

'See what you can organise and tell me. In the meantime, I'm going to try to get hold of Miss Campbell. I'll be interested to hear what she has to say for herself.'

Chapter Thirty-Four

February 2020

Seville was tired and jaded from travel, but her many soil and water samples needed analysing. Her old tutor from university recommended a good laboratory in Durham. When she decided it would be simplest for her to bring everything to the laboratory, her tutor invited her to meet for a drink. She thought he was curious about what she wanted analysing and interested in where and what she had gathered.

Seville left the Eurostar at St Pancras and trundled around to the London apartment. She abandoned all her cold-weather clothes and packed a small backpack to cover her for the next few days. Barely an hour later she made her way to Kings Cross and boarded a train to Durham, still wheeling the large case holding all her samples.

On the journey, she caught up with her emails. Many were about snowmobile hire and courses; she would need to unsubscribe from all these sites. She was so busy deleting emails she almost deleted an email from Jason, and her hand trembled as she opened it.

Jason's mail included many attachments, detailing various

'incidents' of industrial pollution from chemical manufacturing. The companies responsible were all owned by Gaia Chemicals, and the man she'd seen in Russia and at her father's New Year's Eve party was the CEO of Gaia Chemicals. The name, Donald Brown, came up in the list of company directors.

In his email, Jason expressed concern about the relationship between her father and George Fenton, the man from Gaia Chemicals. He was concerned that when he suggested Atlas should check what they sold that this company manufactured, her father forbade any investigation. Jason asked if she would speak to her father about this.

Seville wondered who owned Gaia Chemicals, it was not a public company. She had no idea how to find out such a thing, but she thought the journalist, Colin Wilton would know how to investigate these matters. Her instinct told her that her father was in some way involved.

Her tutor met her at the station, eager to hear what she had been up to. She only told him part of the story but even that censored version interested him. She described the glowing lake, he assumed phosphorous was dumped there and perhaps also zinc sulphide. He would inform the laboratory as both were dangerous.

Seville passed a pleasant evening in the pub with her tutor and a couple of students from her year who had stayed on to complete their masters. The snow in Durham was on a different scale to Siberia. The cosy pub, the crisp fresh air, the carelessness of the conversation made her feel utterly relaxed.

When asked where she was going next, she realised she had no plan. Her focus was on Norilsk for so long she had not thought about what she would do afterwards. Apart from anything else, she needed the results from her samples. They left the bar at throwing out time, and slightly drunk, she went back to her hotel.

When she took her phone from her handbag, she saw several missed calls from Colin Wilton. Excellent, she thought. I'll ring him tomorrow and see if he can get me more information on Gaia

Chemicals. She wondered why he was calling her, but she was too tired to return the call that night.

Her mobile phone woke her at the unearthly hour of seven-thirty the next morning. She squinted at it to see who could be ringing so early. Taras, she sighed, it must be a civilised time of day in Siberia, if not in Durham.

'Hello.'

'Seville, it is Taras.'

'Yes, what do you want?'

'Is that any way to speak to your friend, is sneaking into Russia and not telling me any way to treat a friend.'

'Sorry.' Seville thought she knew why Colin had rung.

'So, I read about the swimming exploits of Ophelia Macbeth, now I would like to listen to the tale of the investigative exploits of Seville Campbell. Can you come to Paris?'

'Come to Paris, when? I've just got back home.'

'But Seville, you are a jet setter, I think. These people they come, and they go all the time.'

'I'm not a jet setter. Can't you come to London?'

'I cannot come to London, as I can no longer get a visa for Britain. I do not understand why, and it concerns me. I need to meet with you soon, my boss has permitted me to go to Paris next week and Colin can make it too. What day could you be in Paris?'

Seville considered, it put off having to decide her next moves for a few days at least. She could return to London, wash her clothes, pack clean ones, and go to France. 'How about next Wednesday? she said.

'This works for me, where will you stay.'

'I know a cheap hotel in the 19th arrondissement; I'll email you and Colin the details.'

'That is good,' said Taras. 'Colin and I need cheap. Make your notes before you come, you must tell us everything.'

Chapter Thirty-Five

February 2020

Ross met Albert Tolstoy at the Oxo tower, in a discreet corner of the bar. Novichok was in the news again, this time a French investigative journalist collapsed in Paris with symptoms of nerve gas poisoning. Ross wanted assurances the production facility at Norilsk was secure from any publicity, though it was difficult to question Tolstoy without revealing his own involvement.

'Why are you concerned? Where could be more secure than a closed city?' said Tolstoy. 'Access to Norilsk is tightly controlled. The national press cannot go there. No one can leave without a permit, and I can assure you no one working at Northern Chemicals will ever obtain such permission.'

'I feel responsible, I introduced you to Gaia Chemicals, I would not want my friends to think I had given them a bad business connection. Is it possible for anyone to get authorisation to visit the city, I know some of our people are authorised?'

'A small number of tourists are allowed. They sail up the river to Dudinka and can take a day trip to Norilsk. People like to say they visited a forbidden place. This is fashionable with young people, even my daughter asked for authorisation to go, her generation likes to be able to boast they travel everywhere.'

Ross shook his head, marvelling at the foolishness of youth. He could not imagine anything worse than staying in a grim Russian closed city. Just as well, he thought, he prevented Seville from obtaining a visa to visit Russia. She had expressed an interest in Norilsk, and he wouldn't put it past her to join some river cruise and abscond from an organised trip.

'My government has a way of dealing with publicity,' said Tolstoy.

'Indeed,' said Ross. The French journalist was an example of how the Russian authorities dealt with unwanted publicity. 'What concerns your government most now, Albert?'

'They are concerned about movement between us and China. We closed the border at the end of January, and although necessary, it has caused much inconvenience. But we must protect our country against this virus.'

Ross frowned; he heard a lot about this. He read up on the reports from WHO after George's comments, there had been many SARS-like diseases in Asia, and none exported to the West.

'Is that necessary, isn't this an Asian disease? I know China locked down their city of Wuhan, but it is a long way from your borders.'

'Ross you must take this seriously. Already we are aware of two cases in Russia, though they are both Chinese. It is a pity we did not close the border earlier. The issue is freedom to travel, too many of our citizens travel the world so it is difficult to contain the disease. Forty years ago, there would be no problem.'

'But Albert, there's always talk of pandemics and nothing much comes of them.'

'That does not mean it will not become true one day,' said Tolstoy. 'We should not panic, but one must be cautious.'

Ross thought about Tolstoy's words as he returned to his office. He decided he would ring Ganak, what was the point of owning a pharmaceutical company, if you didn't get the low down on disease and plague.

***

The conversation with Ganak troubled Ross. He appeared to think he had alerted Ross about the dangers of this virus. Ross told him he was in the position of the boy who calls wolf. After so many scares about potential worldwide pandemics, Ross had better things to do than take alarm at each new one. He needed to understand if this was different.

'Tell me Ganak, how important is this?'

'There are cases in France, the USA and the Middle East as well as the well-documented ones from China and Southeast Asia. Exact details are difficult though it is certainly a coronavirus. Public health experts feel China was slow in sharing information until they locked down Wuhan.'

'Yeah well, the world splits into two parts, one part airs its dirty washing all over the media, the other part hides it in the depths of the laundry basket. I think China is in the laundry basket clique.'

'Ross, I think this may be momentous news, the foundation of worldwide fame,' said Ganak.

Typical Ganak talk thought Ross, fame for Ganak as the developer of a world-saving vaccine. He did hope Ganak had not manufactured the virus.

'Never mind fame, I want facts, is a worldwide pandemic brewing?'

'Ross, I cannot give you a straight answer, there are numerous variables.'

Ross sighed, he thought science was supposed to be about straight answers, a question asked, the answer yes or no. Why all this hedging of bets?

'What is the view of the public health people, what does WHO say?'

'They are saying we must be prepared.'

Ross wanted to slam the phone down, be prepared was as good as saying nothing. 'Ganak, I'm not a bloody boy scout, should my business be taking any actions? Do not say be prepared, tell me specifics.'

Ganak sounded huffy, no doubt he expected praise for being so clever as to prepare for a virus of this sort. 'Do not travel, that is the best advice I can give and avoid large crowds, particularly indoors.'

Ross wrote it down in his desk diary, no travel no crowds. He wondered how Madrigal would take to such instructions.

***

Ross forgot about worldwide pandemics when he spoke to George the next day. They met for lunch; this was not a matter to discuss over the phone. They were back at bloody No. One Piccadilly, with snotty waiters giving him the evil eye because he did not want to eat a gigantic roast dinner in the middle of the week.

'Everything sorted in Russia?' said Ross.

George frowned, 'yes and no.'

Ross clutched his head. 'Don't you start George, I had a painful telephone conversation with Ganak yesterday which was all yes maybe, no, maybe. I need straight answers.'

'OK, let me tell you a story. The Norilsk police contacted Ivan Popov on Saturday 1st February at 9.30 a.m. Siberian time. Inconvenient for Ivan as he had flown to London on the 31st of January for a meeting with me, and the time in London was 3.30 am. He said it took him some time to realise what they were talking about.'

'Yes, I can understand that. He said nothing indiscreet I trust?'

'He was, as always, a master of discretion he assured me. He asked Donnie to check out a new installation between Norilsk and Dudinka, a short way beyond the airport. Now at that time of year, no one drives any further than to the airport along that road, and all the traffic going there ends at about five in the afternoon. So, no chance of any witnesses to an "accident." He sent him to a derelict factory a few kilometres or so past the airport. A reception committee waited for Donnie, with instructions to drive his car off the road, out there, no transport and you're dead. No one survives a night in the open. They would come back in the morning and check life was extinct.'

'Sounds like a valid plan. Idiot American drives the wrong way going back to town, tries to turn around, loses control, into the ditch and then hypothermia takes all,' said Ross.

'You would think so. Anyway, the police informed Ivan of the death of a business visitor of his, a Mr Donald Brown. His car had crashed, and Mr Brown unwisely left the car and tried to make his way to the airport in a snowstorm. Unfortunately, being the back end of beyond, they close everything at night as flights only operate in the morning and early afternoon. Mr Brown managed to make it to the gates and perished there. Tragic.'

'Tragic but bang on plan I think.'

'Mr Brown had a companion, a fellow American,' said George.

'Oh yes, the alleged friend, so Donnie took him with him.'

'The friend was an employee of the nickel mining company. I don't understand why he was with Donnie, but he was. This chap survived the accident.'

'How the fuck did that happen? We knew he might have someone else with him and the instructions said no survivors. Donnie must have set out without the other chap, so why didn't they deal with him when they came back to check first thing?'

'The friend did not need to make it through the night, he was rescued during the night.'

'What? Who the fuck was driving from nowhere to nowhere in the middle of the polar night in a fucking snowstorm?'

'Now the answer to that question is remarkably interesting. Three girls driving around the countryside found him. Two Russians and one English girl.'

'Fun night out in the arse end of nowhere?' said Ross. 'Were the police making this up? Did they ask trick questions to see what answer Popov gave?'

'No, one girl was making a film about an English swimmer coming to Russia to swim outdoors in ultra-cold places. The sort of novelty nutter thing that is all-over YouTube. They decided a snowstorm was the ideal time to go out and film a background atmosphere of dark, sinister roads in wild weather. They were coming back to town and saw the crashed car.'

'Now that's exceptionally bad luck.'

'Oh yes. The companion was still alive, so they picked him up, and they drove to the airport to try to find Donnie. Luckily, he was dead, or they would have rescued him too and then the shit would have hit the fan. They found Donnie's body, took the American to hospital and called the police.'

'What did they make of it?'

'They asked Popov if he sent Donnie to the derelict factory. He, of course, said no, he said he thought Donnie was going back to town. The police assumed some deal with the Russian mafia had gone wrong, I think they expect American businessmen to be doing deals with the mafia. This all made sense to them, and they accepted the other chap got caught up in it by mistake.'

'Did they question those girls thoroughly; I would think the Russian authorities wouldn't be too happy about a group of girls racketing around restricted areas.'

'I don't think they questioned them at all. The girl making the film is the daughter of our friend, Albert Tolstoy.'

'What the fuck. What's Tolstoy's daughter doing in Norilsk? I suppose the police would be cautious in dealing with her, Albert has considerable clout in Russia.'

'Indeed. The authorities knew about her making a film about the local swimming club. Before she went to Norilsk, she filmed another mad swimming club at Krasnoyarsk. The police never checked what was filmed, just assumed it was all to do with swimming. The girls were booked on an early flight, and they weren't going to upset Albert Tolstoy's daughter.'

'Rather lax of them. Young girls driving around a restricted area with a movie camera does not sound ideal. Mind you, Albert told me his daughter applied to go to Norilsk. He said it's fashionable for the young to say they have visited a closed city. Any reason to worry?'

George leant back in his chair, an unusually serious expression on his face. 'Yes, I think we have a reason.'

'OK, you've got me concerned. Why should we be worrying?'

'The story of the English swimmer intrigued me. I also wanted to discover what the press said about this accident,' said George.

'If I know my friends in the North, it sounds like the sort of accident that isn't reported in the press.'

'You are right, but a heart-warming story about an English girl coming to see if she is tough enough to match Russian swimmers does get reported. The video is on YouTube, the article and photos are in the media. I have a copy of a photo here.'

George passed a photocopied page to Ross. He took it and stared in shock, he recognised that girl.

George read from another photocopy, 'the name of the English swimmer was Ophelia Macbeth. I was surprised to read that, because unless I am mistaken, she is the double of your daughter, Seville.'

Chapter Thirty-Six

February 2020

Ross told his driver to take him back to the office. He was glad he wasn't driving, waves of anger coursed through his body, and if driving, he would be in danger of committing an act of road rage. He saw himself stopping his car, stepping out and shooting another driver with the handgun he kept in his glove box.

Ross was not a man given to anger, because little made him angry. In the things that mattered he got his way, and why would you waste your time getting angry about things that did not matter. He was the master of the body swerve, he moved out of the way of hassle and left it to someone else.

His biggest mistake was having children, hell he was not a man who could only express his virility by breeding. Children did not enrich his life; they were nothing but problems once they became old enough to hold their own opinions. Sacramento was an obvious nuisance, and he thought Havana was lining herself up to be double trouble. He needed to make sure she stayed in California; he would not let Suzie play that trick on him again.

But Seville, she was trouble in a powerful way. Drink, drugs, teenage pregnancies, anorexia, Jesus, even crime, he could deal with all that. You sent them to the best rehab or specialist that money bought. Those failings were all understandable in the children of the rich, all wealthy parents bore these crosses. What he did not understand, was a child who took such a moral high ground, one that interfered in matters she shouldn't interfere in, who put the environment over family loyalty, a child that didn't value wealth and influence.

George's revelations shocked Ross. He knew Seville had not gone to Norilsk only to swim, she talked about going there to investigate pollution. She overheard George and Donnie talking about the manufacture of chemical weapons, and she was obsessed with water. What if she ganged up with Madrigal on this clean water for all issue? What if she found out his links to all this and exposed him? He did not want people to know the extent of what he owned, the true reach of his power.

George felt anxious and George was not a natural worrier. He needed to clip Seville's wings before she did any more damage. She had involved Tolstoy's daughter and he would bet Albert was unaware of this. He had to disable Seville and must act quickly; he would contact Albert Tolstoy and tell him what his daughter was up to.

They reached the office and his driver parked on the deserted street. Ross left the car and went to the night entrance. Security appeared surprised but let him in, and he took the lift to the marketing floor and Jason's office.

He assumed Seville had in some way conspired with Jason. He saw them talking together at the New Year's Eve party. Jason had become interested in Gaia Chemicals. Seville knew about Donnie, hell, she'd found his body for God's sake, and about the issues with the Northern Chemicals factory at Norilsk. He suspected she had gone to investigate that, not to swim. So, what information had she shared with Jason, what did he know?

Ross thought Jason was new to concealment, naive enough to leave incriminating evidence in the office. He had prepared the presentation about unethical and environmentally unfriendly companies for a board meeting, and any further research into Gaia Chemicals would probably be in the same place. He opened the door and glanced around the room.

A green light flashed on Jason's desktop computer, the laptop in its docking station. Like most senior employees, Jason used his personal laptop for working from home. A poncey looking tray held neat rattan containers, pens in one, scissors and a ruler in another, paperclips, and a container full of memory sticks. Ross picked up the entire box and took it to his office.

He turned on his desktop, inserted each memory stick, and checked the files on them. None were password protected. The third stick held the information. Copies of many news articles about chemical spillage and pollution. Most weren't from the national press, they were reports at the local level, particularly the ones outside Europe.

A spreadsheet showed each incident, the date it occurred, the name of the company and if it was a subsidiary of a larger one. Gaia Chemicals featured on most. Jason created a PowerPoint presentation with the names mapped like a family tree, and the name at the head of the tree was World's End.

A note at the bottom of the page recorded World's End was an anonymous limited liability company registered in Liechtenstein, with no information on whom the directors might be. Jason's treachery was revealed, and a buzzing sound and the fuzzy feeling of white anger overcame Ross. He fought to keep control; he clutched his desk to prevent himself from flinging the monitor across the room. He tried to ignore the shady figures who struggled to emerge from the dark shadows in his office, all whispering advice on how to deal with Jason.

Ross sat and lowered his forehead to touch the cool brushed steel. He fumbled at a drawer, took out a bottle of pills, and swallowed two, breathed deeply and calmed himself. He was in control once again, and he would sort out the problem.

Ross decided he would deal with Seville first and then Jason. He would need to be inventive; Jason had inveigled his way into Ross's family circle. The situation was not as simple as merely sacking him with a payoff.

Ross knew a man who ran a company specialising in keeping an eye on people, and he would put them on Seville's case from tomorrow. He needed to get a handle on what she was doing and decide how to act. Seville was of age, which limited his options.

He leant back in his chair and pondered on how in today's world, a father kept control of his daughter. It was harder than it used to be. Even the countries with positively medieval attitudes towards women seemed to have laws nowadays against affirmative action. There was something to be said about a time when a woman needed a male guardian's permission before she could do anything.

Chapter Thirty-Seven

February 2020

Seville smiled to herself as the Eurostar pulled into Paris. She found she enjoyed this sensation of perpetual motion, somehow travelling was easier than staying still. When she disembarked from the train in Paris, she felt a sense of excitement and freedom.

Going to the hotel seemed like coming home. A pleasant thrill of anticipation filled her at the thought she would meet Taras soon, it was five months since she had last seen him. She wondered if he was looking forward to seeing her, or whether this was part of his work obligations.

Colin Wilton stood in the reception of the hotel, apparently having difficulty in making himself understood, so Seville intervened. They had already agreed to meet Taras in a wine bar by the Seine. She beamed with pleasure as they entered the place, and she saw Taras, sitting at a table and reading a newspaper. He hugged her and kissed each cheek, then hugged Colin with equal enthusiasm.

Colin pulled away saying, 'don't go all French on me, Taras.'

They ordered wine and made themselves comfortable, and Seville prepared to explain herself, waiting to see which one would start the interrogation.

Taras began. 'So, Seville, you decided you would go to Norilsk?'

'The opportunity came up, and I didn't want to involve anyone else in possible trouble.'

'Very noble,' said Taras. 'So how did this opportunity come?'

'Vera had an idea, she is Vera Tolstaya you know Taras.'

'Is she now, ha, Sacramento must be careful, or he will end up at the bottom of an oil well. Her father is an extremely powerful man, but why would a girl like this go to Norilsk with you Seville?'

Seville explained and her companions looked increasingly interested in her story. Telling her story made her feel slightly uneasy as she remembered both were journalists. She took a sip of her wine and thought of the permanent acrid odour and taste that hung over Norilsk. When she talked of Lena and Irina, she felt a pang of guilt, Vera and herself were merely tourists, they were tourists throughout their entire lives. They visited and moved on, Lena and Irina did not have that ability.

She ended her tale and drank more wine. She had a dizzying urge to become completely drunk, to loosen all inhibitions, to cry out to the world the tale of unfairness. What was the saying? "Some are born to sweet delight, and some are born to endless night," the words of William Blake. She thought of Irina, a wild Slavic poetess, surrounded by smoke and darkness, a fitting subject for a Blake illustration.

'That's some story,' said Colin as she finished. 'When will you receive the results of your samples?'

'In a week. It's hard to decide where to begin. What should we do with the information we've gathered?'

'Let's see what the samples show,' said Colin. 'From my end, I think I can sell a story about a British owned company manufacturing in Russia and causing bad pollution. The more dangerous the chemicals found, the stronger the story is. If you find any evidence of the manufacture of chemical weapons or nerve gas, then we've got a front-page article.'

'It is harder to make a scandal of this in Russia,' said Taras. 'There could be outrage that a British company is polluting our land, we only allow Russians to do this. But we will want this in our news feed if there is evidence of chemical weapon manufacture. The nerve gas will not be news.'

'What about my father?' asked Seville.

'But Seville, your father's company cannot be involved in this, Atlas does not manufacture or sell chemicals,' said Taras.

'Your stepmother is part of the clean water brigade,' said Colin. 'Let's face it, your father is probably friends with loads of dodgy businessmen, it goes with the territory. Just because you saw one of these directors at his party doesn't mean he's involved in this. Still, you know what, I'll poke about a bit and see what connections there may be between him and that man from Gaia Chemicals.'

'And what of the other man, the man who died?'

'Now that sounds dubious,' said Colin. 'Taras, you say this was not reported in the press.'

'No, much was written about Ophelia and her amazing swimming, but nothing about an accident. What was the name of the man you rescued, Seville?'

'It was Andy Baclanova, I remembered it because he was so American, and his surname sounded Russian.'

'I will ask for information on him, I have contacts who can check if he left the hospital yet, and what address he gave.'

'If you get the address, I'll contact him,' said Colin. 'It might be enlightening to hear what take he has on the accident. Have you worked on any interesting stories Taras? I like to keep up to date on what my rivals have an eye on.'

'There are always events to interest a journalist in Russia, our problem is writing about them. The growing story is this epidemic in China, we share a border with China, and we have closed that border.'

'Maybe it will become a bigger story, though there is a desire not to alarm people. Now politics are settling down again in Britain, the environment is the major concern. Let's hope it stays that way.'

***

The next morning Seville woke up to find items of interest in her inbox. Vera had emailed a video to her, and Jason had contacted her again. She decided to save the best for last and opened Jason's email first.

'Hi Seville, I've done some digging and now I wish I paid more attention to my chemistry lessons in school. Gaia Chemicals developed an award-winning pesticide last year, though they do not manufacture this in any of their factories, but in factories run by Northern Chemicals in Russia.

'The ingredients in this pesticide are the same as those used in Sarin and nerve gases such as Novichok, so this company may be involved in the manufacture of chemical weapons. I believe this was your concern when we talked about the chemical weapon attack in Syria at your father's party.

'What does worry me is an initiative for increased transparency in business, that I supported on behalf of Atlas, appears to have been abandoned. This is since your father withdrew his support. I don't know what to think. Is it possible to meet for lunch sometime, I'd love to hear your thoughts? Regards, Jason.'

Seville wasn't sure what her thoughts were. Her father was in some way involved with the man from Gaia Chemicals, and as far as she had seen Ross had no friends, but only business contacts. When it came to business, her father was always the one in charge, no one would ever tell him what to do. She thought about his interaction with herself and Sacramento, the relationship was all about control. Had he business interests beyond Atlas? If so, he would be the man at the top.

She sent a reply to Jason, suggesting some dates for lunch, then opened the video attached to Vera's email. It was not the swimming video, but the one she had constructed to show the pollution. Seville read the email.

'Ophelia, this is our Shakespeare moment. I need to edit this film once you can tell me what chemicals and minerals have infected the earth in these places. We cannot release it until a few months pass. If people see it too soon, they will start to think of those girls who were filming in the area, and it could be bad for Lena and maybe for me. Please view it and let me know what you think.'

Seville played the film; it was impactful and alarming. Vera was undoubtedly talented, and she could imagine this going viral. She decided to show Colin and Taras after breakfast.

***

Colin and Taras sat awkwardly on the bed while Seville positioned the laptop on a table. She clicked on play and plaintive jazz echoed through the room. They watched without speaking, the film made the expedition appear even more dangerous than it had felt at the time.

The final scene was an image of the Russian president. He filled the screen shaking hands with the British Prime Minister, and a voice said in English, 'My name is Ozymandias, king of kings. Look on my works my children and despair.' The picture faded away to the accompaniment of Irina's maniacal laugh.

They were silent for a moment, then Seville spoke. 'Vera says once I have the results of the samples we took, then she will also run a banner at the foot of the video. It will show the details of all the chemicals found in the ground and the water, along with the names of the companies mining and manufacturing there.'

'That is a disturbing film,' said Taras.

'No shit Sherlock,' said Colin. 'I think your friend is right, wait a few months before releasing that into the world. You need to stay anonymous. Seville, I suggest you avoid Russia for some time, but the next time you go there you may wish to do so on a different passport.'

'Travel is becoming a difficulty for all three of us,' said Taras.

Colin said, 'yes I cannot obtain a visa for Russia under my name, nor can Seville and you, my friend,' he turned to Taras, 'appear to longer be able to get a visa for Britain. We are all undesirables.'

***

After arranging to meet for dinner that night, Colin left to catch up with an old colleague who now worked on Le Monde. Taras and Seville decided to visit Montmartre and climb up to the lofty eyrie of Sacré Coeur to gaze across the city. They went inside the basilica to look around.

The church had a calming spirituality, an impression of blue and gold, the scent of incense and soft light from banks of candles. Seville lit a candle and said a prayer that Lena and Irina would be safe. She knew not what God she was praying to, but it did not matter, it was an expression from the heart.

They went outside and gleefully spotted landmarks, the Eiffel Tower was easy to identify. They looked around the panorama, then Taras stiffened and nudged Seville.

'Do not turn around now, but I think someone may be following us.'

Fighting the impulse to turn and stare at the surrounding people, Seville continued looking at the Eiffel Tower. 'What do you mean? Is someone watching us, what do they look like?'

'They have an eye patch and are wearing black leather gloves,' said Taras. He laughed as he saw Seville's surprise. 'I joke, but I see a man in a navy jacket who seems to go wherever we go. I am paranoid, in Russia, we worry about being under observation.'

'No, you are right to be cautious, but who would want to follow us? Why would anyone wish to spy on us?'

'It may not be us; it may be me. Maybe I caused concern somewhere, remember, I could not obtain a visa for the UK. We will ignore them, we will show them I am a tourist, meeting my English friend and seeing the sites of Paris. There will be nothing for them to report on.'

On impulse, Seville grasped Taras's hand, and he did not pull away. They walked down the steps and the steep streets of Montmartre hand in hand. Seville could not imagine that anyone would be interested in her movements in Paris, a visit to meet friends in Paris was an activity to expect from a rich man's daughter. If someone was following them, it would be Taras whom they were spying on.

They met Colin for a lengthy dinner and consumed a considerable quantity of food and wine. All were infected by a sense of recklessness, as if they were setting out on a journey from which they may never return. Colin had undertaken to investigate whether there were any links between Atlas and Gaia Chemicals. Taras would focus on pollution from foreign-owned companies in Siberia. Seville would provide whatever information she could and was going to continue with her investigations into polluted water supplies.

Colin left to catch up with another contact and Taras and Seville ambled down to the Seine. They held hands and Seville's fingers tingled from the strangeness and intimacy of it.

'Are you not swimming tonight?' said Taras.

'Come and swim with me.'

'I have not brought any clothes to swim in,' protested Taras, 'and it is cold, it is February, Seville.'

'We could skinny dip.'

'My God, Seville, you want to kill me?' Taras put his arm around her. 'I can think of a better reason to take all our clothes off than to die of cold.'

Seville did not resist the embrace, her mind raced, what was she committing herself to? Taras kissed her, no greeting kiss on cheeks, and with a sense of release, she abandoned herself to the moment.

***

Colin and Seville said goodbye to Taras the next morning, he had to meet a colleague to discuss the French response to the coronavirus. Seville said her proper farewell to Taras in her room, in front of Colin they took leave of each other like friends rather than lovers. She agreed to come to Novosibirsk once she had sorted out her immediate affairs at home. She had made a commitment, though she did not yet understand exactly what that was. Seville anticipated seeing Taras again in a few weeks, if she could have seen into the future, she would have gone to Novosibirsk with him then.

An air traffic control strike had grounded planes, so Colin was returning to London by train. They boarded the Eurostar and made themselves comfortable.

Colin leaned forward and whispered to Seville, 'don't look now but I think we are being followed.'

Seville turned around in her seat and looked up and down the rows of seats. 'Is it a man or a woman?'

'I did say don't look now,' said Colin. 'There is a chap about five rows back, wearing a navy quilted jacket. He followed you and Taras into the restaurant last night, talked to reception and went away, though he was outside when we all left. I must say he doesn't appear Russian, so I don't think the FSS are keeping an eye on you.'

'Taras thought someone was following us yesterday, but we both thought they were following him, we didn't notice anyone follow us to the restaurant,' said Seville. 'Why would anyone want to follow me?'

'That was what I was going to ask you. Would your father put a tail on you?'

Seville frowned as she thought about this. 'Well, he's capable of that but I can't think why. Unless he is involved with that man called George. I guess if the man called George was concerned about me, he might have me tailed, what do you think?'

'I think I don't like it.'

'Colin, would you be able to check who ultimately owns a company, a private company?'

'Is this Gaia Chemicals?'

'Yes, I have a suspicion my father may own that company. That would explain a lot of things. I told him I wanted to visit Norilsk and after that, I couldn't get a visa anymore. He's seemed unusually interested in my activities lately, and I don't think this is a sudden expression of fatherly concern.'

'It is quite a specialist skill tracing details of private companies if the owner wants to hide their involvement, but I know some people who could help. If your father is a major investor in a company like that, he may send professionals to spy on you.'

'It's just the sort of thing he would do.'

'More worrying than being watched is this strange 'accident' that happened to the other man from Gaia Chemicals. I think you need to be careful Seville. Where are you planning to go once we're back in London?'

'I was going to go to my father's apartment while I worked out what I should do next. But Colin, he is my father after all.'

'So, if you find out your father owns Gaia Chemicals do your investigations stop because your father is involved?'

Seville didn't reply straight away. She considered her parents and wondered if her mother loved the concept of her more than the reality. Truthfully, she had no idea if her father loved her. He treated her with the same amiable indifference he displayed to everyone else he was involved with socially. He was a polite stranger to her.

'No, it would make a mockery of what I want to do with my life. If I am going to make people aware of how their access to clean water is endangered, I cannot choose who to expose. And this is so much worse, imagine profiting from manufacturing products to kill and injure people.'

'Well, an entire armaments industry is devoted to doing just that. The UK made 14 billion pounds from weapons of mass destruction in 2018. You'll get them on chemical weapons though, even our government agrees they're illegal.'

'I only intended to call companies out on pollution, I never thought it would go further than that. It would be great if you could find out about the ownership of Gaia Chemicals, I'll be going back to the London apartment, so I can meet you at any time.'

'That sounds like a bad idea to me. I think you need to get away from observation. Let me make a call.' Colin got up from the seat and made off down the carriage. He came back and sat down looking self-satisfied.

'And your plan is?' asked Seville.

'OK, you may not like this because my plan involves going on another journey. Go back to your father's apartment tonight and pack a bag to cover you for a couple of weeks. I will book a courier who will come this evening and collect your bag and take it to where you and I will be going. Do you remember when I bumped into you on Skye? Well, I was visiting a friend; I rang him, and he's happy for you to come and stay awhile. No one will expect you to be there.'

'Who is your friend? Are you sure they are OK having a strange woman to stay with them?'

'My friend is the well-known singer and environmental activist, Paul Turner. He lives in splendid isolation on Skye.'

'But what if they follow me?' said Seville.

'Have you ever read the Thirty-Nine Steps? Tomorrow you will stroll down to the shops as if nothing is happening. Go into Waterstones through the main entrance in Torrington Place. I will distract anyone following you, go out through the Gower Street exit and I will arrange for a car to pick you up there. They will drive you to Euston Station. I will meet you at the entrance to platform one, and we will take the train to Glasgow. We'll hire a car in Glasgow and drive to Skye, it will be simple.'

Seville shook her head and exhaled loudly. 'Goodness Colin, how exciting, it's like going from being an ordinary person to some sort of spy or secret agent. I may find life boring when it goes back to being normal again.'

'What is normal, will you withdraw from fighting the capitalist forces? We don't live in ordinary times anymore, that's the truth. Just think, two weeks in Skye with an environmental celebrity.'

'I'd rather spend the time with an environmental scientist than a celebrity. Hey anyway, I'm a celebrity too now, Ophelia Macbeth, the mad English winter swimmer. Swimming in the sea off Skye in February will be nothing to me.'

Chapter Thirty-Eight

February 2020

Jason entered his office clutching a coffee in his reusable bamboo cup, and an almond croissant, his guilty breakfast treat. Dido did not approve of croissants; he couldn't remember why. It was too difficult to keep up with all the reasons as to why one should not eat something.

He felt at a bit of a loose end. Lady Fakenham's initiative appeared to have been dropped and no new project had come along to fill his time. So, he invented his own mission, to pull together a biography of his boss, Ross Campbell.

He was an interesting subject; Jason started on LinkedIn where he gathered a few basic facts about the start-up of Atlas, its development in the US, then Ross's move to Britain and registering Atlas as a UK company.

The most information about him was a page on Wikipedia, and Jason suspected Madrigal had written this. The Wikipedia entry scarcely mentioned his past wives and children and went on at length about his current family and his philanthropy in the UK.

Jason found various articles about Ross on newspaper websites. Most were about Atlas or Book of Friends, they noted his attendance at prestigious functions, the Sunday Times and Forbes rich lists mentioned him. Tatler, Vanity Fair and, to Jason's surprise, Horse and Hound, all featured stories about Ross Campbell. Jason presumed that an old friend of Madrigal's was editor of Horse and Hound.

The curious thing was, Jason could not find any details of his life before Atlas. No information on his childhood or his education, no mention of parents, siblings or even cousins. Like the Roman goddess Minerva, he appeared to have sprung to life, fully formed, in his early twenties. A god of wisdom, strategic warfare, and commerce.

Successful men from humble beginnings often liked to make sure everyone heard how they managed through sheer hard work, or outstanding genius, to make such a success of themselves. Those from privileged backgrounds tended to be less forthright about their advantageous roots, but in their cases, their early years were well documented. Ross never spoke about any of this.

Jason wondered whether Ross had something to hide. He asked Dido if she knew where Ross was born. She said she had no idea and appeared surprised Jason should be interested. He noticed Dido took little interest in other people. He originally put that down to her being so involved in what was right for the planet, but now he wondered if she was just self-obsessed.

Jason's investigations troubled him. He had seen Ross as a hero since he first joined Atlas. Ross gave him this prestigious job. He supported worthy causes, he lacked prejudice, both women and people of colour occupied senior positions in his company. It was difficult to drill below this façade, impossible to find the real man.

Ross's daughter thought he was involved with people and companies who did not match the ethical and environmental standards that Atlas apparently upheld. Jason would have dismissed this as ludicrous. He started his investigation to protect Ross, to show him the businesses he and Atlas should distance themselves from. But Ross told him to close these investigations down, and this, along with the lack of information on the man, sowed a seed of doubt in Jason's mind.

Jason made a date for lunch with Seville, and he hoped she would answer these questions about her father. She must know where her father was born, and some details about her grandparents. He supposed such information might be irrelevant, but he found it unnerving that a person so high profile in some ways, could be so anonymous in others.

He tipped out the pot of memory sticks on his desk. The IT department frowned on the use of memory sticks, but everyone used them. The company laptops were never as good as people's personal laptops, so they downloaded files to memory sticks and took them home. Of course, only senior management got away with this practice.

Jason rummaged through the sticks, unable to find the one he wanted. A prickle of unease trickled down his back. This stick held the files documenting his investigations into Gaia Chemicals. It was not a file he wished to share with anyone apart from Seville. He checked his desk drawers and his backpack in case he had inadvertently taken it home, but it wasn't there.

He realised he would sound paranoid if he asked security to check the CCTV cameras to see if someone entered his office after he left last night. Maybe a cleaner knocked over the pot containing the memory sticks and accidentally stood on the missing one. Then threw it away to hide the evidence of the mishap. A happy thought, though it seemed unlikely.

Only Ross could be interested in his memory sticks, but Ross left the office before him last night. That thought comforted him, no one else would be interested in his research, and Ross left before him. He told himself he had nothing to worry about.

Chapter Thirty-Nine

February 2020

They said goodbye at St Pancras, Colin disappeared into the depths of the underground and Seville left the station to walk home. She paused in front of a shop window to check for the reflection of a man in a quilted jacket. It all seemed unreal, like being part of a computer game.

She thought she must contact Jason and postpone their lunch. She would explain why she had to go away and warn him to be careful. The world had shifted in some imperceptible way, and she should not take it for granted her father would do her no harm. She felt she had regressed to her early teens when inexplicably, the people she thought would take care of her had abandoned her to that institution and left her powerless.

But she was an adult now and could not be sent somewhere she did not wish to go. Someone cared for her, a man who called her a rusalka, a man who desired her, who maybe one day would love her. She was a different person to that terrified, yet defiant girl.

Seville was glad to get back to the apartment block, the concierge at the door would not allow any uninvited strangers in. The concierge rang residents to tell them of any visitor, but she guessed someone would be watching the single entrance to the building, to follow her if she left.

She called her father at Atlas and his secretary said he had gone to Cambridge, so she did not have to worry about him turning up. She decided to sort herself out, pack for her next trip, drop the bag off with the concierge, and have an early night.

The idea of going to Skye excited her, Colin told her Paul Turner's house was by the sea, so she should be able to swim each day. It was strange to think of staying with someone so famous, Madrigal would love an introduction, she thought. She wished Taras could be there with her and decided to ring him once she arrived in Skye.

By ten p.m. Seville was ready for bed, her muscles ached with tiredness. It would be good to stay still for a while she thought, a house somewhere remote, by the sea, would be ideal. She laid in her bed, her mind racing as she thought about last night and Taras. It was as unlikely and strange as all the other recent events, though what was abnormal about forming an intimate relationship with another person?

Somehow her life had become filled with drama. Tomorrow she would go to Waterstones and would deliberately throw off a man who tailed her, then run away to Scotland. She would meet Colin at the entrance to platform one at Euston, and they would escape. It was like a spy movie, and she wondered when she would see Taras again.

***

Seville awoke disorientated, with no idea as to what time it might be. She thought a noise in the apartment woke her up, but it could be in a dream. It sounded like a door flung open and hitting a wall. Her heart beat fast, and she put her head back on the pillow, and felt sleep on the edge of her consciousness.

She heard the bang again, and the sound of footsteps moving rapidly through the apartment. Seville sat up as her bedroom door opened and lights blazed on. Two people approached her, and one bore down on her before she was able to call out or scream.

She was aware of a needle and a sharp pain; she saw a stretcher on the floor and a woman pulled back her duvet. Unable to move, two people lifted her to the stretcher and pulled straps around her. She fought against slipping into unconsciousness as the people carried her on the stretcher out of the apartment into the lift.

Seville blinked against the bright lights in the reception area and heard the concierge say, 'just as well she managed to ring you.'

'The stretcher-bearer replied, 'yes we got the emergency call, if she hadn't rung straight away it might have been too late.' Then they were through the doors and out into an ambulance, and Seville could no longer hold on to consciousness.

***

She was strapped to a stretcher and in a vehicle moving in a choppy manner. Seville gradually realised she was in a helicopter and a sense of panic rose in her. She dug her nails into the palms of her hands to stop herself from screaming and breathed deeply, trying to calm herself. Her stomach swooped as the helicopter started to descend, and she wondered where they were taking her, was it a place she would recognise?

A woman leant over her and smiled, a kind smile. She held a syringe in her hand, 'we need to sedate you again until we've got you settled in. Don't worry, you'll be alright now you are here.'

How bizarre, thought Seville. I was alright. Who are these people? Are they linked to the people who were following me or has something else happened? She fought the drowsiness again as her mind reeled with questions. Heavy doors opened and then her stretcher was raised, and carried out of the helicopter, down a ramp and into a dim dawn light. She saw the sea and colour on the horizon, and then she lost her battle to stay awake.

***

Seville woke up abruptly to find herself on a narrow bed in a bright room with high, multi- paned windows. There were no restraints, so she got up cautiously and went to the window.

The view outside was discordant, she overlooked a terrace and below that a strictly manicured lawn with equally well-manicured flower beds, and the feel of a well-tended English garden. There were no trees, and the lawns ran down to a drystone wall. Then any resemblance to a cultivated garden ended, after the wall was rough heathland, with sheep grazing and strewn with boulders. Beyond the heathland was the sea, blue with the waves making small white horses in a brisk wind.

She gazed out of the window and thought of Colin waiting outside Waterstones. He would ring her and get no answer. How long would he wait before he went to check at the apartment? Would the concierge tell him she had been carried out on a stretcher, transported to hospital? Would he check the hospitals to find where she was, and what would he do when he couldn't find her?

She looked at the window itself, constructed so it only opened a small way. Seville went to the door and found it locked. She glanced around for her mobile which of course, she could not find. An old-fashioned telephone sat on a table by her bed, and she went to investigate. It said to ring 2 for reception and 9 for an emergency. Seville thought this an emergency but decided to give reception a go first.

'Flett Clinic, part of the Assist Healthcare Group,' said a voice.

'Hello, assistance is what I need,' said Seville. 'I need someone to come and tell me where this is and why I am here. My name is Seville Campbell.'

'Ah, Miss Campbell,' said the voice, in a calm and unhurried manner. 'I will send the Clinic Head Administrator to be with you straight away. Goodbye and don't hesitate to call if you need anything else.' The line went dead.

She considered ringing straight back. Within seconds she heard a knock at her door and the sound of it opening. A smart woman in her forties came in, her face adorned with a corporate smile. Seville fought against her rising anxiety, she needed to stay in control. She had a powerful sense of danger; stronger than when prowling the slopes behind Northern Chemicals in Norilsk. She knew why, here she was alone and in Norilsk they had been four.

The woman put out a hand to Seville and said,' Miss Campbell or can I call you Seville? I am so pleased to meet you.'

Seville regarded the hand with distrust. But concealment was her best policy, so she grasped the hand loosely and shook it. 'You are?' she asked in an autocratic way that did not come naturally to her.

'Of course, I am Serena Hope, I run Flett Clinic. You are entrusted to our care for a while.'

Seville took a deep breath, fighting to keep herself under control. She wanted to scream and shout, to demand to be sent home at once, to cry hot furious tears, to smack the unctuous smile off this woman's face. Instinctively she knew she must not. As a young teen, she gave in to anxiety, panicked and cried and her behaviour convinced people she could not cope, that she was not in control, that she must be managed.

When she was thirteen, her parents sent her away to a place like this. They told her she was in danger of harming herself, so she learnt how to dissemble. Expressing her inner turmoil led to people thinking they knew best what was good for her, so she rigidly controlled herself and kept her anxiety buried. She would not give them any evidence to use against her, no matter what lies they concocted about her.

'Why have I been abducted and brought here?' she said, her voice steady and calm.

'My dear, you are confused, you were not abducted. You took an overdose last night, accidentally I am sure, and you rang the emergency number from your flat. The number goes through to a call centre. The ambulance came to collect you and pump your stomach.

Your parents gave their permission for you to be brought here to recuperate. Both your parents have been anxious about you for some time.'

'Where is this place?' asked Seville, not bothering to deny the concocted story, fighting the lie would make her angry and anger would not be her friend.

'It is a safe place,' said Serena Hope, 'an island off the coast of Scotland. We will help heal your mind from all that anxiety. But today you must relax, you'll find an e-book reader next to your bed, download whatever books you like from our extensive library. Look at the menu and order whatever you want to eat and drink. Relax, and in a few hours your therapist will come and work with you to design a programme of activities, a special diet and the appropriate medicines.'

'Where is my mobile phone?'

'Initially, phones and the internet are not permitted. Social media causes much anxiety for many of our patients. You will find yourself better able to relax without online distractions.'

Seville stared at her in silence, now was not the time to challenge anything. She gave the woman a curt nod of dismissal and sat down at the desk and began to read the various documents there. Serena Hope appeared disconcerted, then turned and left the room. Seville heard the door locking behind her and tears prickled her eyes.

Two days ago, she had walked in the streets of Montmartre, hand in hand with Taras. Two nights ago, they had laid in bed together. She thought she would remember every detail of that night; it was the only night with Taras she had to think about. Seville felt a bitter regret that at Lake Baikal, she had not gone to his bed, then she would have more memories to fortify her.

Chapter Forty

March 2020

Ross met Albert Tolstoy at the Bulgari Hotel. They dined in the restaurant, surrounded by men of a certain age, accompanied by women of a more youthful age. In one corner an older woman hosted a table, her diamond-encrusted fingers gesticulating to the four young men at her table, demonstrated the equality of the sexes. It amused him how Russky the clientele was, if the iron curtain ever came down again, Knightsbridge was fucked.

Tolstoy was edgy, rumour had it he was out of favour with the Russian president, always a risk for a national who appeared too influential and rich. He talked about selling his Moscow apartment and his dacha on the Black Sea. Ross was sure Tolstoy had many assets tucked away from the possibility of confiscation, the Knightsbridge house being one of them.

'You must need a base in Moscow?' said Ross as Tolstoy discussed his plans.

'You are right, anyway, Anna will not let me sell the apartment, it is the home of our daughter, Vera.'

'How old is your daughter?'

'She is eighteen. She is having a gap year before university. This is what they all do now, anything to put off the business of becoming an adult.'

'Albert, I believe your daughter is a friend of my daughter.'

Tolstoy frowned. 'Indeed, what is your daughter's name?'

'She is called Seville.'

Tolstoy shrugged. 'I have not heard that name, does your daughter live in Moscow?'

'No. Let me show you something.' Ross picked up his phone and clicked on a file. He handed the phone to Albert Tolstoy.

Tolstoy was silent as he read, then he muttered a curse under his breath. 'That girl, her mother spoils her. How did you find out about this?'

'A mutual friend of ours, George Fenton, brought it to my attention.'

'Why were our daughters in Norilsk, why would they visit there?'

'My daughter is an environmentalist, Albert. George knows this and it concerned him she should visit Norilsk.'

Albert snorted and handed the phone back to Ross. 'Well, Vera has no concept of the environment. She cares about nothing but clothes and parties. I can see her thinking it fun to make this sort of film. I will ensure she does not get the authority to visit any other closed cities.'

Ross stared at Albert; did he not see this was more serious than a careless escapade? 'I think you should be concerned, Albert. Seville is on a mission to investigate pollution, she asked me if I could get her permission to visit Norilsk, she will not have gone there only to swim.'

'But Ross, what are you worried about, they are only girls, what problems can they cause?'

'Albert, George is worried my daughter stumbled across the manufacture of nerve gas by Northern Chemicals. He is concerned with the use of Novichok on British soil, there may be consequences if any publicity happens. I would be anxious: your president may not take kindly to any involvement of your daughter in this. Now an employee of mine, who met with my daughter, is taking a close interest in Gaia Chemicals. Naturally, none of this affects me, but I am concerned for my friends, and it is my daughter stirring up this trouble.'

Tolstoy appeared troubled. 'Why are your employees taking an interest in Gaia Chemicals?'

'The employee wanted to ensure Atlas did not stock products from any company that caused pollution through their manufacturing. I can deal with him, and I have dealt with my daughter. Now I worry about your daughter.'

Albert looked alarmed. 'How did you deal with your daughter?'

'Seville suffers from some mental health issues. We sent her to a clinic for treatment.'

'I cannot send my daughter to an asylum; Anna would never allow that.'

'Not an asylum Albert, a clinic. Maybe she drank too much Champagne, she took too much cocaine. Mothers understand the need for treatment for these weaknesses.'

'But she is in Moscow.'

'Something can be arranged. Don't let her become a problem, Albert.'

Tolstoy took a deep breath, fell silent, and sipped his drink. 'It is a sensitive time now; Vera might allow herself to become involved in environmental matters if she thought it amusing. The authorities would not receive that well. You must give me time to think about this.'

'Very well Albert, but you need to be quick. Let me know by Friday.'

***

When their dinner finished, Ross decided he would walk home. The night was clear with a full moon and the company apartment a mere three miles away. He walked through Hyde Park and cut through Mayfair. He felt triumphant, he had asserted his authority over the richest man in Russia. It did not matter how rich you were in Russia; the apparatus of the state was always a threat. The most powerful man was the president, but even he could be unseated by the people, unlikely as that may seem.

No one could unseat Ross, though people might cause him problems. Ross did not dance to the whims of any electorate, though to be fair, it would need to be a brave electorate to take on the Russian president. Still, it was possible.

Voices whispered to him as he passed alleyways, calling to him from the dark. Warning him to beware of treachery. He saw Jason Harris, the words 'Et tu Brute,' rang in his ear. Someone had shouted them from the shadowy mews, and a picture of his daughter Seville formed in front of him.

He paused in his stride and took a deep breath. A police car stopped, and a voice called out to him, 'are you alright, sir?'

He would like to go to the police car, put his hand through the window and grab the stupid policeman by his tie. It would come off in his hand, he remembered reading policemen had to wear clip-on ties. He struggled to stop himself from laughing. 'I'm fine officer, just realised I left something at the restaurant. I will call them.'

'Of course, sir,' said the policeman. The car drove off slowly. Ross released the laughter convulsing his body. He grasped the imaginary tie tight, and his admirers applauded him from the shadows.

Chapter Forty-One

March 2020

The world tilted on its axis to a crazy, vertiginous angle for Jason Harris. In three months, his situation changed from being employed by a man he thoroughly admired and holding an interesting, well-paid job, to working for a man who alarmed him, and a job that no longer had any purpose. He did not know how this had happened.

He wondered if it helped that the entire world had also changed, literally overnight. Last night the Prime Minister told the British people to stay home, to only leave their house to buy essential goods or to exercise and not to mix with people outside their own households.

Jason abandoned eight months of not touching alcohol because Dido thought it a poison, and drank an entire bottle of the poison, of a Bordeaux flavour. He surprised himself this morning by feeling remarkably fresh, considering how reduced his tolerance to alcohol must be.

Atlas sent an email to all senior managers with a schedule of Zoom meetings attached. Jason checked the list, and his name was conspicuous by its absence. He wasn't working on any project now, so he guessed he should sit tight and wait for redundancy.

He considered his situation and decided lockdown improved it. No more going into the office and trying to find tasks to occupy the day. He would work on his CV and research companies he might want to work for. He wouldn't have to try to avoid Ross Campbell. Jason was convinced Ross suspected he had been looking into his background and because of this, he was side-lined.

Last week, when Jason turned up for his lunch date with Seville, she did not show up. He had tried ringing her on the mobile number she gave him, and it went straight to voice mail. He rang several times, but it always went to voice mail. This disturbed him, he wondered if she had spoken to Ross, and Ross told her never to speak to him, Jason, again. Now, of course, they had no opportunity to meet for lunch.

The silence from Seville concerned him, and he asked Dido if she knew anything. He made some excuse about promising to get some information for her on water pollution. Dido said how would she know about Seville's movements, that she barely knew Seville.

His relationship with Dido would also benefit from lockdown. He had tired of her, like a dementor from Harry Potter, she sucked all the joy out of life. He considered how to end the relationship and lockdown seemed the ideal opportunity. Jason felt happier this morning than he'd felt for a long time. He would use his spare time to dig deeper into the background of Ross Campbell.

He opened Wikipedia and studied the entry for Ross. It held no information on early years, just the bald statement that Ross Campbell was born on 24th June 1964 in Sheffield, England. No information about his parents, his education, or his upbringing.

The Wikipedia entry began with his early career. 'Ross Campbell first conceived the idea for Atlas whilst working as a counsellor on a summer camp in California. The company was originally set up in 1987 to sell rare and limited-edition vinyl and CDs by mail order. In 1994 Atlas went online and broadened its range to all types of music and books. The range further expanded to include videos and DVDs in 1997. The online shop that sells everything concept launched in 2001 and in 2014 the worldwide headquarter of Atlas relocated to London.'

Details were given of Ross's marriage to Madrigal and the births of their two children, Imogen, and Charlie. This was the longest paragraph. A final entry mentioned in passing the five children from two earlier marriages, without giving any details of those children.

Jason typed in 'what summer camp did Ross Campbell of Atlas work in?' and to his surprise, an answer came up. The camp had a page on various people of note who in the past either attended or worked as counsellors. Ross was among those listed. What amazed Jason was the discovery that this was a Christian camp. Another page detailed how they gave opportunities to young people from troubled backgrounds, both as campers and counsellors. Could that be the reason for no information on Ross as a child? Had he come from a troubled background?

A buzzing from Jason's entry phone interrupted his thoughts. He went to answer it. 'Hello?'

'Jason Harris? A delivery for you mate.'

'OK, I'll be right down,' replied Jason.

He went down and opened the door. A courier handed him a well-wrapped box. Jason thanked the courier and returned to his flat with the package. The delivery puzzled him; he hadn't ordered anything. The box was extraordinarily well secured, he needed a penknife to break the seals. Inside was a second box, equally securely wrapped.

He wondered what this held. It was not a big box, maybe six inches by four inches high and wide, four inches deep. Jason broke through the next set of seals to reveal a box holding a bottle of aftershave. Nothing among the packaging showed the sender. It couldn't be from Dido as she took a strong line against perfumes, they were not vegan.

Who would send him aftershave he wondered? He opened the box and took the bottle out. Contrary to popular fashion, Jason was clean-shaven. He had tried growing a beard, but the results did not please. He shaved most days, but today in celebration of lockdown he neglected his normal routine.

Jason took the bottle of aftershave into his bathroom and put it on a shelf. He would shave tomorrow and try it out then. Today he would be a rebel, he would slouch around in pyjamas and stubble.

Chapter Forty-Two

April 2020

Time marched to the beat of its own drum at Flett Clinic. The boredom of confinement interspersed with various therapies made the days run into each other, and there were no weekend rituals to mark the passing of time. A personal therapist was assigned to Seville, a large, bouncy woman, with a strong Scottish accent she found strangely reassuring. Her name was Anne Campbell, and Anne made much of their having the same surname. She seemed kind.

Seville discovered the official reason for her admittance to the clinic was attempted suicide, that she had a history of extreme anxiety, and was a danger to herself. Her past exile to a place like this for six months as a young teenager gave authenticity to the story. The suicide label rankled, though at times life had not seemed worth living to Seville, she never wanted to admit defeat. Her sheer stubbornness would not allow her to take her own life.

Seville experienced a deep sense of betrayal, she thought her father had orchestrated this, though she did not know why. She presumed he persuaded her mother to play along with it, her mother would see Seville's refusal to follow the career path she desired for her as a form of mental illness. She asked to speak to her parents, and they told her it was not allowed.

Anne Campbell's favourite therapy was talking about what made Seville anxious. After a few sessions where Seville claimed nothing caused her anxiety and Anne watched her with a sad, disbelieving smile, Seville said that environmental concerns made her anxious.

She was surprised to find Anne knew little about the environment and gently rubbished Seville's concerns. In Anne's mind, nothing could happen that scientists would not be able to sort out. They would build barriers to deal with sea level rises, they would invent something to shoot into the atmosphere to correct temperature change. There was nothing to worry about, man was so clever, he, and it always was he to Anne, would find a way to circumvent anything nature might devise.

Every day Seville put a colourful array of pills in her mouth, yellow antidepressants, green anxiety reducers, a strawberry pink vitamin pill. She held them in her mouth, her cheeks bulging like a hamster, then she spat them out as soon as she was unobserved. She focused on keeping a calendar, it would be both dangerous and easy to lose all track of time.

It was hard to gaze at the sea and not swim in it. The clinic had a swimming pool, but swimming in a contained structure seemed unnatural to her. Anne Campbell told her it was too dangerous for her to swim in the sea. Seville asked if other people were staying at Flett Clinic and Anne said yes. She asked if she could meet any of them, she told Anne she was lonely. Anne appeared unsure, she said she would see what she could do.

About a month had passed when Seville noticed a new tension in the staff. Anne escorted her down a corridor, and she saw people talking in small groups, lowering their voices as she went by. In a place designed to cure anxiety, there appeared to be an inordinate amount of anxious people, she thought cynically. She wondered what colour pills they took.

Some days later Anne appeared in her room wearing a face mask. She carried a box of face masks that she gave to Seville. 'These are for you to wear when you leave your room. I need to update you on a couple of things.'

'Update away,' said Seville.

'There have been some worldwide issues while you have been our guest here. You are of course aware of the coronavirus disease, Covid 19, now a major issue in the world?'

Seville frowned; she was aware of a disease that was a major problem in China. The day she returned from Paris she read about an outbreak in a secretive cult in South Korea. Brits evacuated from China, people stuck on a cruise ship, cases in Brighton. It did not impinge in any way on her life, it did not affect her travels in Russia and Europe.

'This disease is now a pandemic. Five days ago, the government put Britain into lockdown and most of the world is the same. All non-essential travel is forbidden, and everyone is instructed to stay home unless they are a key worker. You are lucky to be here, this is a safe place, but we wear these face masks as a precaution against the disease.'

Anne paused and smiled encouragingly at Seville. 'Most of the world is like you now, we are all in lockdown.

***

A week later Anne told her she could attend what she called a zoom coffee morning with some of the other residents. A surge of excitement ran through Seville, her company for the last five weeks had been these pleasant automatons, who spoke carefully and never gave any information on the wider world.

She longed to be part of a group again, one of four, to be having adventures with her crazy angels, to racket around with those wild Russian girls. She wondered if she missed her Russian girlfriends more than she missed Taras. The girls made her life vivid and exciting, in contrast to the dreary calm and caution she always exercised here. But she did miss Taras. She felt a wave of bitter anger this relationship and all its possibilities were shown to her, then snatched away.

She wondered what they all thought of her going missing, how Colin must have searched for her that day. Did Taras miss her, might he even now be searching for her. Seville gazed out of her window and imagined seeing Taras come ashore in a rowing boat, arriving like an old-fashioned hero to rescue her. She chided herself at these ludicrous, romantic thoughts.

She wanted to know what had become of the test results of the samples she gathered in Norilsk. How it was possible to suddenly become a blank space where previously you existed. It was like death, people die, and life carries on without them. She might be dead and in limbo, or purgatory. This place would make a good purgatory.

The zoom coffee morning was a surreal experience. Anne brought coffee and cakes to Seville's room, then set up her laptop on the desk. A babble of chatter filled the room, as smiling faces popped up on the screen. Seville stared at them, unable to focus on the confusing conversations.

Anne clicked away at the screen, typing out some messages and suddenly the screen reverted to one face, that of a girl with elaborately braided hair and beautiful eyes. When she smiled at Seville she smiled with her eyes as well as her mouth and Seville relaxed, it was a long time since she had seen such a genuine smile.

'Seville, this is Charity,' said Anne

'Hi Seville,' said Charity, 'how are you doing?'

'Good,' said Seville, conscious of Anne sitting next to her.

'I'm good too,' said Charity. 'I'm part of a trial, a vaccine is being trialled on me, I must stay here while they check for side effects. They asked for young healthy people, and they're paying £500 a week for four weeks and you get to stay in luxury surroundings. Mind you, this is much more boring than I expected, though I guess it would be even more boring at home, at least we're allowed to mix. Why are you here?'

Seville did not know how to answer. Anne had left the room, giving the illusion of privacy. If she said they had imprisoned her, Charity would write her off as a paranoid patient, displaying ample evidence of why she needed confinement. She longed to tell this girl she had been kidnapped, brought here, and locked up against her will. But that story was more incredible than the story the clinic would tell; that she attempted suicide and had mental health issues.

'I'm being treated for anxiety.'

'I guess everyone's anxious now,' said Charity. 'People are anxious they're going to lose their jobs, lose their homes, lose their lives. Guess few people are going into clinics to treat that anxiety.' She laughed, 'people haven't got the money for that.'

This made Seville feel heart sore, people worried about their livelihoods, and here she was a rich girl. Charity would think her spoiled and indulged by rich parents sitting here in her luxurious retreat from the world. But that was all so wrong, only a rich girl could be confined like this, only a parent with boundless wealth could lock his daughter up in this manner. How to explain herself?

'I would prefer to be anxious at home,' she mumbled.

Charity held her hands up in horror. 'Oh, I'm not criticising you, anyone able to afford it would pay for their child to come here if they suffered from mental health problems. Don't be ashamed.'

Seville wasn't sure how to have a rational conversation. 'I didn't choose to come here; I was made to come here.'

Charity smiled sympathetically. 'Of course, but I'm sure it's for your own good. Anne said you needed someone of your own age to talk to.'

The conversation stumbled on, Charity was warm and friendly, but Seville could feel no connection. Her recent experiences had disconnected her from the normal world, she felt like a conspiracy theorist.

Anne returned to the room. 'Time for your water therapy Seville. I hope you enjoyed speaking to someone your age.' She smiled at Charity. 'Normally poor Seville has to put up with us old ladies.'

'Great to meet you, Seville, let's talk again.'

Anne shut down the laptop and they left and went to the spa and pool area. Seville sensed the approval radiating from Anne. She thought she had passed a test. They wanted to see how she would react with other people. Would she claim abduction, or had all the pills they thought they fed her made her compliant, and unable to remember exactly what happened? She would beat them, she had not let herself descend into anxiety and panic, she kept her emotions under control.

Seville changed and slipped into the swimming pool. She began to swim and thought of women prisoners. Bertha Mason in Jane Eyre, the insane wife locked away by her husband. The widow of Abraham Lincoln committed to an asylum by her son. Rosemary Kennedy, given a frontal lobotomy after her father committed her, and many other wives and daughters, locked up because they did not obey their husbands and fathers.

As she swam mechanical lengths up and down the pool, she considered this news of the world locked down. How would that affect all her friends, were they all confined like her? She thought of Sacramento, was his school now transformed into a true prison or had he been sent home? The concept was incredible, could it be that the rest of the world mimicked her experience. She wondered how to regain her freedom.

Chapter Forty-Three

April 2020

The April weather was unseasonably warm, and the inmates of Flett Clinic were allowed limited access to the grounds. The island sat in a bay, no more than a mile from the closest shore. She hoped Charity would know where they were, but she told Seville the location was kept secret to prevent any journalists trying to track them down and bother them. They all arrived here by helicopter from Glasgow airport. They were somewhere in Scotland, none of them knew more than that.

Knowing the rest of the world was also in suspension was a consolation, though Seville was not sure if that helped her. Without her mobile, she had no way to contact anyone, and no way to find where the people who would help her were locked down. If she left the clinic, where would she go? Her heart told her she should find Taras, though she knew that was not possible. She could not swim to

Russia, nor steal a boat and row there. She had no passport and no access to money.

If she escaped from this place she would not get far, but perhaps she did not need to go far to discover refuge. She was in Scotland, and she had intended to travel to the Isle of Skye. She had an idea of the address, and if her host was still there, he would surely help her.

As she walked around the grounds for the thirty-minute time slot allowed five times a week, she considered the landscape and the possibilities for escape. She checked the outside of the building, focusing on the area around her room. Inmates had rooms with a sea view, whilst the staff accommodation was at the back, overlooking the hill. Her room was on the first floor, with a drainpipe next to her bathroom window, and another pipe crossing above.

The bedrooms on her floor appeared the grandest, with long, multi-paned floor to ceiling windows giving a spectacular view over the water. She always stared up at the windows when she exercised in the grounds, but the rooms were either empty or their occupants too subdued to gaze out of windows. One window had a tan leather chair positioned in front of it, an ideal position to regard the sea, though it was always empty when Seville looked.

Seville began to plan, and the planning soothed her. She would swim away, and she thought the water would be warm enough for her to swim at night, so she would be unobserved. She would not swim to the closest shore. She saw mountains on a distant horizon, which she thought might be about four miles away. In calm seas, this would be an easy swim for her.

She would leave when still dark, an hour or so before sunrise, and by the time the sun came up, she would be well out of sight of the island. She had a good sense of direction, and she did not worry about swimming the wrong way. Depending on the weather conditions and the current it should take her two hours to swim to the most distant coast. No one came to her room before 9 a.m. and she would be long gone by then. If they suspected she had swum away they would search the closest coast.

The problem with swimming was what to do once out of the water. She would need shoes and clothes and swimming would make them wet. She checked her room to see what materials were available to her. A type of wash bag hung in her wardrobe. It had a waterproof seal, and was presumably put there to hold any clothes a patient might soil in their distress. It could be tied to her waist, but she must not make it too heavy, or it would weigh her down.

Seville had rubber shoes for wearing in the spa and the side of the pool. She preferred to swim without them, and they were not ideal for walking over rocky ground and heathland, though better than nothing. Leggings and a sweatshirt could go in the bag, and she would find somewhere to shelter at night.

She decided she would take the first opportunity to escape while the weather remained fine. Her greatest task was to work out how to gain access to the sea as they locked her room at night, and the rest of the clinic as well she assumed. She thought about picking locks, people did that so there must be a way.

Seville spent an afternoon trying to open her door with no success. She could open the yale lock, the problem was the deadlock. In frustration, she examined the windows. A sort of catch prevented the bedroom window from opening fully, it appeared secure. However, in her bathroom, a smaller window, also with a catch, looked easier to dislodge. The bathroom window was small and set high up the wall, an unlikely route for escape.

Seville worked on the catch till she managed to pull it out. She smiled with satisfaction and considered the window. She brought through a chair from her bedroom and climbed up to reach the small window. Seville reckoned she could squeeze through. She had lost weight since her admittance here, and always slim, she was now positively thin. She opened the window as wide as it would go and put her head through.

'Tricky,' she said to herself. This was going to require acrobatics, her room was on the first floor, and she could not drop to the ground without risk of injury. To the side of the window was a solid-looking drainpipe, and she would need to squeeze through and swing herself to the left and grasp it. Hopefully, it would not detach from the wall. She glanced upwards and spotted a helpful drainpipe snaking across above to join the other drainpipe descending to the flower bed below. Checking no one was outside to observe her, she reached up through the window and pulled on the pipe, it felt firm.

She withdrew back into the bathroom. Her best bet would be to exit the window headfirst, grasp the pipe above her head and pull herself out. She would stand on the sill and swing across to the main pipe. If nothing gave way, she should be OK, and if she fell, she would not land on her head.

***

Seville went to bed early that night and fell asleep. She woke with her heart pounding; afraid she had overslept but the darkness of the room told her she had not. She dressed in her swimsuit and pulled the sweatshirt and leggings on.

Exiting out of the window was surprisingly simple, she slipped through without difficulty. The most complicated manoeuvre was holding on to the pipe above while pulling the rest of her body through, that done, she balanced her toes on the windowsill and swung across to the drainpipe. It held her weight, and she slid down the pipe.

On the ground, she paused, worried about triggering the security lights. A cat ran in front of the house and no light came on, so she assumed they set them for a specific time each night. No one expected burglars and escapees to be abroad at this time of the morning.

She glanced back at the clinic, then stood motionless, a light glowed in a window. She held her breath even though she knew they would not hear her from the house. It was the room with the empty tan chair, only the chair was not unoccupied now, someone sat in it. As she watched, the person in the chair got up and pressed against the window. Seville saw her clearly in the light, it was a girl, a young girl. With a prickle of horror, she recognised Vera.

Chapter Forty-Four

April 2020

Ross gave himself the status of key worker. He told Madrigal that with his warehouse workers so busy, he must set an example. Both Mary and the Trading Director seized upon this as a reason for them to come into the office too. Ross thought they came in because they had no life apart from work, and they found it difficult to feel important at home.

Today, the HR Director was also in, her office was next to his, and he heard her weeping while Mary, quite unsuccessfully, tried to comfort her. His mobile rang, he glanced at the screen and groaned, Madrigal, again.

'Hi Mads, what now?'

'Don't you what now me. What do you think I'm ringing you about? Have you any more news about Jason?'

'Madrigal I'm not the police. I'm not investigating Jason's death.'

'Yes, of course, Jason was just another employee to you. Dido rang again.'

'You could try not answering,' said Ross.

'Dido is my best friend. She's in a terrible state and I can't even invite her to come here. The Prime Minister is your friend, tell him to change these stupid laws. It's inhumane to expect somebody who's just been bereaved to stay on their own.'

Ross thought the last thing he wanted was for James Holt to allow Dido to come and stay with them. Lockdown had some quite substantial advantages.

'I thought you said the police were going to interview Dido?'

'Yes, and that made everything worse. They asked Dido lots of impertinent questions.'

'That's what the police do, Madrigal. Still, she was in Sri Lanka at the time of his death, so they can't suspect her of murder. If they have interviewed Dido, she must know as much, if not more, than I do. They haven't spoken to me.'

'I thought they came into the office?'

'Yes, but to see HR, they didn't need to speak to me.'

'What did they say to them?'

'I don't know, I wasn't there.'

'But why? You could have at least sat in on it. Go and find out what they said to her now and call me back.' Madrigal hung up.

Ross smiled to himself, he loved when Madrigal got angry. No one else ever spoke to him like that. Loud sobs came from the office next door. He sighed and prepared to face the drama. He glanced in the mirror before he left his office to ensure he didn't have a smirk on his face.

Ross knocked on the door to alert them of his entry, and hopefully give the HR Director a chance to pull herself together.

'What did the police say?'

The sobbing stopped and the HR Director burst into loud, hysterical tears. Ross flinched. Mary frowned at him and patted her on the shoulder.

'Three weeks, they said they thought he'd been lying there dead for three weeks.'

Well, he wouldn't be lying there alive for three weeks, thought Ross. 'How terrible, what did he die of? Was it Covid?'

'They couldn't tell yet, they said the body was too, too, oh I can't say.'

Ross raised an eyebrow at Mary.

'Too decomposed,' she mouthed at him. She made a face and hugged her colleague, with a blatant disregard for all the current rules.

'They think it unlikely to be Covid,' said the HR Director. 'He was slim, fit, and young. Oh, so young and so handsome.'

Ross wondered what handsome had to do with it. 'Why did it take them so long to find him?'

'His girlfriend was at a yoga retreat in Sri Lanka when lockdown started,' said Mary. 'She only managed to get home yesterday and hadn't got in touch with him before. His father became concerned when he couldn't contact him and notified the police. It was all quite unpleasant.'

Ross coaxed the details of the unpleasantness out of Mary. Jason's neighbour complained to the service company about a bad smell of drains in his apartment. Service companies across the land had enthusiastically embraced the excuse of coronavirus as a reason why they could not promptly fix maintenance problems, so they told the neighbour he had to live with the aroma for a while.

When the police contacted the management company for Jason's block of flats to gain access, they immediately thought of the complaint about the drains. At this point, the HR Director started to wail, and Ross retreated, gesturing to Mary to join him in his office.

It took Mary five minutes to calm her colleague back to the quietly sobbing level. She came into Ross's office, sat, and put her head into her hands.

'This is so terrible.'

'So, what do they think happened, you were in on the meeting with them?'

'They can't tell yet, at least there is no suggestion of suicide, thank God, as we were going to make him redundant, and he must have realised that. He was found collapsed in the bathroom, clutching a bottle of aftershave.'

'So, it was natural causes? He was an irritating twat but not so irritating that someone would murder him, surely.'

'They won't know until they perform the autopsy, and that may take some time with all that's going on now, but yes, the initial assumption is natural causes.'

***

Mary and the Trading Director took their sobbing colleague out for a walk by the river and a beautiful silence returned to the floor. Ross hoped it would be a long walk. He couldn't understand the fuss, Jason wasn't a friend or relative.

He went to the window to enjoy the view of the Tower of London. That ancient prison, used by rulers to incarcerate their enemies. Ross had so much better a view than that from 10 Downing Street. The Tower was a true symbol of power, in contrast to a Georgian townhouse in a London street. He owned this view, unlike that hollow man, the Prime Minister, merely a lodger subject to eviction at any time.

Ross gazed at the ancient building and thought of the most famous people incarcerated there before execution. No winners, all victims. He knew how to successfully deal with his problems, imprisonment or death brought resolution. He thought the pandemic would play into his hands. It would expose more hollow men and reduce scrutiny on the puppet masters.

If Ganak had created this virus he had done Ross a service, and this was the time to consolidate his power. His mind was clear and unobstructed, he sensed no whisperings from the corners of his office. He had succeeded in suppressing those who threatened to work against him, and further success was in his grasp. This was his time, he thought, and he had won every battle. The people who could be a threat to him were gone, or in Seville's case, incarcerated, and she wasn't getting her freedom back in a hurry.

Ross opened his 'Bollocks Bingo' spreadsheet and read it with some regret. Though the others talked plenty of bollocks, none were in the same league as Jason. He wondered if he should change it to a political bollocks expressions spreadsheet. James would become its new champion. Ross added 'world-beating' to the list.

Chapter Forty-Five

April 2020

Vera gazed down on her, Seville waved at her friend then realised that looking from the light into the dark, Vera did not see her. She searched for a missile to throw at the glass without breaking it. Stones surrounded her, but they might make too much noise or break the window. Looking by her feet for suitable material, she thought of her shoes. She took one rubber sandal off and threw it at the window. The sandal hit the window with a muted thud and Vera looked startled, her head moved as she scanned the gardens.

Seville waved, and it seemed Vera knew there was a person down below her window, but she did not wave back. She went back to the building, determined to reach Vera. The drainpipe arrangement by Vera's room was similar to that by Seville's, though climbing up a drainpipe is harder than shinning down. With an effort, Seville gained Vera's bathroom window ledge and a light came on in the bathroom.

The small window opened, and Vera's face appeared in the space. 'Who is it?' she said in English, then she muttered a swear word in Russian. Seville started to work at the catch that prevented the window from opening fully.

'It's me Vera,' she said. 'It is Seville.'

Vera pushed furiously at the window and the catch gave way. 'My God, Seville, am I dreaming? All day I lie in bed and dream, I do not know what is real anymore. This cannot be real.'

Seville grasped her hand, using the forbidden gesture. 'I am real, come on you can climb through here, I am escaping, we will escape together.'

Vera started to cry, and Seville felt warm, fat drops on her arm.

'I do not think I can escape; my mind is clouded.'

'Yes, you can,' said Seville with reassuring certainty. 'I will help you. Come, you can get through this window.'

Vera wriggled through the window and Seville helped her to balance. They slid awkwardly down the drainpipe together, and Seville placed a finger to her lips.

'We must be quiet.'

Vera stood in her pyjamas, looking bewildered and uncertain. 'What do we do now?' she asked. She seemed like a different girl from the one Seville knew, she had an air of defeat about her.

'Did you take the pills they give you?' asked Seville.

A flash of spirit came over Vera's face, 'they gave me pills and I spat them at them.' She became dejected again. 'But they gave me injections that I could not resist.' A triumphant look crossed her face. 'So, I pretended to take the pills, and I spat them out once they had gone. For a week now I have not taken any.'

Seville felt glad Vera had learnt how to resist, no obvious rebellion, never let them know that you were subverting their rules.

'Well, we are going to escape now, I have a plan, come with me.'

'But how?' said Vera. 'We have no transport; they will find us.'

'We are going to swim,' said Seville. 'This is an island. We will swim but not to the nearest coast, we are swimming to the furthest coast, and they will not think to look for us there.'

Vera flopped to the floor; her spirit left her. 'But how far, I cannot swim like you, Ophelia, I can barely swim at all. I have no energy.'

'I will help you. We will swim slowly as far as you can go, then we will turn on our backs and I will tow you till you can swim again. It will be easy.'

Vera's head came up, tears streaming down her face. She laughed; a wild Irina laugh.

'My crazy angel friend, we must be real, I cannot do this. If I try, we will both drown.'

Seville regarded her friend. Vera had no shoes or swimwear, only her pyjamas. She did not look capable of swimming a hundred yards let alone four miles. A sense of sorrow overwhelmed Seville.

'I can't leave you here, maybe I could tow you the shorter distance, if we go back to our rooms now and tomorrow night, we leave at one a.m., I'll tow you to the nearer coast, and we will have time to get away.'

Vera shook her head. 'No, our best chance of escape is for you to go now. Swim to the far coast, you will have a better chance of getting away. If you escape you can get help and come back and rescue me.'

Seville stood irresolute. She did not want to abandon Vera though what Vera said made sense. 'I hate to leave you here.'

'Yes, but you would hate me to drown even more. Oh Seville, just seeing you has made me feel so much better. Now I have hope. Swim away and come back and rescue me.'

Seville paced up and down considering what to do. The sky began to lighten, and she had to decide.

'OK, I will come back by boat or kayak. I will come at two a.m., so every night you must watch out for me at that time. Give me at least a week, then start to look out for me. Can you get back to your room?'

They both regarded the drainpipe doubtfully and Seville said, 'I will go up first and help you up.'

It was difficult, Vera was not strong, but Seville pulled her up, and they balanced on the windowsill, while Seville held open the window for Vera to climb back. Seville became anxious that soon it would be sunrise. They clasped hands again through the gap.

'I will be back, watch out for me.'

'Thank you, my friend, I will wait for you, good luck.'

***

The early morning air was not cold. Seville tiptoed down the lawn, leaving footprints in the dew and climbed over the drystone wall. She made her way across the heathland, startling the sheep, till she reached the shore. She left a footprint trail to the south of the island; she would enter the water as if she was going to swim to the nearest shore.

Seville pulled off her sweatshirt and leggings and placed them in the waterproof bag which she tied around her waist. She walked into the sea, small wavelets moving over her feet. Even in the crepuscular light, she sensed the beauty of the scene.

She swam around the island to the north, then struck out to those distant mountains. A glimmer of light came from the sky and a pale mist hung over the sea. The water was unusually calm, with no sign of any white horses today. The sea around the island appeared rimmed with mountains, as the first strands of dawn light came up in the east.

A weight rolled from her heart and shoulders and the tension and anxiety left her. Seville thought the sea would rise and consume mankind before mankind irrevocably despoiled the sea. We may have less of the earth to live on, we may have less freshwater to drink, but the sea will remain, mysterious and eternal, or as her Russian friends would say, deadly beautiful.

Chapter Forty-Six

April 2020

No one watched the beach, no one saw Seville emerge from the water into the unseasonable sun. She staggered as she came up from the shore, then sat down on the fine white sand and gazed around. A strikingly beautiful scene, the curve of the bay leading down to the clear turquoise water, the view framed by misty distant mountains, a semi-circle of paradise. The wind was still, and the only noise a gentle lapping of the waves and the mournful calls of sea birds.

Seville untied the bag holding her clothes from her waist and turned to examine the shoreline. Heathland and sand dunes surrounded the beach, and cabins and some low white houses stood behind the dunes. She went to investigate, moving cautiously so as not to be seen. Many of the buildings had a clear view of the bay, but they looked like holiday homes. Seville saw no sign of life, no smoke from any of the chimneys, no parked cars.

She walked through a flat, empty area that was probably a campsite. Seville stared through the window of a cabin on the edge of the site, she saw a desk and some office equipment, and a rack holding tourist pamphlets and maps.

Her heart lifted. She had no idea of where she was, apart from knowing she had been on an island off the coast of Scotland. Judging by the sun and its position to the mainland, she assumed it was the west coast. The information in the cabin might show her location, and once she knew that she could plan to complete her escape. Seville tried the door and found it locked; she shook the handle, but the lock was secure. She went back and gazed in; the pamphlets were too far away for her to distinguish any writing on them. She pressed on the window, and it stayed firm too.

Seville slumped to the ground, and started to shiver, although sunny, the April morning was not warm enough to wear only a swimsuit. She opened the bag tied around her waist and took out the sweatshirt and leggings. The waterproof seal had remained intact and kept her clothing dry. She pulled the garments on, and her shivers subsided.

She considered the cabin again, she needed to get inside. There might be someone living in these dwellings, but she did not want to reveal her presence, she was a fugitive. She peered through the window and checked to see if a lock or just a catch secured it. It appeared to be a catch.

Seville considered the structure and decided if she broke the pane next to the catch, she would be able to open the window and climb in. The damage would not be much she told herself, she would leave the window closed when she left the place and send money for the repairs.

She picked up a rock, took off her sweatshirt and wrapped it around her hand. Her first blow was not hard enough, she had not truly committed to the act. She tried again and this time the glass shattered, she knocked out the loose shards, put her hand through the gap and released the catch. The window opened, and she climbed through.

Seville crossed the floor to the rack holding the pamphlets and riffled through them. She glanced down at a single-page flyer on the desk, a picture showed the beach and Mellon Udrigle campsite. It could be a place name from Lord of the Rings.

So, she knew the name of this place, now she needed to find out where it fitted into the geography of Scotland. A map hung on the wall, and she scanned the place names, trying to find one she could recognise. Gruinard Bay, Loch Ewe, Loch Gairloch, these meant nothing to her. She looked westwards and recognised a name, that of the Isle of Skye. Now she had her bearings.

A pang of hunger interrupted her thought process, and she searched around the office for anything to eat. She opened a small fridge in the corner, but it held only some milk, well past its best by date. Seville looked through the desk drawers for old chocolate bars and found none, but a tin of barley sugar twists, it was almost full.

She gave a quick prayer of thanks to the Gods of the sweet tooth and returned to study the map. The barley sugar twist tasted marvellous. Skye was the obvious destination, Sacramento may still be at his school in Dunvegan, and Colin's friend, Paul Turner, lived at Milovaig. Even if Sacramento was not at school, Paul Turner was likely to be at his house. She did not have his exact address, but she was sure she'd find him if she got to the village.

Seville found a ruler and measured between her destinations, trying to work out the distances. Over a hundred miles she thought, it would take her five or six days. She would need to stick to roads, short cuts across moorland and mountains often proved to take much longer, and she was not equipped for hiking. She studied the map for the best route.

The most obvious path, walking down the road to Laide, was where they would most likely be looking for her. She went back to the shelves and searched for the detailed Ordnance Survey maps. She found one covering this area and spread it open across the desk. She smiled; a swimmer had other ways to complete a journey.

Seville sat with paper and pen, jotting down her route, the mileage, and likely travelling time. She could reduce the length of her journey by swimming. She would avoid Laide by taking a track across the peninsula and swimming a short distance across Loch Ewe to the next peninsula, then come ashore in a bay below the hamlet of Cove.

To shorten her journey, she would need to swim twice more, one a short hop across a loch, the other a serious endeavour. She would swim from Redpoint to the beach at Staffin on Skye. She reckoned this was about fifteen miles, a distance she had swum a few times before. It should take her about seven hours, though that would depend on tides and currents.

Seville searched the shelves for tide tables and found a book about sailing around Skye. Tides ran westwards according to the book, which would work in her favour as her way was to the west. She studied her notes with a mixture of excitement and apprehension. It felt so good to act after weeks of inactivity.

She was, of course, ill-prepared for this adventure. No hiking boots, no backpack, no tent, no cagoule and worst of all, no food. A tin of barley sugar twists wasn't going to get her far. She made a pile of her Ordnance Survey maps and got up from the desk to search the cabin for useful items.

She discovered a waterproof cagoule, four pairs of thick wool hiking socks, a box of six Tunnocks tea cakes, slightly out of date, a thin polar fleece blanket, and a swim bag. The swim bag was a treasure, a waterproof bag to store all one's possessions in, then inflate and tie around the waist. This meant room for the maps and the blanket.

Seville filled the bag with her loot and tied it around her shoulders. She would walk and swim to Poolewe and find somewhere to sleep, tomorrow she would make her way to Redpoint, and the following day, she would swim over the sea to Skye.

***

Seville trudged into Poolewe feeling stiff and hungry. Tunnocks tea cakes were great at giving an initial sugar rush, but not sustaining for the long haul. She crossed the peninsula from Mellon Udrigle along a rough farm track, then swam across Loch Ewe and walked along the metalled road to Poolewe. The roads were deserted, not a single car passed her. It was like being the last person alive.

She walked down the street past closed shops and heard the engine of a car. Instinctively she backed into an alleyway as a black SUV, with the Flett Clinic logo, cruised slowly by. Her heart started to beat faster, and she pulled back into the alley. They were out looking for her, and she was glad she had not taken the road from Laide.

The sound of the car faded away, and she opened her map of the area. Seville decided to spend the night at a National Trust property, Inverewe Gardens, just outside Poolewe. She walked along the shore to avoid the road and scrambled up into the gardens. She was hungry again and couldn't face another tea cake, but she thought there must be something to eat in the shop if she managed to break in. The gardens were deserted.

She broke into the café. She nearly cried when she found freezers packed with meals, she assumed the cooks had frozen everything they had prepared to prevent it from going to waste. A brief thought that the power in the kitchen may be turned off disturbed her, but the cooker worked, and her meal was the best she had eaten for a long time. A sofa in the staff sitting room made a comfortable bed, and she slept peacefully.

After a delicious and sustaining breakfast, she considered what she might steal from the freezers. If she packed away a couple of vegetarian frozen meals, she would eat them cold once they thawed out. It would not be the same as the tasty meals she ate last night and this morning, but it would be food, and better than tea cakes or barley sugar.

Seville studied the map to look for any other way to Redpoint that would avoid walking along the main road between Poolewe and Gairloch. The sight of the SUV, presumably searching for her, made her anxious. But without proper footwear, there was no other realistic path. She would listen out for traffic and get off the road if she heard a car.

People were queuing outside a small grocery shop when she walked through Poolewe. They turned to stare at her curiously, and she realised she must make an eccentric sight in her oversized cagoule, gym leggings and rubber shoes. She quickened her pace, anxious to get away before anyone challenged her. Her stomach was pleasantly full and the sun so warm, and she took the cagoule off once she left the village.

One car passed her on the road from Poolewe to Gairloch. At the sound of the vehicle, she got off the road and crouched down in the gorse. She lay on top of her fluorescent orange swim bag, to prevent the bright neon colour calling attention to her presence. A battered old Land Rover drove past, sheepdog in the back with its head sticking out of the window.

Gairloch was also unnervingly quiet. The golden sands and sparkling water called to her, but she walked on. Despite the lack of people, this seemed too major a place to stop for lunch. She would eat her Tunnocks teacake once she was on the small road to Redpoint. Seville studied the map again, it showed rivers, waterfalls, and lochs all near the road, but she resolutely disregarded these temptations. She promised herself she would come back one day, and camp and swim in these enticing places.

Seville wondered if 'one day' would ever come again. If her life, if not everyone's life, had irrevocably changed forever.

***

Two days after she swam away from captivity, Seville woke on the beach at Redpoint and gazed over the sea. It was an astonishingly beautiful place, the mountains of the Inner and Outer Hebrides framing the view. The day was clear and sunny, and she could see her destination, all she had to do was swim across in a straight line.

She ate her breakfast of cold cauliflower cheese, and she thought it tastier than the cold vegetable lasagne she ate last night. The thought of the challenge ahead filled her with swooping excitement and a sense of guilt, because she was glad Vera had not come with her. But she would return for Vera, she would keep that promise.

Seville packed her belongings in the swim bag. One last tea cake would be her reward for success. She thought she would be hungry tonight. She drank all the water in her water bottle and filled it from a stream. Safe drinking water could always be found in the Highlands of Scotland.

She ran down the sand to the water and turned her face towards the sun. It should take her about seven hours, and if she became tired, she would rest on her swim bag. The water was deliciously cold, she felt alive and calm. Seville had no fear of drowning, she thought she would be safe while she swam across the sea. She had evaded her captors, and she thought they would not catch her now.

Chapter Forty-Seven

April 2020

Ganak Reddy picked at the skin on his index finger and took several deep breaths. For all its first promise, 2020 was turning out to be a shit year. He'd seen so much potential, a pandemic he predicted now ravaged the world, and he was ahead of the game, the man most likely to develop a vaccine.

He expected worldwide recognition of his name. His role as the CEO of the company that developed the vaccine and the man with the foresight to predict this, gaining him acclaim. He thought his position would become unassailable.

But events did not appear to be happening as he forecasted. Ross bought a major US pharmaceutical company, Smith and Smith. Ganek expected this to increase his power, expected to become CEO of the joint company. Now it was looking like he might be the junior partner. The amalgamation might diminish his authority. Ross was cagey about stating his plans and that always meant treachery.

He thought Ross a treacherous swine, but Ganak was also well versed in these dark arts. He held his fire and considered what action he should take. Then events slipped from his control and now Ross had the upper hand.

Ganak arrived at Flett Clinic to review the results of the vaccine trials on his guinea pigs. He would also use the opportunity to catch up on how his 'hostages' were getting on. Treating the daughters of two of the most powerful men in the world at his clinic, made those girls his hostages in Ganak's opinion.

When he arrived the previous afternoon, the clinic director, Serena Hope greeted him. They drank tea together while she fluttered her eyelashes at him. Ganak was aware of the effect he had on many women, and Serena gave out all the signs. She appeared to have dressed up for the occasion, he assumed tight pencil skirt and stiletto heels were not her normal attire for a day's work at the clinic.

It was his cross to bear. Ganak did not advertise his homosexuality apart from in certain circles. As far as his family in India knew, he was a dutiful heterosexual son, married but sadly without any children. It would be difficult to produce the children as he never had sex with his wife. He paid her well to keep up the pretence.

His meeting with Serena Hope today was quite different. They woke him up and told him a hostage had escaped, and of course, it was Ross's daughter. He screamed and shouted at Serena and the lumpen therapist. However, screaming and shouting made no difference to the facts, Seville Campbell had managed to abscond last night.

'I don't know how she got out of her room,' sobbed Anne Campbell, the therapist responsible for Seville. 'The door was locked when the assistant went to her room this morning.'

'How she got out is our second priority, our number one priority is to find her,' said Ganak. 'What do we know so far?'

Serena tugged at the hem of her skirt and steepled her hands. 'We believe she swam off the island. Security saw footsteps on the grass leading down to the shore of the loch. We think she swam across to Gruinard House, or further down to the bay. Probably

Gruinard House, as it's the shortest distance and has a jetty where the boats dock.'

'She hasn't taken a boat?' said Ganak. 'She might be anywhere if she stole a boat.'

'I have already checked,' said Serena. 'No boats have been docked there for a while.'

'Where would she go to?' Ganak studied the map spread across Serena's coffee table. 'Inverness is the nearest city, and the closest settlement is Laide, though Laide is tiny.'

'It is hard to imagine where she would go. She will not have any money, if she goes to the police they will call here and then obviously they will send her back. I would think she would stick to main roads, or she risks getting lost. She has no map and no food and is not dressed adequately to attempt to cross mountains or moorland,' Serena informed him.

Anne Campbell burst into loud sobs again. 'Oh, the poor wee mite, this is terribly dangerous for her.'

'Do you want me to inform her parents?' said Serena.

'No,' said Ganak. 'Let us try to find her before we worry them.' There was no way he would tell Ross his daughter had gone AWOL unless he absolutely had to. He picked at his finger again and considered if he could turn this to his advantage.

Ganak studied the map once more and wondered where a body would turn up if the girl was unfortunate enough to drown. He decided it would be best not to ask his companions' opinion on this, he'd bring up drowning if they did not find her. It must be a possibility, Ganak could not even begin to imagine how anyone would be so foolish as to attempt to swim a mile in the sea.

He thought of telling Ross his daughter was drowned. He had an intuition that would be an outcome to his daughter's incarceration that Ross would not regret too much.

Chapter Forty-Eight

April 2020

Seville waded into the water and struck out towards those distant mountains. The first chill faded and with every stroke, she became warmer and full of energy. She concentrated on her rhythm, turned her head, and breathed in time with each movement of her body. Seville swam out for about twenty minutes, then paused and trod water while she considered her surroundings.

She thought she was already about a mile from the shore, the current worked in her favour and pulled her across the top of the Inner Sound. To her left, she saw the Island of Rona, to the north, distant but visible in the clarity of the day, the Isle of Lewis. Straight ahead, looking deceptively near, the Isle of Skye framed the sea.

Both water and sky were a sapphire blue, and all she could hear was the gentle whoosh of the sea and the cries of sea birds overhead. Her swimming fell in rhythm with these sounds, and her breathing matched the swell of the waves. Her mind was as clear as a crystal bowl, and she placed her thoughts in it, to consider without distraction.

She thought of Taras and longed for the physicality of him, thought of their ease of companionship. If he saw her now, he would shake his head and laugh. He would say 'you are a force of nature, Seville.' That is what she felt like, a force of nature. An elemental fury that would not be subdued filled her, and swimming released that force.

She thought of governments and their wish to constrain and manage people. All governments hated nomadic peoples, they found them hard to control. Was a wild swimmer a temporary nomad while they swam? The act of wild swimming was anarchic, unorganised, and free. An expression of power, an individual's freedom to make a choice. Wild swimmers did not conqueror their environment, they worked with the environment they found themselves in. They conquered their fears, they looked out for each other.

She swam on at a constant pace, occasionally treading water to appreciate the transcendent beauty of her surroundings. On her left, now level with Rona, she spotted the squat white lighthouse too clearly and she realised she had drifted south. She corrected her course to head slightly northwards. She must land on a beach as she did not want to find herself washed up against rocks.

Now when she gazed south, the ominous peaks of the Cuillins, high and menacing in the distance, dominated the view. She had no idea how long she had been swimming but thought she could swim forever. She began to feel hungry, she thought of her Tunnocks teacake, a symbol of sugary delight.

Seville was thirsty so she paused and trod water. She'd tied her water bottle to the swim bag and hoped it hadn't absorbed any saltwater. She fumbled with the lid and accidentally dropped it in the water, adding her own plastic pollution to the sea. She drank and emptied her full bladder into the ocean. The urine would be less polluting than the plastic.

The sun moved towards the west, so she imagined it must be about two pm. If that was right, she had been swimming for six hours. The coast of Skye looked near, and she noticed a waterfall gushing down the cliff face to the south. She saw Staffin Island and knew she had to swim to the north to avoid the rocks at the southern bay.

She felt almost sad her epic swim would soon end. Swimming in the sea was simple, on land, it was not always so clear what she should do next. But she was hungry, thirsty, and beginning to get tired. Her body fell into such a rhythm that her muscles did not ache too much, but she reckoned she would be stiff tomorrow. She hoped she found a comfortable bed for the night.

The coast came up faster than she expected, and Seville lay on the sand, like a beached mermaid, with the water lapping at her legs. Buildings towards the east of the bay looked like holiday homes, and she presumed they would be empty. It seemed strange to stand, she thought she still felt the swell of the sea and swayed to an imaginary motion as she got up and opened her swim bag.

Seville wrapped herself in her blanket and rummaged for the tea cake. She bit into its glorious, sticky sweetness and enjoyed the sugar rush through her body. Lying back on the beach she regarded the sky. Still an impossible cerulean blue, with a few, determinedly white clouds.

She stood and walked along the deserted beach. Her father was behind her imprisonment, of that she was sure, and he would think he had won, that she could never succeed in any battle against him. But she was his daughter, like him, she played to win and she rather thought he had won this battle.

The End

Afterword

The Man Who Bought the World is the first book in The **Swimmer's Almanac** trilogy.

The Swimmer's Almanac Trilogy

Book One

The Man Who Bought The World

Book Two

Journeys By Water

Book Three

The Legend of The Water Woman

To be published 2025

Author Page

I have a magpie mind and I am always taking notes as a person or situation captures my interest. The idea for this story came to me after I came across the photography of Elena Chernyshova. Elena's atmospheric photos of Norilsk are quite beautiful, even though her subject matter is often disturbing. Her images in *Days of Night/Nights of Days* are well worth taking a look at.

Details of this and other sources of inspiration can be found on my website
                www.fionalamontandmjritchie.co.

Wild Swimming

There is something immensely powerful about scrambling into a river or lake or running into the sea. Perhaps it's because we always need to brace ourselves against the potentially cold water, there is a moment of hesitation before committing ourselves, an element of risk.

In recent years wild swimming has become more popular, but it is not an activity to be undertaken without managing risk. First you need to be able to swim. No matter how tempting it is to wade into a river or lake in hot weather, remember just one step can take you out of your depth. Cold water shock can be a danger, so always enter gradually, make sure other water users can see you, and ideally swim with a companion. Stay safe and enjoy the water.

Printed in Great Britain
by Amazon